THE ELEMENTAL CHRONICLES

Awakening

THE ELEMENTAL CHRONICLES
BOOK ONE

Awakening

ROSS KINGSTON

First published in 2017 by Ross Kingston

Copyright © 2017 Ross Kingston

All rights reserved. No part of this publication may be reproduced, stored in a retrieval system or transmitted, in any form or by any means, electronic, mechanical, photocopying, recording or otherwise, without the prior written permission of the publishers and copyright holders.

A record of this book is held at the National Library of Australia.

ISBN 978-0-6481126-0-0

Project editor: Kaitlyn Smith
Proofreader: Claire Bradshaw
Designer: Lorena Susak
Cover illustrations: Livia Prima
Map artist: Marc Loths

This book has been typeset in Palatino

Printed and bound in Australia by SOS Printing Group

10 9 8 7 6 5 4 3 2 1

Keep up with The Elemental Chronicles on www.tecseries.com

*'Open your eyes and see for yourself
what is impossible, and what isn't.'*

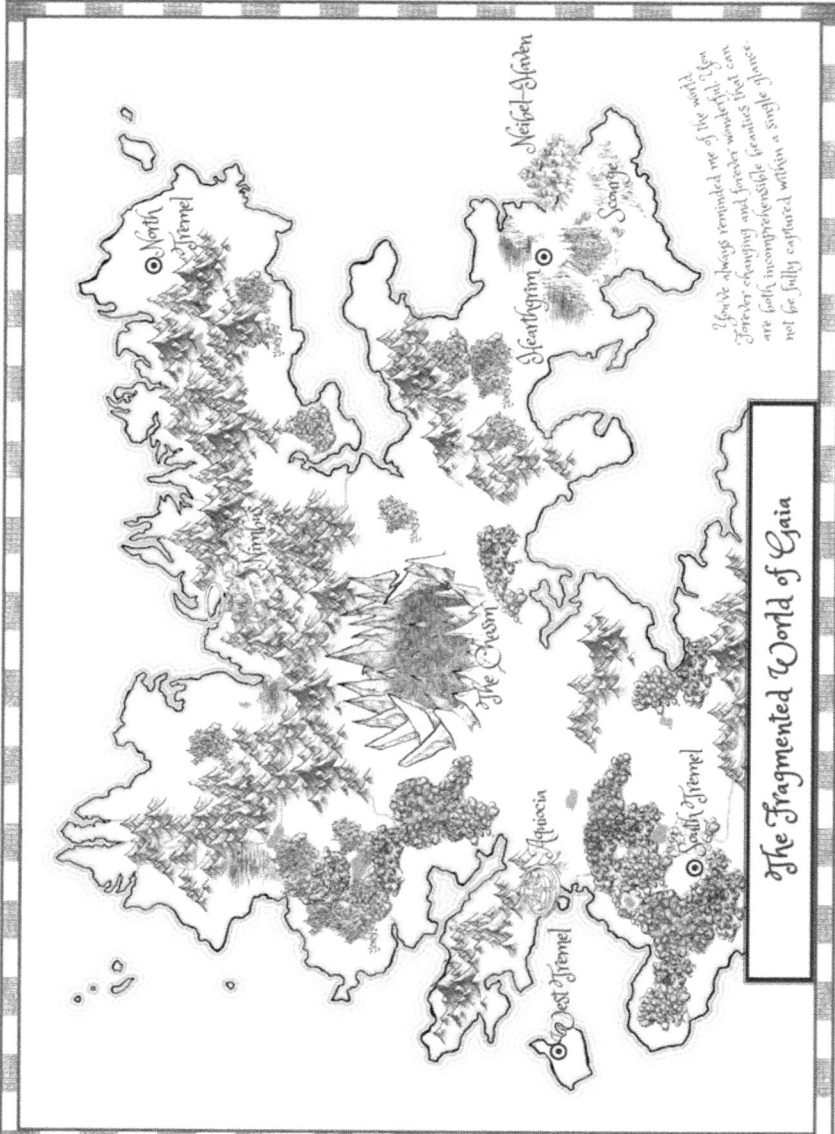

PROLOGUE: PECULIAR GOINGS-ON

The rough, dirt path leading to the hamlet's entrance was deserted. The pair of guards stationed at the rugged yet sturdy gate shifted restlessly. Bored with their shift and bored with their jobs.

Nothing ever happened within the hamlet of maybe fifty people, but the self-proclaimed Mayor was known for his paranoia – hence the massive timber gate they were forced to watch overnight. The guards didn't have much to complain about in truth. They didn't have to go through any strenuous training for the position and the most they ever had to do was occasionally break up a bar brawl when clients of the dingy pub got a little too much cheap mead in their stomachs.

"What's the point of having us here in the middle of the night?" groaned the shorter of the two, scratching his shadow of a beard. "Nobody ever comes here unless they need to rest before the last leg of their journey to Aquiocia anyway."

"Search me, Chief," replied the lanky youngster of barely seventeen.

The term "Chief" was loosely used, referring to Jemur. It wasn't so much that he had any authority, as that he was the oldest of the guards. At thirty-five he joined the guards after suffering an injury. Physically, no wound could be seen, but he would deal with constant aches and pains; randomly and with little notice. This was often the way with spell-inflicted injuries.

"I'm just getting old," he would joke with the other guards.

"The Mayor is just worried about the ghost, I'd wager!" Isaac added, with a slight hint of excitement sneaking into his voice.

Jemur had to physically refrain from rolling his eyes at the youth's enthusiasm. It wasn't the first time that Isaac had brought it up; it wasn't even the first time that night. Isaac's desire to discuss the "ghost" had only intensified since rumours of an unknown figure appearing in graveyards had reached their tiny hamlet.

"Isaac, for the last time – it's not a ghost," Jemur replied with a measured breath. He didn't want to discuss it again, but they didn't have anything better to do.

"Then what would you call it?"

"A lie, mostly," Jemur muttered before catching a glimpse of Isaac's disheartened expression. As far as the older man was concerned, there was no reason why the kid would want to believe in a myth about a man who'd slaughtered countless people.

"I heard it was a knight," Jemur said finally, his partner's eyes widening in interest.

"A – a knight?" Isaac repeated.

"Aye. Apparently he wandered the land after some stones or something. I heard he started with no one at his side, but he'd recruit the strongest of opponents to join him."

"How'd he recruit people?" Isaac wondered, his eyes never leaving the older man. "Why'd they join?"

"They say they didn't have a choice. He was a picky one, and they say he recruited through death . . . or something," Jemur added with a shrug.

"Who are 'they'?" Isaac probed.

"Oh, I dunno, kid! This all happened two centuries ago – *if* it ever did! Give me a break! I'm gunna take a piss!" Jemur's grumbling ceased when his eyes caught sight of a silhouette in the distance. Only noticeable by the full moon's light overhead, the figure seemed to be content to simply stare at the pair.

"Hail, traveller!" called the kid in a friendly greeting.

"Enough, Isaac, be patient. Allow whoever it is to come to us," Jemur muttered, unease growing.

After a minute of waiting and no movement, Jemur started to get impatient.

"Well, are you going to come to us or . . .?" Jemur's question was cut short when the silhouette vanished, reappearing a few strides away.

The guards immediately drew their swords as Jemur spat, "Sorcery!"

The once indistinguishable figure was a knight, but bore no emblem of any kingdom. Instead, the knight was outfitted in dark purple, full plate armour from head to toe. Along the surface of the metal ran thin, intricate lines with translucent energy coursing through them.

The lights emitted from the travelling energies didn't discriminate in colour, shifting from the most searing crimson to the calmest of azure, the most peaceful of emerald to subtle sienna. Isaac noticed they always returned to a harsh contrast of black and white wisps that attempted to counter each other as they raced over the knight's armour, never following the same path twice.

The armour itself seemed to be of no material that the unnerved pair had seen. With the amount of time that Jemur had spent checking the wares of merchants at the gate, he'd assumed he'd seen all the metals that the lands within Gaia had to offer. To gaze upon the almost ultra-violet plate was both a refreshing and disconcerting experience.

The knight's face was hidden beneath a heavy, violet helmet that gave away no features. Its design was simple and fully enclosed – save for the eye holes, which faded away into an abyss of blackness as the guards gazed into them. Although where he sourced it from remained a mystery, he wore the same heavy style of armour that only the strongest knights wore within the most powerful of kingdoms – usually generals who had proven their worth in battle. The only reassuring thing Jemur could perceive was that the knight appeared to be unarmed. It was a fragile reassurance at best, after the seamless teleportation.

The knight seemed uninterested in the guards, his gaze directed straight ahead at the gate between them. Instead of moving, he addressed them in a voice that even one who had never witnessed magic could recognise as magically altered and enhanced. The voice was soft and yet forceful.

"Open it," the knight ordered.

"Forget it; your display may scare some, but not us!" Isaac answered defiantly.

"Foolish. My time here is limited and not to be wasted," the knight replied, disappearing from view again.

This time his reappearance was not apparent to the guards.

"H-he fled?" Isaac asked, allowing the breath he'd been holding since the knight appeared to escape his lungs.

Jemur had no chance to reply before the gate exploded behind them with the deafening din of shattering timber. The lumber that the gate was comprised of flew past them, with a large chunk impaling Jemur. The blow killed the older man before his body was lifted into the air and tossed down the dirt path.

Isaac, who was standing to the side of the gate, glanced towards the body of his Chief before spinning around to look inside the town. The knight was there, his armoured hand still glowing with a strange aura as he lowered it. The knight turned away, looking around at the town. People were piling out of their small dwellings to investigate. The night air filled with the terrified screams of women and children as they recognised the abomination from the stories told around the land.

There was only one heavily armoured and ruthless man with the supernatural strength for such destruction. The villagers had reason to be terrified of the figure in luminescent plate mail and it was just one part of the legend that Jemur had missed.

It was Lucian.

Fierce cries of brave men were heard as they picked up whatever weapons they could find and charged the knight.

He stood with an eerie composure until the first villager reached him. A bearded man, heavily under the influence of alcohol, swung a rusty longsword erratically at the threat. The knight moved with unreal speed, practically disappearing from the blade's fury and catching the man's arm. With a twist of the knight's arm, the drunk's wrist snapped.

The knight ripped the sword from the drunk's hand and smoothly impaled him through the stomach, before tearing it from its new home. The man's body was left to shower the ground in blood and booze. The men didn't hesitate in their charge, with another ten of them following the first man's lead.

Isaac then witnessed firsthand the slaughter of the men he had grown up with, the knight spinning and pivoting, taking limbs and heads from his victims. It was like a macabre version of the dances the prostitutes who visited the hamlet used to do with ribbons and lace. Only this time, the dancer had a sword in each hand and the people he was entertaining found no happy ending.

Most of the villagers had already fled for their lives by the time the murderer had finished. With a vicious slash across the last remaining man's chest, the knight turned his head in the direction the villagers had run. He took a single step to follow when Isaac appeared in front of him.

With his sword drawn and his knees shaking almost as much as his voice, he addressed the knight with false bravado.

"Y-y-you won't get past me, you – you monster!" Isaac spluttered as the knight faced him for the first time with any real interest.

"You still resist?" Lucian's cruel voice tore at Isaac's frail courage. It wasn't so much a question as an accusation that was given to someone right before their execution.

"I can't let you hurt them anymore!" Isaac insisted as the knight stared at the kid with his seemingly hollow eyes, but Isaac refused to step aside.

"You're an interesting one indeed," the knight said, "perhaps even useful."

The knight disappeared, and Isaac felt a flash of pain. It lasted only a split second. His world was doused in a bright light, compared with which the sun seemed dim. After it subsided he was standing in the same spot, still facing the knight.

"Look down," Lucian ordered.

Try as he might, Isaac couldn't resist. His gaze descended towards the earth and alarm raced through him at what he saw.

He was lying on the ground! Yet here he stood!

"Your soul is bound to me now – your body an empty shell. You will do my bidding. My magic allows you to interact with this world; you will not die so long as I exist and wish it so," the knight explained without a hint of emotion. "This place does not hold what I am looking for. If it did, I would have had a far greater resistance to contend with. Burn everything."

Isaac willed himself to stop, to run, to swing his blade at the knight – to do anything. Instead he took one last glance at the dissolving body lying before him, before dropping his blade and making his way towards the pub's cellar, where the villagers kept the explosive powder.

CHAPTER 1

AN UNEXPLAINED CONTRACT

The sewers of the great city of Aquiocia were less than desirable in a lot of ways. The least appealing aspect, according to the man being pursued, would have to be the lack of light, despite his familiarity with the maze he was running through.

I might know this place like the back of my hand, but damned if their lanterns aren't an unfair advantage.

The risk of misjudging the walls within the darkness was enough to make any man slow, and this one longed for the light of day. Being underground left the sun's rays moot, but his desire for the sun stemmed from the fact that his life became a lot less interesting – even boring – when it was out.

Boredom isn't an issue to me. Boredom means that I'm not required to do anything strenuous. Boredom means that I can sleep.

The thief's hand habitually pushed back the stray hair from his eyes as he raced through the dark corridors he'd memorised years ago. Boredom was not a luxury he could indulge in at this moment and he begrudgingly accepted that fact as he maintained his speed.

He wore all black, covered by a dark, violet-hooded cloak, designed to meld with the shadows as he underwent various contracts. Wrapped around his waist was a thick, black belt with thinner counterparts hanging loosely from its length. From the ends of them, twin sheaths housed the thin blades that the thief preferred, hanging loosely and shifting slightly as he ran. The narrow scabbards served both as a home for the sharp blades and a way to dampen the noise of their movements. Thanks to the thick, cushioning material surrounding them, they were all but silent.

He had realised at a very young age that people's eyes were attracted to motion. While they were busy watching the dancing blades as he moved, they overlooked what his hands were helping themselves to. Sometimes it bought him a split second; other times it rewarded him with a clean escape. Every time, it had saved his neck. It was his own idea, and one that was often questioned by both amateur duellists and seasoned assassins. Neither of which received the simple explanation behind the odd practice.

This attire had done nothing for him this time, however. Once he found his mark – a beautiful blue stone the size of a lady's fist – a band of soldiers was there waiting for him.

Now he was fleeing for his life.

"If I believed in a god, then this would be a good time for me to curse him," he muttered to himself, only slightly short of breath as his feet swiftly raced across the cracked stone beneath them. He was lazy, but he wasn't unfit. Another misconception that his enemies often constructed.

He could hear a trio of royal guards yelling out to him from the darkness behind. The only things he could make out from the view over his shoulder were their lanterns and the glint of steel from their drawn blades. He was surprised there were any left following him from the secret treasury; he'd thought he'd lost them.

All this for a stone? Don't make me kill you lot, he thought as he felt for the daggers dancing at his side. Rounding a corner sharply, he focussed on losing the knights.

The thief had little luck as they followed him around the same corner and the pursuit continued.

I'm almost out of options.

The thief started turning at every corner he came to in an attempt to lose the knights in the labyrinth of the sewers. The effort went unrewarded since the knights had the light from their lanterns by which to navigate the darkness. He didn't risk creating his own light in fear of making it even easier for them.

The guards approached another corner and as the first turned he saw a brief flash: the glint of steel from the thief's dagger slashing his throat. The second guard reacted to the attack, raising his sword as the thief predicted he would. He was already crouched down and bringing his second knife across to the gap in armour at the knight's kneecap. The soldier desperately swung his blade as he fell. The wails were broken by the clatter of his sword meeting the stone floor.

The final knight emerged from around the corner to see the thief greeting him with venom in his green gaze.

The thief had light brown hair that fell across eyes which held a calm hue of slightly diluted emeralds. He was roguishly handsome with stubble lining his striking jawline. His facial features were set in apathy as boredom took reign within his mind. It was unnerving to see so little acknowledgement written upon the thief's face, save for those vicious eyes glaring at the knight through the collected light of fallen lanterns. They burned with a loathing of the remaining soldier that seemed out of place on his otherwise emotionless face.

"Run," he growled at the quivering man and without a second thought, the knight fled back the way he came. The coward's departure left the thief to turn his attention to the wounded and whimpering excuse for a man, who was grasping desperately at his bleeding knee.

"Please – don't –" the paling man begged.

"How did you know I would be coming for the stone?" the thief asked, producing the large sapphire-blue stone from his pocket. "What's so special about it that you'd set a trap?"

"They know about your organisation, the Captain set this up, he . . . He said –" The knight seemed to hesitate. The thief raised his hand menacingly and he continued in a hurry. "He said the stone was to be kept from the Princess and used to lure out your leader, not you!"

"Well, sorry to be such an inconvenience, but the reward was too good to pass up," the thief retorted sarcastically as he knelt down to eye level. "You know, I don't enjoy taking the knights' lives but I can't risk it."

With that the thief slashed the knight's throat: a quick and humane ending. He wiped the blood from his blades on the guard's cape and kicked the lifeless bodies into the murky water.

The thief grimaced as he watched the bodies sink, dragged down by their armour. He didn't like killing. He also didn't dislike it. But it did take more effort than what he felt he was paid for. Satisfied that the lifeless bodies weren't going to return to the surface, the man turned and continued to the only place he had ever called home.

❖

Beneath the beautiful city of Aquiocia, in the heart of the sewers, was the Underbelly. Thieves, murderers and run-of-the-mill pickpockets looking for fortune had made their home within the civilisation, having been turned away from the world above. The number of malcontents and downtrodden continued to grow, although they were not without talent. Along with the questionable trades, there were also those skilled in the more mundane, those who had fallen on harder times as the kingdom above them changed.

These somewhat morally challenged people – if willing – would be sought out if their deeds were recognised by the organisation known as the Guilty Blade. Providing that the guild had a use for them, they would be offered a home within the Underbelly in return for their contribution to the underground society. Led by a man known to the people simply as "Setz", the Guilty Blade watched out for its own, and governed the Underbelly.

The thief walked instinctively through the streets of the Underbelly towards his own personal hovel. He had grown accustomed to the dirty paths that served as streets, all of which eventually led to the enormous pillar in the centre of the underground town. The stores and traders fanned out from the central point of the civilisation. Further out still were the homes of the Underbelly's residents. While most of the housing was made from second- or third-hand resources, the lofty ceiling of thick stone high above them provided the people with far more than just the illusion of safety and comfort. Perhaps it was the strange, glowing orbs drifting across the ceiling and offering light to the residents, or maybe it was the knowledge that Setz's trained assassins were watching over every single one of them. These assassins boasted the ability to watch over the residents beneath the ever-present orbs' light and yet remain hidden from view. It was a difficult concept for some to understand, as well as a testament to Setz's ability. He led and trained these exceptional warriors of the shadows. It was a constant reminder of his presiding power in the region.

The street that the thief was traversing was littered with small, makeshift stalls where anyone part of the Underbelly family could stop and purchase day-to-day necessities, just like on the surface. People had set up lives underneath Aquiocia much like they would in any normal city; the difference was that the goods sold by the vendors were often obtained through less than honest means. It was a fact that this led to the Underbelly's residents often having valuables that were a season behind what was considered "high fashion" by the surface dwellers' standards. It was also a fact that very few cared for.

None of this was the thief's business.

He was the one Setz picked for particularly dirty or high-risk jobs because he refused to join the guild. Because of this refusal, even if he was captured, the thief couldn't give away secrets of the Guilty Blade. But that was just another thing the thief didn't care about as he opened the front door to his dirty little home and was greeted by the only two young ladies to whom he was truly loyal.

CHAPTER 2

A GRIEVING PRINCESS

Often referred to as "Sanctuary" by the less fortunate, the city of Aquiocia was truly a spectacular sight to indulge in regardless of the beholder. Her beautiful gardens and glamorous houses were lined with canals of sparkling, running water. It was the dream of many men and women alike to be able to claim that they were a part of her beauty. Situated on the side of the Blue Crystal Mountains, anyone entering the massive, silver-lined cerulean gates of the city for the first time was immediately entranced. Stepping inside the walls revealed a grand path of pale blue stone leading to the city centre. From the front gates, the Aquiocian palace was visible in its awesome splendour in the distance. Branching off early from the great path led to what was known as the lower-class housing.

Name aside, the residents there were anything but destitute. The somewhat smaller houses shone with polished blue stone, directly sourced from the mines within the Blue Crystal Mountains that loomed behind the grand palace. These smaller abodes had a certain modesty about them, with only small amounts of silver engraved upon the front doors as the houses' numbers. It was a system designed so – should trouble arise – people could refer the number of the closest house for the guards. The closer to the palace, the more impressive the adornments upon the houses. Some spent their entire lives trying to encase their house in more valuables or jewels than their neighbours, in an attempt to outdo them. They became so focused on this competition that the problems outside the kingdom were often overlooked.

The image of the city wasn't the only thing that threatened to make the eyes of newcomers bulge. There was also the astounding amount of commerce it brought in. Traders and merchants alike gathered in the centre of town around the larger-than-life statue of Alicea – the current Princess of Aquiocia – to trade their wares in hope of one day finding a more permanent place within the city.

The young Princess' parents had erected the statue before they died. Her mother and father had been adept at swordplay and magic, yet both were killed eleven months earlier on the Plains of a Thousand Blades. The late King and Queen had travelled to the Plains to try to find a peaceful resolution for two warring entities of immense power. Tragedy – that no one could quite explain – had struck and the young Princess' parents had met their end on the field of battle. There was no more to the story; both Princess and civilian alike were forced to swallow the vague reports and rumours supplied by those who investigated the scene.

Alicea had been expected to take on the role as acting Queen until a more suitable candidate could be elected by the Council of Aquiocia. However, Alicea had no interest in the Queen's duties she was obligated to undertake, and had allowed the Council to take care of such matters. Stricken with grief, she had taken to hiding away within one of the guests' chambers on the lower level of the palace. As a result, she was as far away as possible from the royal quarters on the third level, along with anything that might remind her of her late parents.

The battle on the Plains was the last anyone had seen or heard of the two forces clashing. When it went quiet, strange happenings around the land had begun, seemingly at random. Rumours of an old enemy of the land had resurfaced but, as the Council of Aquiocia had assured everyone, they were just that – rumours.

❖

Locke's footsteps echoed up the corridor of the west wing as he made his way to the Princess' newly adopted bedchambers. It was a walk that he had grown tired of.

Sixteen years, Locke thought bitterly. *Sixteen years of servitude but never knighted or truly recognised.*

But that cruel reminder always came in second to the real reason he dreaded this walk every morning. He knew as soon as he knocked on the door to the Princess' chambers he was in for another round of arguing so fierce that it made any spar he had been in throughout his thirty-six years seem trivial. Now, he was frowning at the thought of another round with the Princess as he came to the door leading to her chambers. A smile forced its way to his worn face at the irony that with his large six-foot-three masculine build, the tiny, sharp-tongued lady on the other side of the door held such control over him. The thought was cut short by a silvery, feminine voice from beyond the door calling out to him. The pleasant sound was at odds with the message its owner was delivering.

"I know you are there, Locke. I'm already up, so you can

forget about waking me and go back to whatever it is you do all day."

Locke sighed to himself before opening the door and entering the chambers.

"Milady, you know I have to escort you to the audience hall."

"I don't think so. I have no desire to sit in a chair while a bunch of prince suitors from around the world put on the facade that they are the one for me," the Princess replied dryly.

"They merely want to meet you. Your parents were very happy –"

Alicea snapped.

"You stop right there, Locke! My parents were an exception and the men out there are not here for me. They want the kingdom and its money and I –" Alicea's voice caught in her throat. "– I won't let my parents' death be tarnished by their daughter just handing over the kingdom they died for. They would want me to find someone who wants me, just me, not all the perks that come from marrying *the Rose of Aquiocia*."

Locke looked over the young Princess for the millionth time. At the age of twenty she stood just shy of five-foot-three, with long hair that cascaded down to her lower back in ebony waves. The natural sunlight often set her hair ablaze with its crimson reflection, a colour lost within this chamber, poorly lit by a single torch. Locke often thought that the length of her hair would be a nuisance, yet with every movement the Princess made, it was never found strewn across her face.

Probably a result of the constant maintenance from its owner, Locke thought with amusement, looking at the countless jewel-encrusted clips throughout the Princess' perfectly arranged hair. As a result, her hair did nothing to hide the once stunning smile that Locke had almost forgotten, its existence now lost in the void of quiet misery that had taken hold of the lady sitting before him.

The Princess' features were delicate and untarnished, with skin that, while somewhat pale, was flawless and free of any blemish. Her soft jawline met with a slender neck that followed down to the short, but developed, frame of a young woman. Her petite figure was garbed in a thin, yet modest, dark blue dress, lined with elegant patterning; long, white stockings covered her legs underneath. While she was currently better dressed than most of the people in the kingdom, Locke knew that the effort in her image had dwindled and the outfit was one that suggested she was still not interested in moving from her chambers.

Her right hand was adorned with half a dozen silver rings on various fingers, in contrast with the simple silver chain around her neck. Upon the chain was a small jewel in the shape of the flower native to the Blue Crystal Mountains known as the Aquiocian Rose. While her body was not one that anyone would consider imposing, a certain fierceness could often be seen within the Princess' eyes.

Ah, her eyes, Locke thought, almost dreamily.

Big, curious and beautiful, the Princess' eyes were a cold, pale blue. Many men found themselves captivated by the ice-blue gaze of the Princess, a gaze that often erupted with colour when she was overcome with intense emotion. The radiance of her eyes was just one feature on a long list of alluring qualities that had earned her unofficial titles from people all over the land such as "the Jewel of Aquiocia" and "Aquiocia's Rose."

Now, they held a different shade that he had not seen in years: almost completely grey, with only the slightest hint of blue left.

The same shade I saw sixteen years ago when I found her being tormented by thugs near the markets, he thought. *She's scared. She may be approaching full adulthood, but to lose everyone like that . . .*

"When you're quite finished gawking at me like an entranced drunkard, I'd appreciate being left in peace," Alicea announced, her eyes flashing with anger.

"I apologise, Princess," Locke responded quickly, finally averting his gaze. "I'll tell them that you have taken ill, and to come back another day."

"You can tell them to go home!"

Locke exited the Princess' chambers, walking back the way he came. As he reached the audience hall, he cursed his weakness for the Princess' feelings, along with the fact that he had been entranced by her again.

I'm not doing the late King and Queen any favours by bending to their daughter's whims . . . Locke thought before reaffirming his resolve to the Princess. *They were never as important to me anyway.*

CHAPTER 3

FOR THE GIRLS

"RUFFIE!"

A grin broke across Rufus' face as a pair of twins launched themselves at him, wrapping him in a tight embrace.

"You are finally –" started Lori.

"– back from your mission," finished Tori.

"Don't even start with that shit, you know it drives me crazy," Rufus said in exasperation as he looked down at the twins.

Although their thin structures and facial features were predominately the same, Lori always wore her long, blonde hair in a ponytail, whereas Tori let her similarly coloured hair fly free. Both had eyes of vibrant jade and while Lori's held wisdom beyond her years, Tori's were fraught with a youthful mischief. You could also tell them apart simply from their speech. Tori's tone was always a little harsher and more insensitive, while Lori's voice was soft and sweet.

Before the twins had left Setz's careful watch, he had informed them of the real reason they had ended up in the organisation – their late father making an attempt on their infant lives. The revelation had humbled Lori with the fact that she had been given a second chance at life, while turning Tori bitter against anything to do with the knights and, to a slightly lesser degree, royalty itself.

"Did ya kill many knights, Ruffie?" enquired Tori.

"Tori! You shouldn't be so bloodthirsty. Besides, the contract said *no killing*," Lori finished smugly.

"Enough, you two! Lori, don't be like that and Tori," Rufus continued after a moment of hesitation, "yes, there were some casualties." He never liked lying to the girls.

"Did you kill them? Slash them? Stab them? Make a necklace out of their tee—"

"TORI!" Lori's voice rose to a familiar, scolding pitch.

"You have a wild imagination, Tori, I won't deny you that." Rufus looked on, rubbing his temples in fatigue. "But the sun was well and truly set before I left the Underbelly, meaning you two should be asleep."

"Aw, but –"

"A very good point indeed," a deep voice from behind the small group rumbled and Rufus instinctively reached for his blades, his nerves still on edge.

"Setz!"

"Lori, Tori, good to see you both. Now bed," commanded Setz and the twins scampered off to their shared bedroom.

He then turned his attention to Rufus.

"Are you going to release your grip on those or attack me with them? I only ask because the knights never got a chance to."

Long since aware of the fact that Setz always seemed to know everything, Rufus' hands relaxed before eyeing up the tall, darkly cloaked man in front of him.

Setz stood almost as tall as Rufus and his face was scarred almost beyond recognition, though no one but Setz knew what the damage was from. The scars helped preserve the older man's age at around fifty, but Rufus always felt that he was much, much older. Whether that assumption was borne from the Guildmaster's demeanour or otherwise, he couldn't tell.

Though obviously elderly, Setz moved with an unnatural grace. His feet seemed to glide across the room under his pitch-black cloak, leading him to examine the various mundane items within Rufus' small home. He had unkempt, pure-grey hair, which fell over his face as he shifted. His eyes appeared to be brown, although once the light hit them their amber hue was revealed.

"Speaking of questions that should be asked, why were there knights waiting for me? You said it was a jewellery bust. Obviously that's not quite the whole truth, what with me having to run for my life as soon as I reached the stone. What's so special about this damned rock?" Rufus demanded, eyeing Setz for any trace of emotion and seeing none.

"That hardly matters at this point, Rufus," Setz replied after a moment, changing the subject smoothly. "I have informed the grocers and traders that your credit is good for your reward, as usual. For the girls and all," he said with a slightly condescending tone, continuing to look around Rufus' hovel.

He seemed to take careful note of the dirty sheets across his hammock and the unclean spare clothing hanging from a rickety railing that looked as though Rufus had installed it himself on the wall.

"Answer my question, Setz," Rufus commanded, beginning to undo the countless belts holding his attire together. "I'm not one of your lackeys. I don't blindly follow you."

Setz gave no response, continuing his visual tour of Rufus' home.

"Well, if it doesn't matter, then it won't matter if I keep your precious little stone?" Rufus pressed, changing his tact as he produced the gorgeous, fist-sized sapphire from one of the countless hidden compartments in his attire.

"Very good, you hold onto it," Setz conceded carelessly, leaving Rufus staring at him in surprise while continuing, "I have another job if you are interested."

"Why would I be interested?" Rufus asked in irritation.

"For the twins' wellbeing, of course," was the emotionless response.

"Are you blackmailing me now?"

"Do not think of it that way. If you do this I will see to it that you will have more favourable living arrangements – and who knows? The girls may even be able to bathe this year," Setz added snidely as he glided towards the door.

"Is that what this is about? You are still upset about the fact they left your grip? I never wanted that. I care for them, yes, but I made it clear that I didn't have much to give –" started Rufus, before getting cut off by Setz raising his hand.

"Enough self-pity. If you want the job you will come to me tomorrow. The usual place." Setz was almost out the door when he turned back to Rufus.

"Oh, and Rufus? Try not to be so short-sighted. What's coming is bigger than you, the girls or even myself. You have great things ahead of you; whether they are for good or otherwise – well, that's up to you."

With that he was gone. Rufus pulled out the stone and stared at its brilliant, cerulean hue. As it shone back at him, he muttered to himself, "It's like he tries to confuse me."

CHAPTER 4

THE GUILTY BLADE

Looming over Rufus was the heart of the Guilty Blade. It was fashioned out of one of the great pillars erected under the earth by workers centuries ago to stop the sewer canals from collapsing in upon themselves. Setz had ordered it hollowed out some time ago and converted into the head of the guild. Even hollow, the silo-sized pillar stood strong. It was rumoured that magic helped it and, while anyone who had met Setz knew that the claim was possible, it hadn't been confirmed.

Rufus was always going to agree to see Setz – they both knew it. He had lived in the Underbelly for a few years now, ever since he had been approached by one of Setz's best men after seeing Rufus in his adolescence pick the pockets of fourteen unsuspecting people in a crowded marketplace.

It was a grand day right up until Setz's man sprung me. "Scouting for talent", what a joke, Rufus thought bitterly. *Still, I will never forget his face when I said no to joining Setz's organisation.*

He chose not to think about Setz's indifferent reaction to his blatant refusal. The Guildmaster had shrugged and allowed Rufus to dwell on the outskirts of the Underbelly with little responsibility and the protection of the guild.

This didn't sit well with some of the others under Setz's

command, but no one dared question Setz's decision. Nor did anyone know the reason why he kept Rufus so close, allowing certain freedoms that others didn't have. Setz wasn't one to share his thoughts with just anyone and so the mystery, along with the disapproval of many people, remained.

What an odd turn, Rufus thought as he approached one of the many entrances to the pillar. *Whatever, it doesn't matter right now.* As he entered the unusual structure, his eyes met with a group of Setz's finest assassins, covered from head to toe in their typical black garb. The only thing that gave their rank away was the red trim on the cuffs of their uniforms. It was so faint that only those who knew what they were looking for would recognise it.

Rufus impatiently made straight for the stairs, not wanting to start any trouble with them, despite their loathing for one another. He'd slept poorly in his hammock, opting to pace around his home most of the night – a practice he was almost certain the twins had been aware of in the room above him. It seemed to Rufus that the higher up the chain of command the officer was – indeed, the closer they were to Setz – the more they resented him for not joining their ranks and openly bared their hostility towards him.

Rufus climbed the stairs, not stopping at any of the many floors as they circled around the wall of the grand pillar before coming to an abrupt end. At the top of the staircase was a seemingly frail wooden door with little in the way of distinguishable features. He knew better than to try the doorknob if he didn't want to be sent flying down the stairs from the enchantment. It stopped anyone without the Guilty Blade's mark branded on their left forearm from entering. The tattoo of a crimson rose with black lining and dagger crossed over was magically branded into the skin of all members within the guild. As such, Rufus' skin remained untouched by the enchantment.

"The damned outcast wants to get in again, huh? I swear you get more face time with the boss than anyone else."

Rufus turned; one of the assassin elites had followed him.

"Relax, Outcast. I was told to come here and let you in," continued the man before turning the doorknob. "You know, you really get on my nerves. But I'll do you a favour while you're out on your special little quests for the boss. I'll look after your little girls for you *real good.*"

Rufus met the man's seedy grin with a smirk. It hadn't been the first time the twins had garnered unwanted attention, and it always ended the same way.

"Feel free to try," Rufus said, closing the door on the uncertain man's face.

He took his time to look around the room, as he always did, for it held much wonder to the thief. Both walls were lined with every type of blade you could imagine, from short and longswords to heavier blades such as broadswords and the like. But the one that always caught his eye was behind Setz's desk, hanging in front of the Guilty Blade's flag that took up the entire back wall. It was just one single longsword as black as night except for the beautiful red ribbon that curled around its hilt, up past the hilt guard, and coursed along its dark blade. It curled around it three times before seemingly disappearing into thin air. Looking at it in awe, Rufus could swear that the ribbon was moving along the blade in front of his very eyes, slithering up the length of the sword only to reach the tip, disappear, and start again back at its hilt, in a never-ending cycle.

It's like a living shadow . . . One with a mind of its own.

The crimson flag with jet black knives behind the weapon was lost on Rufus as he openly stared at the peculiar blade. The blade itself gave off small wisps of what appeared to be smoke, though the thief couldn't be sure. He'd heard rumours about when the blade had been delivered. According to the stories, the blade could not be wielded by humans; it apparently took the life of anyone who ever tried. With the mention of a curse, stories had quickly become too far-fetched for Rufus to take seriously.

"Rule twelve, Rufus." Setz interrupted his thoughts, appearing from behind him and taking his place behind the large desk. "Don't touch what is likely to get you caught, hurt or cursed."

"You have too many rules! Spit out your proposition already. This place makes my skin crawl," snapped Rufus as he looked around to make sure they were indeed alone. It was a pointless practice. If Setz wanted him dead, he would be surrounded in the time it took to draw a single breath.

Setz paused to look over Rufus with a humourless expression and shrugged. "Very well, Rufus. Your job is to kidnap the Princess of Aquiocia."

A moment of silence settled with only the sound of a crackling fire in the room as Rufus let Setz's revelation sink in. Then, the bewildered thief lost his self-control. He burst into laughter at the idea, before forcing a straight face and taking a mocking tone.

"Oh, sure! Not a problem, I was planning to do that this

afternoon anyway, right after meeting with the girls for tea on the surface!"

"I have no idea why you would be laughing, but I will take that to mean you are happy. Tonight is the ceremony to commemorate the sacrifice her parents made. The Princess was due to make a speech but has refused," Setz replied softly, looking over the papers on his desk, utterly unabashed by the thief's outburst. "This means that she will be hiding out in her chambers while the majority of the guards are either guarding the ceremony or too drunk to gather that a poorly dressed man is stealing their Princess."

Rufus ran his hand through his hair and started to pace around the room while Setz patiently waited for his reply.

"Right, let's overlook the fact that this is the perfect way for me to get myself killed. How the hell do you propose I get in, get to her chambers, and get her out?" Rufus asked, listing his first issue with the ridiculous plan.

"We have located her chambers. She hasn't resided in the royal quarters since her parents' deaths, so it will be easier for you to access. Some hired explosive experts will create a distraction, which the knights will assume is our retaliation to their intrusion last night," Setz finished curtly, taking a quick moment to scratch at a document before him with a dark feathered quill.

"You're assuming a lot here," Rufus quipped, peering over the desk, trying to see what Setz was writing.

"Our presence has been noticed. Even before your display of incompetence last night, our existence had been known for quite a while. The Council of Aquiocia is starting to catch onto many little pieces of information in their paranoid attempt to keep control," Setz replied, simultaneously insulting both the Aquiocian government and Rufus.

"Hasn't the Princess been grieving or some such rot for the past year?" Rufus grasped at his failing argument. "What use could you possibly have for an emotionally crippled Princess?"

"That doesn't concern you, Rufus. Not yet, anyway," Setz said coldly. "You will also watch your tongue in regards to our Princess."

"Yes, it bloody well does concern me! I'm the one doing the kidnapping! It more or less has everything to do with me!" Rufus yelled. "And I will speak about the Princess – who has done nothing for the past year – however I damn well please!"

"It's not all about you, and I take that to mean that you agree to the plan. Your target is at the base of the east-wing tower of the palace on the ground floor," Setz explained quietly, now watching the dying flames in the heart of the fireplace. "You will meet your contact where the wall meets the mountainside. I've drawn a map of where you need to go to meet with the contact. I have also included the full details for you to familiarise yourself with before you leave tonight."

Setz gestured towards his table and Rufus saw a scroll sealed with a red ribbon. Setz waited for him to pick it up before continuing.

"When you get past the wall, head through the gardens to the door directly ahead. Upon gaining access to the palace, you must hug the wall until you get to a corridor lined with portraits of the royal family. At the end of that corridor, your target will await," Setz explained step-by-step to a dumbfounded Rufus.

"Right. You make it sound simple enough, but I think you overlooked a couple of things. Like the numerous guards with sharp pointy weapons and how I'm supposed to get out with the Princess?" Rufus replied dryly, scratching at his stubble.

"Simple solution: kill any that get in the way. It's unfortunate that I have to give that order but it is of paramount importance that the Princess be brought to me," Setz replied with pursed lips. He looked genuinely regretful. "As for getting out, I'm afraid that is your responsibility. Be inventive."

"That's the one thing you have said to me that has made any sense. Why me?"

"Perhaps an assassin would be better," Setz conceded with a slight nod. "But if one of them were captured, the Council would find the brand on their arm. I would go myself but I am unable to. You are the best choice as you do not have the brand."

"What difference would it make if they found the brand on someone's arm?"

"Rufus, what do you think a paranoid council would do to the people in the Underbelly?"

Rufus took a moment to think before answering when he realised the Guildmaster was finally looking at him directly.

"I'd say they probably aren't particularly happy that there are countless people living outside their rule?" he guessed with an unsure wave of his hand.

"Exactly. Now imagine if they found one of our people within their palace walls. Imagine what they would do if they found one trying to abduct the Princess."

"They would come down here in force," Rufus realised in defeat. He knew then that he was the one to attempt the kidnapping.

"Then you understand."

"Will the Princess come willingly?" Rufus asked. It almost looked like the question surprised Setz.

"No," the Guildmaster replied shortly. "She will fight you every step of the way."

"I'd best get some rest then. Wouldn't want to be tired for what could very well be the night of my death," the thief announced.

"Rufus, if I may offer you some vague and cryptic advice," Setz started. Rufus stopped his march to the door.

"Do you give anything but?"

"If I'm right in what I'm organising here and the pieces all fall into place as I hope they will, you may wind up bound to something you will wish you weren't."

"I don't know what you're talking about, but if I don't like it, I will walk away," Rufus quipped as he made his exit, leaving the Guildmaster to stare at the dying embers of the once roaring fire.

"So you say," Setz muttered with the faintest hint of a smirk.

CHAPTER 5

WHERE STEALTH FAILS, STRENGTH PREVAILS

Just outside the confines of the palace's outer walls, a cloaked figure snuck cautiously along the length of the stone perimeter. He had steered clear of the main gates, glancing around after each step, still edgy from the ordeal the night before. Although he was unlikely to be seen, as he'd left the residential areas behind in his pursuit of the eastern wall that he was now hugging, he still couldn't shake the nerves that riddled every one of his muscles. A quick glance over his shoulder at the lights congregating in the far west helped alleviate some of his anxiety. Most of the residents would be making their way to the festival.

What is wrong with me? Rufus chastised himself in an attempt to rally his senses. *You're a petty thief and killer. Now you want to kidnap a Princess?*

He didn't *want* to do any of it. Setz had made him take this task. Right?

Rufus couldn't remember the Guildmaster saying that he had to take the job – and yet, he remembered feeling pressured to do so. He jumped at the sound of a stick under his own foot. He'd lost sight of his task, but even as he attempted to focus on staying quiet, his mind wandered.

I've been feeling out of sorts the past day or so. Perhaps I need sleep, he thought as his hand rested on the side pocket of his trousers.

As he closed in on what he thought must have been the location marked upon Setz's map, Rufus' mind finally focused on the task at hand.

The walls surrounding the castle all reached the same height, but everyone knew that the ground was higher at the eastern wall, built into the side of the mountain. This made the impressive wall become a shorter version of itself, barely half the original height. It was an obvious weak point in the castle's defences and one that was fiercely guarded at all times.

This'll be easier than I thought, Rufus mused as his hand finally left the pocket and reached for the thick rope bundled and tied to his lower back. *Just have to watch out for guards . . .*

There would be resistance. He'd have to lead the guards away or strike quickly and silently to remove them before, somehow, tethering one end of the rope to the top of the wall and scaling it.

Rufus soon realised that his fears of being caught were unfounded when he saw half a dozen knights sprawled in the dirt along with a short, stocky man in the middle of the unconscious bodies. From the light of the full moon, Rufus could make out that the man stood a head shorter than him, with medium-length brown hair sticking out in all directions as if he had just woken up. He wore pelts of various animals sewn together into a vest. Crossed in front of his broad build were arms the size of Rufus' legs. The stout man wore plain brown trousers with tears here and there. His boots were of tanned leather and completed the primitive and yet rugged look. He took a swig from a wineskin that was slung over his shoulder.

Most noticeable was the giant grin the man wore, filled with humour even though there was little to laugh about. It was infectious and even Rufus had to roll his eyes away from the man to stop himself returning the smile.

"I s'pose you're the one I'm meeting. I gotta tell ya, I prefer to meet women out in the dark, but, uh, I guess a man can't be helped in this instance," the man addressed Rufus in a deep, rough and yet friendly voice.

"Ah, that's refreshing, someone with a sense of humour." Rufus grinned as he leant up against the wall. "Not to be rude, but why are you here?"

"To help ya. Setz said ya weren't too bright, didn't know ya had a bad memory to boot," laughed the man before extending his arm. "Name's Arok. Weird name, I know, inheritance thing an' all."

"Rufus," the thief replied, introducing himself but not returning the gesture. "How do you propose to help?"

"When the distraction goes off I'm gunna throw ya over the wall," Arok replied casually as his hand fell back to his side with a dismissive shrug.

Rufus looked up at the wall. "How do you plan to throw me over it?"

"I could stand here and explain to ya the hows and whys or I could throw ya over, go get paid and get back to Tremel," Arok smirked.

Before Rufus could reply, there was an explosion in the distance from the western side of the city. Arok leant down, wrapping his arms around Rufus' shins.

"Time's up, handsome. Up and over and all that!" The barbarian laughed as Rufus flailed vainly against his strength. Before Rufus could protest, he was already airborne.

The thief soared straight up the side of the wall, clearing it by about an arm's length. Smiling in both surprise and relief at the display of Arok's superhuman strength, Rufus briefly saw that he had been flung over the path atop the wall. Fear gripped the flying man as he realised what went up, usually came down.

CHAPTER 6

WHAT A PICTURE IS WORTH

The Princess of Aquiocia sat alone in her chambers, staring at her canvas with an intense gaze that threatened to burn through the material she was sweeping with her brush. Her mind was lost in concentration as her hands swiftly yet carefully traced patterns across the surface. The seemingly random lines steadily formed a whole image with each precise stroke. Within half an hour of undivided attention, the Princess had produced the spitting image of the city of Aquiocia from the viewpoint of a trader approaching the main gates and first gazing upon her glory.

Every detail was included, from the cracks in the pavement to the blue and silver trimming across the bright armour of the guardsmen at the front gate. Those with a keen eye could make out every water drop in the spray from the fountains littered around the walls. Alicea's hand only slowed its feverish pace when she started painting the silhouettes in the centre of the masterpiece. One was a man of reputable stature, dressed in the splendid, almost sky-blue that was the royal garb, with a glittering gold scarf slung casually around his neck and falling neatly down his back. His head was adorned with a gold crown, encrusted with countless tiny sapphires and diamonds surrounding a larger sapphire in the middle. It clashed against his brown hair and almond eyes but the sheer majesty of the man could not be quelled, regardless of his attire.

The man's arms held a woman close. He was looking down at her youthful face, which denied the forty-something years it had weathered. The youth was within her smile and her blue eyes. Both features being massive and dazzling, it wasn't difficult to see where the young Princess had inherited them. Unlike her own, the late Queen's eyes never differed from the lucid, deep blue of an ocean at midnight.

Alicea's stony expression turned to one of pain as she recalled the numerous times the King would laugh and buckle under the gaze of what he considered "so many sapphire-eyed beauties" frowning at him at once. Her pain turned to outright anguish as she remembered the Queen's reply. "Well, if you'd act like the adult you claim to be instead of a fool, Alicea and I wouldn't have to scold you!"

Alicea pushed the echo of their laughter from her mind and raised her paintbrush once more.

Her expert strokes quickly revealed the Queen also wearing the royal colours of sky-blue in the form of a dress that complemented her slim body. As she looked up at the man with a smile lighting up her face, her shoulder-length flyaway hair did nothing to cover up the look of adoration and happiness that radiated from her when her eyes locked with the man's.

They were happy, Alicea thought bitterly. *Why can't I have that?*

As Alicea added more detail to the man and woman, a single tear rolled down her face. With each stroke of the brush, more and more features formed to recreate the King and Queen. As the picture came to life, the same sadness that had tormented her for almost a year swelled within the young Princess' heart. It was always impossible for her to forget anything, let alone that which caused her pain.

Eventually, her concentration broke, forcing her to place down her paintbrush, stand up and walk to the window. As she dried her eyes, she looked away from the main gate and instead fixated her gaze on a point in the distance where the ceremony was taking place. She felt her heart lift ever so slightly at the light from the fires and the joyous music blending with the laughter and mirth her people were emitting.

"At least they can still enjoy themselves," Alicea whispered to herself. The thought comforted her slightly.

As she went to turn away from the window, a bright flash caught her gaze in the furthest corner of the festivities as a distant rumble met her ears. As the flash died out, a purple cloud of dust erupted into the air.

"What in the world?"

Unable to make out what was going on from her slight vantage point, she ran to her chamber door and flung it open to peer down the deserted corridor.

Not a soul. Terrific. Well, at least the guards are there to help anyone that may be hurt.

Thinking better of the idea of walking the empty corridors of the castle alone, the Princess decided to close her door, turn its key and sit on the end of her bed. She knew that Locke would be there any minute to fill her in and act as the ever-protective guardian he wanted to be. With a sigh to herself at the idea of him fussing, she turned and looked at her painting before quickly snapping her head away. The irritation of his fussing was preferable to facing the sadness that her own creation had brought.

Why are there no guards in the corridor? Alicea wondered. *Why does that matter? I am not scared to walk alone . . .*

Rising to her feet again, she attempted to will her legs to walk out towards the chamber door. They followed her mental order for a single step before she was confronted by the overwhelming urge to stay where she was.

"Gah! What is wrong with me?!" she yelled against the silence.

The window! Her body was already in motion before the thought had settled.

Taking another look, the Princess could see the festivities in full swing despite the disturbance. About to retreat within her chambers, she noticed the courtyard just below was filled with knights. They were pouring out from the palace and stopping before the great gates leading further down the mountainside to the upper residential area. Somebody was yelling at the forefront of the soldiers.

Locke! Alicea realised. *What is that silly man doing?*

The Princess' attendant was issuing orders to the knights even as the gate slowly opened. As soon as the great barricade lifted, the men marched out into the streets.

"No, that's fine. Please, don't feel obligated to watch your posts!" Alicea quipped under her breath as she caught sight of the next interesting development.

There were people running away from the main crowd. She saw a few smaller groups fleeing in the opposite direction of the festivities. The people in the streets were pushing and shoving each other to get free, but the Princess couldn't make out the cause of the disturbance.

Is anyone going to tell me what is going on? Alicea thought, frustrated by her own inability to leave her chambers.

CHAPTER 7

AN UNCONVENTIONAL ENTRANCE

"Ooof!" Rufus groaned as his backside collided with pavement.

Quickly stifling any further verbal complaints in fear of attracting attention, he studied his surroundings. He also used this time to make mental notes of anything that would draw attention to him, or worse, get him killed.

The courtyard mentioned in the brief, Rufus deduced as he took in the massive fountain in front of him.

He had landed looking back the way he had come. His eyes adjusted slowly and he saw a statue twice his size. It was a monument in the image of the late Queen. The detail was delicate and thorough in catching every feature with uncanny precision. The creator was obviously very skilled, though Rufus found it difficult to care at that exact moment. The statue captured the image of the Queen standing with her palms together as though in prayer, with water shooting out of her fingertips and collecting at the base of her feet, which stood in a shallow pool.

If I remember right, she was supposedly a great mage.

Surrounding the fountain in a semi-circle were three rows of hedges, each standing two feet tall. Rufus quickly noticed the native flora of Aquiocia blooming from their well-maintained stems. Their shiny blue-and-silver hue contrasted against the green hedges splendidly, with the silver outline of the petals catching the moon's rays to illuminate the blue heart of the roses.

Rufus realised that he'd managed to land on the cobblestone path leading from the palace entrance to the fountain. Everywhere else here seemed to be thick, soft grass.

Before he had a chance to curse his misfortune and bruised backside, he spotted two lights in the distance. Rufus recognised them immediately as the same lanterns the knights who had chased him the night before had carried. Crouching behind the hedge closest to the fountain, the thief could hear the bare feet of the knights slapping against the path towards him.

Rufus felt a false sense of security behind his organic wall.

Why aren't they wearing their sabatons?

"This is why we need guard towers out here on the flanks. If we had them, we'd be able to tell if you actually saw anything and we wouldn't have to stop our drinking on your account," complained a voice.

"Considering we are supposed to be guarding the Princess' door, I'm sure we can stop drinking for a couple of minutes to investigate," came a wavering second voice in between hiccups. He seemed nervous about the fact that they weren't at their post.

"Who would want to see the Princess anyway? Useless wench hasn't made an appearance out of her chambers since the King and Queen went and got themselves . . . Well, you know. That said, at least the precious little prinny hasn't gone and got herself killed on a foolhardy quest of revenge," the first added thoughtfully.

As they got closer Rufus realised that his luck had turned.

They were intoxicated, and from the lack of metallic clinking he wagered they left their armour behind.

"Lower your voice. Just because everyone is at the ceremony doesn't change the fact that there are still plenty of ears in the wall to overhear your ramblings and – who are you?" The second knight cut off from his lecture, looking directly at Rufus crouching behind the hedge.

"Oh! Gentlemen! I apologise, I must have fallen asleep! You see, I'm the gardener. Please don't report me to the Princess!" Rufus lied to the sceptical-looking knights, an anxious hand running through his hair as he got to his feet. The poor lie allowed him a moment to locate the other knight, now directly behind the rose bush and shaking his head at his partner.

Well, they were never going to buy that anyway . . .

Rufus jumped backwards, preying on his opponents' sluggish reactions to create distance. His right hand darted to his sheathed dagger and with lightning speed he had drawn the blade, loosened his grip and let it fly free to bury itself in the first knight's chest, puncturing his heart. As blood spilled from the knight's wound, he collapsed in a heap against the stone. The second knight drew his sword and slashed wildly at Rufus' throat from across the hedge. Rufus nimbly jumped backwards and attempted the same move on the second man, bringing his remaining dagger from its sheath and launching it over the rose bushes at his target. The intoxicated knight drew and flailed his sword. His effort was rewarded when the dagger deflected off the waving blade and into the fountain's pool.

"Not sure if it was skill or booze that saved him there . . ." Rufus muttered as he looked at the knight swinging his sword at the rose hedge to get to him.

As the sword's steel bit at the hedge, the blade ravaged and scattered the roses. Rufus spun away and leapt into the fountain to retrieve his dagger. Mid-pivot, a rose glided up the side of his cheek and its long thorns cut through the soft flesh from just below his eye to just above his eyebrow. The momentum of him turning was the only thing that had stopped the thorn from piercing his eye.

Oh, how poetic, cut by a rose's thorn. At least its poison isn't dangerous . . . Rufus thought as he splashed through the pool towards the glint of moonlight on steel. He wrapped his hand around the dagger's hilt, stumbling for a second, with one eye closed due to the escaping blood.

He turned around to see the out-of-breath knight step over the gap in the hedge that he had carved. With a quick wipe of the blood around his eye, Rufus leapt out of the pool at the knight. He barely noticed the roses around him steadily changing in colour as he brought his dagger down towards the knight's head. His steel met his opponent's as the knight parried the clumsy blow. The clash sent Rufus sprawling to the ground.

Wasting no time, the knight brought the tip of his sword straight down at Rufus' chest. The thief rolled away, barely avoiding being executed. Rufus used the momentum to leap to his feet, hurling his blade once more. This time the blade dug into the knight's unarmoured shoulder, forcing him to drop his sword to the ground. The knight fell to his knees in pain, desperately trying to pull the weapon from his shoulder. Rufus ran forward, bending only to lift the abandoned sword from the ground. Raising it with two hands, he brought the sword up from the pavement and right across the knight's neck, ending the struggle in one fluid movement.

Rufus dropped the knight's blade in disgust and tore his own out of the corpses before wiping around his eye with his sleeve. A cursory pat-down of the bodies revealed a set of keys that he immediately pocketed. He stayed low, keeping an ear out for any sign of reinforcements before letting out a soft sigh of relief. *Either the castle's knights are all passed out from alcohol, or Setz's distraction has worked a treat. I should have learnt not to doubt his schemes by now . . .*

Deciding that the creepy silence was indeed a blessing, Rufus made for the door the knights had come from, figuring that was the entrance that Setz had mentioned. Upon reaching it, he made use of the key he had acquired from the now near-headless guard and peered inside, finding himself staring down a corridor. One way seemed to be a dead end but the other opened up into a much bigger room, which he guessed was the audience hall.

Taking a deep breath, Rufus took his first step into the beautiful castle of Aquiocia in search of his target – the precious little prinny herself.

CHAPTER 8

BROUGHT TOGETHER BY FATE AND MONEY

Rufus' pace was quick yet silent as he made his way down the corridor. The unease resting deep-seated in his chest was constantly antagonised by every door he snuck past. Each one he passed was one more that could open and blow his cover in an instant.

His hand instinctively reached up, running its fingers over the scratch he had received from the rose in the conflict earlier. The bleeding had stopped, although the stinging sensation had not ceased. The sting itself didn't bother him, nor did the fact that the rose's poison would never let it fully heal. It was the fact that the only thing that had managed to injure him so far was a goddamn flower.

Peering around the archway into the hall, his stomach plummeted as he took note of the numerous knights posted in every corner. He counted eight armoured men on the ground floor with swords, patrolling around a large fountain in the middle of room. A further ten were on the balcony, pacing back and forth, armed with crossbows.

Well . . . Rufus thought. *This is a real 'I-should-have-become-a-blacksmith's-apprentice' moment. What am I supposed to do?*

As Rufus pondered his next move from behind the arch,

a tingling sensation started to spread through his leg and a cold chill crawled through his entire body. He stepped back behind the cover of the archway and reached into his pocket to find the all-but-forgotten stone. Rufus examined the item curiously as it gave off no reaction except the cold sensation surrounding it.

What's with this thing? he wondered before his thoughts were interrupted by the sound of crashing water in the audience hall.

Rufus' neck nearly snapped as he turned back into the hall, panic filling his chest at the idea that his cover had been blown, but what he saw bewildered him. The fountain had erupted, spraying water skywards before doing the most peculiar thing he had ever seen water do. The sparkling liquid was gathering on the ground in small streams before moving as one towards an archway across the hall, much like a slithering snake, fleeing from a larger predator.

The guards were responding as guards should, stabbing at the water in both fear and surprise as the liquid made its retreat towards the exit across the great hall, effectively leading the guards away. One man called out, "This is sorcery, men, we will follow it to its source!" and was joined by the others.

Rufus was unsure if the guards had any real idea of how sorcery acted, not that he could have corrected them. It was a topic that he hated after all.

Within a minute all the guards had filed out of the hall, chasing the living water. The crossbow-wielding men atop the balcony followed in tow as they rushed down the stairs and joined their fellow soldiers. Rufus forced his legs to move in spite of his hesitance to run into the hall. Waiting for a hail of crossbow bolts that never came, his eyes darted along the length of the beautifully and artistically lined walls before they found his target – the very next corridor on the left. He sprinted down the new corridor, hearing the clinking of metal behind him.

Did I overlook some of the guards?

When there was no sign that anyone was coming after him, he looked up the new corridor lined with portraits of royalty. He was pleased to see a single door at the end of it, signalling that his mark was close.

Providing Setz's intelligence was correct, the Princess should be in there.

The young thief took in the residents within the ostentatious, jewel-encrusted frames and scowled in distaste. A frame alone could feed a pair of mouths for months.

Pompous bastards, the lot of them.

One portrait caught his eye and he even risked a moment to absorb the image. At the bottom of the painting was the name "Alicea A. Aquiocia".

His eyes wandered upwards and he immediately felt a strange and powerful stab of emotion. The woman in the portrait was striking indeed. The thief had seen the statues of the Princess within the city as many times as anybody else, but the sculpted stone didn't capture the Princess in the same way as this artist had. The statues didn't show the lustre of the hair that fell to just below her slender waist. They didn't capture the life in the Princess' eyes or the full, cheeky smile she wore here.

Now is hardly the time to develop a crush on a painting! Rufus' cynicism sobered him and he turned away from the masterpiece.

Upon reaching the door Rufus immediately tried the handle and wasn't surprised to find it was locked. Rolling his eyes, the thief looked at the door closely. It was as grand as any he had seen, a light azure in colour with silver trimming emblazoning the image of a large Aquiocian Rose across its surface. But it wasn't the door itself that he cared about so much as the lock. It was a simple, heavy mechanism that those with ample gold and minimal tact relied upon. Simply put, to one trained in the skills that Rufus was, the lock was a joke.

Rufus smirked as he produced a lock pick kit from his inside pocket and went to work, sliding the thin tool into the large cavity. Finding the flimsy trigger, he released the bolt and the door slowly creaked open, all within a few short seconds.

"Who is there?" a young, well-dressed woman asked as Rufus walked into the room as casually as someone who belonged there.

"I suggest you hold your tongue, Princess, lest I cut it out," Rufus growled, attempting to intimidate the woman.

"Ah, good, I've been awaiting your arrival, Prince Charming," retorted the Princess sarcastically, taking Rufus by surprise and allowing her time to follow up with the question, "What are you doing here?"

"I'm here to take you away. Will you cooperate or not?" Rufus asked, shakily attempting to regain control of the situation by stepping forward.

"No, I think not," Alicea replied curtly, flicking her long hair carelessly.

"I recommend you do or –" started Rufus.

"Or what? You will kill me? My parents have already been taken. Some would say that I would be reunited with them . . ."

Alicea started forcefully before trailing off.

"You don't believe that. I can see it in your eyes. Look, I've been ordered to do this and it will get done one way or another," Rufus said, crossing the room towards Alicea.

"With a single scream you will be crushed underneath countless royal guards. If you value your life I suggest you leave now." Alicea countered with her own threat and stepped forward into the light. She was only a few strides away now.

This made the thief hesitate and take in the woman before him properly. She was certainly the same woman, but the one in the painting seemed full of life and, while the one in front of him had a quick tongue, the fire wasn't there. Either way, Rufus knew that he had to stay the course he was on.

"I've ensured that no one will be coming to your aid," bluffed Rufus, leaping forward.

He wasn't sure if it was his words or something else, but the Princess hesitated just long enough for his fingers to close around her neck and pinch the pressure point, rendering her unconscious and forcing Rufus to catch her. He'd expected more resistance from someone he'd so openly admitted his intentions to.

Forget it, he ordered himself.

With the target subdued, he laid the Princess down on her bed and looked around the room for anything of use. After running his eyes over the painting tools and the rest of the chamber, he made his way to the window and peered out to see the courtyard below littered with guards along with an open main gate. He counted at least forty knights before returning his attention back to the now unconscious Princess.

So much for leading them away, Setz. Did some of them come back? Rufus thought bitterly. He decided that his only chance was going back the way he came and somehow climbing over the wall itself.

And then what? Am I just going to leap off a castle wall with a Princess? I'll surely break something.

With a sigh to himself, Rufus slung the light Princess over his shoulder and made for the door. As his hand reached for the knob, he froze at the sound of panicked voices outside. Opening the door just a crack to make the voices clearer, he heard the guards speaking.

"Are you sure?" asked a disbelieving knight.

"I know what I saw. Two of our men dead in the courtyard with the fountain of the late Queen! Hurry up!" replied the panicked voice.

"Right then! You two! Check on the Princess! The rest of you scour the other gardens and along the wall's perimeter. And you! Lead me to the bodies," said the voice with authority. It was met with a chorus of "Yes, Sir!"

Rufus heard the clinking of armour move off into the distance as two pairs of footsteps made their way to the Princess' chambers. Closing the door quietly, he laid the Princess on the bed in the best sleeping position he could manage before hiding behind the door, barely a second before it swung open.

"Milady! We just – oh, look, she is safe and sound asleep," said one of the knights.

"Somethin' don't seem right. Be careful . . ." said the sceptical second guard as they both crept slowly toward the Princess. "See, that's bruising on her neck! Someone – ergh!"

The brief gurgle of blood was all that was heard after Rufus silently followed the knights, drawing a dagger in each hand

and simultaneously burying each blade into the gaps between the knights' helms and armour and deep into their necks. Wresting the blades from the knights' flesh and sheathing them quickly, Rufus grabbed the Princess and slung her back over his shoulder.

Now or never I suppose, he thought, sprinting out the door and into the corridor.

CHAPTER 9

THE THEFT OF AQUIOCIA'S GREATEST TREASURE

This is without a doubt the worst kidnapping scheme ever concocted, Rufus thought grimly as he hurried down the corridor back towards the audience hall, the limp body of the Princess bouncing on his shoulder.

He knew full well that from there he would have to improvise greatly in regards to his escape plan. The way he got in was quite simply not an option for getting out. As he approached the archway leading back into the audience hall and peered inside, he noticed that it was deserted. He had to move quickly lest the guards come back and spot their Princess being carted off by an unknown man.

As he took in the hall properly for the first time, he was forced to admit it was indeed as beautiful on the inside as the outside of the palace. Its magnificence had been lost on him before as he had been too preoccupied with the guards and the peculiar behaviour of the fountain's water.

Why did the water act like that anyway? Rufus thought before dismissing the question as he shifted the unconscious Princess' weight on his shoulder.

She wasn't heavy, but carrying her wasn't an easy task. While he had her over his shoulder, he wouldn't be able to fight properly and he could forget about outrunning anyone for any length of time.

And the hair!

Rufus pushed his captive's hair from his face in irritation. He was surprised to find it was extremely soft to the touch. He was even more surprised to find himself thinking about the Princess' hair rather than a way to escape.

But does there have to be so much of it? Rufus grumbled mentally.

Looking at the palace's ice-blue walls finally, he stopped in wonder at the beautiful silver lines gracefully racing across the blue stone. In a moment of clarity, he saw that the seemingly random lines of silver were actually tracings of the Aquiocian Roses all across the length of every wall and no two surfaces were the same. It was as if they tied together as one masterfully done piece of art. In the centre of each rosebud there was a torch attached to the wall, their flames dancing across the flowers as they gave light to the great hall.

At the sight of the roses, Rufus' spare hand rose to his face. The dry blood flaked away under his fingers; the stinging sensation, however, was persistent.

Rufus snapped out of his reprieve and focused on the task at hand. Both sides of the hall were mirrored in terms of corridors and rooms. Both had three corridors branching off symmetrically from the hall. Between each of the corridors there were stained glass windows that had faint rays of moonlight pushing through the images and into the hall. Rufus' first impulse was to go through one.

Shatter the glass, climb out, and run for it. Simple, something urged.

Run where, genius? Rufus ridiculed himself. *Run to the giant walls that you can't get over while the knights investigate why one of the windows just decided to shatter of its own accord? Brilliant!*

From his spot in the archway, Rufus could see a staircase leading upwards to the second floor along with three more entrances to corridors along the upstairs balcony. They branched off in different directions to the ones below.

"A layout like this . . . From above it would almost look like a bloody snowflake. An unnecessarily giant snow . . ." Rufus stopped mid-curse.

There was a book he had stolen from the library titled *Aquiocia: The Delicate Snowflake of Gaia,* and as he recalled what he had read within the book as a child, a map formed in his mind. He sprinted straight to the stairs to the right of the thrones and followed their spiralling ascent to the second-floor balcony. He hugged the wall tightly out of fear of being spotted from the bottom level. He wasn't surprised when he heard the steady clinking of armour from above. Knights were beginning to return to the hall.

The royal quarters were located on the topmost floor and Rufus knew it as his memory continued to supply him with the information. Ducking straight down the first corridor to avoid the knights, the thief raced as quickly as he could while weighed down from carrying the unconscious Princess. He knew the second-floor corridors crossed over the top of the bottom in key locations to maintain stability in the higher floors. His memory was proven correct when he reached a cross section at the centre of the corridor. Rounding the corner, Rufus' free shoulder was clipped by something metallic. Barely staying upright, he corrected himself and kept running. He knew what it was even before he heard the drawl of a man.

"What . . ?" the knight managed to spit out as the strange figure that had knocked him off-balance took off down the corridor the knight had just come from.

Should have killed him. The alarm is even closer to becoming a problem. Rufus cursed his own incompetence.

He thought he heard muttering from the Princess on his shoulder but the noise had stopped. She was still out of it, which was about all that was going in his favour. This mistake could very well be fatal, but how was he supposed to fight while he was weighed down like this?

I could put her down. Rufus dismissed the idea immediately. What if she woke up while he didn't have hold of her?

The corridor melded into the next as he continued running straight in a haze of thoughts. As he reached the final corridor, he turned right to avoid the dead end he knew was waiting. Instead, he ran back towards the hall and came out of the archway right next to the staircase as he knew he would. His moment of triumph was cut short as his ears were filled with the sharp sound of bells ringing from around the castle, signalling that Rufus' presence was very well known within its confines.

"Well, my life just got worse, tenfold," Rufus muttered to himself when he felt the woman over his shoulder begin to squirm.

"Put me down, Thief!" came the voice of the Princess from over his shoulder.

"Check that – hundredfold," Rufus corrected before taking the steps two at a time as the lower level of the audience hall flooded with knights. "I will in a minute, Princess. I just have to get out of here alive; that's my priority."

"Oh, give it up, you've failed! The only reason you got this far is that I took to residing in a lower-class suite after my parents died," Alicea yelled while pounding her fists into Rufus' back. "Take solace in the fact that you aren't the only one who has tried and failed. There have been many."

"I'm not like the others," retorted Rufus as he gasped for air. The night's ordeal was slowly catching up with him and the Princess waking up had started wearing him down.

"And what – pray tell – makes you so different?" snapped Alicea.

"I am – considerably – more – handsome."

"Oh, for the sake of all that is holy! Arrogance is hardly a good look for a dead man! If you don't – what's this?" Alicea's anger broke off and was replaced with curiosity as Rufus felt her lift something from his pockets. "A stone? And a strange one at that. It's like its surface is moving."

"What do you mean? Wait, put that back!" growled Rufus as he reached the top of the staircase that was evidently a lot higher than the book had suggested. His words were rushed between gasps. "You can't just rummage through someone's pockets!"

"Uh huh, you have no moral high ground here, Mr. Thief! Not after deciding that kidnapping me was a good way to spend your evening!" came her sarcastic reply.

"This bitch needs a muzzle," Rufus muttered under his breath.

"This delinquent needs a crossbow bolt!" Alicea shrieked in response.

After Rufus didn't reply, she continued her interrogation.

"Why do you have this? It's not part of the castle's treasury.

I'd certainly have noticed something so beautiful," Alicea prodded, calmly embracing the conversation as she caught a glimpse of the guards below.

When Rufus reached the top floor his escape route came into sight. The staircase led to another balcony with large double doors that he knew opened to a bridge stretching down to the ramparts. Rufus didn't have a plan for when he got there but it was a start. Maybe he could find a way down one of the side towers, or if he could get back to the eastern side where the wall was lower to the ground, he could find a soft spot of grass to aim for.

He ran across to the double doors, awkwardly kicking them open and almost falling to his death in the process. He teetered on the edge of the door frame before throwing himself back from the open air he'd almost attempted to traverse.

Rufus swore as he glared at the open air where a deployable wooden bridge should have been. Then he swore again.

"Counting on a platform, Mr. Thief?" Alicea sniggered from her place upon his shoulders.

"Shut up!" Rufus snarled viciously, moving his focus to the strange contraption protruding from the wall.

There was a lever that bent at a right angle in the middle of its length, obviously designed so that someone could manually rotate the lever to deploy the bridge. Even if he had the time, and the free hands to turn the crank, the large padlock holding it in place wasn't going to budge.

The clanking of armour broke his internal monologue of curses.

Damn it! What a way to go . . .

"Where did you find this stone?" Alicea asked.

"Why does that matter, woman?!" Rufus snapped.

"Mr. Thief, I suggest you speak to me a little more nicely," the Princess said in a grim tone.

"Why the hell should I?" Rufus grunted, spinning and looking down at the soldiers now filling the second floor. There was dozens of men and women clambering across both balconies; he was surrounded.

"Because, you're going to place me on the ground gently, and then ask me to save your life."

Rufus barked a laugh.

"Alternatively, I could embrace death by hurling you off this balcony. I don't beg, Princess."

"I'm not asking you to beg, I'm offering you a way out," Alicea said with a little more force. "Put, me, down."

He didn't know if it was the way the Princess spoke, or the sound of metal on the staircases, but Rufus did as commanded. Effortlessly swinging the Princess off his shoulder, he growled, "Betray me and I will end your life before they can end mine."

"Don't be such a brute," Alicea replied, clicking her fingers towards the wall beside the staircase they'd just ascended. "Press your back up against that wall."

"Why –" Rufus broke off upon catching the cold gaze from the Princess.

The thief eyed the staircase as he followed the orders of his former captive and awkwardly placed his back towards the stone wall. The firm sensation of the stone didn't help the feeling of being trapped when he saw the shadows on the stairs. Here he would die, pressed up against a wall by order of the woman he was supposed to have kidnapped.

Then the wall was gone. He was falling.

A surprised yelp escaped his throat as he fell through the air. At least, it momentarily *felt* like falling. He was actually stumbling backwards until his ankle found something solid and he fell onto his back. He braced, waiting for pain but instead finding the softness of bedding.

What is going on? His mind raced as his body flung back upright and faced the way he'd come.

His bewildered expression was met by a stone wall similar to the one he'd pressed his back against a moment before.

Across from the foot of the bed was a large writing desk with half a dozen bound scrolls littered across it. Upon the walls were countless ribbons and gem-encrusted weapons. Rufus had seen that sort of weapon before, ostentatious and impractical – they were ceremonial. The kind given to someone in honour of a great deed, generally held in the company of a lot of people with deep pockets dying to be picked.

He knew where he was even before the shadow of someone emerged from the stone. Immediately on his feet and primed with weapons drawn, Rufus recognised the Princess. It took her a moment to examine the chambers with a doleful expression before pointing at Rufus' weapons.

"Away," she ordered. Her voice was commanding, her eyes shaking at the sight of the weapons.

"You're a mage!" Rufus declared.

"The magic is not my own. Put the weapons away, now."

He didn't like being ordered, but he did as commanded.

"What are you doing here?"

"Where else would I be? Come." Alicea flicked her hair and dashed towards the door.

Rufus had no choice but to follow in bewilderment.

"Now," she began, opening the door a fraction and peering out, "this is the barracks of the Warmaster and his elite guard. Obviously, these are the Warmaster's personal quarters. They are away from the city and have been for some time."

Rufus didn't say a word. What was he supposed to say?

"Most of the guards will still be investigating the palace; now is our time to leave. The main gate is our target and there are two entrances to these barracks. One from within the palace, one from outside."

"Princess," Rufus started, finally finding his voice. "If you are coming with me, can't we just walk out? Can't you just give the order to leave us alone?"

"Hmm, I'm not sure." Alicea brought her hand to her cheek in mock thoughtfulness. "I've often pondered if my knights would pause long enough to find out if I wanted to be kidnapped or not before killing my assailant."

"Point taken," Rufus conceded as he reached to pull open the door, only to push it closed again. There were knights walking into the barracks, three of them.

Alicea looked at Rufus with a puzzled look.

"You said there wouldn't be anyone here!" Rufus accused.

"I humbly apologise, Mr. Thief. This is my first time commandeering my own kidnapping!" she hissed back.

"What do you want me to do here?"

Alicea's hand flashed forward to Rufus' side, relieving him of one of his blades and handing it to him.

"I want you to kidnap me."

❖

"How does one *lose* a Princess?" one of the knights laughed, the youngest of the three. "Where do you even go to look for –"

The young man physically choked on his words when he saw someone appear from the Warmaster's chambers. The two others, who had their backs turned, spun on the spot with expressions of surprise at the sight of their Princess walking slowly with a man looming behind her and a long dagger at her throat. She whimpered as the cold metal brushed her neck.

To the knights, she was terrified. To Rufus, she was committing to the role of captive. They were both right. While there was a perpetual anxiety resting within her as she was steadily led across the silent room, it was the blade that sparked the true fear. It was the sort of weapon that wounded and maimed. It was the sort of weapon that killed. It was the sort of weapon that had resulted in the eradication of her family.

This man is not going to kill me, Alicea tried to reassure herself. *He doesn't even have a firm grip on my arm. He isn't going to hurt me.*

The thoughts did nothing to alleviate the trepidation nestled inside her. She wouldn't know any measure of peace until the blade was removed from her sight.

Involuntary tears fell from her grey eyes as the knights drew their weapons.

More blades . . .

"Ah, ah, ah!" Rufus started, making the Princess jump slightly. "Wouldn't want your Princess to get hurt, now would we?"

The knights stopped in a mixture of confusion and concern. Something wasn't right.

"Now, lad . . ." one of the older knights started tentatively.

"Don't do something you'll regret here."

"Bit late for that, don't you think?" Rufus replied coldly. He was falling into the role of hostage-taker and he exuded a strained calm. "One of two things is going to happen here."

The knights remained silent.

"The Princess and I are either going to walk out of this castle together." Rufus paused to look at each of them in turn. "Or neither of us are."

A few seconds passed before Rufus made his demand.

"Weapons on the ground."

The knights obliged.

"If I think for a second we are being followed or you have retrieved your weapons . . ." Rufus left the threat open-ended as he forcefully dragged Alicea across the room, dagger never leaving her throat.

As they reached the doorway, Alicea whimpered, "Do not follow . . . Please, that's an order."

Rufus was gambling and he knew it as he backed out of the barrack doors, pulling the Princess out of the room with him. He was still watching the knights and a quick glance over each shoulder revealed two options – a corridor or an archway leading to a spiral staircase. A watchtower. He'd only seen them from the outside, but he knew that they reached the ground. What he hadn't considered was that they might open up into the palace itself. The Princess' plan quickly became apparent.

"Door," Rufus growled at the youngest and most uncertain-looking knight. The knight stepped forward hesitantly. "No heroics, kid."

The kid reached towards the door and flicked his wrist,

stepping back hurriedly. The door swung slowly and clicked into place. The moment Rufus heard the click he released the Princess and slammed his long knife into the keyhole. It didn't go particularly deep, but that wasn't his goal. With a grunt, he ripped the weapon from left to right, up and down before pulling it free. The lock was mangled.

"Move," he ordered, though he didn't grab the Princess again. He didn't feel the need to; the Princess looked more than a little uneasy as she wiped the tears from her face and composed herself before walking towards the archway.

It was just an act, right? Rufus wondered. *She looked genuinely upset. No, had to be an act. She followed me, this is what she wants. But, why?*

He felt he should say something, anything, but he couldn't think of anything. They reached the archway and Alicea paused for a moment, staring at the pillar in the centre of the tower. Spinning on the spot, she uttered a single word.

"Run."

His instincts spiked as the sound of metal hitting stone met his ears and the pair began their hasty descent down the watchtower's winding staircase. It was narrow, so Rufus was stuck behind the Princess the entire way. She wasn't slow, moving with litheness he hadn't expected. But, compared to a man who'd spent a large part of his life running, he quickly became frustrated. Whoever was following them down the watchtower was likely to find the others now locked in the barracks, if they hadn't already broken free.

"Halt!" a voice called from somewhere above.

Damn it!

Thankfully, Alicea appeared to have had a reserve of speed

and their feet hit ground level within two more laps of the tower's wall. A knight walked through the entrance of the barracks and Alicea screamed as a dagger flew over her shoulder and lodged itself in the man's arm.

Alicea had frozen to the spot, staring at the wounded man as he looked down at his new wound in shock. Rufus shoved Alicea forward, her small frame easily led by his strength. His free hand formed a fist and punched the unfortunate knight squarely in the jaw. The man fell against the door frame and to the ground.

The fresh outside air hit Alicea's face as her mouth attempted to form words.

"Move, Princess," Rufus growled, realising that they were in the main courtyard. The main doors leading to the castle were closed, the main gate open, and no one stood between them and their escape. Everyone was still within the castle; if they ran for it now . . .

"You . . . You attacked that man . . ." she stammered.

"He will live," Rufus snapped, shoving her in the direction of the gate – their escape.

"How do –"

"I know because if I wanted him dead, I'd have aimed for his neck!"

His tone actually sobered the mortified Princess somewhat. There was a sincerity buried within the viciousness. She stepped forward hesitantly, as if unsure whether or not she could still walk. After a couple of shaky steps, she broke into a sprint, with a relieved Rufus close behind.

The pair of shadows raced across the courtyard, with Rufus constantly glancing back both at the tower and main entrances to the palace. The grand doors didn't budge, which, while he knew it was a blessing, still seemed odd. In fact, the way the soldiers had acted in general seemed peculiar, not that he understood the inner workings of the military. They all seemed so . . . disorganised.

Rufus could see shadows in the tower's entrance, though he couldn't make out anything specific. He'd caught the Princess and was now beside her in their dash for freedom. He caught a glimpse of her face in the moonlight; she wore a solemn expression. Rufus knew that look. She was hurting.

The Princess slowed suddenly, and Rufus matched her speed before scanning the area ahead of them for her trepidation. He saw . . . houses. Houses and streets. They'd cleared the main gate. They'd made it.

No guards at the main gate? Rufus thought in disbelief. *Really?*

Alicea was staring back towards the castle with a frown that was deepening by the second. She looked poised to run back the way they'd come.

"This is still a kidnapping, you realise?" Rufus said softly. He didn't move any closer – he didn't have to. They both knew he could catch and restrain her if she ran.

"I know a ruffian's word isn't worth much, but promise me that man is all right."

"He's fine," Rufus said shortly, meeting the Princess' accusing gaze before continuing. "It hit him in the arm. There were knights coming down the stairs behind us that would see him. He is fine."

For a strained moment, there was a silence between the two.

"Speaking of those knights that were behind us –" Rufus started before Alicea cut him off.

"Take me to whoever sent you."

Rufus' eyebrow rose, but rather than replying, he simply gestured down a side street. With a quick glance back at her home, Alicea fled to the shadows of the city with her assailant.

CHAPTER 10

THE SIDE OF AQUIOCIA THAT ALICEA NEVER SAW

"What are you looking for, Mr. Thief?" asked an impatient Alicea. They had been weaving through side streets and alleys before Rufus had slowed, staring at the ground as he walked. "There will be patrols and they know we are no longer within the castle."

"Hush, Princess, and follow," Rufus whispered with a glance at his captive. She was walking calmly, her back straight and her pale eyes forward. She had held onto the stone the entire escape, but had stashed it away from view when Rufus wasn't looking. Concerned that her captor might take it back while doing her best to seem aloof.

She keeps her cool well given she's being abducted, Rufus thought before scolding himself. Probably because I've practically let her walk free. She could change her mind and start screaming at any moment. I should just knock her out again . . .

But he didn't. Something told him it wasn't needed, or rather, he *felt* it wasn't. Despite the fact he was currently hunted by the Aquiocian military for kidnapping their Princess – one who was doing nothing to hide her presence – he wasn't anxious. He almost felt at ease, as if he'd taken something to take the edge off. He regarded the sensation warily, but didn't fight it.

"Hmph," Rufus grunted as they turned into another side street. Two stalls stood on one side of the narrow road, both closed up for the night. Not that it mattered if they were tended to or not as they were owned by merchants of the Underbelly. Although the assassins within the guild held a certain disdain for Rufus, the merchants looked upon him favourably. He was, after all, one of very few in their society who came with a line of credit directly from the Guildmaster.

The pair entered the alley and Rufus, not skipping a beat, knelt and studied a lid covering a manhole. Alicea looked on with disgust and shifted from foot to foot.

"Mr. Thief, if you think for a second that I'm going to go down into the sewers, you are sorely mistaken."

"Princess, you will do this if you wish to meet with my employer."

The Princess didn't reply. She didn't move as Rufus picked the lock holding the metal plate in place and removed it. It was only when she heard the distant sounds of a crowd that her shoulders slumped in resignation and she lowered herself into the manhole, Rufus following with a smirk.

Rufus smiled grimly when he heard a gasp from the Princess as the pair came to the Underbelly.

Her eyes darted across the makeshift town that so many people called home. From the small huts built from whatever wood and other resources the people could salvage from under the city or sneak from above, to the massive pillar in the distance with the light of fires flickering from inside. The people passing them, in what she supposed could be called the main street, gave Rufus a nod or a small greeting before fixing their eyes on Alicea as the two shuffled towards the pillar.

The Princess' unease grew as they made their way further into the city before Rufus addressed her roughly.

"Listen up, Princess," he began coarsely. "If you leave my side I can't be held accountable for what might happen. Providing we don't go into the deeper regions of the Underbelly, staying with me should be enough protection."

"Deeper regions?" she enquired.

"In every town, city or settlement, there is the lower quarter, if you will. A more violent and straightforward district," answered Rufus. "A neighbourhood that doesn't care who I am, and even less so who you are if they can get the pretty clothes off your back or the shiny trinkets from your skin for themselves."

"So even the Underbelly has an underbelly." Her voice wavered with the weak joke.

Rufus showed his grim smile once more as they got closer to the giant pillar, while Alicea's eyes lingered on the stalls they walked past. The food seemed relatively fresh and some of the jewellery stands had newer trinkets from the merchants above ground. But it wasn't their wares that she wished to discuss.

"How is this place so well lit? Should it not be darker down here?" Alicea asked curiously, a question that Rufus had not thought to ask for months after his arrival. He silently commended the Princess' observational skills and nodded towards the stone above them, which served as a ceiling. Alicea saw the peculiar orbs of light hanging in mid-air.

"Those orbs are one of the results of the Guildmaster's magic. It's an enchantment or something that will give light to those who mean no harm or something like that," Rufus replied uncertainly.

"I'm not sure I understand," the Princess pressed.

"All I know is that if someone is walking around as if they cannot see anything, it means that the Guildmaster's magic doesn't help them. There's no light down here for that person," Rufus continued to explain poorly.

"Oh, I see! It's a defence strategy." The Princess nodded thoughtfully while Rufus stared at her in confusion.

"Go on," Rufus replied, encouraging her.

"I'm willing to bet the Guildmaster takes an interest in those who cannot see within his lair," Alicea continued confidently. "Any intruders would be at a distinct disadvantage here."

Rufus quashed the urge to commend the Princess. Instead he looked forward once more and focused on their destination. The Princess continued to look all around her in wonder, trying to ignore the anxiety in her chest from being stared at.

These people have really made something out of nothing, Alicea realised. *But that aside, they shouldn't be forced to live down here as sub-humans. When I'm finished with this task, I must help these people. If I can . . .*

"Here we are, Princess. The headquarters of the Guilty Blade, the Guildmaster's organisation of assassins, cutthroats and thieves. Please remember that your title means nothing here. In fact, I'd just keep your mouth shut unless spoken to."

Before Alicea could reply, Rufus opened the door to the giant pillar and pushed her inside. The Princess couldn't control yet another gasp escaping her lips as all eyes fell on the pair – from men who looked like mountains of meat with scars littered across their faces, to smaller individuals who were cloaked from head to toe, save the cruel and calculating eyes protruding from their hoods.

"The staircase," Rufus instructed, referring to the archway across the room and pushing Alicea forward with one hand while the other rested on his sheathed blade's hilt.

As they ascended the stairs towards the top, as they passed each floor and caught the eye of more and more thugs, Rufus felt as though it had never taken this long. On the third level, they were forced to stop at a rough voice calling, "Outcast!"

"Do these people know who I am?" Alicea whispered.

Rufus had no time to whisper an answer back.

"Well, well, who would have thought the 'lady-respecting' Rufus would bring himself back a prize like this?" Rufus recognized the voice of Keenin, who had let him in when he was there last.

"Just open the door, Mongrel," Rufus growled.

"Tsk tsk, that's how you ask a favour? You know, if you had've just joined us you could come and go as you please," Keenin replied.

Rufus was about to reply, before being cut off by Alicea haughtily addressing the man.

"I'm terribly sorry to interrupt what I'm sure is a meeting of the minds for the local delinquents, but what exactly do you mean by 'prize'? I am an actual person, royalty if you'd believe, and most certainly not a trophy that Mr. Thief here seized after some glorious victory in battle. In fact, I'd go so far as to say that he is far more adept at running than actually fighting."

Keenin stared at Alicea, slightly taken aback and amused as Rufus shook his head in disbelief. He couldn't work out if he was angry or impressed.

"This is the result of a mission given to me by the boss himself. Are you going to open the door, or do I tell him you refused?" Rufus asked, recovering quickly.

Keenin lost his amused look immediately and grunted in affirmation.

"Fine, follow me."

As the three of them climbed the stairs, Rufus leant in and whispered harshly in Alicea's ear.

"Listen here, mistakes like that can cost someone their life. So, before you piss off the entire guild – belt up about anything royal!"

Alicea smirked before whispering back, "Well, aren't I lucky to have Mr. Thief here to protect me?"

"Mr. Thief is likely to get a bloody knife in the ribs if Miss Brat doesn't shut her mouth," Rufus snarled before pulling away as they reached the door and Keenin opened it with ease.

"I'll just put it on your tab," he muttered, walking back down the stairs.

As the pair entered the room, Rufus turned to Alicea once more in warning.

"Don't bother, Mr. Thief!" she said, cutting Rufus off before he got a single word out.

With a flick of her long, dark hair and a cheeky smile, the young Princess turned to the man at the desk.

"Hello, Setz, I see your ability to make an office feel welcoming hasn't improved."

"Your Highness." Setz rose from his seat and genuinely

smiled for what Rufus swore was the first time. "It has been too long."

CHAPTER 11

THE CALL OF HOME

"You ready, Arok? We haven't got time to mess around," called an impatient voice from a horse-drawn carriage. Arok lumbered across the open field away from Aquiocia and towards his companion.

"Just relax, had to take care of something for an old friend of my father," Arok responded as he leapt on the back of the carriage behind the man at the reins. "Why so impatient, Stiff?"

"The name is Stefan and you know it. We need to get back, I got word from Garnet," Stefan explained. As Stefan lashed the horse with its reins, Arok looked at his companion with interest.

Stefan was a few inches taller than Arok and his opposite in almost every way. With emerald green eyes and perfectly maintained blond hair combed across to make a single fringe down the right side of his head, he struck a handsome figure.

He had donned a perfectly pressed wayfarer's outfit designed for travel and, while Arok couldn't for the life of him work out why Stefan cared so much about his appearance, they had quickly become inseparable since their first meeting.

Stefan had come to Arok's home village of Tremel a few months earlier in a state of delirium. The man couldn't recall where he was from or why he was stumbling through the forests on the outskirts of the Aquiocian kingdom's influence. His sudden appearance had borne some scepticism within the village's residence, but Arok had insisted the man be subjected to the challenges of Tremel to prove his worth. Stefan's skill with the bow had quickly demonstrated his prowess in hunting and providing a service in return for their hospitality. The man had continued to earn his keep in more ways than hunting, often accompanying Arok on errands issued by Kurok, father of Arok and Chief of their village.

"What does the old crow want now? Get it? Old crow? Cause she can turn into one." Arok chuckled at his own pun.

"Yes, yes, very humorous. She brings word that Lyrium has found the lost ruins in the forest," Stefan replied quickly.

"What? Damn it, we are a week away at best on this half-dead horse!" snapped Arok.

"Well as we both know, if we were to take two horses from Aquiocia we could halve the time –" started Stefan, only to be interrupted.

"Not gunna happen, Stiff! Not touching the stupid beasts," Arok declared, expressing his well-known disdain for horse riding.

The pair sat in silence for a time, the only sounds being the crunch of the path underneath the horse's hooves, the carriage's wheels, and the occasional lash from Stefan as he whipped the horse.

"Did Garnet say anything else? About the ruins and Lyrium, I mean," enquired Arok.

"Dark, dank and smells different to the rest of the forest. Garnet also senses something – *off* – about the place. She said that the magical energy from within is unlike anything she's ever felt before and yet so familiar at the same time," replied Stefan.

"I asked if you heard anything else, not to confuse me. What about Lyrium?" Arok asked sharply.

"She awaits your return before entering the ruins."

Satisfied with that, Arok settled back in the wagon and closed his eyes.

CHAPTER 12

THE REPETITION OF HISTORY

Far from the castle of Aquiocia on the edge of her kingdom was the small hamlet known as Tremel.

Normally quiet, it was favoured by hunters and the odd traveller who wanted to make use of its limited facilities, such as a warm bed or the stories and laughter of the hamlet's hunters. The village comprised a few lines of huts and tents that circled a massive timber cabin. Being a hamlet where the residents were firm believers of "you make what you live in" and "you eat what you kill," some fared better than others. But there was a certain quaint unity within its culture and – through iron-clad loyalty – Tremel's hunters and warriors were some of the strongest in the land.

In front of the timber cabin was a large bonfire. Surrounded by thick logs designed for sitting, it made the perfect place for the conversations and stories shared at the end of each day. On this night, however, the bonfire did not attract its usual light-hearted stories or jokes. Nor did Lyrium, the Chief's chocolate-brown-haired daughter-in-law, feel any comfort or warmth from the blaze as the discussion she was deeply engaged in sent chills through her body.

"The ruins are all that remain of the temple where our ancestors worshipped Gaia. Despite the fact that our people are divided across the world in different settlements, those ruins were what symbolised our unity centuries ago, when Tremel was also a great city," lectured the Chief, Kurok. "It is your duty, and not my foolhardy son's, to go into the depths and locate the stone."

"What do you mean 'locate it'? You never even explained how you managed to lose the temple in the first place," replied Lyrium.

Kurok sighed, staring into the blaze in the centre of the circle. His scarred and wrinkled face screwed up in an expression that was the closest thing to pain Lyrium had ever seen on it. What was once a thick mane of dirty brown hair had thinned in the past year and had even attracted some stray silver hairs. His physique had also suffered and while he still wrestled with the young hunters, even that very day, they had left him much more exhausted than they used to.

Between the rumours circulating the land, the search for the ruins and other political difficulties, it was a small wonder that Kurok was a little worse for wear. After a moment, he looked back at the young hunter to continue the tale.

"He went by the name Lucian. The story tells that no one ever saw his face; it was hidden from view by his dark purple armour. He wielded two blades – one made of metal that was the colour of the blackest of nights; the other shone with the light sung of by angels. At his command was an army of fallen men and women obeying his every word."

"Fallen men and women? Surely you can't be speaking of Necromancy, Chief?" piped up a fellow villager. Kurok had gained the attention of all nearby.

"No, our ancestors didn't believe it was Necromancy.

Neither do I. They say that it's much stronger because even the best Necromancers can only summon feeble imitations of the victim's living forms. It can't be Necromancy, especially the numbers that Lucian had."

"What makes you think it's the same man? How could it be after two hundred years?" enquired Lyrium.

That is where I come in, young lady, said the soft voice of Garnet, her authoritative voice entering everyone's mind. Whether vocally or telepathically, the older woman spoke as if giving a lecture.

All eyes turned to the tree just outside the circle where Garnet often perched in the form of a crow so she could keep lookout as well as be included in the conversation.

I've been investigating the major cities and even small towns. There have been odd goings-on. One incident is recurring over and over and has formed a pattern. In cemeteries, there has been a sighting of an armoured silhouette.

"But how – how could it be the same person?" pushed Lyrium.

"That we do not know, but we do know he was never vanquished. He was defeated before he could gather all the stones, yes. But the stones' chosen Vassals were disorganised. The battle at Tremel was particularly bitter. They were besieged for weeks and eventually exhausted their resources. The enemy was relentless, and our ancestors tired. The Vassal did what needed to be done. She took the entirety of the stone's power unto herself, allowing herself to be devoured. Her body was turned to stone in exchange for the salvation of her people." Kurok's voice cracked a little from overuse.

"Her sacrifice was not in vain," he continued after a cough.

"It made the land for leagues around the fortress explode with life. Seedlings grew to trees in seconds, shooting up from the ground, either impaling our ancestor's enemies or sending them flying. Undergrowth lashed out with barbed vines, restraining and choking all who opposed Tremel.

"The very ground shook and while our ancestors fled, unharmed by the magic's embrace, the ruins of our once grand castle moved with the rapidly changing earth."

Lyrium paled at the thought of turning to stone. "Such a sacrifice . . ."

"She is with Gaia now." Kurok bowed his head in genuine reverence.

Lyrium found herself doing the same. It took her a moment to absorb the implications of such a sacrifice.

While it forced Lucian to flee, it also created miles of dense forest that kept growing years after, Garnet contributed for the Chief, who was rapidly growing tired of speaking so much. *His swords were all that remained of the enemy.*

"His swords were still here? Where are they now?" replied Lyrium.

His sword's locations are kept secret for the wellbeing of all. They curse anyone who tries to use them. They, like the stones, are not of this world.

Lyrium paused thoughtfully. "Were there no other Vassals?

Kurok's eyes darted back to the feathered lookout. The bird held herself with dignity, chest puffed out slightly and head moving slightly to take in her surroundings.

Only the Vassal of Fire and our own Vassal of Earth even located their stones and were chosen. Scourge, the city to the far east, was annihilated in minutes as the Vassal of Fire was consumed by the power of her stone. She destroyed her entire civilisation in one uncontrolled rampage when her body and soul gave out. The possibility that history might repeat is a fear that we face.

"The power you describe is . . . hard to believe," stammered Lyrium.

"Indeed, it seems the work of fiction. But this is straight from the archive. What happened in Scourge was a tragedy, and the battle that took place here is our legend," replied the Chief. "If it truly is the same enemy as before, then he's grown more cautious. We must be prepared this time. You must gather your stone quickly."

"Even in light of this, I must refuse to enter the ruins without Arok," Lyrium said.

"Yes, he will be back in a few days anyway. Until then, continue your training with Garnet," Kurok replied in a resigned voice.

Lyrium nodded and the bonfire became silent. It was as if the silence was the chance the gathered villagers had been waiting for to throw questions at their Chief as the entire circle erupted in conversation again.

One question stood out: "How do we even know Lyrium is the Vassal?"

Garnet's voice entered their minds once more.

We know as it was Lyrium who came across the ruins, she said shortly before adding ominously, *The ruins have appeared in the centre of the path that hunters take to the forest to search for game. It is a location people walk past everyday but they appeared in front of Lyrium. She did not find the ruins; they found her.*

CHAPTER 13

AN ENEMY OF OLD?

Arok yawned loudly as he awoke in the back of the horse-drawn cart. He looked around through sleep-filled eyes to see trees spanning all directions. Ahead was the bridge that signalled the edge of Aquiocia's patrolled land. After crossing the structure, there were only small settlements who enjoyed the freedom of independence, but also took advantage of relative protection from the great kingdom. Arok and Stefan wouldn't be questioned about coming or going.

After they made their way through the forest they would be on the last leg of their journey to South Tremel. Its name reflected that it was the most southerly of the Tremel settlements and while it was technically just outside of Aquiocia's control, the residents of the small hamlet had accepted the royal family as their lords.

Two hundred years prior, after narrowly avoiding annihilation, Tremel's people had to decide whether to stay or leave. Most left; a lot of those who remained died from illness or fatigue from the long battle. It was only when the royal ancestors approached them and offered help that Tremel offered its loyalty to the crown.

Those who rebuked the idea of an alliance left, forming their own settlements, distancing themselves from the site of their destroyed homes. There had been heavy controversy within the ranks of those leaving about where they'd go. Finally, they split into two factions: one residing on the isles to the west, the other deep within the northern mountains. A fourth faction had formed and cut ties with anything to do with their people and had marched east. No one within the three established settlements felt the need to collaborate their efforts in finding the part of their family that did not want to be found.

Stefan, sitting at the reins, showed no signs of fatigue despite the vigilance he had held over the past three days. Stopping only for the horse to graze on grass and drink from small streams, they had made excellent time by allowing only a few hours of rest each night. Arok stretched himself out as best he could in the back of the cart while Stefan rolled his eyes over the top of his grunting and groaning. The pair reached the stream and Stefan directed the horse straight to the water. The liquid passed by swiftly, coming up past the bedrock to the grass, showing that the area upstream had had some heavy rain recently.

The pair hopped off the cart to change roles, Arok taking the break to wash his face and drink from the stream as Stefan stretched out his limbs. Now that they were approaching the edge of Aquiocia's area of control, Stefan would remain in the carriage to rest.

"We have made exceptional time, Arok," Stefan stated as Arok sat down in the shallows to enjoy the cool water after turning his nose up at the taste. He craved wine, dipping his wineskin in the water to create a diluted substitute. "We could very well be back in South Tremel in four days, three if there are no interruptions."

"Not soon enough if you ask me. Those ruins . . ." Arok paused thoughtfully.

"I'm sure Lyrium won't go into them without you. She isn't that reckless."

Stefan was about to add another point to his argument when Arok saw his eyes widen. Before words could be spoken, Arok leapt up and ran for the cart as arrows flew into the water where he had been sitting. Stefan pulled his longbow off his shoulder and nocked an arrow in less than a second. He stood up straight with the arrow drawn back, aimed towards the trees. Calm washed over him as he took control of his breathing and felt the slight breeze telling him things that only he could hear.

Things like disturbances within its flow, people moving through it. It had told him that the people were within the trees directly across from them and not very deep within the forest. It told him that his arrows would veer slightly to the left when firing at the trees. The arrows that had been fired at Arok were designed for short bows and would have found their mark if he hadn't moved. They found no assistance from the wind.

"How many, Stiff?" Arok growled.

"There are several taking cover, but . . ." Stefan let his arrow fly. It soared across the stream, piercing one of their opponent's skulls who had chosen that unfortunate moment to poke his head out from cover. ". . . They seem to be amateurs at best."

Arok took on the role of sentry, peering towards the trees and glancing behind them. Stefan casually avoided enemy fire by moving slightly to either side before returning his own. The enemies hadn't realised that, despite their numbers, they were at a severe disadvantage. Stefan outmatched any opponent in ranged combat, even before taking into consideration the fact that they seemed equipped with short bows.

Stefan killed two more within the trees: one who was playing lookout and the other as he was climbing to a vantage point. Both were dead before they hit the ground. As he lined up another shot the brush behind him burst with movement as two of the bandits sprinted towards the lone archer, short swords drawn.

Arok had been waiting for this and was instantly upon them. Putting his shoulder up and his head down, he charged past the surprised Stefan and intercepted one of the attackers. The assault smoothly lifted his enemy off the ground and sent him sprawling back as the second reached Stefan.

He brought his blade into a downward swing, which Stefan smoothly avoided by moving mere inches to the left before slamming the point of his arrow into the man's jugular. The vicious wound prompted a geyser of the man's blood to spray up Stefan's arm and face as the man went down, choking to death.

"Ergh, see now *this* is why I like to fight at safe distance," groaned the disgusted archer. "Arok, don't kill that man just yet, keep him down."

His partner grunted in affirmation as Stefan approached the bridge with his eyes on the trees. Taking his first step onto the bridge, he heard the enemy call "Retreat!" and three silhouettes broke their cover and sprinted into the forest. Stefan drew his longbow again before lowering it after realising he had no chance of getting a clean shot without giving chase.

Stefan returned to his partner and stood over the pinned

man, who was wearing a nice assortment of bumps that were already starting to bruise.

"Who are you, bandit?" Stefan asked civilly.

"You ain't getten noffin from me!" the bandit spat.

"Arok," Stefan said calmly as Arok produced a hunting knife, gently pressing it to the man's throat.

It seemed to dawn on the man exactly what his situation was as the adrenaline of battle subsided and his face gave way to a look of hopelessness.

"Rolik, name's Rolik," Rolik the bandit answered.

"No, no. You misunderstand. I don't give a damn about your name. I want to know why you decided to attack us. Was it just money? A bounty perhaps? I'll make it simple: was this random? If not, who sent you?" Stefan replied impatiently.

"Dunno his name. Some knight. I didn't even see his face," Rolik started and his speech quickened when he saw Stefan's eyebrows rise in doubt. "It's true! He told us to kill anyone from South Tremel with somethin' to do with some bloody ruins or some shit. I didn't understand, nor the other boys – we just took the coin and found out the Chief's son was coming back this way."

Stefan glanced at Arok before returning to Rolik.

"Why target Arok? Who was the knight?"

"Beats me. He was wearing dark purple and black armour, real scary man. Somethin' wasn't right with him. Took the job 'cause we were scared ta pass it up," the man stuttered.

"Humph. Disarm him and let him go, Arok."

"What for? The bastard tried to kill us," Arok asked angrily.

"Because a knight of that description means that bandits who can barely string a bow are the least of our problems."

Stefan grimaced as Arok reluctantly set his captive free.

"What do you mean, Stiff?" Arok asked as he climbed to his feet.

"I mean that we have a new enemy. Or rather, a very old one."

CHAPTER 14

THE LATE KING'S ADVISOR

Rufus stared in bewilderment at the friendly nature of the conversation between the Princess and leader of the Guilty Blade. Not only did they know each other but they seemed to be on extremely good terms.

What's going on here? Rufus wondered to himself.

"Oh, don't act so surprised, Mr. Thief. Setz here once sat on the Council for Aquiocia and was my father's advisor. That was before he disappeared, of course," Alicea said impatiently as though she was relaying information she considered to be common knowledge. "I had figured out who your client was as soon as I worked out what kind of person you were."

"Don't be so harsh on the lad, Your Highness. He had no clue why I wanted you taken from the castle and I deliberately kept that part hidden. He thought it was just a kidnapping. Besides . . ." Setz added with a slight hint of humour, "the confused look has come to suit him rather well, as he wears it a lot."

"Oh, shut it, Setz," snapped Rufus. He had no interest in any of this as long as he was paid and Lori and Tori were safe. "Where are the girls?"

"Yes, of course, you will find them where your hovel was," Setz replied.

"*Was?* What have you done?!" Rufus demanded, his temper rising sharply. "You swore that –"

"I've kept my word," Setz quipped. "Go and see for yourself. You are dismissed."

Without a word, Rufus rushed out of Setz's office to go home and more importantly see how his girls were holding up.

I swear if he has hurt them I'll cut his throat out and leave him in a pool of his own blood, he thought viciously. *That is, after I get someone to open the door to his office, of course.*

❖

As Rufus approached his home he stopped in surprise, staring at what stood before him. In one short night Setz had turned his hovel into a small house. All the outside walls had been reinforced with timber of quality from the forests just outside of Aquiocia. They were most likely from Setz's own stores. The timber was thick and glossy, making his house much less likely to cave in upon itself.

The hovel looked more like a home. Two small rooms seemed to have been built on either side of the main structure. In the centre of the two add-ons was the original ground-level doorway and second-floor window above. The door itself had been replaced and the whole structure had been painted black, save for the door and window shades being a clean white colour.

The odd colour choice didn't concern Rufus as he followed a roughly paved footpath leading to his new doorway. On either side where there had been filthy, cold stone was now dirt, along with some sort of green plant making its best attempt at life. There was also a waist-high fence that had been erected around his home, making for a modest front yard. It wasn't really capable of holding anyone out, but showed that this was indeed private property and the boundary was not to be crossed.

The scene was completed by two cloaked men who stopped him at the entrance of his new gate. They flipped off the hoods of their cloaks before addressing Rufus in gruff yet respectful tones.

"Rufus," grunted the first man, who was clearly the elder of the two. He was in his early thirties with a neat beard and a fair share of scars on his arms. "Name's Gerald, head of a small party of mercenaries. We came to Aquiocia from our village after it was destroyed recently. We were searching for work but the guards . . ."

"They don't see our worth like Setz does," finished the younger, fresher-faced companion, as Gerald nodded in affirmation.

"That's a very nice story, but save it. Why are you here?" Rufus asked suspiciously.

"Well, as already said, Setz was more welcoming. He hired us as guards of this house – your house," finished Gerard, a little put off by Rufus' brashness. "So – er – if that's alright, we took the job."

Rufus took the measure of the two men in front of him. They were down on their luck, much like he had been before he got involved with Setz many years ago.

You weren't so different; you were hungry and cold once, his conscience whispered to him. *On top of that, Tori and Lori would be safer with someone watching over them while you are away.*

"I'll be checking with Setz to make sure this is all true, of course. But, as long as you are telling me the truth, I have no problem with you keeping the job," replied Rufus thoughtfully and the two mercenaries relaxed.

"Good choice," Gerard replied, his confidence returning. "Rest assured that we will take this seriously."

Rufus nodded and pushed past his new guards, making his way along the short path to his house in a daze of fatigue and surprise. He hadn't realised until now just how drained he was. Being awake for over thirty-six hours coupled with the excitement of the break-in to the castle had finally caught up with him.

"Ruffie! You're home!" The twins rushed to Rufus as he walked through the front door and hugged him tightly.

"Yes, hello girls," replied Rufus shortly, exhausted but happy to see the twins nonetheless as his tired eyes looked around the small house.

Setz had even been to work in here, reinforcing the walls from this side along with the roof. Parts of the wall on either side of the main room had been knocked down in the image of new doorways. Curtains hung over each of the doorways, one in blue, and the other in pink. The twins finally had their own space, a bedroom each.

Where the rickety stairs once stood a new heavy set had replaced them, made of the same sturdy timber as the beams that now reinforced the house. He took the stairs two at a time out of habit, but sluggishly. By the time he reached halfway up the stairs, he could see a large tin tub with an odd cylinder leading into its confines. There was a second cylinder coming out the bottom of it that went under the floor and he realised that it must lead out of the house. He had seen the contraption before in houses he had been tasked with breaking into. It was a bathtub, and by twisting a knob on the top pipe, hot water would be sourced from within the mountains. Only the rich above the surface had them. Even fewer had the luxury in the Underbelly.

He returned to the ground floor, looked longingly over to his hammock in the far corner and realised it had been taken. In its place was a bed tucked into the corner.

"Setz came in and changed everything!" started Lori as Tori nodded.

"Yes, I got that," replied the exhausted thief as he made his way to the new bed and basically threw himself onto it. Tossing this way and that, he let out a loud grunt.

"Girls, have you seen my hammock?"

Rufus looked over to see his hammock in Tori's hands while she smiled mischievously. "They were going to throw it out, but I swiped it for you."

"That's my girl," Rufus replied, taking it from her.

Standing on the bed to place the metal links back within the hooks that were thankfully still protruding from the ceiling, he climbed onto his hammock that now hung over the bed.

"Tell us about your mission, Ruffie!" Lori exclaimed.

"Tomorrow or something, girls," Rufus replied, throwing his cloak and boots off the side of his hanging bed. "Right now I'm exhausted, and you girls should be asleep anyway."

"We were waiting for you," Tori replied indignantly.

The next words out of Rufus' mouth were muffled as sleep claimed him.

❖

The Princess strolled around the leader of the Guilty Blade's office, taking in everything from the flag in the back down to the trinkets on his desk. Her tour halted briefly when she caught sight of her reflection in a hand mirror upon Setz's desk. She quickly produced a comb from within her dress and, with masterful strokes, began to fix what was an atrocious state for her long hair to be in. The Guildmaster waited patiently as his guest continued to eye the contents of his office.

A necklace, a few rings, arrows, a short blade here and there, and a pitch-black blade behind the desk. She spent a moment allowing herself to be entranced by the dark beauty of the seemingly moving metal before snapping back to the matter at hand. She pulled out the stone she had taken from Rufus and placed it on the desk, where Setz eyed it before turning his gaze towards the Princess.

"I apologise for the somewhat primitive way I got you here, Your Highness," he began somewhat stiffly. "But with the Council in control of the kingdom, I could hardly count on them being supportive of me walking into the castle and taking you away."

"Your justification is not necessary, Setz. I understand that you have always done what you thought was best for both myself and the kingdom. But I would like to know why you wanted me here?" replied Alicea.

"Yes, quite right. Tell me, Your Highness, how much do you know of these stones?" he enquired, and received an answer in the form of a blank expression. "Not a lot then, I assume. Some two hundred years ago now, these stones were discovered, though not all at once, nor were they all in the same location."

"You speak in plural, meaning there is more than one?" she asked.

"Indeed. I believe there are six, from what my sources have gathered over the years," replied Setz. "My reports and research indicate that they hold one of the major elements within each one. That would make six in total."

"Well then, we have the one of water in our possession," the intrigued Princess replied, stowing her comb away and nodding approval to her reflection.

"Oh, and how do you know that?"

"When it's touched," Alicea placed her hand upon the stone, "you can see the ripples through the colour of the stone. It's like it's responding to touch; it feels like water."

The stone responded to the touch and the ripples started to move, creating a beautiful outwards effect, like throwing a stone into a lake.

"Unbelievable – so I was right. I didn't dare believe it," Setz mumbled, then turned to the questioning look on Alicea's face. "My apologies for being vague, Your Highness. But this is a huge revelation. Not just anybody can make the stones respond, for example . . ."

Setz finished his point by touching the stone himself, and – while it was indeed still beautiful – the stone lost its rippling effect and went back to its original cerulean shine.

"What does this mean?" Alicea asked, curiously holding her hand to the stone, removing it, and then repeating the action.

"It means that we are one massive step closer to putting an end to the danger that is threatening this world," Setz replied as he tapped his hand on the table thoughtfully.

"Are you referring to the two people who were at the Plains?"

"Yes, exactly. If you can learn to wield this stone's power then we will be closer to ending this," Setz said. "The only catch is finding the other stones and the appropriate people to wield their power. We will have to somehow find a way for you to harness the power within this one, along with convincing others to help you."

"Why has this become my responsibility?" Alicea asked. There was only curiosity in her tone, no complaint.

"Given the evidence before us, it appears you're a Vassal."

"So . . .?" Alicea pressed, fishing for something more.

"I apologise. I should have opened with the fact that the late King and Queen wished for it to be this way," Setz said tentatively.

It worked, and while it held a measure of sadness, she smiled at the mention of her parents.

"I assume you know where to find these other stones and people?" Alicea asked.

"I'm afraid not," Setz replied and Alicea's face fell. "But I know where to start: South Tremel."

"Are you talking about the small settlement to the south? Why there?" the Princess enquired.

"That's where Lucian met his downfall at the hands of the Vassal of Earth. She turned herself to stone in exchange for forcing him to retreat. No word has been heard about the stone being found, only that the ruins of the fortress have been located very recently."

"How was I unaware of that? So, the stone could very well be within those ruins? That's convenient," Alicea said thoughtfully. "Then I will be off after resting. The quicker I get out of town the less chance the royal guards will locate me."

"The information regarding the stones was always kept away from you by your mother's request. I am uncertain as to why," Setz answered and quickly continued when the Princess' eyes narrowed. "It is approaching dawn now. So, we will leave at nightfall."

"I don't think it's wise you come with me, Setz. These people need you," Alicea said, surprising the Guildmaster. "I've had barely a glance at this underground city, but I can already see they depend on you."

"Your Highness, I simply cannot allow you to go alone. You will need an escort."

"I already have one," replied Alicea briskly. "Now, where can I rest?"

"I've seen to it that you get appropriate resting facilities." Setz pointed at the wall covered in the flag directly behind him. Alicea nodded, seeing the outline of a doorway behind it. Turning back to the Princess, Setz's scarred lips pursed slightly. "Do you think that dragging him along is going to please him?"

"Don't act like you didn't plan all of this," Alicea grinned. Setz actually smiled at the Princess' observation. She was as agile-minded as ever.

"He still won't be happy," Setz warned, his smile fading as quickly as it came.

"He will do as he is told!"

With that declaration, she stepped around the desk and disappeared behind the large flag.

"This is going to be interesting, if nothing else," Setz said to himself.

CHAPTER 15

AN UNLIKELY PAIR

"Alright, that's enough sleep for you, Mr. Thief!" the Princess declared loudly to Rufus, still unconscious in his hammock. "We have stones to find and roads to travel and all those other exciting activities ahead of us."

Rufus stirred at the sound of the Princess' voice and rolled over to look at her through tired eyes that struggled to focus on her blurry outline. As his vision came into focus he noticed that she had changed attire, donning what appeared to be a modified wayfarer's outfit. As more detail became apparent to him, Rufus saw that she had dark leggings along with long, impractical white boots. But it was her tabard that caught his eye.

It was made from the beautiful azure silk that Aquiocian royalty wore. The kind that light played havoc across, making it appear as if she had shimmering water draped casually across her. Down the centre of her top was the image of an Aquiocian Rose, stitched with the precision of a master tailor. The craftsman had caught every detail from the blue petals to the silver trimming of each petal.

Her long hair was tied back into an extensive ponytail that fell down her back. A few long wisps flew free on each side of her head and Rufus figured that it was deliberate. He knew nothing of hair styling so he decided it was best to ignore it. Her rings had been removed from her right hand and were now hanging from the silver chain around her neck with the pendant, a development that – had she still been in his care – Rufus would have loathed. The Princess was practically asking to be robbed.

"You almost look like a regular traveller until you open your mouth."

"Mr. Thief," began the Princess impatiently, brushing off the insult. "Do you intend on lying around all night or are you going to escort me?"

"Well, currently I'm wondering what the point of hiring guards was if they can't even keep one loud-mouthed woman out," Rufus mumbled as he got out of his hammock. "Why are you here? My contract has been completed."

"The stone you gave me – there are others like it. We are going to South Tremel on the closest thing we have to a lead to gather the others."

"Lovely!" Rufus exclaimed sarcastically. "You go on ahead and I'll catch up later."

"No, you are coming with me. Setz's orders."

"Look, Princess, I don't report to Setz. I only take on the jobs that suit me and offer a decent reward," Rufus replied stubbornly. "To be honest, running around the world after pretty rocks calls for a pretty high price."

"Yes, I know about your money-orientated nature," responded an exasperated Alicea. "I also know of your obligation to the girls."

"Leave Lori and Tori outta this," Rufus replied viciously.

Alicea saw every part of Rufus' body tense and she knew

that she'd found her leverage.

"I'm a Princess, Mr. Thief. I'm sure I can compensate you for your troubles afterwards."

Rufus paused as he considered the Princess' new tact.

With a piece of a castle's wealth I could make sure the twins never had to worry about money again. I might even be able to ensure some kind of future on the surface for them; even I might be able to pursue something I want and get out of this way of life. Rufus looked longingly at his hammock. *Well, worst case scenario, after it all I'll be able to get some sleep.*

"Fine, I'll just have to let the twins know before we leave."

"No need, I have already spoken to them. Girls?"

At Alicea's call, the twins appeared from one of the bedrooms. Tori was wearing her mischievous smile while Lori's eyes were wide with worry, both of which immediately triggered Rufus' concern. Before he could open his mouth, the twins spoke.

"You aren't thinking of backing out, are you?" Tori asked loudly. "You know you have to do this. I mean, how often does a Princess come and ask for help? You know I hate the royalty and especially the knights, but . . ." Tori's voice trailed off and her twin weighed in.

"This is a chance for you to change things, Ruffie," Lori finished softly. "You can do it."

Rufus stared at the twins and, for the first time, he realised that they had grown up. A lot of time had passed since the girls first clung on to him. He was reporting back after a job: dirty, lightly bleeding and more than a little pissed off. He'd tracked and eliminated half a dozen bandits who were attacking merchants on the forest line. It had been another job that he was the "best candidate for" and had earnt him his hovel. Setz had been training two boisterous girls in combat, pitting them against each other.

The second Rufus had walked through the door, Setz had clicked his fingers and the girls had pounced. The surprise had worked, somewhat; Rufus had barely fended off the pair before being told that they were training in "tandem tactics" by the Guildmaster. Something had sparked during the spar between the twins and Rufus and he often woke up to the pair shaking him in hopes they could "continue their training". As blasé as Setz seemed, Rufus could tell it bothered him.

Now, after months of trying to shake them off and years of living together, it was finally apparent to him that they had become independent women – wonderful, talented and mature women. As this thought came to him, his heart swelled with pride as if they were his own daughters.

"You two." Rufus' voice threatened to break before he could say any more and the moment got the best of him as the girls rushed to hug him tightly.

"We are going to be fine, Ruffie," came Lori's muffled voice, buried in his chest.

"Aye, we got jobs to do!" chimed Tori's voice. "So be a man, and help the Princess!"

Rufus laughed loudly and turned to Alicea, whose smile had broadened at the scene before her.

"It seems that we will be spending a little more time together after all, Princess."

"As much as I hate to say it, I look forward to it, Mr. Thief!" she replied with a flick of a stray hair.

❖

"How do you – this damned beast won't cooperate! Why is yours doing what it's told?" spluttered a flustered Rufus, struggling with his new brown steed.

"You have to respect the horse and coax it gently, otherwise it won't cooperate with its rider," Alicea repeated for the third time.

She was quite comfortably sitting atop her own grey mount called Cedric who, compared to Rufus' new friend Everett, was the very definition of cooperation. The two had set out after Rufus had packed basic supplies and the prairies of Aquiocia were bathed in the dying light of dusk. The pair had been led out of a secret passage of the Underbelly by Setz and emerged from a trapdoor under the stables owned by a farmer named Advik. Advik was one of Setz's many supporters on the surface and had little qualms with helping them.

The stablemaster had prepared two of his better horses that had made the trip to South Tremel a few times before. However, while the horses and Princess knew what they were doing, Rufus certainly did not. He had never ridden one. Even with Advik's advice and Alicea's continuous mentoring, he was still only slowly getting the hang of controlling the beast and was rapidly losing the battle of patience.

The horses seemed to know where to go for the most part. It was only when they had reached the point of the journey where they'd had to break off the main path to avoid detection that Rufus had to take full control. Control that the horse was reluctant to relinquish.

Seeing him struggle, the Princess directed her horse up

beside his. "Look at what I'm doing."

Rufus snarled back, "You're just sitting there; you aren't even pulling on the reins!"

"Exactly," smiled Alicea. "I've directed him and then I have allowed him to take the lead. Now try relaxing."

Rufus looked at the Princess riding comfortably and imitated the pose. He hesitantly relaxed his grip on the reins slightly and the reaction was immediate. The horse calmed a little and walked in a straight line for what Rufus swore was the first time since he had led it off the path. The horse pottered on at a comfortable pace, its head bobbing ever so happily, and Rufus nodded at Alicea, who returned with a somewhat cheeky grin.

"Honestly, Mr. Thief. I can't believe you have never ridden a horse. One would think that in your line of work a horse could serve as a great escape tactic."

"I'm afraid it's more of a burden than some might think," replied Rufus, still overly proud of his progress as Alicea's eyebrows rose questioningly.

"Well, think about it," explained Rufus. "Most of my work takes discretion and hiding in the shadows, so to speak. I can't just gallop in and declare, 'Everett and I are taking your valuables now! So, if you could just kindly load them up on my steed, we would appreciate it greatly.'"

The Princess laughed at this before posing another question. "How did you come into this line of work anyway?"

"I had what my mother used to call 'sticky fingers,'" Rufus shrugged, looking dead ahead.

"I see. I'm sorry," Alicea offered.

"You're sorry? For what?"

"The way you mentioned your mother, you used past tense.

I know what it's like to lose someone. I'm sorry for your loss." It was Alicea's turn to look dead ahead to avoid the eyes of her companion.

Rufus was about to point out that he didn't miss his mother, or his father for that matter. He could barely recall the robbery in which he'd lost them and their faces eluded him. But for now, he didn't correct her.

He didn't admit that his time at the orphanage was etched far more prominently in his memory. He didn't tell her about the other kids. He didn't tell her how they almost starved on a daily basis, or that it was his "sticky fingers" that had kept him and the others fed. He didn't mention that the reason they were to be punished was his thieving, or that he'd led them all to escape.

He didn't correct her that it was the friends he'd once had that he missed. The friends he'd gotten killed.

He thought of the huge double doors of the orphanage . . . He remembered lifting the heavy barricade with the help of four friends, though there had been dozens silently cheering them on. He'd managed to pick the locks of his own dormitory before hitting the others, each with a dozen kids of various ages. The differences between the orphans didn't matter as they had two things uniting them. Hunger . . . and Rufus.

Rufus had presented each of them with food at some point in the months he'd been there, seemingly pulling it from nowhere when they needed it most. The quickest way to earn a starving kid's trust was to produce fresh vegetables from the kitchen that served thin soup once a day.

Not enough, was the one thought Rufus often tormented himself with.

"Your scar . . ."

The voice broke through his recollection and his hand instinctively reached for his eye.

"What about it?" Rufus asked, forcing himself back to the present.

"It is not from a blade. Yet it was bleeding when we met," Alicea observed, greatly understating the situation in which they'd met. "If my theory is correct, it'd have only recently stopped stinging."

"How do you know that?" Rufus asked, his eyebrows rising slightly.

"I've seen countless soldiers return from battle, Mr. Thief. Some bruised, others much worse. I remember each and every one." Her response was cold, though Rufus couldn't discern why. "Such a thin wound . . . You came very close to losing your eye to a rose."

"How –"

"Have you ever heard the legend behind the roses, Mr. Thief?" Alicea asked abruptly before continuing without waiting for a response. "The flowers change from azure and silver to crimson and black whenever there is hate or conflict nearby. If left like that for too long, they wither and die with the people around them. They say that once you are cut by an Aquiocian Rose, the sting lasts for hours until you become familiar with it. It becomes a part of who you are. Then, whenever the one you love most is in mortal peril, the sting returns. As the Aquiocian Rose senses the strife surrounding it, its sting informs its bearer of their true love's turmoil," Alicea explained wistfully. "It is not uncommon for a couple to deliberately prick themselves on one as part of their wedding ceremony. My father spent weeks searching for the perfect flower, one worthy of my mother. They say he told everyone at the ceremony, the entire kingdom, that he'd failed in the impossible task. Isn't that beautiful?"

Alicea turned to see Rufus' deadpan expression.

"I don't have a 'true love', so I guess the 'call of love' will go unanswered."

"I apologise. I hadn't considered the possibility that your ability to appreciate romance might be akin to your understanding of the concept behind clean clothing."

Rufus remained silent, gently encouraging his steed as if he hadn't heard a word.

"Mr. Thief, what I mean is –"

"I KNOW WHAT YOU MEANT, NOW SHUT IT!" he roared as Alicea was forced to turn away to conceal her cheeky smile.

He's so easy.

CHAPTER 16

A FORBIDDEN RITUAL

Far to the east of Aquiocia, with countless houses hidden behind walls, at the top of a large hill was the city of Neibel-Haven – home to scholars and mages alike. A dirt path wound its way up the side of the hill and while there were many paths leading to the city, there was only one entrance: a large gate guarded vigilantly by a military that was somewhat lacking in manpower.

What truly set Neibel-Haven apart from other cities were the massive towers within its confines that rose behind the city's barricades. From a distance, the towers looked to be a part of the ramparts but they had been built within the wall's perimeter itself. It had seven towers in total; the six that were dedicated to each of the primary elements were situated in an outer ring, away from the centre of the city, which was where the seventh and largest of all stood. The outer towers were largely identical, made of strong stone from the northern mountains.

They were simply adorned with a few windows reflecting the many levels within and a banner, decorated with an emblem displaying the element that was studied within. Each of the banners that fell from the roof was wrapped around the tower on its way to the ground. The walls of the grand constructs glowed ever so slightly with powerful magical wards, each ethereal light a different colour depending on the field it was dedicated to.

There was a burning red for Fire, a serene blue for Water, a verdant green for Wind, a calming brown for Earth, a mysterious purple for Darkness and a soft white for Light.

Each tower reached for the sky, achieving lofty heights. Each was centuries old, with the seventh – known as the Celestial Tower – in the dead centre of the city. The name of "Celestial Magic" was given to all forms of magic that didn't fall under the normal categories of the primary six. While all the elements were equally mysterious, Celestial Magic was elusive for very different reasons. Although the seventh tower had been standing as long as the others, it had only recently seen regular use.

Neibel-Haven was often referred to as "invincible" by both resident and outsider. In the past, the layout of the city's iconic buildings had proven siege-impossible, as any would-be invaders encountered great difficulty charging up the hill as a rain of spells fell upon them from above. Unbeknown to most, however, an eighth tower had been built. Unlike the others, it was built within the mountain itself five years ago, mirroring the Celestial Tower above. This tower came into existence when the Magic Council of Neibel-Haven lost its leader, Professor Lazear, half a decade ago.

What the scholars and other citizens also failed to realise was that the head Council member had never left the city itself. Instead, he had taken to residing within the underground tower.

Working feverishly on his experiments with only his most

trusted advisors, few though they were, he had come closer and closer to success as the years went on. The numbers were kept small for the sake of secrecy, with Lazear putting the labourers to death after the construction of the tower out of fear of his operation being discovered or worse, shut down. It wasn't a precaution he wanted to take but it had been necessary.

His five straight years without the light of day were finally showing promise. His next potential breakthrough was dragged into the laboratory in the form of a struggling young red-haired female. The pair restraining the prisoner were led by Lazear's right-hand man, Chase.

"Here she is, Sir," reported Chase with hesitation before adding, "awake and alert as you requested."

"Very good, Chase. She will need to be conscious for this," replied Lazear. "Bind her in the usual spot and we shall begin."

The men dragged the screaming woman over to the furthest side of the room and secured her feet to the ground with chains and her arms in the same ones hanging from the ceiling. The two men bowed deeply – one of them handing Chase a small bag of accessories belonging to the prisoner – and left the room, leaving only Chase, Lazear and the woman.

"Professor," began Chase over the wailing of the lady. "Don't you think that maybe this has gone far enough? I mean, the other women . . . They just mutated. What's to stop this one?" Chase trailed off. He'd been feeling uncertain about the experiments for a while now, but she seemed different. When he had gone to fetch the latest prisoner from the cells – when he'd laid eyes on her – he'd wanted to stop.

The Professor eyed his young trainee. The boy was only

twenty, naive and unsure of himself. He had grown up in Neibel-Haven and even though he was quite accomplished at Fire Magic he preferred the sword, wielding an enchanted longsword draped across his back. The blade had been crafted by his father when Chase expressed interest in swordplay at the age of twelve – under the condition he didn't shirk his magical studies. To solely be a swordsman in the city of Neibel-Haven was a somewhat shameful existence. It wasn't long before the other kids nicknamed him "Firesword" for his tendency to light up his blade during duels and manipulate his magic into his swordplay, making the messy brown-haired young man lethal in any confrontation.

"What brings on this sudden change of conscience, Chase? You said you wanted to learn more and you have. You wanted to help create a weapon to fight the threat coming, a goal almost accomplished," replied Lazear.

"Sir, I just need to know that the end is in sight. So many lives have been destroyed," began Chase, glancing at the bolted door to his left. "I just need reassurance."

"I have traced back this one's ancestors and I believe that she is the descendant of Scourge. If this woman isn't the one . . . perhaps we have indeed failed. But this one is our greatest hope. If one more life is to be sacrificed for the greater good, don't you think it should be so?" enquired the Professor.

"I will stand by you through one more, Professor," replied Chase in a somewhat defeated tone. "Maybe we can be heroes yet . . ."

"Oh, Chase . . . It's much too late for me to be a hero," the Professor chuckled to himself. "Now the stone!"

As Chase went to the box on the bench in the middle of

various tools used for both torture and medical attention, the screams stopped. Chase looked back to see the Professor lifting the woman's chin, looking deep into her eyes.

"What's your name, girl?" enquired the Professor as the lady remained silent with defiance. "No matter . . . Temperance," the Professor ended dismissively before continuing his monologue to the surprised woman.

"Allow me to explain why you're here," Lazear began as Chase placed a beautiful red stone in his outstretched hand. The stone outshone any ruby and it looked as though there were burning embers within.

"This stone holds great power. It's the source of the power the Vassal of Fire once wielded. I – no, *we* – are going to imbue your body and mind with it. The Fire and Blood Magic used will not be pleasant, but at the end – should you survive – it will give you great strength. Strength the world will soon need."

"You mongrel. I won't survive this. All you are is a murderer!" came the coarse voice of Temperance.

"Then you will be dead, therefore you won't be worried about it," came Lazear's curt reply.

"You! Chase, is it?" sputtered Temperance. "Are you really going to stand there and allow this?"

Temperance's words fell on deaf ears and silent lips were the only response she received as the troubled young man looked on. All he could do was take in the woman's image as he handed over the stone to his master and watched, anxiously fiddling with the spectacles in his hand.

There is something different about this one.

Guiltily examining the bound woman, Chase took in her

tall and full-figured frame, garbed in a full-length orange and pink dress. There were tears here and there in her attire, but it wasn't that which caught his eye. The young man felt like he was in the presence of a scholar. There was a deep intelligence within her eyes, but he felt it was more than her physical appearance that gave this aura.

Another thing that caught his attention was the unusual colour of her eyes. They were of a deep emerald hue, with amber specks littered throughout. Chase compared them to pleasant meadows with scattered embers just waiting to catch fire.

"So, you'd just stand there and watch? Fine," said a suddenly submissive Temperance.

"Very good. Cooperation is key, after all. You may enter!" Lazear called towards the door Chase had just entered, which opened. Six cloaked figures walked in. They gathered around Temperance in a semi-circle with Lazear dead centre, palm outstretched, stone in hand. In a barely audible whisper he said, *"Infirilis."*

With that single word, the stone erupted in blinding red light and the cloaked figures started murmuring an incantation under their breath. To Chase's astonishment, the stone began levitating from Lazear's hand before a beam of orange fury shot from the relic and into Temperance's chest.

Her reaction was delayed before she began to scream in agony.

Lazear grinned to himself at this breakthrough and called to the encircling figures for more power. They nodded and obliged by becoming more audible in their vocalisation. The stone shone so brightly that Chase could no longer watch it as it floated closer towards Temperance. Though it trembled within the blaze, it never strayed from the blistering path leading to its target. The stone was mere inches from her chest when Lazear could taste success. He drew his small knife. The cloaked figures followed suit and produced their own small bladed weapons, gliding them deeply across their own palms and adding the essence of blood to enhance the foul magic's power.

The stone responded by launching the remainder of the path, sinking into Temperance's chest. Chase saw her face clearly for the first time since the spell had been initiated; he saw panic, pain and, most prominent of all, rage strewn across her face as the young woman's eyes flashed a blazing crimson. Her body ignited with a flare so hot it melted through the smouldering chains binding her and forced the sorcerers to the ground. When the last of her bindings dripped away, she collapsed in a heap on the ground.

Lazear was the first to recover his bearings and approach the exhausted lady.

"It worked! Success, I –"

"Fool!" came a voice from the heap. Before the stunned men could react the body of the tortured lady rose slowly from the ground, unfolding like a puppet. Hovering a foot above the ground with her arms hanging limply, the baleful blaze in her eyes bore through her tormentors as she spoke in a deep, reverberating voice that was too masculine to be called her own.

"This war that you think you are fighting . . . just became direr . . ."

"You have beco—" Lazear began, attempting to gain control of the conversation.

"Silence, Maggot!" cut across the new being that was once Temperance. As she raised her hand in front of her face it ignited in the same searing heat that had encased her moments before. The heat forced the men to cower and Chase drew his blade out of instinct. The entire chamber was beginning to feel like the inside of a soup pot over a roaring flame. "The stone tells me things . . . It has told me what it has seen transpire here . . . You preyed on defenceless women in the name of whatever you told yourself to make you sleep better at night . . . They were innocent! You will all pay for this . . ."

CHAPTER 17

THE PAST IS ALWAYS CLOSE BEHIND

"Temperance, stop, this is not how it was supposed to be!" screamed Chase as he picked himself up from the rapidly heating ground.

The Professor's research room was in disarray. The cloaked figures had charged Temperance to subdue her, only to meet the searing inferno that erupted from her fingertips. The flames had scorched the figures as they were blasted back. Now they were burnt beyond recognition, lying dead on the ground.

Temperance ignored Chase's plea and instead looked towards the ceiling, her face twisted into a cruel smile. It was an expression that – although Chase knew next to nothing of the woman – he knew didn't belong on her face.

"This city will meet the same fate as Scourge did all those years ago."

The woman was a sight to behold. She began to hover higher in mid-air, as if supported by the very air devoured by the flames around her. Chase could tell that her movements were controlled – too controlled. Something about her didn't seem right, as if her body was moving against its will. However, whatever was resisting was frail at best. Her body was completely engulfed in an incandescent inferno that alternated between a furious orange and a brilliant white. Whenever the flames flashed white they threatened to blind anyone looking directly at her, and the heat was something else entirely.

Chase was familiar with the sensation of nearby fire but, as he stood across the room from the woman, he felt as though the very flames surrounding her body were licking at his skin. Looking down, he noticed that the hair in the gap between his shirt and glove was lightly singed.

Temperance lifted her hand in the direction of the bolted door in the back of the room and a tremendous ball of fire burst forth from her fingers. The blast collided with the door, blowing it off its hinges and showering the room in sparks as its conjurer turned her attention back to Chase.

"Ah, the young fool. Consider this a mercy. Instead of burning up like your colleagues you will be ripped apart by that which you created!"

"Stop this –" Chase's sentence was cut short as Temperance's blazing aura picked up in brilliant white fury and she opened her palms towards the floor.

A fierce stream of energy raged from each hand and she directed them straight up. The torrents of raw energy devoured the stone ceiling above her before moving onto the ceiling above that. Her endurance seemed endless as the concentrated power soared ever higher until the interior of the tower above could be made out through the molten hole in the ceiling. Having blasted free from the dungeon, she took flight into the Celestial Tower directly above. Chase hesitated as he made to follow after her, his eyes darting at the now wide-open door that was until moments ago sealed tight.

His stomach recoiled, not so much from fear, but from the guilt assaulting his conscience that accompanied the people emerging from the next room. The term "people" was a generous one as the silhouettes stumbled into the dying light of the torches. They had four limbs, a head and a torso, but all features had been razed, leaving only dark, cauterised skin. The mutations varied in height but were all deathly thin with what remained of their flesh falling in places from their bones.

Every lumbering corpse had eyes glowing the colour of the stone they had been afflicted by. They illuminated the area around them with the sinister glow of what remained of the magic that had consumed them. The fire of the stone had burnt away everything about these people, including their skin, clothes and identity.

Clothes? Temperance's clothes did not burn away. The flames didn't touch them. Is she in control? Chase's mind whirled with possibilities, all fuelled by tainted hope.

Shaking his head slightly, the young man focused on the issue at hand. He couldn't let the mutations past. *Mutations? That's what you think of these people?* Chase kicked himself internally. He didn't need guilt-ridden thoughts like that right now. One of the taller mutations lunged at him clumsily, only to be impaled by the man's sword with ease. Chase kicked the mutation back, freeing his blade.

"I am truly sorry to you all," Chase addressed his now focused visitors as he ran his hand across the flat of his blade.

He felt the energy leave his body and attach to his blade before flicking it up into a battle-ready stance. The mutations quivered with anxiety as his sword erupted into flames, the steel sheathed in its own personal inferno.

"But if I'm to correct my wrongs, I must live."

Three of the mutations attacked from his left. One received

a fiery blade across its middle, another a swift kick to the jaw. The head of the final victim fell as Chase fluidly brought his weapon through its neck.

More mutations emerged from their former prison. They all lumbered slowly into the room before catching sight of Chase. They stared at the young man with their lifeless eyes, almost as if they recognised him but couldn't place where they'd last seen him.

I will be smothered! he thought grimly. *I have to end this now.*

Chase tightened his focus and allowed more of his magical energy to flow into his blade. The energy joined the rest within the weapon and as a result, the flames turned white hot and the air thinned around it as the blaze greedily consumed its fill. He took a deep gulp of hot air to steady his nerves; he wasn't accustomed to using so much magical energy at once. He was risking sudden exhaustion. Chase swung the searing blade around with ease and in quick succession raked the tip along the ground on either side of him. He knew that it was the magic, not the physical exertion, that was taxing him so greatly.

As the blade slashed at the stone floor, the sparks ignited. Fuelled by Chase's magical energy, a wall of flames erupted from the ground on either side of him that branched out diagonally from the man and trapped the mutations. The mutations showed their first obvious emotion since being released: panic. They tripped over one another, shrieking so fearfully that Chase's insides froze despite the heat in the room. His desire to collapse and block his ears was stifled by the knowledge that if he didn't finish it, he was dead. It wasn't a way he wanted to meet his end – at least, not yet.

Instead, he took a single step away from the flames and forced his quickly tiring mind into imbuing his blade with energy once more. This time he stretched his arm to full length, his blade's tip aimed directly at the centre of the screaming, disorganised ranks of his enemies.

"This is it," murmured Chase before crying out the incantation for the spell: *"Infirilis: Infer Impus!"*

He felt his body drain of all energy as the blade's metal hissed and burst into flames. Chase didn't know if the enchanted blade had a limit, but he knew he was approaching his own at an alarming pace. The blade of his sword had doubled in length with swirling orange-white flames reaching out in an attempt to find release from the magical binds their master had in place. Before long, Chase had called forth enough energy that the length of his blade had tripled, with every piece of it fighting against him.

Sweating profusely from both exhaustion and the heat, Chase finally released his ties to the magic. Unrestrained, the lethal force launched forward in the form of an enormous sphere of incandescent wrath towards the screeching mass of mutations. The hellish magical assault collided with the sound of a bomb. The unfortunate mutations were lifted from the ground, thrown backwards, crushed and pinned against the walls of the tower before falling to the ground. Any remaining resemblance to humans they had was eradicated with the blast.

His magical energy completely left him; the walls of flames shrank before they fizzled out. He tried to resist the exhaustion; they might not all be dead and he had to find Temperance. Chase willed himself to walk towards the exit, but his body collapsed. His flame-free sword fell from his grasp as his consciousness faded to black.

CHAPTER 18

TO BE A HERO...

In the back of Chase's mind he could hear people talking around him. Their voices sounded distorted, as if far off in the distance. He tried to catch what they were saying but every time he thought he understood a word, the voice seemed to muffle itself. After a while of trying and failing to hear what was being said, all he could tell for certain was that one sounded female and the other male.

Chase felt rough hands grab his shoulders and shake him violently out of his exhausted slumber, though his mind remained sluggish.

"Who is he?" came a female's voice. "What is he doing here?"

"I have no idea," replied the worried voice of the man.

Something within Chase's mind broke through the exhaustion, a thought, a fear. *Temperance!*

Chase's eyes flitted open and saw the man and woman above him, looking concerned. With a grimace he forced his body to move.

"Where is she?" Chase groaned, pulling himself into an upright position.

The pair shared a confused look, before the man addressed him.

"Son, you have expended a tremendous amount of magical energy and –"

"No, Temperance has to be stopped!" Chase argued, trying to struggle to his feet as he looked towards the hole in the ceiling.

Even from within the underground tower he could hear the screams and destruction above.

Tower? Chase let the word roll around his mind. *I suppose it is more of a pit now. In a way, it always was.*

He took stock of his options, as few as they were. He would waste too much time if he went out the secret passage leading to the surface. Temperance couldn't be left to her own devices any longer. If it hadn't been too long already.

"How long was I out for?" he yelled frantically at the two confused scholars.

"A blast erupted from the floor about ten, maybe twenty minutes ago," the man answered uncertainly. "What was that energy?"

Chase didn't answer as the guilt clawed at him.

Why has it taken me so long to develop a damned conscience?

The countless women used for experiments, the long hours finding and tormenting subjects, trying desperately to find someone compatible with the stone.

We wanted to help save the world, to be bloody heroes, and now what? We succeeded and already I have had to resort to slaughter just to justify what I'm doing. And Temperance . . . he thought viciously. He blamed himself for everything, and why shouldn't he?

"Son, whatever it is that was going on down here and whatever part you had in it needs to be put aside for now," the elderly man said rationally to the torn Chase. "Right now, if you have any small hope of stopping whatever or *whoever* that is, you need to get up there. Now."

"I'm aware," he snapped.

"We can help," started the shy lady. "We use Levitation Magic."

Chase stopped and thought about it quickly. He hadn't even wondered how they had gotten down there from the high ceiling above.

A rare talent, and a useful one.

"That would be greatly appreciated," Chase said, hope replacing his anger.

"It would be our pleasure," said the elderly man before the pair took their places on either side of Chase. "I will bestow some of my magical energy upon you to use when you are up there. My apprentice here will be doing the same." He tilted his head slightly towards the woman.

"Of course, Sir," came her eager reply.

"Good, now let's see to getting you up there," said the man as both he and his apprentice raised their hands and spoke words of the ancient magic. *"Aisuir: Risius!"*

Chase's feet started to tingle and as he looked down he saw a pale lilac glow gathering at them. He was already a few inches off the ground, and ascending every second. He looked around himself in wonder as he steadily rose higher and higher. The sensation was wonderful and one he'd never thought he would experience. Very few mastered it; fewer still shared it.

"Now!" he called to the woman.

"Sir!" she cried in affirmation.

"*Aisuir: Shairus Terrous!*" they called together and less than a second later Chase felt a surge of rejuvenation.

It was like he was getting the benefit of a good night's sleep in mere seconds. He was enjoying the feeling so much he almost didn't notice when he was standing on solid ground above the hole in the ceiling. Chase looked over the edge to see the pair exhausted on the ground; casting two spells at once was no small task, even for accomplished magicians.

"Thank you both so much," he called down. If he lived he would have to seek them and thank them properly.

Chase dodged and weaved through chairs and other furniture as he made his way to the tower's exit. He spotted a trail of black coursing across the floor and up the side of the far wall. The windowpane was melted back and scorched thoroughly.

He was unsure of what he would do upon confronting Temperance. All he knew was that it had to be done to save everyone and to redeem himself. He had to do whatever it took – to be a hero. If that was still in reach.

CHAPTER 19

I'M NOT A WEAPON

The ruckus from outside grew louder as Chase ran for the door, his heart racing at the thought of what he might find. He swung the door open sharply as a loud explosion echoed throughout the city and debris flew around the area. A large stone narrowly missed Chase as he stepped out of the tower.

He scanned the area swiftly for damage before Temperance's piercing red-white aura caught his eye in the middle of the main square about a hundred yards away. It looked as though she was surrounded by mages dressed in various coloured robes. Glowing lights flashed and he realised that the city's mages were firing off spells of every element in her direction.

Chase set off at a sprint towards the chaos, leaping over mounds of rubble, his boots crunching on stray debris. There were bodies everywhere, either dead or receiving medical attention from the mages gifted in the healing arts. Everyone looked terrified and Chase felt the guilt gnawing at him again as their sanguine gazes fell upon the one man running towards the commotion.

They don't know you are involved. Don't let paranoia beat you. The authorities of Neibel-Haven will do that later.

Temperance had damaged the tower dedicated to wind. A terrifying thought occurred to him. *This woman commands enough raw power to puncture the magical barriers and crumble the stone! She is going to raze the entire city!*

Temperance was looking worn down. Her aura wasn't as bright, and she wasn't flinging the balls of fire as frequently. As he got closer, he realised that the rage on her face had not dispersed; it had grown more manic as the group of mages tried to pin her down with their energy. Supernatural lights were connecting each mage with Temperance, ripping her energy from her. They were attempting to drain her.

This is dangerous, Chase thought, assembling the pieces. *Temperance is special – she can handle this magic better than them. They'll shrivel and die trying to take that energy.*

Temperance's face turned from surprise to a foul scowl as she spotted Chase making his entrance and drawing his blade from its sheath. She brought her energy to the surface and the aura grew and changed back to white-hot again.

"How dare you survive, you maggot!" Temperance shrieked at Chase in a combination of a male's and a female's voice. "How dare you?!"

She ended the sentence with a high-pitched screech, raising her hands, letting loose an erratic burst of flames. Her aim was hindered by her fury; instead of hitting Chase with the flames, they soared past his head as he dove to the ground. The attack crashed into the same tower he had emerged from. To everyone's relief, its barriers held strong against the flame's assault.

"Let's take this monster down!" called a voice from the group of mages.

That's Mordrik, the city's Archmage! Chase realised. *The damned Magic Council!*

Mordrik's words inspired the mages who were magically connected to Temperance and their worn faces had renewed determination plastered all over them.

"Stop it! Her energy will kill you all!" Chase screamed over the din as the Archmage looked for the voice.

"Chase? How is this possible? I thought you died years ago!" Mordrik called from the other side, barely audible over Temperance's shrieks.

"Just stop it!" Chase turned his cries to Temperance. "Temperance! You need to stop! The experiments were to save lives!"

"Enough of your lies! Lies! That's all you are . . . lies!" the poor woman screamed, gasping for breath between words.

"These mages will drain your energy! You'll die and they'll die alongside you!" Chase argued.

At this Temperance threw her head back, laughing before doubling over in pain, wailing from the bottom of her lungs.

"Good! Let them all die! Die with me! Liars must –" Temperance screamed, her aura flickering from bright white to a dull red. "He's coming . . . It's coming!"

"What's coming?!" Chase asked in panic.

Temperance collapsed to her knees, looking up at Chase as he ran towards her.

"Stay away from –" called Mordrik, his warning drowned out by Temperance's wail as she told him to get back.

Chase ignored her words. He knelt an arm's length from her and looked the tormented woman in the eye. The aura had weakened and yet that uncomfortable heat still washed over him. He was sweating from exposure within the first few seconds and he knew that if she flared again, it would be over for him. Temperance seemed to fidget and twitch as if she was anxiously awaiting something.

Her clothes are undamaged still?

"It's – it's coming – Ch-Chase is going to die!" Temperance spat between laughing and crying, a symphony of painful sobs and manic joy.

"Temperance, what is coming? What is happening?"

"It's in here with me . . . It's big, it's . . . so strong . . . It . . . it will kill . . . everyone!" Temperance squealed in pain.

"You cannot let it in, Temperance. Fight it!" Chase demanded, fear slowly taking a grip on his voice.

"Why should I? You . . . mongrels . . . You are the real monsters . . . .Scourge . . ." Temperance spat a hint of sadness at the final mention of her ancestor's home.

"What about Scourge? It's why we did what we did!" Chase pleaded.

"This is how Scourge died, you fool!" Temperance screamed at Chase's dumbfounded look as he tried desperately to put the pieces together.

"I see . . . its memories . . . The destruction of Scourge . . . He did it . . . It's coming . . . and again . . . Neibel-Haven . . . doesn't care or help . . . It brings destruction . . ."

"No! This wasn't our goal; we wanted power to protect!" Chase yelled. Tears started to well in his eyes, partly from the severe heat washing over him, and partly from the full impact of what he had done.

Whatever was inside Temperance had caused the destruction of Scourge over two hundred years ago. He'd helped reactivate it.

"You have to fight it! We can make sure this never happens

again. Please, Temperance!" Chase begged.

"No! You're lying . . ."

"We know the cause now! Nobody else needs to die. I want to help you!" Chase continued to beg. "I wanted to save lives, not end them. Just give me a chance!"

Temperance looked into the young man's watering eyes. His skin was singed and peeling from the flames and a voice of reason broke through her manic mindset.

He is putting himself through this for me – why?

"What . . . do you want?" Temperance asked, her own voice returning shakily. She struggled to her feet, watching Chase curiously.

Chase rose with her, taking a step towards the broken woman, and reached out, touching her searing arm. He ignored the pain of his burning flesh and let his sword arm fall to his side.

"I just want to help people."

Temperance looked down at his smouldering hand on her arm before looking to him. Her aura vanished as she collapsed into his arms. Chase knelt on the ground, cradling her, the heat from her body almost instantly returning to normal.

"I'm not . . . a weapon," the exhausted woman whimpered before losing consciousness.

CHAPTER 20

THE VASSAL OF WATER

Alicea stood under the waterfall almost at complete peace within herself, the water gently flowing over her naked body as it relaxed for the first time since Rufus had barged into her chambers. The water gathered around her waist, offering a refreshing and cool sensation in the late afternoon sunlight. They had stopped to rest when Alicea had noticed the sound of running water. She had found herself drawn towards it and had dragged the confused thief with her in search of the source.

It's odd that Mr. Thief couldn't hear it, the Princess pondered. *But given the distance I heard it from, I suppose it's odder that I could. What is this rock formation even doing here? It's as if the earth forced the stone upwards to form a waterfall. How is that even possible?*

She stood at the centre of the cascade, her hair released from its restraint falling past her shoulders into the water, becoming one with the pool around her waist. Her clothing rested on a large stone at the water's edge near a break in the pond that stretched out into a river heading south.

Rufus was some eighty yards away in what they had set up as a camp. She had ordered him to prepare food like a "proper gentleman should" while she bathed in privacy – an instruction she'd given very clearly before leaving Rufus. The only thing the Princess had brought into the water with her was the beautiful stone that she felt caused a lot more fuss than any rock rightfully should have.

It sat comfortably in her hands and the idea of leaving it outside the water somehow seemed ridiculous. She'd left it with her clothes, but had retrieved it after being unable to remove it from her mind in her attempt to relax. It was ludicrous, but she knew it wouldn't be returning to the water's edge without her leaving with it. She gazed at it intently with an interrogative stare, as if expecting some form of justification from it. Why did she hate leaving it out of her reach?

Its surface was alive with the same image of rippling water that was at her waist.

Why are you so important, hmm? the Princess questioned the stone in her mind while the ripples on the stone's surface went crazy. It was like a complicated dance performed for her benefit only. *A lot of people have died over magical stones just like you, so why are you so important?*

She reflected on the conversation with Setz on the night of her "capture". He had said that the stones held tremendous power and that only certain people could hope to wield it. It was obvious that she was one of them, although she had no clue how to tap into its secrets. It hadn't helped that her parents had decided not to share any information.

The Princess thought about what she knew of magic, though it was only from what she had read. It was said that almost anyone could wield magic. Everyone had some varying degree of magical aptitude, from insignificantly weak to chaotically strong. She remembered a certain book in particular; it was one her parents had brought home for her from one of their trips to Neibel-Haven. It was called *The Basics and Fundamentals of Magic* and had been written by a man named "Lazear Skyfire", and with ease, she flitted through the pages of the tome in her memory as she'd always been able to do.

The book had gone into depth about the three basic conditions. The first was that the person must have the required amount of magical energy to cast the desired spell. If they didn't, it was possible to exhaust oneself or even die. The tome hadn't delved into how the magical energy was gauged, or even how it came about in the first place.

The second was that the caster needed to know the nature and name of the spell and she had no idea what those names would be. She knew that realistically, the scholars at Neibel-Haven would have the best idea of the right words to say.

Finally, the caster must have the will to control the magic lest it go astray, manifest and make its results unpredictable and dangerous.

Do not overthink it, Young One. Alicea's eyes bulged as a soft, feminine voice entered her mind. *There is a reason you were chosen and even one for why I led you here.*

"Where are you? *Who* are you? Show yourself!" the young Princess demanded, covering herself and regaining composure as her eyes darted around the pond and trees leading deeper into the forest.

I am within the stone, you could say. You could also say I am the stone. I am not trifled by the specifics of it all, the voice continued smoothly as its bearer looked back down at the rippling surface of the jewel.

"State your business, Stone!" the Princess demanded again,

feeling ridiculous for communicating with an inanimate object.

That requires many complicated answers, Young One. However, now is not the time. No, instead I am speaking to you with the intention of teaching you how to wield your gift. If you are willing, that is, the voice said, continually dismissing the tone that the Princess held.

"I'm not certain I should trust you. No one mentioned that you would speak," the Princess bluntly responded.

Caution is indeed a virtue, Young One. It's traits like these that have entitled you to my power and why have you been chosen as a Vassal for me. Whether you elect to inform people of my ability to communicate is your business, as is the illusion of choice that you display here, the voice said before continuing with a hint of amusement. *You know that you will give into curiosity. I've already had a hand in shaping your fate, and you already feel the pull. This is why you dislike being separated from me.*

The dumbfounded Princess stared at the stone in disbelief at the fact that it knew so much about what she felt. It was a strange sensation to find someone, or *something*, holding the upper hand over her. She hated it.

As she tried to rally her thoughts, she conceded that at least one part of what the voice had said was true. She *was* intrigued at what the stone might say or teach her, and she certainly didn't want to be away from it. It seemed that there was some form of bond between her and the stone that had been crafted since their union, and she planned on investigating it.

"Show me," Alicea finally responded.

You will show yourself, Young One, the voice replied. *Now place your hands in front of you, open your palms and let the stone fall to the water.*

The Princess hesitated at first. The idea of letting the stone fall into the water seemed silly to her; what if she lost it? She only did it for the sake of hopefully deriving more from the voice. She opened her hands as instructed and the stone fell from her grasp and hit the water, the ripples branching out from its descent as Alicea fought the urge to bend down and retrieve it from the bottom.

I'm here to help you let your magic take shape. Even I can't tell you what form it will take; but I can show you how to tap into it. Keep this thought firmly in your own mind: if you try to do too much too quickly, you will die. You have me as a source of energy and through our bond you will find it unnecessary to use words of power, the voice explained patiently as the Princess listened. *With my aid, you will find that you can bend the rules of magic. Break them and you will find only death as reward for your insolence. Now, close your eyes, and feel the water around you,* really *feel it.*

The Princess did as she was told, closing her eyes and focusing on the water. The running water gently rained down her face, her shoulders and her breasts. She felt its surface around her waist, the cool sensation against her legs before joining the rest of its essence in the pond.

She felt her senses sharpening to the sound of the water running down the rocks and colliding with the pool at the bottom, becoming again a single liquid mass.

Very good, the voice commended and echoed through her mind. *Now for the difficult part. I want you to command it to your side. Do not be disheartened; through simple will of mind, you can make magic take a shape of which is dependent on the person. This is complicated magic, but you are meant for this, Young One. Now, will the magic and water to take shape!*

The Princess, feeling foolish again, issued a command in her mind. *Take form!* she ordered before standing there, eyes closed and face reddening from the embarrassment of the activity.

This is impossible, she thought.

Open your eyes and see for yourself what is impossible, and what isn't, the voice replied curtly.

Alicea's eyes opened slowly at first before widening in wonder.

Nesting in her open palms sat a tiny bird comprised solely of water. It stood at maybe eight inches tall, its long neck curled gracefully as it looked curiously at the Princess. Its head was twitching slightly at different angles, weighing up its conjurer and taking in the Princess' image for the first time. It was sheer shock that caused Alicea's mind to take a moment in realising that it was a swan. A cygnet.

An interesting form for it to take, Young One. Consider me surprised, and yet I can't think of a form more suited to you.

"It's so beautiful!" the Princess exclaimed, staring at her achievement for another long minute before adding, "But what am I to do with it?"

It will return to simple liquid when willed by you. Water is extremely versatile, though; it can take many forms. The swan seems to be when it's most comfortable, but it can take on the properties of many a weapon or shield, came the voice's reply. *I'm sure you have more questions; however, your companion returns and it's time to move on.*

With that the voice was gone and immediately replaced with Rufus coming closer, cursing all the way.

"Princess? Where are you? I swear if you've gone and

drowned in two feet of water I'll –" Rufus' voice trailed off as he came to the water's edge and spotted the Princess as she spun around in alarm. "Princess, what in the world is that?"

"Mr. Thief! A lady needs her privacy! You simply cannot walk in on me while I'm washing!" The bird flew from her hands as she abandoned holding it to cover herself. With her back still turned to him, she scolded the exasperated thief. "I expected more from you! Honestly, peeking in on me when –"

"Oh, for the sake of all the gods that don't exist, I'm talking about that!" Rufus pointed at the water between them.

The Princess looked down over her shoulder at what Rufus was referring to only to see that the bird had grown in size and was standing upright on the water as a normal bird would on solid ground. Its whole body was a feverish dance of ripples with its wings extending out in front of the Princess and distorting the view of her naked body.

The bird's beak opened and closed angrily in an inaudible squawk.

"Is it going to attack me?" Rufus asked warily.

"I will make it if you don't turn your back while I put my clothes on!"

CHAPTER 21

THE ARCHMAGE'S VERDICT

Chase walked alongside four guards into the Council's chambers located in the impressive building at the rear of Neibel-Haven. It was almost completely hidden behind the towers of the city, a deliberate part of the original design of course; the Council chambers weren't just for the politicians of the city to hold meetings and conduct debates. It housed many a secret, including a library separate from the others within the city.

As a child Chase had been enthralled by the designs on the walls. There were explosions of colour upon each surface as the six elements were portrayed with smaller versions of the enormous banners wrapped around the towers outside. The images now barely even registered to the distracted man, who was being accompanied to the leaders of the city by guards who would kill him without hesitation if given the order.

Or if he tried to run.

Dread filled his veins as he walked the length of the long corridors and into the vestibule which was filled with people running here and there to get out of the chambers. Once a meeting was called, everyone was to evacuate the building with no exceptions. Countless people spotted Chase and looked at him with mixed expressions; they weren't sure of his involvement yet. That was a blessing. Ahead of him lay a white marble staircase with golden railings that led upwards to grand double doors with the image of a seven-headed hydra.

He ascended the stairs and one of the guards pulled him backwards. Before he could say a word, they were moving again. Two guards had taken point and two behind him. Chase groaned inwardly at the display of superiority. Neibel-Haven's actual military was pathetic at best. Standing at, maybe, five hundred strong compared to the twenty thousand mages – they were arrogant. They had long since adopted the attitude that they didn't need magic and were protecting the mages of the city. It was a common belief amongst the military that had been deemed magically inept at birth. Those without talent were not required to perform militant duties; only the truly determined even applied. The instructors were also magically challenged and were sure to impart the belief that it was the mages who were weak onto their subordinates. The jaded leading the jaded.

It was warped logic, but it got the guards by. They were no slouches with a blade, but their numbers lacked greatly. Chase also had the suspicion that if they returned his sword, he'd be able to take the four guards down before they knew what was happening. *Could do it without magic too.* Not that he'd dream of trying to assault the guards of the city he'd almost destroyed the day before. He'd probably done enough.

Temperance had been taken from Chase immediately after she collapsed. Her fate remained undecided and the guilt of destroying her life was tearing at his insides like a wild animal. Even though he understood the city's standpoint, it didn't help reassure the young man in the slightest. He did realise, however, that him being brought before the Council first was a small miracle. The people rushing from the chambers may not know how he was involved but they'd have recognised Temperance. Of course, they wouldn't drag her through first.

What will happen when I get to the panel? Will they sentence us to death? Have they already? Will they understand Lazear's struggle? Will they even listen?

The four Council guards escorting him offered no reassurance to his fears, nor did he ask for any. He figured it best not to strum on the strings of the arrogant. As the great doors to the Council were opened slowly by no one's physical touch, Chase forced himself to exhale.

"Best behaviour," grunted one of the men. "Understood?"

It sounded more like a threat than a question but Chase just nodded nervously. He took in the scene before him as he walked into the wondrous chamber. The colours splattered across the walls of the outer halls and vestibule were not the theme within the main meeting room. Instead the chambers were held up with strong, luminescent-white stone walls that almost glowed from the rays of light offered by a shining globe hovering in the centre of the roof. The orb gave off constant and lustrous light that bathed the entire chamber along with its residents.

The orb was one created to offer light only to those who mean no ill intent to its caster. Being this far within the building, there was no natural light, and with the walls reinforced and the orb only offering light to the allies of the caster, it was a fine place to retreat to, should the need arise.

It was also a great way to test someone's guilt when they

walked into the room. Chase gulped before realising that this was working in his favour. He could see, proving he had no malicious intentions towards the caster. He took note of the six men and women sitting at a circular table with an image of Neibel-Haven's beautiful emblem of the seven-headed hydra in the centre. The heads of the beast were depicted with each mouth spewing forth a different element – an inferno for Fire, a fissure for Earth, a hurricane for Wind, a tsunami for Water, golden rays for Light, shapeless black ghostly figures for Dark.

Even Celestial Magic – though it was not yet considered a true element – had its own section, adorned with glittering stars raining down.

From the centre, the elements expanded outwards in even cones to the perimeter where their respective leaders sat.

The only Council member missing from the table was Mordrik of the Celestial Tower.

Addressing the damage around the city, Chase guessed.

"Chase, excellent. My name is Miranda, acting Head of the Council in Mordrik's place," began the brunette beauty of the Fire Tower.

"This is Midel of the Water Tower, Freid of the Earth Tower, Serell of the Wind Tower, Ezeal of Dark Tower and finally Lepoe of the Light Tower." Miranda casually waved at the people sitting around the table.

Chase nodded with as much respect as he could muster without speaking. He recognised the hooded man in black as Ezeal, as he had often patrolled the streets at night when Chase was younger. There were many times when an adolescent Chase and his friends stirred up mischief in the dead of the night, only to be scared out of their wits by the Dark Mage himself appearing from the shadows. He'd always say that it was to keep them out of trouble but Chase swore he enjoyed it.

He had seen Miranda and Serell following Mordrik around in his time before the underground tower. They appeared as exact opposites with Miranda being a proud, tall and slender woman and Serell an inquisitive, short and somewhat plump older lady, who wore a snappy gold dress with an uncomfortable-looking shining corset to match. Miranda had deep brunette waves that framed her sharp features and kind, hazel eyes, whereas Serell had pudgy cheeks and intense, green eyes that took in everything around her, unhindered by her thinning blonde hair tied back in a bun. The master of Fire was young and in her prime, the guru of Wind elderly and cynical. Out of the two, Chase knew that Miranda was the most likely to hear him out. She might even actually understand.

Midel of the Water Tower was another Chase recalled with ease. It was hardly surprisingly that the woman with long hair dyed the colour of the ocean was set firmly in his memory. Chase had been infatuated with the older woman since he had first laid eyes on her at the age of eight. She was forty now, twenty years his senior. Even after five years underground, he recalled the woman at the centre of his affections as if he'd seen her just the day before.

She curled her wavy blue hair through her fingers and clucked her tongue as she absentmindedly stared at the young man on trial. She had always seemed bored when it came to politics but her sheer brilliance in the field of Water Magic had her sitting firmly on the Council. For all that politics eluded her interests, she was hailed as a wonderful teacher.

Chase felt a peculiar sensation as he recalled the time his

elemental affinity had been determined. It was found that he was aligned with fire and Midel had been there at the time, as testing couldn't be performed without one of the Council members partaking in the ritual. It was strange that he had been so disappointed in being aligned with fire and not water like his love interest had been. Midel had shrugged on that day, wished him good luck, and he had been smitten ever since.

When he gazed upon her now he realised that his crush had evaporated over time. He had grown up.

He looked towards the man named Freid and the woman named Lepoe. He hadn't seen either of them before. With his examination of the members complete, he returned his full focus to remaining calm. He was saved from standing when Miranda offered him the last seat at the table. Chase sat in the seat that would normally be occupied by Mordrik and looked around meekly at the men and women watching him closely. He noticed that Midel hadn't stopped twirling her hair and that the lady named Lepoe was smiling broadly; she gave the impression that she was a person who was always happy.

"Now, as you know, this whole incident has not only put a lot of people at risk, but also requires an explanation on your behalf. I was informed that Lazear's remains were found. While the explanation would be best to come from him, given the circumstances, you will have to suffice," Miranda finished with a wave of her hand.

Chase looked around the table before realising it was his cue to speak. With a shaky breath, he began from the start. He took the High Mages through everything that had happened over the past five years underground. Everything from when he was first taken under Lazear's wing, to the failed experiments, right up until the confrontation in the main square. His audience listened in silence; the only indication that they were even attentive was the occasional raised eyebrows at parts of his story. By the end of it Midel had stopped twirling her hair and wore the first expression of genuine interest she'd had in a long time.

"And here I am," Chase ended, somewhat anti-climactically.

The tension in the chamber was so thick that Chase could have cut it with his blade – if he still had it, that was. The Council members seemed to be trying to wrap their heads around what had been said, trying to find a way of approaching the matter.

"Right, let's put the directly deceitful side of this aside for just one moment. What would you do now? If we were to permit it, that is," Miranda spoke finally.

Chase took a long moment to think before answering. He knew full well that his answer would seal his fate. He knew that tact was the only way he would gain a favourable outcome. Freid of the Earth Tower, however, had a very different idea.

"Well? Out with it, boy!" the elderly man demanded, his mouth only visible through his grey beard when he spoke.

"I – I'm not sure –" Chase stammered.

"Not good enough!" the old man pressed, ever more wrinkles adding to his forehead as he frowned. "A plan! Inkling! A far-fetched long shot of an idea will suffice at this point!"

"I want to help people," Chase blurted out. "That's why this all happened. It's why I believed in Lazear and his ideals. I thought that if I could find a way to make something stronger than those causing the problem, then I could end it all."

"Ha! That didn't work particularly well, did it, boy?" the old man scoffed. "A fine bit of a failure if I ever saw one."

"I tried to do what I thought was right!" Chase argued weakly.

"And instead of helping anyone you put more people in danger, even killing some of our civilians!" retorted Freid, chortling at some hidden joke that made his large belly jiggle under his brown robes.

"At least I was bloody trying! All anyone around here does is practise magic! Hiding the secrets of our craft away in this one location! You never help anyone but yourselves!" Chase was on his feet by this point and yelling directly at the older man. "You're all just cowards! You should be talking with the other leaders of this land and coming up with a plan instead of hiding behind a desk!"

"Oh? Well, this youngster has it all worked out, doesn't he? Go out and risk his neck for others, he thinks. Take a risk to find a solution, he thinks. Why, I bet he'd even take on this foolhardy journey himself, wouldn't you, you imbecile?" Freid sarcastically replied, throwing his hands into the air in dramatic exasperation.

"Damn right I would! If I could sacrifice my life to save others I wouldn't hesitate! I would travel this whole world searching for the other stones alone if I had to, and happily!" Chase yelled at the old man, his voice echoing through the chamber with conviction.

"And that's what I wanted to hear!" Freid slammed his fist on the table, white teeth glinting from under his beard at the now confused Chase. "This boy has the right attitude!"

Realising that he had fallen right into Freid's trap, Chase flushed with embarrassment and sat down quietly. He looked around at the other Council members' faces, which were all smiling coyly as well, except for Ezeal, whose face couldn't be seen under his hooded cloak. Serell spoke next.

"Freid, are you suggesting that what this young man has done was the right course of action?" she asked, in a surprisingly shrill voice that didn't fit her rotund appearance.

"Of course not. He's a bloody idiot! But his heart was in the right place."

"I assume you know this by the extensive amount of time you have spent with him?"

"Serell, if you're so bent on seeing the worst in everyone, that's fine. But keep me out of it!" Fried snorted as Chase smiled appreciatively. He hadn't expected anyone to understand, least of all the man who had started by pressuring him.

"We will discuss amongst ourselves the next step we will take regarding you, the young lady and this whole situation," Miranda interrupted before Serell could reply. "You will have our answer tomorrow, or rather, you will have Mordrik's. Ultimately, we can only advise the Archmage; it is his decision alone. You will await his summons from your cell as a security measure, do you understand?"

Chase nodded numbly, knowing that while it wasn't pleasant, another overnight stay in a prison cell was a lot better than other options.

"Might I ask one question?" Chase requested meekly. "Is Temperance okay?"

"She is alive, if that is what you are referring to," Miranda replied dismissively.

"Not if I have anything to do with the monster's fate!" Serell trilled.

Chase's expression was one of alarm before he saw Freid throwing a curt nod in his direction. He couldn't be certain, but it looked to be a gesture of goodwill.

Is Freid going to make sure she is taken care of?

Chase was escorted from the chambers and outside to another building, then to his holding cell. Relief from hearing that Temperance was alive turned to worry as the thought of what the Council might decide come the following day loomed in the foreground of his thoughts.

Chase was in an uneasy sleep when a guard banged on the bars of his cell. His eyes widening immediately as he sat up and took in his surroundings, he realised that he was still inside the enchanted cage. His gaze fell to where the guard was pointing at the ground to see a plate of fresh bread and fruits.

The prisoners here eat pretty well compared to the stale bits and pieces we dealt with underground, Chase thought to himself, chewing on the half loaf of bread. *Well, if executed, I want to go out on a full stomach. A small win, but given the situation I'll take anything.*

After Chase's meal of bread, he stood up, stashing the various fruits in his pockets. He stretched and saw through his small barred window that it was past dawn. He smiled grimly, knowing his judgement was imminent. Anytime now someone would summon him and he would walk to his fate.

"What did you do, kid? What was with the deranged woman on fire?" the guard asked, his curiosity getting the better of him. Chase turned in the direction of the guard's voice. It was the first time the guard had bothered to address him since his imprisonment.

"I don't feel like talking about it, no disrespect intended," Chase replied.

"No disrespect? You think that's going to fly? The demented woman nearly destroyed the city and you were the idiot responsible. You want to talk about respect?" The guard growled at Chase and watched him closely.

Chase chose not to answer, instead retreating to the corner of his bed away from the bars. The guard, along with everyone else, would know the whole story soon enough and he didn't need to stoke the fire by getting into an argument with him. He was saved another round of the guard's verbal onslaught by a messenger coming up the stairs. The newcomer came up to the bars and with a muttered word, the bars disenchanted and the door swung open of its own accord, allowing Chase to step out.

"I was told to escort you to the main chamber. No funny business," the messenger briskly stated. Chase nodded, following the man as he set of at a swift pace.

As he approached the chambers again, the walk seemed to take twice as long. His nerves started playing up all over again – his fate resting firmly in the Council's hands. He ascended the stairs and entered the chamber. There was no seat for him today as the whole council sat before him at a new table in the shape of a large, ostentatious horseshoe. They sat with rigid posture, looking on edge. It was not a good sign for Chase.

Mordrik wasted no time, his voice resonating through the chamber as soon as the great doors shut behind Chase. It'd been over five years since he had seen Mordrik before two nights earlier, but the man's voice still carried as much as it did when he once regularly drank with Chase's father.

"Good morning, Chase. I trust you found your quarters comfortable?" Mordrik asked rhetorically, his voice practically dripping with sarcasm. "I have been informed of your story. As unbelievable as it is, I have only one question for the likes of you."

Mordrik rose, his eyes never leaving Chase's, his gaze practically burning right through him. The Archmage navigated himself around the table towards the younger man. He seemed to struggle to find the ability to voice his question and instead stood right in front of him for a solid minute before finally unleashing his pent-up anger.

"You vanished, Chase! Your parents were grief-stricken and even left the city! But that clearly doesn't matter – I AM NOT FINISHED, YOU INSOLENT WHELP!" Mordrik's volume found a new level as Chase tried to defend himself. "They left after searching the surrounding area for over a flaming year!" Mordrik's voice was unusually high-pitched for the older man. "Then, after five long years of not knowing if you were even amongst the living anymore, and after you cost me one of my closest friends, you just appear again – as quickly as you vanished, I might add. And on top of all that, you chose to bring danger to this city!"

The verbal onslaught continued on for what felt like hours to Chase, with Mordrik only pausing briefly to catch his breath before finally stopping and glaring at Chase with the same burning eyes. Chase's mind flickered to his parents briefly. They weren't in the city? What had happened to them? He found it difficult to focus on the thoughts with Mordrik's grey eyes judging his very existence. It was as if he expected him to justify what he had done but had given him no insight as to where to begin.

"You said you had a single question?" Chase asked meekly.

"I thought it was apparent!" Mordrik exploded again. "WHY?!"

Chase recoiled from the old man's outburst and took a moment to consider his answer before deciding he deserved nothing but the absolute truth.

"It felt right; I know it might be hard to believe. But all that was going on in the city were the same studies, as if the dangers on the outside didn't even exist," replied Chase. "Professor Lazear may not have been right in the way he wanted to make a change, yet he was the only one who even started looking into a solution. Even now, while I regret what happened, I truly believe that what we were trying to accomplish was for the greater good."

"You want to know what's truly unbelievable, Chase?" Mordrik was back to the rhetorical questions. "The fact that I spent most of the night examining this marvellous upside-down tower built under our very feet and your ridiculous story actually checks out! Meaning it was a direct violation of the Council, and of this city!"

Chase had no response to that and instead opted to anxiously shift his weight from foot to foot in silence. A silence broken by an eager Serell.

"Archmage, have you made your decision regarding the fate of Chase and his tool?"

"Oh, I most certainly have," Mordrik snapped, swiftly

taking his seat at the table once more. "Don't think even for a second that I'm condoning your actions. They were ruthless, horrid and quite frankly the stuff of nightmares. I still don't know what is stopping me from branding you as a monster."

Chase stood uncomfortably waiting for the Archmage's verdict, shifting nervously and squirming under the Council's gaze as Mordrik composed himself. It was at that point the chamber doors opened once more, and led in by two guards was an exhausted Temperance. She was shoved forward, staggering to keep her feet beneath her as she stood next to him.

"Chase Everstrom! I hereby charge you with conspiracy and treason," began Mordrik. His voice commanded all attention back to him. "I find you guilty of misusing magic and endangering the entire city. You are banished from Neibel-Haven for the remainder of your natural life on pain of death, do you understand? You are to leave immediately with only what's on your person. I'll allow you your blade, but only out of respect for your father."

Chase bowed his head as shame and sorrow clouded his face before looking at the pathetic woman beside him. The mention of his father made the exile all the more bitter. He had betrayed everyone and, for a moment, death seemed preferable to living with what he'd done. His resolve barely rallied upon meeting Temperance's terrified gaze.

"And take that monster with you. I pray she doesn't turn on you," Mordrik added. "The guards will return your sword after escorting you outside the city gates and not a moment before. Now get out of my sight, before I turn you into one of those things I found in your little hideout!"

The guards grabbed Chase from behind, twisting his arms behind his back roughly. His burnt hand sent sharp pains through his body as he was led out of the building, with another guard roughly forcing Temperance close behind. As he was hauled through the streets the citizens of Neibel-Haven recognised the pair and before long a crowd had gathered.

"You killed my mother, you monster!" called a young boy.

"Execute the monster!" yelled another civilian.

The crowd started to throw whatever items they had in their hands at the pair, which was thankfully stopped by the guards, who were also getting showered with rocks and various food products. When they finally reached the gates, the guards pushed them through before releasing Chase a short way from the entrance to the city. Another guard approached and threw Chase's sheathed blade at him.

Temperance was released as well – falling to the ground. Chase knelt and helped her to her feet. As the guards turned and walked back to the city, the exiled man and woman did the same in the opposite direction. Battered, bruised and destitute, the pair began the downhill journey into the mountain range along the roughly man-made path away from the city.

CHAPTER 22

AN ENEMY ON THE MOVE

Sitting in a meditative state, on a platform surrounded by crystals of all sizes, ranging from the size of a man to larger specimens protruding from the floor and reaching the ceiling, was a single silhouette encased in dark armour from head to toe. The heavy plate seemed to bend with the body within, granting unrestricted movement despite the thick, unusual metal. Anyone able to get close enough to examine the surface of the knight's choice of protection would be able to make out countless tiny plates of the otherworldly metal linking together to form the whole.

The light of dozens of torches reflecting off the surface of the crystals produced a beautiful aurora effect that danced merrily across the room. The crystals were never the same colour for long; by the time one had determined their hue, they had changed from the flickering lights. Centred directly in front of the sitting figure was a smooth-faced stone. Devoid of the colour the ones surrounding it held, it sat on the likewise transparent platform.

Its surface showed the slightly warped outline of a female with intense and yet relaxed features. The woman had hair the colour of the darkest pitch that fell over one side of a face portraying a look of utter boredom. Her only reaction when the knight spoke was a slight raising of one eyebrow. His voice was distorted and rough from the magic he used to hide its true sound, but she knew its owner well.

"Vassal of Darkness."

"This gets no less annoying each time you do it." The young lady rolled her eyes of apathetic crimson.

"If you were more reliable, I wouldn't have to check up on you through the method of the Gaian Crystals," the man replied softly.

"I was going to contact you shortly, but I suppose now is as good a time as any. I assume this is about the spike in power I felt?" the woman enquired impatiently.

"Then you noticed, and yet I still sense you near North Tremel," the man whispered.

"The people here don't know who I am, or what my followers and I are about. It was a perfect place to rest," the woman explained, lowering her voice to avoid drawing attention. "Besides, if you used your precious energy to actually come into this world properly, then –"

"North Tremel to Neibel-Haven is three weeks' travel at least for normal humans. I expect it done in a week. I will be checking in then," the man ordered in the same dangerously soft voice that cut across the woman's griping. She hated the fact that he never moved when speaking to her. He was always so still, deathly so.

"Wait," the woman interrupted, sensing he was about to disconnect the magical energy needed for communication through the crystals. "It's one of the other Vassals, isn't it?"

The knight's response was a silent gaze and the connection ended. The severed energy left her gazing at the hand-sized piece of crystal she had been given by the man; his image disappeared from its surface and was replaced with her own reflection. She stared at the precious stone for a short while, contemplating what she would have to do should she meet one of the other Vassals. The Vassal of Light had come head-to-head with her on the Plains of a Thousand Blades, and everything that dared to get between them was eradicated in a few short moments.

The dark-haired woman frowned at the memory of the army that had interfered, holding sky-blue flags and waving their audacity as they tried to get between them. They were annihilated almost instantly but there had been some impressive resistance from two people within their ranks. Those two, a King and Queen, had displayed amazing synergy in their magic and it had almost brought about her demise. Then, just as suddenly, something had interfered with their onslaught and she secured victory. She had questioned Lucian about it upon her return but he had offered no information further than saying that he "took care of it".

Enlightening, she thought with another roll of her eyes.

It wasn't their deaths that bothered her; it was the fact that in those few seconds it took for the army's ranks to be destroyed, the Vassal of Light had managed to unleash her stone's potential and flee.

What was that light that she summoned? Pillars of scorching luminescence came from the sky and completely razed the area around me, but I was already hidden. What was she saying before the battle, something about knowing her struggle? That the light would help me? A pathetic tactic given that the woman was almost as gifted in combat as I am. Almost.

Deciding that it didn't matter as the battle had ended in her victory, she turned to the assembly of fifty men and women who had gathered and were staring at their Commander, awaiting their next orders. The Vassal of Darkness straightened her outfit as she begrudgingly got to her feet. She wore dark colours and soft, stretchy fabric designed to enable full body movement without restraint. The material fitted to her skin and covered her entire body save her left arm and the bottom half of her right leg. The black colours faded into purple and various shades of grey across the elastic fabric. The outfit was finished with a clashing crimson belt that held a small satchel on her hip.

Anyone knowledgeable in the art of combat knew that the ensemble was a type of sparring outfit that had been modified and designed to the wearer's individual tastes. She knew there was no other battle gear known to the men of the land that was as daring as the thin material the Vassal of Darkness wore. But, as she said – and proved consistently on the field of battle – it doesn't matter what you wear if you kill the enemy before they strike you.

"You heard the man!" the woman addressed her party of companions as she flicked her dead-straight, shoulder-length hair in irritation. "Get ready to move out! Our destination is Neibel-Haven, and our target is the Vassal that caused the disturbance."

CHAPTER 23

A STRANGER'S KINDNESS

Dusk was approaching on the second day when Chase turned to Temperance, telling her they would rest for a few moments. They had made excellent time down the hills and away from the city, especially for people who had no idea where to go. He knew his travelling companion hadn't recovered from the ordeal as well as he had and it showed. She was often stumbling in her attempt to keep up with him. Chase didn't know why she was following him. The moment they had been banished he had taken the lead as the pair trudged down the large hillside and eventually met level ground. They were travelling east, or so he thought. There was no way of really telling which direction they were going and they had no tools to refer to.

Instead, they followed what looked to be a well-used path and hoped for the best. It was a hope that was steadily becoming less prominent in their hearts as they plodded forth.

Temperance sat on a large rock and Chase looked at the sun setting over the mountains. It was partially to admire the gorgeous display of fiery colour descending behind the great fixtures of the land, a great blaze that steadily disappeared behind a grand curtain of stone and earth. But the real reason was the same one that was at the foremost part of his companion's mind. He didn't want to look at the woman he had taken part in tormenting. He didn't want to face the fruits of the past five years of labour and searching. He had succeeded, and he'd never felt more miserable.

He'd lost his parents too. Or rather, they had disappeared from Neibel-Haven. He hadn't had the chance to ask Mordrik what had really happened. Were they alive? Did they just leave the city?

What did Mordrik mean when he said I had cost him one of his closest friends?

Chase glanced back to see if he could see any sign of Neibel-Haven, though he knew well enough that they had long since lost sight of the city. He'd look at anything to save his gaze from falling on the silent and broken woman.

Apart from the occasional defiant tree poking through the rough terrain, there was no sign of life. The pair at first had enjoyed the lack of people along with the absence of wild animals. But Chase soon realised the issue with isolation as he pulled from his pockets the last two pieces of apple he had stashed away back in his cell. The pieces of fruit had sustained the pair poorly the past couple of days. He walked over and handed them to Temperance and she took them gratefully, though her eyes held contempt etched with fatigue.

Chase turned away the second the fruit left his hands.

Temperance ate slowly as if the act of eating was causing her pain and Chase tried to formulate a plan with his limited resources. They had been on the road, if you could call it that, for over two days, although it felt much longer. There hadn't been any sign of wildlife save for the nights when the howls of the native wolves filled the silence. Repelling the wolves had been simple enough. He plunged his sword into soil, surrounded it with rocks and lit the blade with a little of his energy at night.

It had provided heat and kept the predators at bay. It came at a cost, though, and while the first night hadn't been a problem, the second had resulted in the young man waking up to a flameless blade and scuffling at the edge of their camp. He hadn't done any heavily taxing magic but keeping the flame constant at night was preventing him from resting properly. He didn't know if he'd be able to do it a third night.

He needed food. Perhaps he could trick the wolves.

You don't know how many there are and you are exhausted. Do you really think you can protect Temperance and pull something like that off? his voice of reason questioned him. *Probably not,* he answered. His conversation with himself was interrupted by Temperance speaking in full, if short, sentences for the first time since the ordeal.

"What are we going to do?" she asked, her voice weak.

"Honestly, I'm not sure," Chase informed her. "Unfortunately, we don't have much to work with. I'm trying to get us to one of the neighbouring villages. However, most people who set out for them have a lot more food and a clue where the villages are. Heat isn't an issue as I'm adept with Fire Magic, but that's about all we have in our favour at the moment. If I could hunt . . ." He was rambling and he knew it.

"And if we survive, what then?" Temperance pressed.

"Again, I'm not sure. I never asked the Professor what to do after we succeeded," Chase said, trying to avoid talking about the experiments. The thought of the Professor being dead hit him hard. He'd barely had a chance to think about it.

"I'm supposed to fight the threat that is making all these odd things happen around the world, aren't I?" she asked sadly. "That was the idea, right?"

"You weren't supposed to fight alone. There are other stones," Chase added to the hopeless situation before being distracted by two silhouettes in the distance that were coming their way. "Be on your guard."

As the two figures approached, Chase realised they were both female, one slightly taller than the other and both with long hair. The taller one's hair was deep brown and the other had a lighter shade of the same colour. Both were wearing long brown stockings with green cloth tunics tied with golden belts. His hope for them to be normal travellers was dashed when Chase noticed the glint of steel beneath the gaps of their tunics. He couldn't make out the extent of protection the women wore under their clothing, but they were familiar with both armament and the prudence of not having it on open display.

They were both armed with short bows over their shoulders. The lighter-haired one also had a thin blade at her hip, while the darker-haired lady had what Chase assumed was a heavier blade sheathed on her back with its hilt protruding over her shoulder. The two armed women didn't seem aggressive, putting their hands up to show they meant no harm as they got closer to Chase and Temperance. They stopped just a short distance away from Chase, before the lighter-haired one spoke.

"Greetings, fellow traveller! My name is Katarina – call me Kat – and this is my sister, Amelia," she called out cheerfully as Chase watched closely. "Might I ask your name?"

"Chase, and this is Temperance. We seek no trouble, merely travelling," Chase responded in an attempt at keeping it vague.

"We are headed for Neibel-Haven. Massive spike in power there, disrupted the magical energy wavelengths over quite a distance," Kat said, keeping the conversation alive longer than Chase would have liked.

He took the statement on board. *Did she say magical energy wavelengths?* It was a topic he wasn't familiar with.

"That sort of thing is of interest to you?" Chase asked, his mind drifting to Temperance's outbreak.

"Absolutely, my new friend!" said the cheerful woman with a wink from her large hazel eyes that seemed to be a perfect blend of green and blue. "A power spike is always attracted to its own kind, if you catch my meaning."

"I'm afraid I don't," Chase said, thoroughly confused.

"Kat, this woman . . ." Amelia said, speaking for the first time while looking directly at Temperance. The taller of the sisters seemed more reserved than the shorter.

"I'm aware, Amelia. Here, Chase, take this," Kat said, dismissing Amelia's cryptic observation and handing the wary man two handfuls of dry meat.

"Eat this, but make it last. If you are following this path to Hearthgrim, you still have another two days."

"Th-thank you," Chase stammered, surprised at the generous and unexpected gift.

"No need to thank me. If you want to make it up to me, find the inn called the 'Drunken Smithy' and tell the innkeep I sent you. Take a load off for a few days and we will be back that way," Kat said as she started off towards Neibel-Haven.

"I suggest you do; I feel as though we can help each other greatly. Farewell for now!"

Chase watched as the two women started wandering the way Chase and Temperance had come from. He felt unsure of their suggestion and even more uncertain of their intentions, but upon finally deciding that it was the best plan they had – the only plan they had – he looked to his companion, who was already on her feet and looking purposefully down the rough path they were to take to get to Hearthgrim.

He glimpsed a look he hadn't seen in her eyes before. Hesitancy mixed with something else. She was willing herself to feel something.

"Come on, we can still make some progress before the sky darkens and our new destination awaits us," Chase said to her cheerfully and was rewarded with a tiny smile before a look of distaste took its place.

CHAPTER 24

HOME AND AWAY, AGAIN

Arok entered the gaping hole in the palisade of uneven timber leading to his home village of South Tremel both tired and excited. His happy-go-lucky demeanour was barely hiding the fact that he had missed Lyrium greatly. Stefan bid farewell to his friend at the entrance and went about his own business as Arok headed straight for the Chief's hut. The residents gave warm welcomes and other such greetings as he shuffled through the centre of the small village with haste. Arok returned the greetings hurriedly while his eyes scouted for Lyrium. He was disappointed that he couldn't locate her through the waving hunters as he made his way to the Chief's hut.

His disappointment was quickly replaced with joy as pushed the heavy bear pelt hanging in the doorway aside with a shrug and saw that both his father and Lyrium were there. Both father and lover stopped their conversation as the Chief's son entered the room and Lyrium immediately embraced him.

"When did you get back?" she asked, her head resting on his shoulder, her arms tightly wrapped around him and showing no sign of letting go. Despite being slightly taller than her partner, it was easy to let herself fall into his muscular form.

"Just now, I came here straight away. We would have been

here sooner but we ran into some trouble," Arok replied, returning the embrace.

After remaining silent through the brief reunion, Kurok loudly cleared his throat and Arok let go of Lyrium, turning to his father with a nod of respect.

"It is good to see that you returned unharmed, son. Garnet said she had delivered the message about the ruins?" He addressed Arok in an almost impersonal way.

"She did, and it is even more important that we get in there sooner," Arok responded, his father's face turning curious. "Bandits were hired to kill anyone from this settlement. I don't know exactly why yet."

As Arok relayed the story of the fight he and Stefan were forced into, Kurok almost seem unsurprised. Even with the mention that the one who contracted the bandits was a man in dark armour, his reaction was that of someone resigning themselves to an unfavourable truth.

"I see. So the enemy already knows that the ruined fortress has presented itself," Kurok responded, nodding solemnly.

"Presented itself? Does everybody know what's going on except for me?" Arok asked in irritation.

"I've told you the tale once before, Arok, and now Lyrium knows of it. The ruins have appeared within the forest at a location we have searched before, yet it's only now that we have been able to find them. It was Lyrium's hunting group who found it, though they haven't entered it for obvious reasons," Kurok explained, eyes darting from Lyrium back to his son. "I don't know if it was because Lyrium was there or not, but I do know that the forest senses that something is wrong, and it has its hopes on her."

"Well, I'm glad you waited. But how do you even know it wants Lyrium? I know you've always suspected that it would be her for some reason – why?"

It was then that Lyrium piped up with none of her previous enthusiasm.

"Because when I was there, something was calling out to me from within."

❖

Arok and Lyrium had spent the night in their own room and bed, but they couldn't enjoy it. Instead they had spent the night talking about what had transpired, what might happen within the ruins and their own theories on what everything meant. But now it was dawn and they were rallied once more in the Chief's hut as requested. They were tired and impatient, but most of all they were excited to finally see what was going to happen when they entered the ruined fortress.

Stefan had also attended by request of Arok; the idea that the skilled archer would be entering the ruins with them pleased the Chief greatly. Kurok couldn't offer much manpower to the cause with the news of a potential threat against the town, but he knew Stefan was as skilled as ten men and worked best alongside Arok. He also looked to be the only one out of the three who actually got any sleep the previous night. His cool, calm and collected face showed no sign of the fatigue that was present the day before.

"I understand that you are anxious to get going. I've called you three here not just to wish you well, but to give you something, Arok," Kurok said, directing the end of his announcement at his son.

"We have all the supplies we need, Father," Arok started before being silenced by Kurok raising his hand.

The Chief walked to the back of the room, knelt down and pulled a deer pelt that served as a rug away from the ground to reveal a man-made hole beneath. From the cavity in the floor, Kurok pulled out with both hands a large war hammer. Arok recognised it immediately, despite having seen it only once as a child. Its heavy stone was carved into the image of a minotaur head with its horns protruding outward and its eyes glinting with enchanted gemstones, one of seafoam green and the other of crimson red. From beneath the chin, blood red and emerald green ribbons curled down the hilt, adding a certain beauty to the otherwise vicious-looking weapon.

"Rok's Bludgeon," Arok said, referring to the weapon by its name.

"You remember it then. This is the weapon of our ancestor Rok, the great warrior and shaman who led all of Tremel to the glory it once had before Lucian came. In respect to our ancestor, every descendant of our family has had his name within our own. This weapon was wielded by him through countless fierce battles and was enchanted to never break, thus making it a weapon that will always lend you support. Should you know how to use it," Kurok lectured his son on what he already knew. "Now, seeing you take on this responsibility with the ruins, I wish to pass it onto you, Arok."

"Are you serious?" Arok asked excitedly, shaking with anticipation, not quite believing what his father was saying.

"Yes. May it protect you against any foe you encounter."

Arok took the war hammer from his father, feeling its

weight come onto him as he lifted it up. His father nodded approvingly, seeming happy with his decision to pass the weapon down. It wasn't what anyone would consider a tactical weapon, but with Arok's sheer strength, the Chief knew his son would wield it well. Even if he had little concept of the enchantments imbued within the weapon.

After the three had said their farewells to the Chief, they made their way out of the hut towards the back exit of the wall surrounding the hamlet, the exit leading into the forest. The Chief watched as the three marched into the forest and slowly out of sight – Stefan with his longbow at the head of the team, while Arok stood close to Lyrium, the war hammer resting on his shoulder looking perfectly natural.

Your descendant will make you proud, Rok, the Chief thought. *He will bring honour to our people once more.*

The entrance to the ruins was clear. Massive stone columns lined each side of the stone path towards the tall archway; the stones were devoid of plants, seemingly untouched by nature. The pillars had obviously once supported some form of ceiling but it had been shattered by some unknown force, leaving the sun to shine down on the cracked stone of the columns and path.

To add to the bizarre picture, the ruins were dead in the middle of the dirt path that all three companions had walked countless times on their way into the forest to hunt. The structure they were traversing was obviously designed as a means to screen people trying to access the entrance. There were plenty of places that archers could take cover while keeping watch in all directions. With the right candidates guarding it, it'd be near impossible to sneak past. Fortunately, there were no such guards trying to forbid their entry and even the hunters posted by Kurok that were watching over the entrance quickly dispersed upon seeing Lyrium approach. A few offered satchels of fruit and other supplies, but most were quick to put distance between themselves and the ruins. With a grunt, Arok slung the extra bags of supplies over his shoulder and the march forward continued.

Arok caught sight of an emblem bathed in sunlight above the gaping entrance to the depths. It was depicted as a minotaur's head not unlike the visual one would get by turning his new weapon on its side. It was the mark of Tremel, the same one that had not been used since the fortress' collapse; at least not within the southern settlement anyway. It seemed impossible, yet the ruins were there and they simply couldn't have been missed. With the emblem now in sight, it assured that the once glorious fortress had appeared of its own volition.

"One of you two want to explain how we missed this in the past? A blind beggar could have seen this," Arok asked dryly, looking up at the thick stone columns as he walked towards the entrance.

"It's like they didn't want to be seen . . . As if they were lying in wait," Stefan mused.

Lyrium remained silent as the other two talked. She was listening for the voice she had heard the last time she was here, but only silence greeted her as the trio entered the dark ruins. They walked hesitantly through the archway and into the darkness, feeling the walls for support as they moved forward, led by the light of torches in the distance.

The trio walked towards it cautiously, not sure of what they would find. To their collective relief, nothing out of the ordinary happened as they neared the light. The party stepped into the room with the torches and looked around. Arok was the last to reach the inside and as his feet planted themselves firmly within the room, the grinding sound of stone on stone filled the room.

The three of them spun around to see the light from the end of the corridor disappearing as a stone wall barred their exit. Stefan realised the reason for the trap as he looked around their new prison. It was a perfect cube with all walls appearing the same on the surface and each the exact same size as the others. The one they had entered through had the outline of a doorway, as did the two on his left and right. The wall directly ahead of them, however, held only torches offering light to the cell.

Who had lit them remained a mystery.

Before any of the trio had time to gather their bearings a voice boomed into their minds – a harsh, yet articulate, male voice.

You have returned, Hunter. With companions, no less, the voice echoed within their heads. *It's fine. Someone who can identify that they require assistance is indeed a sign of prudence. However, if you intend on finding the prize these ruins hold, I must test you and I won't hold back, even if you are the ones destined to find it. This trial has been a long time coming and while I still believe you to be inexperienced, the world calls you to arms. It's a cry that neither of us can ignore.*

Arok looked around in a panic but the room held no answers. It was just as it appeared, a small room with torches lining the back wall and the source of the voice remaining unknown.

The time for hesitation is past; you will either claim the prize or rot within these walls along with your companions.

"Who are you? What trial?" Lyrium asked, trying to sound confident despite her shuddering nerves.

Pass this trial and you will have your answers. I warn you, do not become complacent as you are playing by my rules now, the voice replied ominously. *Make your way to the central chamber, and claim your reward from me.*

With that the voice was gone and parts of each side of the room crumbled to reveal a pair of open arches. Both had stairways leading downwards into more of the bleak darkness. The trio looked from one entrance to the other before the men turned expectantly to Lyrium.

"What do you want me to do?" she asked.

"You need to take the reins here, Lyrium," Stefan said evenly. "This is your trial; we are here merely as support. I suggest you make the decisions from here on, starting with the choice of which passage to take."

Lyrium seemed to be in a daze as she looked at her two companions, who stared back, wearing supportive smiles on both their faces. She returned with one of her own, if a little shakier, before looking at the archways and sighing.

"Well, right is right," she said, lifting a torch from the wall before walking to the archway on the right and taking the first step down the staircase with her companions.

CHAPTER 25

A NEW PURPOSE

Chase sniffed in disgust at the smell that greeted his nose like an unwelcome guest.

Hearthgrim's mixed scents from the various smithies littered here and there, along with the farms known for livestock, formed an odour that was less than pleasing to a newcomer's senses.

Hearthgrim was tiny, even by comparison to other small villages. It took mere minutes of walking through the middle of the town to locate the "Drunken Smithy" inn. People could be heard laughing from within the dingy establishment, while others were staggering out of the entrance in a haze of dust. The people exiting were clearly disorientated from whatever house alcohol the unsavoury bar supplied to the patrons.

Temperance noticed a ragged sign indicating that this was indeed the inn mentioned by the women on the road. After reading the sign, she spun around to Chase with a conflicted expression.

"This is the place they mentioned – what do you think? Should we ask the innkeep about what the women said on the road?" she enquired, surprising her companion by even speaking.

Chase hesitated, eyes flickering towards the building and

back. "We don't know who those women were, nor who anyone here is. It is possible it could be some form of trap."

"Those women were armed to the teeth. In our current state they could have put an end to our lives right then and there. And it's not like we have anything of value to provoke being robbed," Temperance countered.

It was the first time that Temperance had attempted an actual debate with him and he was surprised to find that she was rather astute in choosing her argument. Chase was about to respond when his stomach growled violently. He had given most of the food to his companion throughout the trip and it was starting to take its toll. Temperance smiled almost kindly before taking Chase's hand and leading him to the front door, using her free hand to open it before dragging the reluctant man inside.

If the smell outside was bad, inside was atrocious. There were drunks everywhere. A group of burly men were gathered around a table in the corner, playing some sort of dice game and roaring with raucous laughter. Meanwhile, scantily dressed women saw to the drinks at the tables. The bar was littered with people in grimy clothes who only took their weary eyes off their drinks to take a swig before reaffixing their gaze to their poison of choice.

Chase approached the bar, which was surprisingly clean and well-maintained. The innkeep glanced up at the two newcomers. He was the only one in the bar who was remotely well-dressed, his off-white tunic only stained in a few places, his beard roughly trimmed and his thinning grey hair slicked back messily.

He had crows' feet branching away from his eyes like small

spider webs that showed he was a man who had seen a lot of joy in his time. The steely hue of his pupils suggested that he'd seen an equal amount of trying times more recently.

Chase knew that there was more to the man than met his gaze from behind the counter, though he felt it a pointless endeavour trying to figure out what it was.

"You two even old enough to drink?" the innkeep joked cheerfully, a grin breaking through his beard, revealing surprisingly white teeth.

"Greetings, Sir. I'm not sure how to go about this, but a woman named Katarina sent us," Chase said uncertainly.

"Katarina? Oh! Kat? Where are my manners? If she's sent you I'm more than happy to assist in any way. What'll it be? Food? Shelter?" the innkeep enquired.

"We are in need of a place to stay. Kat said to come here and she will be back after her business in Neibel-Haven." Chase left the tale at that.

"Oh? Kat wants you to wait for her?" The innkeep took a moment to look over the pair. "Well, if it's in relation to the operation she is working towards, it's none of my business. At least not at the moment anyways, but I'm happy to give you a room and something to fill your stomach. All for the low price of never calling me 'Sir' again. Call me 'Keeper', nothing else."

Keeper walked around from the other side of the bar and beckoned for Chase and Temperance to follow. The exhausted pair could hardly believe their luck as the man who called himself Keeper led them to the stairs at the end of the bar. The patrons of the filthy pub didn't break in their activities as they were led through the crowd.

Their host seemed to notice Chase's expression and said

with a knowing smile, "Only one rule of Keeper's pub, kiddo. Mind your own damn business. Follow that, and you'll never have an issue within these walls."

Chase nodded slowly and shrugged as if to say, "Fair enough". He was too exhausted to do anything besides focus on climbing the set of stairs that greeted him. Upon reaching the top, they found themselves walking along the corridor of the second floor. Doors on each side of the narrow hallway led to small rooms that were probably available to paying customers. Chase noticed that everything about the second floor appeared to be maintained in better condition than the first.

The observation made Chase think back to the counter they had found Keeper attending just moments before. It had been in almost immaculate condition as well. It appeared that anything Keeper had direct influence over was noticeably better maintained than the other areas within the building. Chase shook his head slightly.

Who cares about how he runs things?

At the end of the hall there was another flight of stairs and at the top was a single door. Keeper leapt up the stairs and pushed open the door to reveal a room about half the size of the entire first floor. In the corner was a massive bed pushed up against the wall. In another corner was a tin tub used for washing with a sheet hanging from the roof for privacy. There were also small pieces of furniture including a table, chairs and even a large mirror, which stood around a few handspans taller than Chase and was wide enough that three people could stand beside each other and comfortably fit in the reflection.

The room was more than they expected.

"It isn't much to look at, to be sure. But I'm sure it will do well enough. Now, I'll bring food in the morning and at night, but let me know if you require more. I'll organise hot water," Keeper listed thoughtfully while glancing at Temperance. "Some clean clothes wouldn't go astray either. All I ask is you both consider your next move carefully. This is Katarina's permanent room and the only people allowed are those with her blessing. You can imagine how few those numbers are."

Keeper made his exit, leaving the two to sit and relax for the first time since their exile before Chase addressed Temperance awkwardly.

"You may take the bed for yourself, and I'll sleep on the floor. It isn't the first time I've slept on a floor, nor will it be the last."

"I want to go to Scourge's destruction site," Temperance declared suddenly.

The sudden assertiveness surprised Chase, but he quickly rallied in the hopes of a lengthier conversation.

"Why would you want to go there? From what I know, the only people who have gone there since the incident were Lazear to find the stone, and scavengers."

"When I was overcome with the stone's power, I could see the memories of whatever destroyed Scourge. I think there may be something still there," Temperance explained hesitantly. "The memories were scattered and inconsistent but I feel as though I should do this."

Chase stared at the woman for a lengthy moment, trying to interpret her intentions. While he wasn't sure of her reasons for wanting to go there, he still owed her something. He didn't have time to speak before Temperance's eyes met his. The embers he had seen in the underground tower were ablaze as the scarlet threatened to consume the green within them as she spoke again.

"I was there before I was brought before the man you called the Professor," Temperance said softly, attempting not to sound accusatory. "I went there to research the ruins. I had always wanted to. I had no idea that I was one of Scourge's descendants or how your Professor knew himself, but I have to go back. If research isn't a good enough reason, then surely the origin of the one chosen by the Stone of Fire is?"

"I want to come," Chase announced a little louder than required. Temperance grimaced, as if faced with something distasteful that she knew was coming.

"I was intending to ask if anyone from the village would accompany me," Temperance replied softly, not meeting Chase's eager gaze.

"The residents seem an unsavoury lot – you can't trust them," Chase argued.

"Then I will go alone."

"Wolves," Chase countered and Temperance sighed. "The only problem left is that I'm not even certain where Scourge is. I've never taken the time to find out," he continued hurriedly before Temperance could argue further.

"I know almost exactly where it is."

"Then it's settled!" Chase declared happily as Temperance sighed in resignation. She didn't want him there, but she couldn't trust anyone else either.

The devil you know . . .

The conversation lulled as Keeper silently entered the room, placed a large plate of food on the table and left.

"It's about a day-and-a-half walk south-east from here.

Hearthgrim was only built soon after its destruction when travelling mercenaries realised that Scourge was never going to be rebuilt again. This village was originally a camp, which grew into a village over time," Temperance explained as Chase lunged at a massive leg of meat. "I didn't realise we were so close to Scourge until I heard the name of this village from Katarina and Amelia."

"What about those travellers, though? I thought we were waiting here for them?" Chase reasoned, as if they had always been going together.

"It took us the better part of five days to get here from Neibel-Haven and we were taking it slow. We could be back from Scourge before they even get here."

Chase smiled, more about knowing that they would be going together rather than the destination itself.

"Very well, we will set out tomorrow morning. We will leave a message with Keeper, but we need to be quick. I'm curious as to what we can help those two with," Chase said, placing his sword on the ground as the innkeeper came in with the hot water in two buckets and clean clothes draped over his shoulder.

"But, we shall discuss it after we have bathed," he added as he grabbed a fistful of food and left the room so Temperance could wash in peace.

CHAPTER 26

A STRANGER'S WARNING

The Council of Neibel-Haven were gathered and seated in their chambers, all slightly agitated and very confused. Two travellers stood in front of them who had the audacity to walk straight in and order that the Council meet immediately.

"I'm sorry, Kat, was it?" Mordrik asked a condescending tone. "You are trying to tell us there is danger coming our way. Indeed, the same dark energy that was present at the Battle of a Thousand Blades. You further accuse us of giving up the upper hand by exiling the monster that tried to destroy our city. How can you say that with such a straight face?"

Kat sighed in exasperation before trying to explain for a third time.

"That's not what I'm saying, old man. What I'm saying is that she, or the dark energy as you call her, is coming here because of the severe spike in magical energy a week past. I don't know why, but the coming threat is intent on finding the other bearers of the stones. Right now, the one I know of is vulnerable, and she has next to no idea how to use the power."

Mordrik exploded.

"So, what gives you the right to walk in here demanding to see the Council, only to undermine my decision to exile a threat to this city? OUR city?!"

Kat exceeded Mordrik's pitch with no hesitation.

"BECAUSE ONE OF THE PEOPLE YOU EXILED WAS A VASSAL! SHE WAS YOUR BEST CHANCE AT REPELLING THE ATTACK, YOU STUFFY OLD FOOL!"

Mordrik looked like he had been slapped while the other Council members squirmed in their seats uncomfortably. They had been told to remain silent by the Archmage the second Kat had finished explaining herself the first time. It was obvious that they each had their own thoughts on the matter they were dying to voice.

Katarina lowered her voice to a normal volume.

"Now is not the time to fight amongst ourselves. You had best prepare for her coming invasion because that's what it will be. She will not care if you exiled the other Vassal; she will destroy anything and kill anyone if it means there is a chance to find what she wants."

"How do you know that this woman would do that?"

"Because I've learnt enough about warfare to know that sometimes the extermination of your enemy is the quickest way to victory."

"No army that has tried to take Neibel-Haven in the past has ever succeeded," Mordrik scoffed proudly.

"True, but no army that has attacked Neibel-Haven in the past has wielded one of the stones' powers."

CHAPTER 27

A THIEF'S IRRITATION IS A PRINCESS' AMUSEMENT

Rufus was talking to Alicea but she wasn't hearing a word of it. Lost in her own thoughts, she stared at her new friend, who had taken to nestling in her lap like a real bird and not one that had been created from water and magic.

Not that I'd know how a magical bird is supposed to act.

They had made camp a day's distance from South Tremel, successfully avoiding the small villages on the outskirts of Aquiocia in fear of Alicea being recognised by any of the villagers. As a consequence, their food had started to run low and sleeping on thin roll-out beds each evening had brought restless nights to them both. Rufus, who would stay up to keep watch most nights, was especially starting to feel the effects of little sleep. Fortunately, he had been able to have most of the fruit and vegetables from the pair's stores as the Princess seemed uninterested in eating them.

For the most part, their journey had been uneventful, with the exclusion of the stone's conversation with Alicea at the waterfall. The Princess kept replaying it over and over in her head, trying desperately to make anything more out of it, but the voice she had heard had revealed no secrets beyond what it had intended to give her. It appeared to be outright ignoring her attempts at conversation as she whispered to the rippling surface of the stone. Frustrated by the lack of answers before her, she turned her thoughts to what she had seen on her little journey. To any merchant it would have seemed a trivial and regular journey. But to the young Princess it was an enormous step away from her comfort zone.

Running across the countryside on horseback with a man she barely knew was something she never considered, especially not a man who had kidnapped her nearly a week ago. She had seen dense forestland, swiftly running rivers through the plains and Aquiocia from a different viewpoint entirely. It was strange to be actively avoiding civilisation when she'd been surrounded by it for her entire life.

The landscape had appeared beautiful and yet, even now as she looked around from her small campfire, she could still sense a heavy unease about the land. It was as if the more her mind was taken off her parents' death, the more she could perceive that there was something wrong in the world. Perhaps an even more alarming notion was the feeling that she herself could do something to help ease the land's pain, as well as the people who called it home.

They hadn't seen another person either, which of course was the whole idea, but it seemed to have disturbed Rufus greatly when she had made the observation a few days earlier. It had been as if she had just brought his fears to the surface. He hadn't offered any insight, though, seemingly distracted the whole time with his eyes always darting from tree to tree, rock to rock, and most of all, to her little bird.

"If Her Highness could tear her focus away from her own royal thoughts and pay attention to the lowly commoner in front of her for just a moment, it would be simply lovely," Rufus said in a sharp, sarcastic tone that made Alicea snap out of her trance. Her little bird looked up at the sound, its eyes narrowing at Rufus.

"My apologies. Is something amiss, Mr. Thief?" she asked absentmindedly.

"I was asking about your little friend. What can it do?" Rufus pointed at the bird with the tip of the knife he was sharpening.

"I'm sorry? Is she supposed to be doing something?" the Princess asked in confusion.

"Well, it would be nice, wouldn't it?" his sarcastic tone returned with a sigh. "It's made from magic, right? So, having it sitting on your shoulder all the time while we are on the move and sleeping in your lap of a night must be tiring, right? At least that's what I've heard – the longer you keep magic active, the more exhausted you become?"

Alicea thought back to when she had first summoned the little bird. She hadn't felt any different herself. She didn't feel the slightest bit of fatigue and keeping the companion with her hadn't had any adverse effects from what she could tell. But Rufus had a point; keeping the water-swan around had to have a drawback, as it was magic, after all.

With my aid you will find that you can bend the rules of magic. Break them, however, and you will find death as reward for your insolence. The memory of the stone's warning rang through her mind.

No, Alicea thought. *This swan is the closest thing I have to a friend. She stays.*

"So, you suggest I dismiss her, Mr. Thief?" the Princess asked. "Will you be the one to tell her that she is being banished because you're an ignorant, fully-grown man with the emotional depth of a thimble?"

"At least tell me why the silly thing is now being referred to as female!" demanded an exasperated Rufus, stowing away the sharpened blade.

"Well, offhand, I would say because she is female?" the Princess replied with a smile at the swan.

"It is a clever trick, but it's just water, Alicea!" Rufus snapped. "Water and magic."

"She's female. When I heard the voice, I hadn't heard one like it in all my life, but for some reason I felt it was female. As it was that magic which made my little friend, so shall she be a female," the Princess reasoned, petting the small bird in amusement at Rufus' outburst.

"Next you will be naming the useless thing," Rufus said under his breath.

"Good idea! What do you think of the name 'Selia'?" she asked, poking her tongue out slightly, which resulted in the thief storming away, muttering something about naming birds as if they were children and collecting firewood with a string of inventive curses tying the two subjects together.

CHAPTER 28

INTO THE DEPTHS

The trio continued their journey downwards in silence. The stairs wound around so much that they lost their sense of direction, taking the descent cautiously. Lyrium held the torch she had claimed in the first room above her head as the hands of both Arok and Stefan rested on their respective weapons.

After what seemed like an eternity they finally touched level ground, gasping as the dark room lit up upon their arrival. Torches on the walls flared up of their own accord, revealing the layout of the large chamber they had found. The hall was almost as wide as it was long, easily able to have fit a string of huts within its walls of solid stone – which, once again, appeared devoid of all nature. Not a single crack or vine tarnished the smooth stone's perfect surface.

At the end of the chamber were great statues of some of Tremel's ancestors, including one in Rok's image holding a massive replica of the weapon now within Arok's grasp. They stood tall against the far wall and matched the height of the glorious chandeliers that hung from the high ceiling. The candles blazed with fire and gave off light across the chambers. The trio had no interest in the massive tributes to the hunters of the past, however, as their attention was drawn to a gorgeous, and equally ostentatious, dining table found only in the greatest of kingdoms.

The lengthy table was lined with trays of food ranging from roast boars to bouquets of exotic fruits arranged in shining silver bowls. For those with a sweeter palate there were daring desserts all the way through to finger food in the form of nuts and cheeses. The food was accompanied by silver goblets of rich red wine at each placing. The spread looked to be laid out for royalty.

However, even this wasn't what the small party's unease stemmed from. Their foreboding feeling came from the people who were sitting at the table, and the people seemed very interested in their new guests. Lyrium noticed them first.

Were these people just waiting in the dark for us? Why'd the torches only flare when we got here?

An impressive, regal man at the head of the table was the first to speak, his full and booming voice echoing throughout the otherwise silent chamber.

"Welcome, guests! We have been expecting you. Please, sit! We have much to discuss and I believe I can be of assistance in your plight." The royal-looking man smiled with a gaudy, gem-encrusted crown sitting on top of his head of messy, dirty brown hair.

Lyrium approached the table cautiously. The only seat vacant was at the exact opposite end from the King. It was considered to be a place of honour; even Lyrium knew that and she wasn't exactly familiar with the social graces of royalty. If the person sitting there wasn't a part of whatever established power was seated at the table, it was considered an invitation of some prestige. It was the seat that, while it may be the furthest from the head of the table, was the one from which an intimate gaze could be held with the host at the other end.

Her eyes darted up the impressive spread of food to each person sitting at the buffet. All present were dressed well in formal attire and beautiful dresses. Though it wasn't the fact that she was underdressed by comparison that worried Lyrium.

Eighteen people, she thought grimly. *We are really outnumbered if this turns bad.*

There was the man at the end, running the festivities as unwonted as they were. He seemed too perfectly put together for a man his age. He looked around forty, but his demeanour housed a certain youthfulness. His slight movements were deliberate and controlled despite his overweight physique. He had multiple chins and a thick neck, but no sweat on his dark brow despite the warmth of the many sources of fire in the room along with his heavy clothing. The man looked as if he should be sluggish, like simple movement should exhaust him. But he moved with the ease of a fit adolescent.

Lyrium looked back to see Arok right behind her to the right. Stefan stood at the entrance, seemingly at ease, but Lyrium saw his eyes weighing up the odds behind his perfectly arranged fringe. From his reaction to the headcount, she could tell that he didn't think highly of their odds either.

Why is he hanging back so far? Then Lyrium realised. *He is lining up the targets. Stefan is expecting a fight.*

Lyrium shot Arok another look as she took her seat. His friendly smile was directed at each of the people around the table while his eyes seemed to show no unease, and no fear.

Arok, how are you always so relaxed? Lyrium thought, both

envious and proud of her lover's trait.

"Ah, good. Now, it is Lyrium, isn't it?" the crowned man asked, and continued before she had a chance to contemplate how he knew her name. "You seek what is at the heart of these ruins, don't you?"

Lyrium nodded, very aware of the many sets of eyes on her before the crowned man continued. As hard as it was, she forced herself to hold the man's gaze so as not to reveal her concern about the numbers.

Why are they staring so much? Shouldn't they be eating?

"You will want to take the route behind the statue of the man on the old King's right, but first I –"

"Who are you?" Lyrium cut across smoothly, taking the crowned man by surprise.

"Oh, I sincerely apologise. Where are my manners? My name is Surok, heir to the throne of Tremel. That is, I *was* the heir before Tremel spilt into four settlements after that battle so many years ago," the almost charming man responded smoothly as he straightened his impressive robe. It was made from the pelt of an animal that Lyrium couldn't place.

"Surok?" Arok spoke for the first time since entering the room before trailing off in thought, ignoring Lyrium's questioning glance.

"Yes. Now, as I was saying. Before you take on that route I suggested you remember this," he continued briskly, turning his attention back to Lyrium. "This is your trial, Lyrium; your companions will only hold you back. I know this very well."

"Oh? And how would you know?" Lyrium asked with a challenging tone.

"You could say that we reside with the one who has set up

this trial for you," the man responded almost offhandedly.

Lyrium stared hard at him, before finally buckling and looked around to the others at the table. The strange guests offered no insight into the man's words or the situation in general; they stared back at her with the same expressions of mild interest stuck on their faces. Confused, Lyrium looked to Arok, who still had a troubled and thoughtful look on his face. In desperation for some advice she looked back to Stefan, who seemed to be glaring at Surok.

Stefan noticed Lyrium's questioning stare and in return gave her the slightest shake of his head, which she took as "don't trust this man". She turned back to Surok and took a deep breath. She hadn't planned on trusting him anyway, but the fact that Stefan acknowledged her confusion helped her confidence immeasurably.

"Forgive me, but you can keep your advice. They are the only ones in this room that I can trust," Lyrium said firmly.

"She's right ta say so," Arok piped up gruffly as he stared at Surok accusingly. "You're a liar. There's no heir, and Surok is my uncle, or woulda been. He died a couple weeks after being born, my father was there. What ya sayin' is horseshit."

The crowned man's reaction was simply a small half smile, almost as if he was amused by the revelation. However, his next words were colder and the trio could feel the malice emanating from the man and filling the chamber.

"I see. So, you refuse to heed my advice, and instead throw delusional accusations around? Well, to your credit, you were right about part of it. You could say I'm not the 'real' Surok, but that's neither here nor there anymore." The man's voice trailed off as he redirected his gaze to his dinner guests, who sharply turned their heads simultaneously to their leader. "Rise."

At this soft command, all seventeen guests rose to their feet, accompanied by Lyrium who backed away from the danger. There was nothing she loved more than a good brawl, but her survival instinct was screaming that it wasn't to be a natural confrontation. Looking back, she saw Stefan nock an arrow and raise his longbow while Arok positioned himself between the party guests and Lyrium.

"What in the world . . .?" It was Stefan who spoke and Lyrium and Arok noticed what he was referring to a split second later.

The guests stood as normal humans would, but the flesh from their limbs seemed to be flaking away. Their faces seemed to be hollower than before, almost as if they were malnourished and losing more of whatever nutrients their body held by the second. The man who called himself Surok spoke once more in his chilling tone.

"I see you have noticed my guests' handicap. Yes, they are fine while they remain stationary or seated, but their movements come at a price. They don't feel pain, however, so I find pity for them has no place here."

"Necromancy!" Lyrium exclaimed.

"No, don't get ahead of yourself, my dear. These people all died shortly after birth. The only reason they stand before you now is because they have been granted the gift from the one within the stone. They were chosen at the time of their death for this exact reason. They were nourished from the magic it gave, injecting the necessities for growth straight into their bodies to allow them to develop into the makeshift adults you see before you."

The trio exchanged startled glances amongst one another before the man continued.

"When dormant, they continue to grow. However, when awakened, the magic alone isn't enough to sustain them. The grip of death, of true death, tightens by the second." Surok raised the sleeve of his robe to reveal an arm that was decaying before their eyes. "Sadly, I'm no exception."

"This is still a despicable practice! An abomination on human life," Lyrium spat. Her anger was starting to get the best of her.

"Perhaps, but my subjects and I need to go back to our dormant state. The sooner we are rid of you, the sooner we can do just that," Surok responded while raising his festering arm towards the trio and issuing a single-word command. "Kill."

CHAPTER 29

DINNER ETIQUETTE

Lyrium cursed under her breath, stepping back a fraction of a second too late. One of the dinner guests' knives grazed her arm before his head was torn from his shoulders as Arok brought his war hammer across the side of the man's face from behind.

"Lyrium, get back, Stefan and I will handle this!" Arok yelled at his love while she nodded, backing away from the table with her small knife drawn. She hated sitting out, but this wasn't hunting, nor was it brawling.

Arok turned and marched towards the crowd of decaying men and women with murderous intent. The man calling himself Surok was smiling villainously. He triggered a level of loathing within Arok that he'd never felt for another human being, or whatever he was. How dare this man drag his heritage through the mud? How dare he claim Rok's name?

Arok didn't flinch as three of the guests charged at him with knives from the banquet. As he expected, an arrow soared over his shoulder and collided with one of the men's heads. The head jolted back sharply and was left hanging loosely from strips of eroding flesh. His march, though, was not hindered in the slightest. Arok grunted as he took a quick step forward, bringing his war hammer soaring through the air in front of him, shattering the near-headless man's ribcage.

The remaining two leapt back out of the range of Arok's wrath as he tried to control the weight of his weapon. He was strong, far stronger than the average man, but the weapon was heavy and unwieldy in the hands of a man who was more familiar with fighting unarmed. Arok's reflexes rallied a second too slow and cost him ground as he had to retreat from his enemies' knives. One lunged forward and Arok ducked down with a smirk. An arrow flew past where Arok's head was half a second earlier, colliding with the rotting man's chest, the force of which made him step back.

Another of the deadly airborne projectiles buried itself in his neck. The impact forced the man to stumble, falling to the ground. He writhed, trying to get back to his feet. Arok roared in triumph as he swung his weapon overhead, jumping towards the remaining man recklessly. Adrenaline was coursing through his veins as he brought the war hammer crashing down on his enemy. The remaining man's brittle bones buckled under the combination of Arok's strength and his weapon's weight. Arok swore he could see a thin cloud of dust rise from the corpse as it twitched violently in its attempt to get back up.

"These things don't even die properly!" Arok exclaimed as he used his foot to stomp on the writhing mass of flesh beneath him, crushing the fragile bones. Three more of the decaying dinner guests stepped out from their chairs and advanced on the trio. Arok stood firmly between them and his companions.

"Arok, do not take any unnecessary risks," Stefan called in warning. He could see that his friend was still getting the hang of his weapon. "We can always retreat to the higher floor."

"If we always retreat we won't get anywhere." Arok's stubborn nature shone through his grim expression. Stefan conceded that his friend was right. It was all or nothing.

This round was different and Arok could sense it. The three advancing forms moved as one, with the two women circling slightly to his flank while the man marched directly at Arok. He had to make the first move. He quickly devised a small yet reckless strategy that was akin to his nature.

"Stefan, the one on my left!" he cried.

"Understood!" Stefan acknowledged as he let fly his nocked arrow at the woman. The arrow had barely found its target before Stefan had readied another.

As he unloaded arrow after arrow, he kept an eye on his ally anxiously. He almost lost complete focus for his target in shock when Arok acted. Arok swung his massive weapon onto his shoulder, gripping the bottom of its hilt and hurling the dead weight at the man advancing up the middle.

Arok's weapon left his hands as he ran directly at the remaining woman, grabbed the arm that held the knife and thrust his fist into the woman's stomach. Her flesh offered little resistance as his bare hand pushed through the slimy texture of almost deceased organs and gripped her spine. He ripped his hand from her stomach and bone structure within her chest smoothly slid from its resting place. Lacking the foundation provided by her flimsy bones, the woman collapsed to the ground. With both surprise and grim humour, he dropped the woman's spine, looking to the other two contenders.

The man was a few feet back from where he was when he had been hit with what must have felt like a charging bull. Arok's weapon was still lodged in the pinned man's chest as he struggled on the ground against the burden.

Meanwhile, the woman on the receiving end of Stefan's arrows resembled a pincushion, filled with the deadly projectiles that at first glance seemed randomly placed. But Stefan had taken the time to pick his targets, striking the nerve centres with an uncanny precision that only he could boast. Before he could commend his partner on this, Arok noticed that "Surok" was looking at the man previously seated to his right. The false heir nodded slightly as the man moved from his spot, drawing a sword from the scabbard that hung from his hip and advancing.

Arok scrambled to retrieve his weapon.

Lyrium looked at the man walking towards Arok in concern. Why would only one man go for her love? Strategy would suggest sending them all at once. She took in everything she could about the man and noticed that he was more sure-footed than the ones before him; the flats of his feet were barely touching the ground as he readied himself. He handled his sword with the calm demeanour of a seasoned swordsman, flicking it casually from hand to hand before gripping the hilt and twisting the blade to point directly at Arok. A challenge.

It seems this man has a lot more skill than the previous ones, so why not back him up with others? she thought, puzzled, as Stefan let fly an arrow directed at the man.

The arrow was caught and discarded as the unperturbed man approached his target.

Arok tore his weapon out of the writhing man's chest, crushing his fragile skull under his foot. The arrow-catching man continued to close the gap towards him. Thirty yards ... Twenty-seven yards ... Twenty-four yards.

"Do not charge him!" Stefan cried, as he started jogging closer. It was a move that he detested and was normally unwise for an archer. The only reason he even considered it was the theory that maybe, if he was closer, he would be able to land the shot.

"Fight defensively!" he added.

Arok trusted his partner and raised his weapon in front of his body. He shifted his grasp, gripping the bottom and top of the handle, ready to parry the incoming blows. Stefan nocked an arrow on the run and let it fly with the assumption that the enemy had less time to respond the closer they were. His theory was quickly proven wrong as the swordsman swiftly raised his sword and the arrow glanced off his blade.

The man followed through, his weapon glancing off Arok's. Arok countered, driving the head of his weapon downwards. His opponent twisted away, spinning gracefully and slicing at Arok's legs. The leather split but his skin remained intact.

How does he fight so well? Lyrium's mind raced to find a solution. *He has so much control over the fight . . . That's it! It's all a show and Surok is the one pulling strings!* Arok took an unsteady step backwards, tripping over one of the defeated corpses. The enemy took the opportunity and lunged directly at him, bringing his blade down. Arok would have met his end if Stefan hadn't reached them, stepping between the two fighters. He had abandoned his bow and grabbed the man's sword arm before it cut his friend to pieces. As Arok scrambled to his feet, his eyes widened at the sight of Lyrium sprinting across the chambers directly at Surok, knife in hand.

Lyrium leapt onto the table. She was so certain that the dinner guests wouldn't react that she ran across its top between them unafraid. True to her theory, the remaining gathered men and women didn't stop her from running past them as she sent cutlery, plates and goblets flying. The smug smile on Surok's face faded as he watched her charging towards him. He greeted the fast-approaching woman with a look of mild surprise, glancing at his champion in time to see him fall.

His concentration on the fight broke and the decomposing swordsman dropped to the ground, much to Stefan's relief. Lyrium smiled, her theory proven correct as she lunged at the now scowling man. She sliced Surok's throat with her small knife and the crowned host stumbled back, staring at her in shock. With a smile that ignored the gaping, bloodless wound across his throat, he addressed her in a friendly manner.

"I say, bravo!" Surok commended. "Such a marvellous display of bravery, cooperation and companionship. I'll admit, for a second I thought I was actually going to have to kill you all, but you pulled through at the very end. For that you deserve only praise!"

"What in the world are you talking about, filth?" Lyrium spat.

"I can understand your anger. It is only fitting, but it is a waste of your energy at this point, I'm afraid," Surok said. "Our bodies will soon give away; your hatred is squandered energy."

Surok raised his arm and the bone was all that could be seen. His flesh and blood alike had taken on the form of dust, which was falling to the floor.

"What trick have you got for us now?" Lyrium growled.

"No tricks; this was all predicted. You came here for the treasure, correct? This was one of the tests, and you have done wonderfully," Surok continued hurriedly before he could be interrupted. "Allow me to explain as much as possible before the force that keeps me here fades entirely.

"I spoke the truth about what door you should take at the back of the room and I *am* Surok – your uncle," he said, with a solemn glance towards the approaching Arok. It was a statement begging to be believed.

"The guardian of the stone employed my assistance before I was even able to understand what it meant to live, let alone serve. I grew under the stone's power and resided here until I was needed. I have now fulfilled my role," Surok explained. "I was to see if you valued your companions. You demonstrated that; you risked your own life by attacking me. Tremel's Vassal of old would be proud, truly."

"Wait – what guardian? What happens next?" Lyrium asked the man who seemed to be disintegrating at an alarming rate before her very eyes.

"I'm sorry. I know little of the guardian itself, but you may see soon enough." Surok fell to his hollowing knees and each word was more strained than the last. "I am truly honoured . . . to have played my part . . . in preparing the new . . . heroes of Tremel."

With that the man collapsed to the ground in sync with the remaining guests. Any sign of life once there was gone in an instant as the magic was finally extinguished. The trio looked around in confusion at the mess of a dining hall, each trying to comprehend what had happened.

"Well then, what now?" Stefan asked as he plucked arrows from the bodies he had shot at earlier.

"We collect anything of use here," Lyrium began shakily. "Then we continue. I'd like a word with this so-called guardian."

CHAPTER 30

THE ART OF BATTLE AND MAGIC

"Get moving! We need the barrier stabilised!" Mordrik called impatiently to the mages running past him as he directed their work.

The city of Neibel-Haven was in a state of panic. Mordrik had declared an emergency defence order and the city's citizens had run to their houses while the battle mages took their positions around the walls of the city. The gates had been shut tight for almost a full day now while they prepared for the upcoming battle. Now, at mid-morning, everyone had been called to arms.

With each of the Council members standing atop their respective towers with growing unease, Mordrik himself ran through the streets, making sure everyone was in position and ready for the attack. The physical walls around the city wouldn't hold the Vassal out and everyone knew it. Mordrik had known it even before Katarina had brought it to his attention. It was designed to keep regular enemy soldiers from gaining access to the city. It would never hold out magic for very long. Not by itself, anyway.

It hadn't taken long for the walls to be swarming with mages in various coloured robes. Those in red were at the front of the walls while the brown robes hung back from the edges.

It was designed with the more destructive fields of magic holding the frontline so they could unleash as much chaos within the enemy ranks as possible, while the more technical of the elements held back, waiting for their chance. The ones in shining white weren't on the ramparts at all; instead they hid within the city, waiting for any injured men and women to be brought to them. Being aligned with Light and gifted in healing made them invaluable in a battle. Throughout their ranks was the odd mage in blue helping out.

"You!" Mordrik called to a young female apprentice mage in midnight-blue robes. "Make yourself useful – go and tell Midel that I'm ready to address the people, so she needs to get her people organised!"

With a loud "Yes, Sir!" the young mage ran off at top speed towards the Water Tower as her superior turned back to the organised mages. With a quick nod of approval, he started at a jog towards the Celestial Tower to take his post at its top.

He ran straight past the Wind Tower and his face grew grim at the gaping hole in its side from the impact of Temperance's assault just three days earlier. The magical barrier was restored around it; however, the stone wall had not been repaired – there had been no time. There had also been strange reports regarding any work done. He hadn't had time to read the report properly. It hadn't been his greatest concern. The Council had met two days in a row just to speak with Katarina and Amelia, and it had taken all of his patience to resist hurling them out of the city.

What had stopped him was an alarming message sent directly to the Council via Mordrik's own Gaian Crystal that hung above them in the meeting chambers, within the orb of light. The messenger had informed them of a small company of warriors led by a dark-haired woman marching towards Neibel-Haven. At first it had seemed a simple coincidence until the report told of the superhuman pace at which the warriors were moving. He knew at that exact moment that Katarina had been telling the truth.

If we can just get the ultimate defence of our city erected we will be able to –

Mordrik's train of thought was interrupted by the sight of Katarina and Amelia making their way towards the main gate at a casual pace. Amelia looked as grim as Mordrik felt. Katarina, however, was smiling as if it were just another normal day. Her smile grew larger when she saw the Council's leader huffing as he came to a stop in front of the two women.

"Don't overdo it, Mordrik. You won't be of any use if you can't even breathe the incantations," she opened light-heartedly.

"This is not the time for jokes, Katarina! Where are you going? What role will you play in this?" Mordrik demanded as he gasped for air, his age showing much more than he would like to admit.

"Amelia and I will be on the frontlines, of course. This is as much our fight as yours, after all," Kat replied matter-of-factly.

"What reason do you have to fight?"

"I'm sorry, I didn't realise we weren't welcome?" Katarina asked mockingly before turning to her sister. "Well, pack it up, Sis. They don't want us to help defend the city!"

Mordrik looked ready to explode at the blatant mockery but composed himself, bringing back the previous conversation.

"Frontlines? You mean to engage the enemy directly? The

idea behind all this preparation is to stop them from getting within the walls!"

"Yes, I'm aware of the plan, old man. But, for all you have in magic you seem to lack in infantry. Very few people in this city appear to have ever picked up a sword. Even fewer seem to know how to wield one," Kat replied patiently. "I'm willing to bet you won't keep the enemy outside your city forever. You will be thanking your lucky stars that Amelia and I are at the front of your army when they break through."

"You speak like two people could make all the difference!" Mordrik spat, his breath having returned. "Do what you like, lead what few swordsmen we have for all I care. Just do not disrupt our strategy."

With that Mordrik set out on his way to the Celestial Tower once more at his brisk pace. Kat watched the man with the smile on her face still intact before Amelia interrupted.

"He may run this city, but he does not see the impact that even one person can make," she said and Katarina threw back her head in laughter.

"Naive and cynical to a fault. He might be gifted in magic, but at the end of the day he really is just a grumpy old man," Katarina responded as the two continued their leisurely stroll to the main gate.

❖

Standing on the rough path leading to Neibel-Haven, at the foot of the last stretch of the mountain's incline, was the Vassal of Darkness. She stood absolutely still, staring at the grand city. She was a little over a quarter mile away from the impressive towers that protruded from behind the impressive walls defending them. She had kept that exact distance for a reason as she contemplated her first move.

She was accompanied by some fifty armoured men and women wielding an assortment of weapons, from swords to halberds, axes to knives, all ready for battle. They only awaited their Commander's orders. The sun was starting its descent as the Vassal looked back at her small army. She knew well that she was heavily outnumbered and yet she remained at complete ease. These warriors were a personal gift from Lucian and she knew well their secret.

These seemingly normal warriors had been chosen by Lucian in his conquest two hundred years ago. As death approached each of them, the knight had bound their souls to his command. Only the strongest and most skilled were chosen and if they were willing, their strength was amplified. These men and women had a presence on this plane of existence, yet their life force had resided within Lucian up until he bestowed them upon the Vassal of Darkness. Anyone could see and interact with them, yet they had no existence at all without a tether to someone boasting enough magical aptitude to serve as a conduit. Once the tether was released or severed, they would fade from existence and find a true death at last.

Most importantly to her campaign, for as long as she was alive and had enough strength to keep them bound with her magical energy, they could not be defeated and were powerless to resist her will. They were invaluable tools, and she recognised their worth.

When Lucian transferred his command of them to her, she had felt both his and their energy. She hadn't been able to make out anything about Lucian's aura; it had been shrouded in magical wards to prevent prying. But the soldiers were willing. This made them stronger as a unit and the drain on their leader's energy was less severe as she didn't have to mentally force them into submission.

The Vassal looked down at the clear surface of the crystal she used to maintain contact with Lucian. After applying her magical energy to the connection, she sent a simple, one-word message.

"Ready."

Keeping it short and sweet allowed her to preserve every ounce of energy she could. Almost instantly she felt Lucian's energy gather around the crystal in her hand as she knew it would. The knight's concealed face appeared on its surface and he replied in short sentences.

"Attack as ordered. I'm standing by to offer the agreed support. Do not fail me. This should be a simple task," he said softly and his face disappeared from the crystal's surface.

"Aye, because I'm thrilled to be here doing your dirty work!" the Vassal snarled when the connection severed.

The Vassal took a moment to mentally prepare.

There must be thousands of mages in that city. Their magic is trivial apart from the leaders, but combined this will be difficult. I hold the stone's power and have it fully under control but I must not take risks. I must trust in whatever assistance Lucian offers.

It was then that she noticed above the centre tower was what appeared to be an odd star-like light. It was uncomfortable to stare at, its luminescence making her eyes itch from the sheer brightness. Before her eyes could adjust it erupted, its radiance fanning out, spreading across the sky before descending. The light collided with the dirt about one hundred yards from her, shaking the earth violently. Dust, rocks and plants were sent spraying through the air as the barrier covered the entire city. Its beautiful light was patterned by shining magical energy and made it look like a giant blanket of stars.

Neibel-Haven's so-called "ultimate defence". I suppose they knew of my coming. I can't sense the source of the power spike, but there is something inside those walls equally as powerful. Maybe they were concealing it. They have a secret they aren't letting on, she thought, ever analytical.

Having studied the history of Neibel-Haven on the journey to the city, she knew that the barrier would reflect spells aimed at it from the outside, along with preventing any mortal human from getting past the radiant star-like cloak. It was designed to keep the enemy at bay while the citizens showered them with their own spells. Oddly enough, however, they hadn't opened fire. Then the Archmage's voice erupted around her and her small army.

"My name is Mordrik, Archmage of this great city. We have been informed of your coming, Vassal. We know what you want!" Mordrik took a dramatic pause in his speech to let the effect of his words sink in before continuing. "But, if you insist on attacking this city, you will find yourself beaten down and buried. This is your one and only chance to turn around and leave. You are outnumbered by over a hundred to one. Make the right decision."

This made the Vassal smile. The man named Mordrik had severely underestimated her. She enhanced her voice by releasing a miniscule amount of magical energy, projecting her voice towards the city in reply.

"One hundred to one, I like those odds. Let us continue this conversation after I've made my way into your precious city."

CHAPTER 31

THE ULTIMATE DEFENCE

Mordrik was stunned by the confidence his adversary displayed. He stood atop the Celestial Tower, overlooking the men and women assembled along the city's walls. The other Council members were atop their respective towers, all staring directly at the star-like wall they had combined their energy to erect.

It was a spell that had been designed long ago when the leaders of Neibel-Haven from generations past realised the power of the combination of certain elements. A prerequisite of being one of the tower leaders and a Council member was proving you had the aptitude to take part in erecting what had come to be known as the Great Celestial Ward. Mordrik felt reassured. The feeling of relief was short-lived as one of the messenger mages came up from behind him and addressed him in a trembling tone.

"Sir, the enemy marches!"

"Then it's only to their deaths. Show some courage, lad," the Archmage responded calmly.

"Sir, the barrier does nothing to impede their march!" the messenger cried.

"What?!" Mordrik yelled in confusion before snatching the lookout's telescope on his right and shoving his eye into the lens.

The Vassal of Darkness hadn't moved an inch, but that wasn't the issue. Her small army was walking calmly up to the barrier separating them from the city. They paused briefly to look up at the beautiful wall of stars before marching into it. The barrier reacted only slightly as the first enemy came into contact and a woman wielding a short bow was showered in brilliant sparks from the barrier. It should have been a painful disintegration of her entire body as it turned to dust and yet she passed through without hindrance. The woman was followed by the rest, one by one, walking through with as much discomfort as if it was a gentle breeze.

Mordrik couldn't explain it at first.

The wall destroyed anything living that may choose to walk through it. Then realisation hit him. The Archmage immediately channelled his magical energy to project his voice throughout the city of terrified citizens.

"The enemy we fight is not amongst the living," he started, his men growing more panicked with each word. "This is not the end. While our enemy walks the earth unworthy of life, it also means that we have no reason to show them mercy. Destroy them all. All towers, open fire!"

An explosive cheer met Mordrik's command. The robed men and women upon the walls raised their hands in unison. Defying fear itself, they unleashed the fury of their respective elements. The otherworldly enemies quickened their pace to a run towards the walls with no hesitation and no fear as the spells exploded around them.

Balls of fire burst around the enemies, scorching them. Water barrels were hurled from the wall, shattering on the ground, the liquid within manipulated to smash into the enemy. The mages dedicated to the studies of Earth Magic and the war strategies for Neibel-Haven pooled their energy together to shift the soil beneath their enemies. They exposed trap holes for the otherworldly soldiers to fall into, only for the hole to close in on itself and bury the unfortunate soldiers. Those who managed to avoid the traps and onslaught were greeted by violent bursts of wind, forcing them back.

To Mordrik's surprise the opposing force didn't seem interested in the idea of retreating, as if they were more than happy to march to their death. He had never seen a group of men and women so willing to throw away what little of their lives they had left. It was an unnerving sight. He watched the battle through his telescope as one of the men carrying a blade moved a little further ahead than the others, only to be launched back by a fireball that seemed to have been dedicated solely to him. Another swordsman was sent sprawling to the ground by an unexpected gust of powerful wind, only to be devoured by the earth he landed on.

This isn't a battle; this is a slaughter, he thought to himself, smiling grimly. *The fool leader of this army clearly thought too highly of her one little trick. It cost her dearly before spilling even a single drop of our blood.*

It was only a few minutes before every man and woman on the opposing side of the wall was either lying on the ground or buried under it. Mordrik addressed his men once more, projecting his voice across the city in the same booming fashion as before.

"You have all done marvellously; protecting our great city with the magical prowess we are known and feared for! Now, everyone rest while the mages dedicated to Earth clean up. It will be a fitting burial for the people who tried to invade our home."

With his words the men rejoiced, a little tired but unharmed. The mages aligned with Earth raised their hands once more and the ground shifted around the bodies of their enemies, swallowing them beneath the soil. The action had left the mountainside scorched and wind-torn in some places, but otherwise untouched. The mages all fell to the ground, grateful to finally join their comrades in rest as Mordrik issued the order to dismiss the barrier.

It was an order the Council members were happy to follow as the barrier ebbed away at their finite energy reserves. The barrier slowly faded from view, its shining stars burning out one by one. As the final shimmering light faded out, Mordrik addressed the Vassal once more with his deep and powerful voice.

"This is the end; your foolishness has cost you your army in a matter of minutes. Tell me, will you be so foolish as to give up your own life as well?"

❖

The Vassal of Darkness wore a look of almost complete apathy. She had seen men die before her and this had next to no effect on her conscience. Besides, he'd done exactly what she had predicted. Instead of biting back at the Archmage, she sent a short message through the crystal to Lucian.

"Barrier down."

His concealed face once again appeared on the crystal's

surface and he nodded slightly. It was what they had both been waiting for.

"I trust that you are ready? This is all I can do to help you over such a distance. It will exhaust my reserves. Even manipulating the power within the Stone of Light that you obtained and bending it to my will, my abilities are limited across the chasm between the planes," Lucian whispered.

"You have been amassing energy for a week, and you are complaining about being exhausted? That's reassuring," the Vassal replied sarcastically, before continuing, "Of course I'm ready, I wouldn't have come here if I wasn't."

"Very well. You may begin," Lucian replied, ignoring her jab, disappearing from the crystal's surface.

The Vassal of Darkness pocketed the crystal, taking a deep breath while looking up at the city ahead of her. She exchanged the clear Gaian Crystal for a different stone in her satchel. This one had the appearance of a large, perfectly cut amethyst, about the size of her fist. As soon as her fingertips caressed the stone, its surface exploded with movement. The stone looked to have a hundred slender shadows coursing around inside its confines like sinister, formless snakes looking for their prey.

The stone brought no emotion to the Vassal's blank face. For all her expression offered, she may as well have been looking at a clump of dirt. She had no reason to feel attached to this stone; it was a tool. A tool to fulfil her – no, Lucian's – wishes. She couldn't remember where she had obtained the stone. She couldn't remember a great deal from before a few years ago. When she asked the forgotten knight why her memory was wiped and why the stone belonged to her he had replied, "It was the other side to a bargain that allowed the person you were to be released from her pain."

It had made little sense to the woman and she hadn't probed further. She wasn't one for riddles.

She had elected not to reply to Mordrik's message, instead raising her right hand in front of her face.

Lend me your strength, Stone. Help me to help you.

Will there be blood? came the stone's reply in a slithery, snake-like hiss.

More than even you know what to do with, she responded in her mind.

It had become alarming how bloodthirsty the stone had become over the past few years. While the Vassal was unable to recall a time it wasn't violent, she was sure that its voice and intentions had once been much more peaceful.

Then take it.

The Vassal involuntarily gasped as she felt a dark presence engulf her body. She embraced the sensation of something sinister slithering through her veins. It coursed through every inch of her body, burning like a poison threatening to shut down her entire system. It felt invigorating.

The Vassal had used the stone's power many times before but each time the level of energy it offered the wielder seemed fiercer and more volatile than the last. The bulk of the power racing through her seemed to redirect to her hand where it was summoned. Once it had gathered, the burning sensation rested there. The Vassal smiled ever so slightly, raising her glowing extremity above her head, issuing the command in her mind.

Rise!

The purple energy burst forward from its home. It flew

straight upwards before sharply changing direction, aiming towards the city. It soared across the centre of the field where the battle had taken place minutes before.

Mordrik stared in horror at the dark light sailing across the sky towards their city. Had he left them defenceless in his arrogance?

The light stopped its travel suddenly and instead hovered in mid-air above the mountainside where the slaughter had just taken place. The darkness split into countless smaller versions of the violet burst and descended on the field in seemingly random places. The earth seemed to welcome the light as the force passed through the soil and deeper into the ground.

All was silent for a long moment. The Vassal had stopped moving, as had everyone within the city. They were waiting for the point of the action taken to be made apparent.

Mordrik laughed, heartily bellowing, "Really? She finally makes a move and she can't even – oh, for the sake of all that's holy!"

Mordrik's boast was abandoned as he looked at the battlefield again in horror. From the very earth, hands protruded, bodies of their enemies following as they dug themselves upwards. Each fallen soldier was coated in the same dark purple glow that was hovering in the air moments before. The Vassal's smiled widened. She knew that she'd successfully caught the mages' attention in a way that threatened to break their morale. Flicking the dark stone away, she touched her Gaian Crystal one last time.

This is my last message. The enemy is sufficiently unnerved. I'm making my move now and I trust you will make yours.

CHAPTER 32

A FORGOTTEN KNIGHT'S CREATION

Lucian stood for the first time in two weeks. His body offered no grief despite the time sitting perfectly still, as he gathered magical energy from within the former Vassal of Light's stone. His whole body tingled, threatening to overflow with power.

The time had come; he had known that one of the other Vassals would make their presence within the world known. He had been preoccupied with tasks that prevented his intervention in the world's proceedings. His attention had been divided for too long, and for good reason. However, when one of his targets made its existence so blatantly obvious, he was forced to pay attention. It would be foolish to let his prey think they'd escaped detection, to risk them learning how to control their power. The Vassal of Darkness had allowed the Vassal of Light to escape a year ago. Another oversight such as that would be . . . unfortunate.

They may have secured her stone, but it wasn't the point. The Vassal still lived somewhere. Being separated from her stone would be both physical and mental torture; Lucian took some solace in that fact.

Now, another Vassal has made their debut.

He supposed he was feeling "curiosity". It had been many

a century since he'd felt it. What was the spike in power that had made Neibel-Haven his target? Or rather, *who* was it? And if they were gone, what was the power sitting within the city at this very moment? He had sensed something within the walls of the city through the connection with his subordinate, but he hadn't had enough time to delve into the specifics of the entity.

There was no way to control the power of the stones to the point that you could so easily conceal its magical presence without training. All mages, especially the Vassals, practically oozed magical energy. Without proper tutelage in concealing it, anyone who knew what to look for would pick up on their energy levels.

The initial spike was reckless, bent on destruction. Now, the one within the city is at ease. They are not one and the same; there are two, he pondered. *The first is wild and more prone to exposing itself again. It'd be wise to seize this new one first.*

Lucian walked out of the crystal-adorned chamber, following a long corridor. The precious minerals had their place here as well: jutting out of the floor, walls and ceiling at precarious angles. Anyone attempting to navigate the perilous corridor would have done well to exercise caution.

A fear better left to the mundane susceptible to such wounds, Lucian thought as he briskly made his way down the centre of the corridor. His reflection bounced off the polished stones and despite the odd angles of the crystals' surfaces, his form did not distort. Even the mirrored doppelgangers of the knight appeared as he intended – as a whole.

He came to a door comprised of thick metal bars rising from the ground towards the lofty ceiling.

Hungry pairs of tiny yellow eyes watched him from the other side as he approached. The cruel eyes never blinked or shifted their gaze, as if their owners were waiting for the knight to lower the gate so that they might feed upon him.

The "Talice", as Lucian had dubbed them, were mutations of his own design.

The beasts had slender bodies encased in scales the colour of onyx that no mortal blade could pierce. Their tails' scales got even more resilient further along before finally ending in a deadly curl like a farmer's sickle. They had four similarly lean legs, each armed with razor-sharp talons, serrated on both sides. Their claws were designed for ripping apart their prey and had been proven effective, even against armour.

Their long bodies followed through into almost elegant, curved necks ending in heads that seemed too big for them. Their faces were home to beaks large enough to lift a human, and sharp enough to cut one in two. Then there were the pairs of small, beady eyes, still watching him.

They each had four thin, bat-like wings protruding from their backs. Each wing was half the beasts' body in length. While their wings generally dragged across the ground, they allowed the beasts to fly and were also suitable for gliding or battering enemies.

Lucian looked at his four creations and almost felt pride. They were incapable of speech but they understood a few choice words they had picked up through their existence within Lucian's castle.

"Blood, flesh, death," Lucian whispered. The words were greeted with a joyous chorus of high-pitched shrieks from the monsters as they threw their long necks back.

Lucian was satisfied. Lyndell had opened the way for them and the monsters were ready. With the barrier down, this battle was as good as won.

The beastmaster pulled down on a crystal to his right. The great gate started to descend into the floor below him, the Talice shivering with excitement. They understood that they were about to have a grand time. Lucian stepped into the dwelling, the scent of rot and bodily decay greeted him in full force, but it did nothing to churn his stomach. His senses of smell, taste and touch had all but become obsolete over his vast lifespan. They only told him what was relevant.

The Talice shifted away from him as he made his way to the centre of the great chamber. The monsters knew to keep a safe distance from the knight at all times but especially times like this, when he produced a stone shining with the light of the angels. The stone had been acquired by the Vassal of Darkness after defeating the Vassal of Light at the Plains.

He took one last look at his creations before turning around to the great doorway he'd entered through. Raising his hand, he muttered a single word.

"Open."

The force that came from his release of magical energy could be felt for leagues, even through the walls of the crystal castle, as time and space were torn away and a portal replaced the large gateway. Before Lucian stood a pleasant birds'-eye view of the city known as Neibel-Haven. He could see the mages running around the city like pitiful ants escaping the threat of a boot coming down on their home. He saw the Vassal of Darkness' army crawling from the ground, marching once more towards the city.

There is still no sign of the mysterious power source.

As he turned to the Talice, he already felt his magical energy draining and he hastily issued his command.

"Kill them all!"

The Talice shrieked once more before bounding towards the portal, excited by the thought of the flesh on the enemy's bones. One by one, the four creatures pushed their way through the portal. As the last one passed through, Lucian severed the connection and the portal vanished from existence.

The knight fell to one knee, his energy failing to keep him upright. He had other resources that he could have bent to his will, but he had wanted to attempt tapping into the energy of the stone formerly belonging to the Vassal of Light. His task was complete, but the stone had been reluctant in sharing its power and it took much more effort than he'd predicted to seize its spoils. He knew it would take an immense amount of time and effort to completely harness the stone's power, but it'd take far more than that to deter him.

Do not fail me. I'm yet to fully reap the rewards of this Vassal's stone.

CHAPTER 33

THE PRINCESS WITHOUT A KINGDOM

Rufus and Alicea came to the crudely crafted entrance of South Tremel. Its roughly erected walls were barely taller than Rufus, made from the strongest timber that could be found in the neighbouring forests. They were clearly built by heavy hands, but their sturdiness was unmistakable. Around its walls was a stream that looked like a small moat of sorts. As Alicea eyed the stream in each direction, she noticed that the water passed the small town by emerging from one edge of the forest and disappearing behind the town. The stream's water was clearer than even the water at the palace.

It's pleasant, if a little primitive, Alicea thought, leading her horse towards the entrance where two figures stood.

The settlement's primitive appearance masked the strength of its occupants. Alicea knew this from her studies of the neighbouring villages littered around Aquiocia. The remaining citizens of Tremel may be separated into four different hamlets after the battle two hundred years ago, but they were still some of the most feared warriors on the battlefield. When it came to brute strength, a Tremel warrior could not be bested.

All too often the tales of Tremel's warriors were spun without mentioning the other reason the hunters were so formidable. Having once been the protectors of the stone that harnessed the power of Earth, it stood to reason that those with a strong magical affinity to Earth would take up the art of magic. Thus, a Tremel shaman was not a magical opponent one should cross lightly.

Alicea smiled in greeting at the two people at the gate. One looked little older than Alicea. The man had donned a massive black bear pelt that was too big even for the muscular frame of his body. His pelt's arms were wrapped around his neck in a rough knot, serving as a beastly cloak. Beneath that he wore only black trousers, his torso left bare and displaying an impressive image of well-defined muscles, tattoos and scars.

The other looked a lot older, perhaps in his late fifties, over thirty years older than the first man. He wore a deer pelt over a roughly spun brown tunic and trousers. While he seemed to be of insignificant size compared to the mountain of meat beside him, the younger man looked at the elder for encouragement before addressing Rufus and Alicea.

"Halt! You are not from this village. State your name and – oh forget it – who are ya?" the young man asked.

"Princess Alicea of the Kingdom of Aquiocia, and this is Mr. Thief," Alicea responded briskly, having decided earlier that honesty was the best course of action.

Rufus disliked the idea and had protested for the better part of the morning. Alicea had listened to his concerns at length before ignoring them entirely.

"Mr. Thief? Parents had you pegged early, eh?" the young man laughed.

"The man's name is not what is important here, Breant." The older man cut through the conversation smoothly with his slightly raspy voice. "Please forgive the rudeness of youth,

Your Highness. He has barely hunted his first trophy and his talents do not lie in diplomacy, as you can see."

Breant's face grew hot as he took a step back. His eyebrows rose as he spotted the tiny swan made of water poking its head out from the Princess' satchel. It looked around for the source of the commotion, puffing its feathers and uncoiling its neck upwards to glare at the man with indignation. Though the bird wasn't a normal sight to behold, its disgruntled, unwavering gaze told him that it didn't appreciate being disturbed.

"Please, no need for apologies. I can understand that my sudden appearance might spark surprise, especially with the young ones," Alicea responded kindly.

"Don't even bother, it isn't worth it," Rufus muttered to Breant before he could point out that the Princess was no older than himself.

"Thank you, Your Highness. My name is Gramere. I serve the Chief as one of his advisors. I also had the pleasure of meeting your parents from time to time when they came for their visits to our humble village. My thoughts often stray to their heroic sacrifice," Gramere said sullenly before continuing, "I know that this may seem offensive, but I cannot allow you to enter the village without some form of proof of your lineage."

"Of course. You say you met my parents – then perhaps you recognise this?" Alicea began as she reached for the necklace around her neck. She separated the rings and revealed the beautiful pendant with the image of an Aquiocian rose. Its petals were made from beautiful sapphires and finished with thin elegant silver threads coursing through each one.

Though the pendant was clearly priceless, it was the rings that caught Rufus' eye. They seemed to glow in the late morning sun, each ring emanating a different colour. The light was gone as quickly as it appeared and the thief knew that he had to be imagining things.

"Ah, of course, your mother wore it at all times and with pride. It seems that you are either telling the truth or are an exceptional thief indeed," Gramere said jokingly. "Please, follow me."

A bewildered Breant was left to stand guard, watching them leave with the reins of two horses and the disappointment of an interrupted staring competition. As Gramere led the two through the open streets of the tiny village towards the Chief's hut, Rufus' eyes darted everywhere, soaking in the village's quaint culture – from the roughly built huts that served as shelter, to the various people running errands. Finally, they rested on another gate leading out of the village and straight into the forest, where hunters were emerging with freshly killed game slung over their shoulders.

He thought the idea was wonderful: hunting what you eat and building what you need. It all seemed a much simpler way of life compared to thievery and kidnapping. He couldn't help but think what it would be like to live out here. It was tempting and with a glance at the distracted Princess, he allowed himself a moment to dream of the possibility after the job was over.

Maybe after it was all over he'd retire to this village if they'd have him.

While Rufus daydreamed of a life after his big payday, Alicea was more focused than she had ever been. While she had been told that South Tremel was her best bet by Setz himself, she didn't know what she would find, or even what she was looking for. Despite the lack of information, she knew that there had to be merit in coming here if Setz had suggested it. As they came to the entrance of the most impressive hut of all, their guide called from the outside.

"Gramere and company wishing to enter!"

The announcement was acknowledged with a rough grunt to enter and they pushed the large pelt in the doorway aside. Rufus nodded in approval at what greeted them inside. The walls were lined with pelts of every animal one would expect to find in a forest. The skins of deer, bears, wolves and others that he hadn't seen before hung from the walls as a testament to the Chief's hunting prowess. Even before Rufus had laid eyes on the bearded and scarred leader of the town, he already respected him on some level.

"I'm Kurok, Chief of this village. I must say that I have issues that require my attention, so if you can make this quick, do so," the Chief addressed the pair, barely glancing in their direction.

"Allow me to present Princess Alicea of the kingdom of Aquiocia," Gramere declared.

If Kurok was surprised, he showed no sign of it as he stood from his chair of animal bones. He approached the Princess, stopping an arm's length away and stroking his beard thoughtfully before speaking once more.

"Well then, haven't you grown? I haven't seen you since you were but a newborn. A pleasure, Your Highness, to be sure," he said warmly.

"I wish we could have come under better circumstances, Chief Kurok," Alicea said. "But, as I said . . ."

"Aye, Setz sent you, I'd wager. About the stones and all that," Kurok finished her sentence for her as he paced around his hut, examining the pelts on the walls as if for the first time. "I have to say, it all seems a little far-fetched for my liking. Not that the stories are without credit. I just wonder if sending good people into danger for these stones is even going to pay off."

"Might I ask why you seem so pessimistic?" the Princess asked.

"Everyone is running after these stones, from what Setz has said; my own son and his companions are no different. But what did the stone's power give us in the past? It decimated Tremel, which was, up until two hundred years ago, known as the 'Forest's Impenetrable Fortress'. Damned rock killed its bearer and the forest changed from its natural shape, consuming the entire place! Until now, its ruins couldn't even be found."

"Until now?" Rufus piped up. "Meaning you found them? That seems like an excellent place to start looking for answers."

"No, it wasn't found so much as *they* found Lyrium," Kurok sighed, still examining the wall of trophies. "They reappeared and Lyrium, my son and his friend are inside searching for the stone. Nobody else may enter."

"Why not just storm the place? It's not like there would be much of a threat left after this much time," Rufus replied.

"Because the stone called to her." Alicea looked at Kurok intensely, her eyes reading every line upon the Chief's face as he finally turned away from the wall. "That's why, isn't it? The stone called for this woman, Lyrium?"

"You speak as if you know more about all of this than I do," Kurok said accusingly as Alicea presented the beautiful blue stone from her satchel.

"You could say I know firsthand," was her simple reply.

Kurok stared at the stone. Its texture looked as if it was that of clear water's surface. It had small ripples arching out of it as if someone had thrown tiny pebbles into its pristine waters and disrupted its solid nature. He examined it closely before shifting his gaze up to the Princess' likewise blue eyes, trying to comprehend the implications of what he had just been shown.

"Setz sent word informing me that you would be coming here in search of the ruins and the possibility of finding the stone that lies at the bottom of its chambers," he began slowly. "But he somehow failed to mention that you already had one in your possession."

"If I might be brutally honest, I know little of these stones. I was oblivious to the fact that this one even resided within my kingdom. It was only when Mr. Thief and I met . . ." the Princess replied, hesitating on the last word as she looked at Rufus.

Kurok nodded, first at the Princess and then to Gramere, who was standing silently to the side of the doorway. The older man sprang into action, bringing two chairs of bone from their place against the wall and placing them beside the visitors. As the pair sat, Rufus nodded towards the older man in thanks before turning back to the Chief, who was staring at him expectantly.

"What?" Rufus asked.

"Princess," Kurok said without taking his eyes off Rufus. "I'd like to hear of your meeting."

"Certainly, I was –" Alicea started before realising whose recount he wanted and joining him in staring at Rufus.

The thief began his recount slowly, picking and choosing the details he offered to his new audience.

"Mr. Thief, is it?" Kurok asked.

"Most call me Rufus."

"Right. Rufus, stop playing games and spit it out," the Chief said roughly. "We don't have all day for you to decide what you do and don't want to share."

Irritation flashed across Rufus' face. It was difficult to hide certain parts of the story and, while he didn't care what they thought of him, he was accustomed to keeping the details of his jobs to himself. Setz didn't like his operations widely known and Rufus hated explaining himself. Normally, that combination worked well together. Now, however . . .

"Mr. Thief," Alicea addressed him softly. "I suggest you focus on your current job, rather trying to hide the previous. Speak."

She's right. Do this job right and you might not have to do another . . . he concluded.

Rufus proceeded to indulge Kurok with everything he knew regarding the events leading up to that point. He revealed everything from the order to steal the stone itself, to the kidnapping of the Princess. Alicea listened intently while Rufus spoke, happy to finally hear the thief's side of the story while she combed her hair. She'd been fighting a losing battle with it throughout the last few days of their trip.

My appearance is unacceptable. It must be corrected.

When the story ended, Kurok leant back in his hand made seat of animal bone, stroking his beard once more.

"Aye, seems feasible." Kurok nodded at Rufus' blank expression. He didn't think *anyone* would believe such an outrageous tale but the Chief seemed to accept it.

"So, they had a stone the whole time . . ." Kurok mused, shooting a meaningful look towards Gramere.

"My guess is they had no one to wield it," Gramere offered.

"Unlikely, Gramere," Kurok replied dismissively. "You met Adele; nothing got past that woman. The question I have is 'why didn't her daughter know she was a Vassal earlier?'"

All eyes were on Alicea, who looked to be struggling with something. Her hand had disappeared into her satchel as she looked at the others. Only Rufus realised that she was petting the bird hidden within.

"Your Highness, are you alright?" Kurok asked.

"You speak of my mother so casually. I dislike that," Alicea said.

"I apologise, Your Highness. I only meant to point out that she obviously had a reason to not tell you about the stone. The Council might have also been aware of its place within your kingdom . . ."

"Yes, well, perhaps speculation on my mother isn't the most prudent use of our time. I wouldn't know if the Council knew of the stone; I have been unable to partake in the affairs of my kingdom since the incident at the Plains."

The Princess' voice held an air of finality. Kurok took the cue and dropped the subject.

"What would you and Mr. Thief here do now?"

"Okay, I've kept quiet about it, but my name is Rufus," the thief piped up in irritation.

"Hush, Mr. Thief," Alicea replied, softly patting his knee in condescension. Her mood had already improved. "You said that a party has entered the ruins. Are you certain that nobody else can enter?"

"That's correct, the entrance has sealed itself," Kurok replied, nodding with worry lines prominent on his face once more.

"Then there is nothing else we can do at this point. Until this is resolved one way or another, whether they emerge successful or the worst is confirmed, I guess we wait," Alicea said in a straightforward tone. "If you would be so kind, I would appreciate your facilities to rest and wash."

"Of course, Your Highness," Kurok said, gesturing towards his advisor. "Gramere will see to your every need. Welcome to South Tremel. We will try to make your stay as pleasant as possible."

The Princess nodded in thanks, rising from her seat and following Gramere out of the Chief's hut with Rufus in tow.

"Why did you ask whether anybody else could enter the ruins?" Rufus whispered to the Princess as they followed the Chief's advisor.

"I would think that was obvious, Mr. Thief. I was gauging whether or not it was possible to follow them," Alicea replied with a tone that suggested that the idea was completely rational.

"Do you often try to volunteer people to charge into dangerous situations on a whim?"

"If that is your juvenile way of asking me if I will try to help others, then yes. I will be volunteering us to do a great many dangerous things if it is so required."

"You will have to learn that I have a mind of my own and it generally steers away from diving into unnecessary trouble," Rufus snapped.

"And you will have to adapt to the fact that I do not care what your mind dictates, as you will do as you are commanded," was the Princess' cold response.

CHAPTER 34

THE VASSAL OF WIND

Katarina and Amelia stood atop the main gate to Neibel-Haven. The sisters were surrounded by two hundred knights in shoddy armour that looked to have been salvaged from the discard piles of various smiths. The men and women were staring out at the mountain range where the revived dead were crawling out from under its surface. They shook within their mismatched armour, glancing at each other's mortified faces with matching looks of disbelief and fear.

These were people of Neibel-Haven who weren't gifted in magic. They were offspring of the bread-bakers, the cobblers, the merchants. They were the ones who were brave enough to pick up a blade to defend their city of magic despite their pitiful magical aptitude. They were the mundane and Mordrik had discounted them.

In a sense, he was right to do so. Katarina looked at the pathetic assembly of feeble excuses for warriors. Their bravado was gone in the face of a real enemy, but she didn't see them as worthless. In fact, in her opinion, they were the bravest people gathered to protect the city that day. They had no magical prowess, yet they stood strong, if uncertain. She was about to say something to them when they moved as one towards the ladders to climb down behind the wall.

They're going to guard the main gate, she realised as all but the archers left. *They are more organised than I thought.*

Amelia was looking over the edge at the undead warriors resuming their march with Katarina at her side, casually propped against the outside of a guardhouse built into the wall, staring towards the portal forming in the sky. She had known something big was going to happen. There was no avoiding it when it came to fighting a Vassal, but the appearance of the portal had surprised even her.

The Vassal had help – powerful help. Katarina couldn't begin to fathom the sheer scope of magical energy required for the feat, let alone the person who had channelled it.

It didn't add up that a single woman who had travelled across the land to be here had the ability to rally the reserves to conjure the portal while continually resurrecting her own troops. To make matters worse, Katarina could see the shadow of some sort of beast bounding through the portal. It was running awkwardly, wings flapping erratically, through the otherworldly window. It was a peculiar sight to behold, considering it was in the sky and appeared to be running vertically downwards.

"Enemies from the ground . . ." spoke Amelia.

". . . and enemies from the sky," finished Katarina.

"The ones from the sky could land within the city," Amelia surmised. "Despite the enemy's ability to resurrect her men, those beasts are the greater threat."

"Then we are in agreement," Katarina said, pushing herself from the wall and walking towards her distracted-looking sister. "What is it?"

"Nothing – I mean, I just wish Sister was with us now more

than ever," Amelia responded bitterly.

She was the oldest and toughest, but battles always opened old wounds for her.

"As do I," Katarina replied, resting her hand on her sister's shoulder. "But she *is* with us, supporting us through all of this."

It was the same line she always fed her sister, but Katarina had nothing else to offer. Thankfully, the sentiment was often enough.

Amelia sniffed, placing her own hand on her sister's.

"Now, shall we greet our new guests?" Katarina asked, laughing at the joke that only the two of them were in the mood for. Some of the archers frowned at the pair, clearly disapproving of this outburst.

"I thought you would never ask!" Amelia responded, back in good spirits. "Let's rip them apart!"

If the fellow soldiers were surprised by the sisters' exchange, then they were bewildered by what happened next. The pair stepped away from each other before nodding, simultaneously releasing their magical energy. At first, a simple breeze could be felt rallying to their mental call. Before long, the air itself could be seen around them. The archers stepped back in awe as the wind currents picked up speed while they circled their masters.

Soon neither Katarina nor Amelia could be seen within their personal tornados. The archers cried out in alarm, shielding their eyes and backing away from the force that felt like lashes to their skin. From their point of view, the two women were being consumed by magic. As the soldiers struggled to respond, the wind started to thin out, congregating around the women's feet. Nothing below their lightly armoured greaves could be made out by the onlookers. The din that came from the roaring element was deafening at first but as it thickened at their feet, the sound become more peaceful. Like a gentle breeze making its way through a forest.

Both the sight and the sound of Wind Magic were foreign concepts to the archers watching on. Outside those studying within the Wind Tower, it was uncommon to find someone who knew that wind could take on a physical shape. It was a presence much more visible, and equally more dangerous than its natural counterpart.

Katarina's laughter could be heard over the thinning gale. "Hold the main gate, will you? We'll be back soon, promise!"

Katarina turned to Amelia with a big smile and calculating eyes.

"Stay close!"

Amelia grinned widely before shouting back, "But of course! For the three!"

"For the sisters!" cried Katarina. With that they released their energy, launching themselves into the sky. Propelled by their overwhelming energy, they cut through the air towards the spawning beasts.

Katarina saw the first beast break free of the portal, followed swiftly by two more. She barely felt the tug on her magical reserves as she ascended higher into the sky and took stock of the monsters they faced. They were armoured by durable scales and while they had wings, she doubted their flying capabilities. They seemed to struggle against their own descent, flailing this way and that through the air. Their limbs lashed out in every direction as their thin, wide wings beat against the air around them before the beasts finally got their bearings.

Everything about them looked sharp, dangerous and evil. Their four wings had black membrane sheeted between thin bones. Scrawled all through the black surface were countless veins the deep red of dried blood. Katarina hadn't noticed them at first until she saw the sun glance across the beasts' shining scales. She had no idea what they were, and she didn't really care; she only knew that she had to protect the city below her. With a quick glance back, she wasn't surprised to see Amelia trailing behind.

The middle sister had always been the best flyer and, with a little training, the best swordswoman of the original three. She always reached the enemy first, and she wouldn't have it any other way. Even though the sisters' creed was all-for-one, any one of them would give their life to protect the others.

Katarina's mind flashed to their absent sister, banishing the memories before they could take shape in her mind. She would deal with missing her sister after they'd eliminated the enemy. If they could, that is.

As she closed in on the first atrocity, her hand reached for her sword, infusing her energy into the sheathed blade. Flying did nothing to drain her, but she felt the enchanted blade drink deeply from her reserves. It was necessary if she wanted results. She called to the wind around her and it answered, pushing her faster through the air; she was soon upon her enemy. Her weapon remained sheathed until the first beast noticed her presence.

The cruel yellow eyes met those of the soaring warrior for a fleeting second. They each took in their opponent. It was meeting of human and beast, warrior and atrocity.

Then she struck.

Katarina drew her thin blade in a brutal and precise swing across beast's wing as she flew past. It slid across the thin membrane without resistance, as if cutting through paper. It all happened in a blink of an eye and Katarina adjusted her magical energy accordingly to come to a stop. Now a safe distance from the threat, she stood as comfortably in mid-air as if she was on solid ground, assessing her enemy.

She cringed as the injured beast shrieked in pain, surprised by the sudden attack. Her blade shone with coursing wind currents so fine that touching them could result in a lost finger. The speed at which the currents whirled around the blade was pure elemental magic, designed to slice through anything it came in contact with.

Katarina wasted no time in projecting her body at the beast once more. She flew forward, ducking a wild swing from her enemy. She lashed out with her enchanted blade, slicing another of its wings on the way through to safety. As the fresh wave of pain took hold, Amelia appeared above the wounded enemy. Having chosen her bow rather than her sword, she drew back and let fly an arrow infused with her own energy that collided with the beast's back. The assault dented the scales and the impact sent the handicapped beast sprawling downwards.

The sisters had no time to admire their work as their enemy violently collided with the city's fortified walls. Their attention was drawn by two more beasts making their entrance to the world with piercing shrieks. The sound made the sisters' ears ache. First it just seemed like their natural cry, as their glare shifted directly towards Amelia; however, Katarina realised that the shriek was a form of attack. If they were closer, the vocal assault would go from being uncomfortable to straight-up painful.

The remaining beasts were more prepared. They knew of the airborne assailants, and were gliding through the air towards their prey. Amelia noted a fourth beast within the portal before engaging the two bearing towards her. She effortlessly glided over the top of the first, but misjudged the second. The beast's talon pierced the chain mesh protecting her and racked across her arm and breast.

She dropped her bow, channelling her quickly evaporating energy into flying away as the beasts flailed through the air after her, wings flapping wildly. It was strange that the wound didn't hurt a great deal. Amelia glanced down at the large hole. Where her armour had been moments before, now she only saw blood.

How does it not hurt?

She was in shock. Her adrenaline shot her into immediate shock – whether as a defensive reaction or otherwise, it didn't matter. She was thousands of feet in the air, with her energy draining and her mind losing focus. There was only one thing to do and Amelia knew that her window to achieve it was closing each second. Her sister would be at her side any moment. She had to move fast.

Amelia took the risk, stopping mid-air and turning to face her pursuers. She waited anxiously through a haze of dizziness for the last possible moment. She channelled her energy downwards, then directly towards the beasts, flying smoothly under one's scaled stomach to confront the trailing other. Narrowly avoiding another wound, this time from the beast's sharp beak, she curled herself around its armoured neck.

She could feel the rough scales tearing at her clothes and fractured armour. It shredded them with ease while she desperately held on with one arm. The other hung limp, sending bloodied rain to the earth from the deep wound. She could feel her grip loosening, her skin being torn. She released all that was left of her magical energy into her new mount. A thunderclap was heard by all below as the force of a raging storm was released directly into the beast's body.

A flash like a lightning strike launched the dead monster downwards as Amelia was hurled from the carcass. The doomed meteor collided destructively amongst the enemies advancing below. The surprise assault hindered them greatly as the Vassal's magic took hold, attempting to revive the undead warriors.

Amelia started her own involuntary descent towards the ground with both body and mind beyond exhaustion. Katarina had sheathed her blade and made it to her sister, catching her in mid-air. The magical energy channelled around her feet, supporting both of them.

"The portal . . . has closed . . . Two beasts remain," gasped Amelia with the strength of a sick child as she looked over her sister's shoulder.

"That doesn't matter, the stone will –" started a panicked Katarina.

"The stone will not heal my wounds. They are to be . . . fatal." Amelia coughed violently, blood spraying on herself and Katarina's face, neither moving to wipe it away.

"Sister! Hold on, this isn't –" Kat stopped as Amelia shook her head.

"I will be with our sister. It's not so bad."

"Then I'll go with you! There is no point without you!" Katarina cried, tears mixing with her sister's blood on her usually cheerful face. Amelia shook her head before smiling, the expression fighting the pain valiantly.

"I'll take my place within the stone with Sister," Amelia started before reaching with her shredded arm into the pocket where Katarina kept the stone. "We shall . . . both . . . aid you together . . . remember? You said . . . we are always . . . together."

The stone in her hand was the hue of a beautiful emerald and its surface was in motion, a swirling vortex of wind and lightning flashing from within. Tears flooded Katarina's eyes as her sister clasped the precious stone to her torn chest. The stone glowed as two thin tendrils of light burst forth and connected with the dying woman's eyes. It was taking its prize.

The vortex within responded by gathering speed, becoming more violent as lightning lashed inside the stone. The disaster within the fist-sized emerald signalled Amelia's arrival, her power and its own becoming one. Amelia's body had already started to disintegrate just like their sister's had done years before. Her flesh was lifeless, but that wasn't the end of the process. The fading colour and flaking skin was the first stage. It fell from her body, disappearing into the wind like the ash left by a ravenous blaze.

Next was the feeling of sand falling through Katarina's fingertips as her sister's body steadily degraded in her embrace. Amelia's features were already gone, and it was a sight that she'd seen all too frequently. Her blood-stained tears fell onto the dusty body, becoming one with the dissolving shell that was her sister.

People grieved and moved on as the person's life force returned to the world. Not those she loved, though. Not the ones close to her, and not the ones touched by the stone. It wasn't enough that she saw them die; Katarina would witness the process of decay eating away at the very element that had given her sister life. In the end it left her body looking like a clay sculpture before the artist had applied the features that had made it real. Katarina's own hands could be seen where her sister's torso was just moments before. Her palms found the large emerald as it sank downwards through the grey soot that remained.

A piercing shriek interrupted Katarina's grief and she looked up to see the beast that Amelia had eluded making its way back towards her. A quick glance behind her revealed the last beast soaring towards her from the other direction. She turned back to see the last remnants of dust catch the wind. Taking the precious stone, Katarina let go of her sister.

She projected herself higher, until she was far above the battlefield. Looking down, she saw the beasts doubling their efforts to catch her. The cold wind started to chill the air she was inhaling, causing her lungs mild discomfort. She needed to be higher. The beasts seemed unaffected by the cold and while they weren't gaining great momentum, they were following her lead without a problem. Katarina knew that should she wish it, the beasts would never catch her. But that wasn't the plan.

When she found that she could barely breathe she halted her ascent, looking down at her pursuers. They were still bounding towards her.

Good.

Her tears had dried on her blood-splattered face and her voice was strong when she finally screamed at the top of her lungs. She directed her magical energy to enhance her voice so it was loud enough that everyone on the field of battle, those sheltered in Neibel-Haven, and especially the Vassal beneath her could hear.

"YOU HAVE GONE TOO FAR! YOU HAVE KILLED AND MAIMED COUNTLESS INNOCENT PEOPLE AND IF YOU HAVEN'T TAKEN THEIR LIVES, YOU'VE TAKEN WHAT THEY HAD TO LIVE FOR! PREPARE YOURSELF FOR THE WRATH OF THE THREE SISTERS!"

CHAPTER 35

THE LAST DEFENCE

Mordrik's attention kept swapping between what was happening above and below him. He was as surprised by Katarina and Amelia taking flight as everyone else who had witnessed it. His men were in fine shape; even the large beast that had fallen onto the wall hadn't managed to kill anyone. Thankfully the monster was dead – whether from the impact or the fight above, Mordrik neither knew nor cared.

But Katarina had disappeared from view. With the aid of the telescope and from what he could tell from his place atop the tower, Amelia had been hurt, or worse. He was unable to help the two women and even if he could have, he wouldn't have.

Mordrik scanned the clear skies for Katarina, pondering her intentions. She had flown into the clouds, far beyond sight even through the telescope. Her presence on the field of battle had only been confirmed by the aggressive message she had declared moments before. His eyes narrowed as dark clouds began to gather in the previously clear sky. In the distance he saw the clouds spawning in small amounts and being dragged from all directions.

In the eye of the gathering storm, the sky was still clear, as if the clouds met a barrier they couldn't pass through. Instead, they settled for circling it as they grew in strength. He knew magic was the culprit; no natural storm could gather that quickly. He also knew that it had to be one of the sisters. Flight alone was not an offensive or aggressive way to utilise magic, regardless of elemental alignment. This display was different.

Any mage would be able to feel the nature of the energy forming above them. They would be able to feel what drove the gathering of volatile energies. Its anger hung in the air like a thick, invisible fog; even Mordrik felt mildly stifled by its embrace. He could feel it settling on his old, wrinkled skin. He felt Katarina's rage laced with sadness, and with that he knew what must have happened above them.

Realising that only allowed for the tension in the air to hit home within him. The old man forced it from his mind in fear of it compromising his attention to the conflict. He turned his focus back to the battlefield and his eyes fell on another of the unidentified winged beasts, lying dead across the path travellers used to reach the city.

Its impact had shaken the ground, but not swayed the enemy's resolve. The crushed enemy had just picked themselves back up, continuing their march. They were undead and yet they were completely unharmed.

How is that possible?

Mordrik had fought against the undead personally on a few occasions throughout his life and every time he had been confronted by them, he'd simply blown the atrocities to bits. No body, no problem. Once you destroyed the vessels that the sorcerer was controlling, it was simply a matter of killing them, usually with relative ease. Necromancy took tremendous skill, energy and focus. Because of that, mages could spend decades upon decades perfecting the art only to find they were defenceless should it fail.

It meant that it wasn't Necromancy at all that he faced now. The only time in all of history that magic such as this was chronicled was in the tales of the knight named Lucian. He had called himself the "Forgotten Knight" . . . Mordrik moved his train of thought back to the issue at hand. He was being distracted far too easily. Meanwhile, his men were tiring and he could see it. The mages dedicated to Earth Magic were trying to rest after shifting the soil in an attempt to bury the enemy.

Other mages were slowly exhausting themselves, killing the undying enemies time and time again. They needed a plan, and quickly.

The great barrier was of no use and the first of the enemy troops had made it to the gate. Some had started battering at it, axes and other sharp weapons clanging off the stone. It wasn't long until their allies with mauls reached the gate. Their strikes began reverberating through the gate itself. Their attacks barely damaged it at all, but the mages on the other side flinched with each powerful blow their last defence took. Some of the enemy troops had attempted to climb the walls only to get blasted back towards the ground. Each enemy that returned to the ground filled the mages with a fickle relief.

Who would have thought that our city's walls would keep out enemies more effectively than our great barrier?

Mordrik allowed himself a bitter smile at the thought and took another look towards the sky at the growing thunderclouds. There was an occasional streak of blue electricity flashing across them. He forced his gaze away, redirecting his telescope downwards to where the Vassal was standing. She still hadn't shifted from her original spot, just out of range of the spells flung around the battlefield.

She knew exactly what we were capable of and kept herself safe to grant unnatural life to her troops. It doesn't matter how long she waits – she knows she has the advantage.

Mordrik adjusted the magnification of the telescope to get a clearer look at his enemy. As the Vassal's face came into focus her head snapped towards him. She stared right at him, wearing a hint of a wry smile on her otherwise bored face as she raised her hand in front of her. It was completely engulfed in dark energy, obscuring the Archmage's view of her.

What is she planning? Mordrik wondered as she let fly the violent blast of dark energy harnessed in her hand. *She couldn't be aiming for . . . the gate!*

Mordrik channelled his energy to give an order to fortify the gate but it was already too late. The energy left the Vassal's fingertips and flew across the field, zigging and zagging erratically as if it didn't know its own target before turning suddenly, flying directly for the gate. The gate caved upon impact, blowing the strong stone doors inwards to the main courtyard, instantly killing dozens of the soldiers waiting to engage the enemy.

The collision between magic and rock had also caught a few soldiers of the enemy force in the blast. Mordrik knew there was difference between the outcomes. The enemies would get back up; his men wouldn't. True to his thoughts, the supernatural enemy rose again, starting to trickle through the destroyed gates. His men rallied, despite their exhaustion and fear, running out from their hiding places and towers, launching spells at the invaders.

Neibel-Haven's small army of swordsmen rushed towards the enemy. One of Neibel-Haven's soldiers impaled an axe-wielding bandit, sliding his blade through the enemy's ribs. The glowing man stumbled back, sword still lodged in his stomach. The wounded warrior let out a loud laugh and charged at the unarmed soldier, neatly taking off his head with his sharp axe and leaving the man's neck a fountain of blood.

No blood comes from the enemies' wounds, and yet it is repeatedly made apparent that my men can bleed.

Mordrik unleashed a furious attack of his own from above in the form of a heavy fireball. He directed it away from his people, towards the gate, its detonation scattering half a dozen of the enemy's men. The Archmage composed himself out of fear of losing his temper and hurting his own. His heart was torn in two directions as hope came in the form of six figures running towards the immortals. It was the other tower leaders joining the fray.

Dread squashed the hope in his chest as he watched the men he'd just scorched get to their feet.

CHAPTER 36

A SISTER'S FURY

Her body had started going numb from the cold, but Katarina held her position suspended amongst the clouds. Moisture had started to chill on her nose and fingertips, leaving a cold, burning sensation. The flying warrior felt the frigid air enter her lungs painfully before exiting, leaving them raw and dissatisfied. Her head spun; her vision was slightly blurred. There wasn't enough oxygen getting to her blood. The stone clasped in her hand could stave off fatigue, but it could do nothing for suffocation.

She didn't care. It didn't matter that she could hardly breathe. Her breath came in short bursts as she channelled her remaining energy to keep herself afloat, leaving the immense store of power within the stone for what came next.

Looking at the stone now resting in her hands, she saw its surface still very much alive, the twisting cyclone within. She tapped into the stone's stores with her mind and was greeted with an onslaught of overwhelming raw power that she was unaccustomed to.

The power of the stone is truly terrifying, she thought. Usually I'd turn to my sisters . . .

The power within seemed to be questioning her, made

curious by her sudden attempt to utilise it. It wanted to know what it was that she desired. The answer was simple: she wanted to borrow its strength to win. She wanted the power to eradicate the evil before her and to protect those within the city. She wanted to avenge her sister, and every other person who'd fallen victim to the cruel campaign of her enemy.

The stone's energy pressed against Katarina's mind as if trying to consume her, approving of her desires. She welcomed it. The stone's power washed over her, overflowing into the chilling air around her. The clouds surrounding her steadily darkened, taking on deeper and deeper shades of brilliant violet before her eyes.

Small arches of blue lightning ripped through the clouds like sharp claws, each one slashing in random jagged directions before disappearing from existence. As more energy came to her, the bolts became more frequent until it appeared there was always lightning in the clouds.

She felt alive.

Her personal vortex of wind whipped up faster around her with new life as her fatigued mind awakened, sharper than ever as the clouds grew angrier and more violent. Thunder boomed, drowning out the shrieks of the two approaching beasts.

The storm had expanded, filling the entire sky for leagues. Katarina's view was that of an unnatural, yet beautiful wonderland of clouds shifting restlessly as they devoured more of the blue sky. The gorgeous magical essence continued consuming every inch of the sky except for a small thirty-yard radius around its conjurer. Before long, the magic finished expanding. It held its position in the air, awaiting a command.

The vicious beasts closed in with Katarina firmly in their sights. The city ignored, they were only interested in killing the one who had defeated their kin earlier. Katarina watched their approach, completely at peace for the first time since the battle had begun. As the beasts entered her sanctuary of clouds she slowly raised her free hand towards the enemy and clicked her fingers.

The clouds instantly responded with a fierce bolt of lightning streaking out of them, colliding with the closest beast. The electricity engulfed its body, tendrils of blue lightning coursing over it. The beast shrieked in pain as the surge found its way to its victim's wings. The deadly current burnt the thin membrane to a crisp, flowing through to the tip where it dispersed, leaving the enemy flightless, but death claimed its body before it even began to fall.

The second beast kept true to its advance and Katarina flew into the purple sea of clouds. It was invigorating. She flew blind through the thick blanket that was her magical manifestation, yet she had never had such clear vision. She didn't spend a single second lost within the immense shroud as the mixture of her own power and the stone's gave her body new life. She was alert and her senses were attuned to her situation like never before.

She was ready.

After navigating through the clouds for a lengthy moment, she dropped from the shroud of sinister violet. She fell beneath the darkened sky, looking back up at the great anomaly. There was still an hour or two of life left in the sun that was descending over the mountaintops but it was all but lost on the field of battle. She smirked bitterly as she gazed at her creation. The beast was lost within the purple haze. It was a fitting development, in her opinion. None of the people below knew why they were in their current situation, so why should the enemy?

For my sisters, she thought as she clicked her fingers at the clouds, this time releasing energy across their entire expanse.

Blue electricity was seen once more, this time arching across the unnatural clouds in all directions. It charged through every inch of the cloud-like canopy, burning the image of a massive, supernatural spider web upon its expanse. The sound of rolling thunder was accompanied by the strident screech of an abomination meeting its end, its desperate cry resounding across the hillside. Katarina's senses dulled momentarily as the stone attempted to replenish her energy. A cruel smile formed on her lips as an unrecognisable, singed body fell from the clouds towards the earth.

This is what everyone who harms innocents will face from now on, she thought as she watched it fall.

She was too far up to see any details; she could barely even make out Neibel-Haven. She hadn't realised how high she'd flown. She projected herself downwards, diving towards the ground.

She reached out with her mind, trying to sense the Vassal's energy below. In response she felt Dark Magic press against her mind. The enemy wasn't trying to hide her presence. Katarina altered her course, making a direct line for the source. She could feel her enemy's strength along with another overwhelming presence nearby.

It had to be her stone. Her theory had been correct.

She'd assumed the two forces that collided almost a year

ago were the Vassals of Light and Dark. It hadn't been a proven theory, but given the legends surrounding the other stones, it seemed the most likely. She had visited the site of the confrontation shortly afterwards and the aftermath lingered with dregs of their magic still present in the air over the frozen wasteland. She'd spent days flying over the abandoned battleground, trying to analyse the remnants of energy, gathering insight into what the battle was over. It hadn't been easy; there had been a third force, one without a stone. But she had felt the nature of the two main forces that had collided. One of the culprits held fierce indignation and desperation. The other boasted malice and apathy in equal portions. The latter was beneath her, attacking the city that Katarina had taken it upon herself to protect.

Let's see how you fare against your own kind, she thought with grim determination as she approached the ground.

CHAPTER 37

AN IRRESISTIBLE OFFER

Alicea stirred from sleep in her primitive yet comfortable bed made from bone and pelt. The exhausted Princess had lost consciousness as soon as her head hit the pillow made of owl feathers.

The Princess had slept deeply. Her dreams filled with raging battles between unknown armies and skies occupied with flocks of birds formed from water. They were identical to the one currently standing on the frame at the end of her bed, eyeing a recent intruder suspiciously. Alicea opened her eyes to focus on the intruder, finding Gramere, with Rufus standing behind him. Upon seeing the thief, the sleepiness in her eyes was replaced with irritation.

"Mr. Thief, I'm trying to rest. I went to bed for that reason," Alicea snapped, lifting her blanket up to her chin. "Look away!"

"Yes, I can understand why you would be upset at getting a meagre eighteen hours' sleep, but Gramere has a message I think you should hear," Rufus groaned sarcastically, turning away as he helped himself to the bowl of fruit the villagers had offered the sleeping Princess.

"Eighteen hours?" Alicea said, sitting straight up in alarm, looking at the older man, who had averted his gaze. "What's the message?"

"Allow me to apologise for disturbing you, Your Highness. Our head shaman heard about the stone you have in your possession and she has some knowledge regarding both it and magic. She has offered to tutor you if you are interested," Gramere said in a kindly, almost fatherly tone.

"Really? She could teach me how to use and control this?" she asked before shaking her head and reaching for her comb. "It doesn't matter. I'll gladly take any offer of assistance in understanding any of it!"

"Splendid! She will meet you at the training field in one hour. If you follow the road outside the north-east gate, you will arrive there in no time. I could gather some guards if you like?" Gramere offered helpfully.

"No need, Mr. Thief will accompany me. I sincerely thank you for everything, Gramere!" the Princess said hurriedly, waiting for the older man to bow himself out before rising.

Rufus looked up from his feasting with a mouth full of wild berries to see Alicea wearing a nightdress made from light brown leather. It was bizarre to see the Princess in the clothing of the rough-and-tumble villagers. It was even stranger that she looked even more beautiful in it than she had in her travelling gear or even the fancy attire of the castle. As soon as Alicea caught him staring, she clicked her fingers and pointed towards the wall.

"Did you jus— " Rufus started as he turned away again.

"Finish the food in your mouth before addressing me, Mr. Thief. I believe you to be human, despite the contrary animalistic evidence you present to me at times."

"Never mind," Rufus muttered, after finishing his fruit.

"Very well, wait outside. I need to change." Alicea ordered the already departing thief.

❖

Alicea and Rufus followed the path through the forestland, the Princess with a purposeful gaze focused straight ahead. Rufus walked with more caution, his eyes darting from tree to tree. He had been in too many ambushes to walk calmly through any area where enemies could be lurking. His fears were unfounded, however, and they arrived at the clearing mentioned by Gramere without a single trace of any threat.

The training ground was a sizable open field. A small river ran through the middle, branching off its main course into countless smaller streams.

Littered across the field were around a dozen stumps of trees that had been cut down, each one levelled to just above the height of Rufus' knee. Alicea and Rufus both turned their attention to one lone tree that had been allowed to grow in the centre of the field. It was nothing grand; its trunk rose from the ground over their heads before three branches jutted out in different directions. Each branch was adorned with a modest number of browning leaves, showing that autumn was starting to take its hold despite the green grass.

The branch closest to them was occupied by a crow. A crow that stared directly at them.

Alicea started to walk towards the tree, assuming that whoever they were to meet would notice them standing in the middle of the field. Rufus followed slowly, eyes still racing around their surroundings. As they approached the tree, they both jumped when a voice entered their minds.

So, the allure of knowledge was indeed enough to entice you, Princess.

Alicea searched around her in alarm as Rufus smirked, "The crow."

Alicea's attention quickly turned back to the feathered occupant of the branch.

Interesting that the lowly thief was the first to figure it out.

"I don't know about lowly, but how do you figure I'm a thief?" Rufus replied, indignant at the insult.

Perceptive maybe, but quick to focus on the unimportant. Not fitting for a guardian, the voice said with distaste.

"Please forgive Mr. Thief! Are you the one we are to meet?" Alicea asked the crow.

I am, the crow replied. *But before we begin I'd like to know how serious you really are about learning from me. I have conditions, and will not waste my time on the lax and lazy.*

"I am committed," Alicea replied quickly.

Perhaps now, but my methods may not be suitable for such a sheltered girl. If you wish to study under me, you must supply a reason why you wish to learn. If it is acceptable we will begin immediately. If it is not, you will leave this place, along with your chance to learn. Now, what is your reason for coming here?"

Alicea looked at the crow for a moment, thinking how best to answer before deciding on the truth.

"I wish to learn so that I may better understand the concept of magic, these stones and my capabilities," she answered, pushing her hair back thoughtfully.

Why? the crow asked.

"To become stronger," Alicea replied confidently.

Why? it pressed further. The crow's repeating of the question took the Princess aback. Had she answered wrong?

"Because . . . Well . . . There are so many people in need, and a danger approaches the land. I've been told I can help, so I will," the Princess answered weakly.

Why?

"Because it is my duty!" Alicea replied fiercely.

Why?

"Why is it my duty? Because I choose it to be so! I will not stand by while people are in need. I've felt the bitterness of losing that which I love and I wouldn't wish it upon anyone!" Alicea replied. It was the closest to actually losing her temper that Rufus had seen. Her face was a little flushed and the coolness of her words ebbed slightly. She didn't like when someone else was in control of the conversation.

The crow silently gazed at the Princess for a minute, its beady eyes of the blackest black. Rufus swore the crow gave off the impression that it knew Alicea better than she knew herself, though he couldn't place why. The crow measured the sincerity of her words before opening its wings in what looked to be an effort to leave.

The Princess' stomach fell.

Did I answer incorrectly?

Rather than taking to the sky, however, the black bird started a slow descent towards the ground. Its beady eyes emitted an ethereal green aura as it touched down in front of the pair. The emanation continued to spread throughout its feathered body until it was completely cloaked in the light.

Rufus pulled Alicea back behind him in caution.

Before their eyes, the crow changed shape. The feathers started to withdraw as its body expanded. Its wings and clawed feet mutated as they grew into human arms and legs, starting at the size of an infant's and developing as if years of natural growth were taking place in seconds. The crow's chest was now featherless, replaced with human skin of shining bronze, stretching as the curves of a woman started taking shape.

The bird's hard beak retracted back inside the crow-woman's head and was reshaped to lips as her eyes expanded. They grew into the human face that was forming but retained their black hue. The feathers upon her head were replaced with long, black hair, which fell across her face.

For a few seconds, the woman appeared as young as Alicea. But the transformation wasn't complete. The Princess watched in awe and mild horror as the woman aged decades in front of her. Wrinkles spread and deepened upon the woman's face as parts of her black hair faded to grey. The dark orbs that were her eyes grew misty, like a light fog lingering upon a lake of pitch. A now human woman of more than fifty years stood in front of the pair and turned away. She walked behind the tree and picked up a brown dress, which she fluidly slipped over the top of her head, concealing her naked body before returning to look at Alicea critically.

"A fine answer," the woman said to the bewildered Princess. "You have conviction if nothing else. Perhaps you know not your true purpose yet, but that conviction is invaluable. I will teach you, should you agree to my remaining condition."

"What is it?" Alicea asked, regaining her bearings.

"While you are my student, you are not royalty and will not be treated as such. I do not take on many students, but the ones I do are pushed to their furthest limits. The fact that you once resided in the comfort of a kingdom means nothing here," the woman answered.

"Understood. I'm Alicea the student so long as you are my teacher," Alicea replied without hesitation.

"And I am Garnet, Head Shaman of South Tremel. We shall begin immediately. So listen well," the older woman said with a stone-faced expression.

"First, the basics," she continued briskly as Alicea snapped to attention. "Magic must never be taken lightly as even the simplest of spells can go wrong and cause harm to yourself and others. You obviously have had some tutoring in the art of magic from one source or another."

Garnet took a second to look at the aqueous bird on the Princess' shoulder. The Princess' strange companion looked up from its unnecessary preening as if it knew it was being referred to.

"It may be acting like a pet, but that is because that's how you, the sorcerer, think of it. It needs to be more than that. If you wish to make it an effective means to defend yourself then it will be more taxing on your mind and body. I have chosen this location as there is water at the ready. Water is both the element and nature of magic that you are aligned with."

Alicea nodded, so far following her new instructor's every word. Rufus had taken to sitting underneath the lone tree, sprawled out with his eyes closed. Alicea sighed at the sight.

Mr. Thief can fall asleep anywhere.

"Am I boring you, Alicea?"

"No! Of course not, I –"

"So, in short, the dangers of magic include fatigue and even death if misused," Garnet resumed her lecture coolly. "Before casting a spell, you must be mindful of how much energy it will take and the intended result."

The Princess nodded quickly to show that she was listening and the older woman continued.

"Mages have multiple ways of using their magic, but they only need to be skilled in one. For example, incantations or 'Words of Magic' can help the sorcerer reach for the spell they desire. These words will do nothing to expand their personal energy reserves. With the right words, a fledging mage could attempt to conjure a fireball with the destructive capabilities of razing a street of houses. But without the required energy reserves, the mage would find himself dead from over-exhaustion before he had conjured so much as a spark."

Alicea nodded again, her mind briefly wandering to when she'd conjured the swan. Had she run the risk of dying there? Was the swan considered a large magical feat?

"Another powerful option is to utilise magical tools," Garnet continued. Alicea refocused on her instructor's words.

"Now, these do the exact opposite and primarily focus on taking some of the burden of casting upon themselves. These can be a wide variety of items. Most mages adopt tomes that previous mages have stored a portion of their energy within as they studied its contents. Tomes are a very common choice, but there are countless alternatives that can serve as a conductor of magical energy waiting to assist the wielder in their endeavours."

"Like my stone?" Alicea asked with wide eyes. She was captivated.

"Exactly. The bearers of these stones have an incredible advantage over any other mage in the sense that these stones provide an energy pool unrivalled by any magical tool known to this world. Other objects have limits before the energy imbued within it will force the item to disintegrate. The stones, however, may have a limit, but one hasn't been discovered yet. You will not exhaust yourself as quickly, but this does not erase the danger completely."

"Why not? If a mage could cast spells indefinitely, they'd be invincible!" Alicea replied.

"Banish that naive thought immediately! I did not say indefinitely, for that is false!" Garnet snapped. "All the magical energy in the world won't protect you from a knife if you can't command it correctly! Secondly, you forget that tools can only take a portion of the burden from the caster. Even if the stone were to take half of the burden from casting, you will still be taxed a portion of your energy as a price. As such, you will be inevitably faced with the ever-present risk of fatigue or death, as with all magic."

Ashamed, the Princess stared down at the ground. It was partially because of the scolding she was not accustomed to receiving, but it was the folly of her suggestion that triggered the shame. She had said something stupid and had been chastised appropriately. It was unpleasant and yet strangely welcomed by the young Princess. Alicea only looked back up at her teacher's face when she had begun lecturing once more in a slightly kinder tone.

"Now that we have touched on your stone and the benefit it provides, we will talk about your choice of magic, or rather, the magic that has chosen you – water."

Garnet walked towards one of the branches in the stream with Alicea following her. Standing at the water's edge, the shaman pointed at the clear liquid as she addressed her new student.

"This is both your weapon and your shield. As long as

there is water, you will be equipped as best you can be for the purpose of utilising magic. Do you know what the benefit of mastering this element in particular might be? Think about its nature."

Alicea stared at the water gradually passing by, happily altering its course over the rocks and sticks in its way before continuing.

"It's flexible?" Alicea answered with a nervous shrug.

"Exactly. Of the six primary elements, it is the most flexible because you can alter it to your liking and needs. Water can take on the shape of almost anything. From a small bird," Garnet nodded towards the swan, "to a snake in the grass, from a spear to a near impenetrable shield. We are now going to see how you fare at its manipulation."

Garnet turned back to where Rufus was napping under the tree. "Thief, on your feet!"

"Hmmm, what?" Rufus groaned sleepily. "What do you want, Feather Face?"

"My name is Garnet. Now on your feet!" Garnet repeated.

"And my name is Rufus, and I'll do nothing until respect is shown," Rufus retorted, suddenly alert to the awful idea that he might have to move.

"Mr. Thief! You will assist right now!" Alicea yelled.

"Here I thought I worked for a Princess, not a student!" Rufus grumbled as he followed the command.

Garnet smiled and turned back to Alicea as Rufus leant against the tree, unable to hear the pair as they spoke.

"Now, strike him with your bird."

"What?" Alicea asked, her usual composure disappearing.

"It's in a weak state of magic so it won't hurt him too much.

Now, mentally take control of the magical energy and order it to attack the thief," Garnet explained to a hesitant Alicea.

"Are you sure that's wise?" she asked.

"Positive. I have a clear idea of your bird's strength; it will cause no real harm. Besides, we have to get him moving," she replied.

"Hello? I'm standing up, what did you want?" Rufus called out.

"I'm going to hit you with my magic bird!" the Princess cheered.

Rufus' face dropped as he stared at the women.

Alicea's face screwed up in concentration. She could feel her mind grasping at the lucid energy of the bird on her shoulder as it had the liquid of the waterfall. It surprised her to find that it was a simple feat and that the bird offered no resistance, allowing itself to be consumed by its conjurer's consciousness. Unsure of how to proceed, she mentally screamed the first order that seemed appropriate.

Attack!

Rufus' eyebrows threatened to jump off his forehead as the bird took flight from Alicea's shoulder and soared directly at him.

"I hate this damned bird," the thief muttered.

Rufus hesitated. He didn't know whether to move or strike the incoming bird, what was needed for the training. His hesitance cost him; he reached for his blades just as the bird collided with his face, forcing his head back into the tree with a dull *thump*. The bird burst into countless droplets as it connected and its former body rained down to the ground.

"Be quick! Make it reform and strike again!" Garnet ordered

as her student grasped at the now scattered fragments of magical energy.

It wasn't as simple as taking control of the bird as a whole, but she found that it wasn't necessarily that difficult either. Despite it being her controlling it, watching the shimmer of sunlight upon the gathering water made the Princess feel as though a miracle was happening before her eyes. Pride filled her chest as each tiny droplet found its place on the growing form that was her shattered friend.

When the cygnet had reformed, it instinctually took flight, soaring into the sky in an arc before swooping back down on Rufus. It already knew what was expected of it.

"No you don't!" Rufus cried, ducking to the side and letting the bird collide with the tree.

The thief's relief was short-lived as the liquid started to reform again from the shower made from the collision. It had started the process of reformation even before all the drops had hit the ground. It was learning, as was the Princess.

"What is wrong with you?!" Rufus bellowed at the Princess as the bird propelled itself at the unnerved thief yet again.

"Faster! You need to make this second nature to you. This is your weapon – so *wield* it!" Garnet ordered the stressed Princess to keep full control of the magic that was her pet. Reforming and commanding the bird wasn't difficult, but each time it happened she felt a slight tax on her energy. It was almost irrelevant, but it was there.

Rufus drew one of his long daggers and hurled it at the approaching bird with perfect aim. The sharp blade pierced the surface of the creature, the force pushing it back against the tree with the blade pinning it to the trunk. His eyebrows rose at the sight, surprised that it had worked, as the bird squawked silently. Its slender neck flailed as its body squirmed in an attempt to break free.

"Enough!" Garnet called as she trotted up behind the thief. Looking at the pinned bird, the Princess' instructor turned to her student, who was following closely. "What's wrong with this scenario?"

Alicea stared at the scene in front of her. First at her bird, then to Rufus. After a moment, she turned back to Garnet, failing to see the issue.

"You are still in the mindset that what you control is a pet. If he had thrown his dagger into water it would have passed through. Here, however, it's as if he has struck a real bird," Garnet explained.

"I – I see," the Princess said, looking at the bird critically. Until now, she hadn't seen an issue with treating her companion any differently to what it appeared to be.

"How are you feeling? Do you feel any fatigue?" Garnet asked, looking over the Princess critically.

"No," Alicea said uncertainly. She felt slightly tired, but she wasn't ready to stop. She would persevere.

"Good then. Thief! Remove your dagger from the bird and we will try again!" Garnet ordered.

"Is free will a foreign concept to you pair?" Rufus groaned, only to be ignored as Garnet pursed her lips at her student.

"We will keep at it until you either understand what I am teaching you, or you collapse from exhaustion. I'm not fussy about which comes first."

CHAPTER 38

A PRINCESS' PROGRESS

The sun had started to descend behind the distant mountains, its brilliant crimson hue lighting up the dying sky. It resulted in a harsh and beautiful clash of colour, setting the scene for the training.

Alicea was mentally exhausted and having difficulty focusing on the tasks set by Garnet. The exercises included guiding the bird through complex obstacle courses; deconstructing and reconstructing its form a set amount of times within a designated time limit; and, her personal favourite, ordering it to chase the disgruntled Rufus. It was exhausting, but the training had already borne fruit. She could now make the bird reform twice as quickly as her first attempt. She also had better control over its flight patterns and could make it collide with Rufus with increasing frequency.

She'd asked Garnet countless questions and received stilted answers. The shaman seemed far more interested in teaching at her own pace and had snapped about "learning the basics first" when Alicea had asked about the bird's ability to fly when it was made of water.

Rufus had developed his own strategy for his adversary. He ran across the field, using the tree stumps as obstacles to jump over or even hide behind as the bird soared overhead, all the while waiting for his chance to either slash at it or pin it to the tree. On one occasion, he had even managed to tackle it out of the sky before ending up in a ridiculous wrestling match that had the Princess chortling from across the field. Even now, he was racing across the field, looking back over his shoulder at his aerial opponent. The swan was gliding through the air, stalking its target from a safe distance.

Its trajectory changed as it swooped, narrowly avoiding smacking into the back of the man's head. He lashed out at the bird quickly, barely missing his target as Alicea made it flap feverishly to gain altitude. Rufus turned and ran once more, this time towards the tree. Alicea had fallen for this tactic once before and made her aqueous flyer arc around in the sky, circling the tree from above before mentally ordering it to dive-bomb Rufus.

The thief quickly stepped to the side, leaving the bird to meet with the ground, splashing everywhere before reforming between the blades of grass. It began flapping its still-forming wings furiously in an attempt to leave the ground again, but Rufus brought his foot down on the bird and its body crumpled into a heap. He let out a triumphant cheer as he turned to see Garnet shaking her head in disappointment and tapping her foot. She looked ready to scold her student again when she must have noticed the same thing Rufus did.

Alicea stood a short distance away, and she was smiling. It was a bad sign and Rufus knew it, even before he felt something crawling up his leg.

Looking down, he saw that his trousers were drenched with water that was coursing up his right leg. Rufus started to panic as the water reached his chest and soaked his clothes.

He noticed that once it reached his neck, his trousers were dry again as if they had never been affected. The water was stretching to its limit as it climbed his frame and it wasn't able to cover his whole body at once.

It was a nice realisation up until it had consumed his face. Rufus clawed at the globe of water building around his head, trying to remove the liquid as he choked, but it just reformed around its claim. Eventually ceasing his futile efforts, he looked at Alicea in alarm. The water suddenly leapt from his face, merging in the air in front of him. In less than a second, he was eye to eye with the bird he had crushed moments before, its wings beating just enough to keep it airborne.

Both bird and thief glared at each other for a moment in an intense staring competition. Everyone present was unsure of what would happen before the bird lashed out with its long neck, striking Rufus' face and sending the startled thief stumbling backwards to fall on his backside.

"Enough!" Garnet called. "Impressive work! Well done!"

Alicea released the connection with the magic and sat immediately. She was finally at the end of her tether and breathing heavily as Garnet continued to speak thoughtfully.

"At first I thought your pet-like style was a bad sign, but you seem to have developed your own way of doing things. This is good," Garnet praised, as she watched the bird take off into the forest. It was free of its conjurer's control and heading off to forage.

"I thought I needed to be rid of that part?" Alicea rubbed her temples. She couldn't remember the last time her mind had actually been tested. It felt sluggish, as if wading through waist-high water.

"At first I thought so. It's quite unique and I thought it would be worthless and hold you back. But if you develop this style, perhaps you could make for an above-average mage. At the very least, your enemies will be surprised. But we need to work on something bigger and more threatening than a small bird, although its flight is an exceptional ability," Garnet explained before smiling. "The way you switched its nature to that of water so seamlessly was unexpected. Other mages take years to accomplish a move so effectively."

"It was strange," Alicea began slowly, reliving the moment in her mind. "It was like I felt his clothes, like I was clinging onto them and using them to climb. It was like part of me *was* the water. Is that normal?"

Garnet took a moment to look over Alicea, her face deep in thought.

"I'm not sure if it's normal, but it could be very useful. It sounds as if the magic itself has a consciousness, perhaps one that you can tap into and tell it what to do based on its own set of senses. Quite intriguing," Garnet said with a hint of surprise in her voice. "Everyone is different; it is possible."

"That means I would have more control!" Alicea exclaimed excitedly.

"Yes, but you had best be careful when you do it. I cannot be sure, but if this is indeed the case, I can foresee a terrible side effect," Garnet said in a concerned voice.

"Like what?" the Princess asked.

"If you can tap into the magic's senses, you may be able to feel its pain. If that's the case, when the thief stomped on the bird it would feel as if you just got crushed yourself," Garnet explained.

"But I wouldn't be hurt at all," objected Alicea.

"Not physically. But if your mind suddenly registered excruciating pain, it could debilitate you at a crucial moment of combat. Your mind is a powerful tool, for better or for worse," Garnet speculated. "If you could somehow learn to switch the link off and on between the magic's consciousness and your own at will, it would make for a very interesting style of magic-wielding. But that's enough for today. It's best if we make our way back to the village before dark as it's important for you to rest between this training. We don't want to push you too far, too fast."

"Yes, I think rest would be wise at this point," the Princess said, getting to her feet slowly and brushing down her blue tabard. Her head was spinning mercilessly with fatigue when she noticed that Garnet had returned to her crow form. *I must report your progress to Chief Kurok and in turn, he will inform Setz. Both will be very interested to hear how today went,* Garnet's voice resonated within Alicea's mind. *Just so you are aware, Alicea. You have done magnificently and I look forward to training you further. Seems you are indeed the daughter of Adele.*

With that, the crow took to the sky, soaring in the direction of the village, disappearing into the trees. Alicea made a mental note that Garnet had mentioned her mother and smiled; it was the best compliment anyone could offer her. Rufus jogged over to the Princess. He seemed a little out of breath but fine nonetheless, which surprised her.

How can someone so lazy display such a level of fitness?

"That was a neat trick with the water at the end there. Didn't see it coming," he commended the Princess.

Alicea looked up at the thief, her eyes shimmering with pride and a wide smile etched across her face before she collapsed into his arms. She had reached her limit. Alarm raced through the thief's mind until he heard deep breathing coming from the limp Princess that he was holding upright. Grimacing, he lifted the Princess into his arms and held her close to his chest.

Typical. Picks up spell-slinging in one day but can't even mange to walk back to the village without my help.

CHAPTER 39

DÉJÀ VU

The party of three descended flight after flight of stairs for what seemed like hours. Every time they came to flat ground, their hopes rose only to be dashed brutally when they found yet another flight of stairs. The walls were lit by regular torches, all exactly five yards apart with the fire's light glowing ominously in the dark. Rather than the blaze of the torches banishing the darkness, the bleakness threatened to swallow the weakened flames.

As the trio hit flat ground yet again, they proceeded forward, refusing to allow themselves to hope that maybe their downwards journey was over. Instead of finding another staircase, they came out into a chamber. It was narrower than the grand hall in which the decaying corpses had been floors above, but it was almost double the length. More a corridor than a place for people to congregate.

It was around twenty yards wide with its walls adorned with countless unlit torches. It didn't surprise the small party when the heads of the dead torches suddenly caught fire. They lit up the chamber, revealing several identical wooden doors lined up along each of the walls.

Lyrium looked back at her companions and forced a nod. Arok and Stefan were oblivious to the unease on her face as they nodded back in confirmation, slowly advancing on the first closed door to their right. The few steps seemed like an eternity to the young woman. She couldn't quite confirm why she felt so unsettled, but it had something to do with her surroundings. It was different from being confronted with the undead in the above chamber; this was far worse.

She had felt fear then, of course. She had been terrified for her own safety along with Stefan's and Arok's.

That was his uncle and he just handled it . . . Oh, Arok . . .

But this was different. It wasn't fear so much as anxiety and foreboding discomfort. On the higher floor, the threat was evident and their opponent directly before them.

This game was different. This game was one of the nerves, and Lyrium hated it.

Arok readied his large hammer and Stefan stood back, drawing his bow. Lyrium grasped the doorknob, her hand shaking so badly that the knob rattled beneath her grip. Breathing deeply, she swung the door open. Despite its age, the door glided back smoothly on its hinges. It opened into the room slowly before gently coming to a stop against the stone wall with a soft *thump*.

The trio stepped inside to find a disturbing sight. It was a well-lit room and yet there didn't appear to be any source of illumination, be it flame or magic. Strangest of all was the presence of a window, despite being so far underground. Even from across the room, they could see the darkness of outside.

A bed, big enough to fit all three of them, was made up in the corner of the room. It had a beautiful red pelt serving as a cover across a luxurious feather mattress. It was obviously of Tremel origin. A wardrobe in perfect condition stood a full head and shoulders taller than Stefan in the other corner. It had resisted the test of time better than any object had the right to. It was as if the beautifully crafted piece of furniture had been constructed not five minutes ago, shining with fresh lacquer.

With a nod to his companions, Stefan lowered his bow, opening the doors carefully only to find perfectly preserved full-length dresses hanging from the wooden beams within. Arok checked under the bed for anything out of the ordinary, rising when his eye was caught by something on the bedside table. There was a small, pink box resting on the side bench, which Arok picked up curiously. Attempting to flick it open, his eyes narrowed when it remained shut. Grasping it with both hands, he tried to pry open the fragile-looking item to no avail.

Grunting with disgust, he put it back on the table and turned to Lyrium, who was examining the window in the back of the room. Trying to dismiss the fact that he had been defeated in a test of strength by a tiny box, Arok joined his lover at the window.

"What's wrong with this picture, Arok?" Lyrium asked, barely whispering.

Arok nodded in agreement. "What's a damned window doing underground?"

The glassless cavity revealed the forestland surrounding their village in the darkest night. A single tree was illuminated by the moon's light, leaving its brethren in shadows.

Arok leapt onto the sill of the window to investigate, only to be stopped by an unseen force pushing him back. It was like invisible hands ushering him away from the window.

It was Stefan who spoke next, turning his attention from investigating the room to his comrades instead.

"I'm of the impression that we will find no answers within this room, only more questions," he began, mildly exasperated.

It was unusual for the man to sound so frustrated but given the situation, the others couldn't fault him.

"I'm with Stiff," Arok agreed, producing a piece of fruit from his pocket and chewing on it. "Like why I can't climb through a window? Or why there's one even here?"

"Or why it is so easy to see in here when it's so dark outside and there is nothing here giving off light?" Lyrium added.

"Or why everything here looks like it was used yesterday instead of two hundred years ago and –" Arok grumbled before being interrupted by the flick of a hand from an alarmed-looking Stefan.

The three of them stood silent for a long moment. Arok and Lyrium directed questioning expressions at Stefan, who seemed to be listening intently to something in the distance. Arok's hand moved instinctively for his weapon, stopping when the sound Stefan was hearing finally met his own ears.

A soft melody, but he couldn't place the instrument. Was it perhaps a lute? No, not quite. A harp maybe? That was closer. The melody was quiet yet steadily filling the entire room. It was hauntingly beautiful, constantly keeping a slow pace in between each note. At times it seemed the entrancing tune was threatening to come to a stop, only to resume once more, split seconds before the last note disappeared completely.

It was soothing; however, Arok couldn't help but notice that it was also very sad – depressing. The longer he listened, the more the song began to weigh down on him. But even as the song's melancholy tune washed over him, his heart held no desire for it to stop playing. It was only when his eyes met Lyrium's that he noticed her face was as white as a sheet and snapped out of the trance.

In a panic he grabbed her by the shoulder.

"What is it?!"

Lyrium just stared straight ahead at something behind him. Arok turned slowly, following her gaze, and realised that Stefan had already located the source of the song. Upon the dresser, the pink music box had opened and protruding from its confines was a small statuette of a young girl with long brown hair cascading down her back.

The young girl was dressed in the black gown of one in mourning. She had a red book in one hand, and the other held a ragdoll in the shape of a grey hare. Her head was tilted to the side, as if looking at the trio with a subtle hint of a lifeless smile.

Arok leant closer, bending down to take a better look at the contraption that had captivated him and his companions. On either side of the small girl there were the strange powders he had seen the ladies in Aquiocia wear. He also noted that the underside of the lid, which now served as a backdrop for the statue, was fitted with a piece of glass, his face reflecting back from its surface.

It's one of those – oh, what are they called? Vanity boxes! That's it! he thought, trying to get rid of the sense of unease eating away at his insides.

He was about to stand up and explain to the others that they were getting wound up over nothing when he noticed something odd in the reflection of the glass. He could see the back of the statuette; between her thick hair there was something small poking out, as if it wasn't a part of the figure.

Arok leant in until he was as close to the glass as possible, his face parallel to the statue as he looked into the glass. Close enough to recognise the mysterious item for what it was. It was a tiny knife. Its hilt was protruding from her hair with just the slightest hint of its blade free of the statue's spine. Captivated and unsure that his eyes were telling the truth, he stared at the knife lodged in the statue's back for a few moments before his blood turned cold. There was red liquid slowly oozing from the tiny wound. Unable to react at his normal speed, he pulled his head back slowly.

Arok examined the face of the statue. Its lifeless smile was now stretched ear-to-ear, forming an exceptionally cheeky expression. The joy in the girl's unsettling smile held the innocence of a child who had just pulled an outstanding prank on her friends. Arok leapt backwards with a yelp, pointing at the girl. His back slammed into Stefan's legs, almost toppling the confused man in his haste to get away.

Lyrium had snapped out of her trance and was kneeling beside her lover, concerned and confused as Arok spluttered, "Back – wound – blood – it's *alive!*"

Stefan looked up at the box, which had snapped shut during the confusion. Its music had ceased but he had seen nothing of what Arok was trying to describe. It took a few minutes, and an equal amount of draughts from a wineskin, for Arok's nerves to calm enough to explain properly.

"A place like this is enough to make any man start to see things," Stefan offered his friend as Lyrium shook her head.

"I believe you and we will find the cause soon. I promise, my love."

Stefan looked like he was about to dispute the idea then thought better of it. Instead he stood, straightening his bow and stating, "There is nothing to stay in this room for. There are many other doors that may hold answers and I suggest we move to the next one."

Having no other better suggestions, Lyrium and Arok nodded and rose to their feet. Arok shakily found his balance and the three filed out the doorway. Passing through into the corridor, they glanced up the empty hallway instinctively as they approached the door directly opposite. The door swung open as easily as the first, gliding smoothly on its iron hinges with the same *thump* as it hit the wall behind it.

What the trio saw inside did nothing to alleviate any of their accrued tension. The same out-of-place window loomed in the corner. The same cabinet and bed were illuminated by an unperceivable source.

To Arok's revulsion, the pink vanity box sat on the dresser, unopened and undisturbed.

The three stepped in cautiously and were met with a disturbing case of déjà vu. They split up to investigate as they had before. Stefan went to the tall dresser to examine inside, Arok to investigate under the bed, and Lyrium proceeded to the window to look out at the forest in attempt to get an idea of their location.

What met her eyes was not what she had hoped, though it was as she expected. Her eyes took in the dark night, the shadows devouring the trees with an insatiable hunger. The flora was soaked in the bleakness, save one in the very centre that was illuminated by a single moonbeam above it. Everything was in the exact same place.

"Exactly the same!" Lyrium exclaimed. "How is this possible?"

"In many fortresses it is the norm to have everything the same in residential quarters," reasoned Stefan, his voice filled with controlled unease.

"But the window shows the exact same garden, as if we are in the exact same room. And there is still nothing to explain why the rooms are so well lit!" Lyrium said, fear gripping her near hysterical voice.

It was only the men's unsettled nerves that prevented them from realising that it wasn't simply the ambient déjà vu that was distressing Arok's lover. The fear ran far deeper. Stefan was about to speak when he noticed Arok clutching something to his chest. It was a ragdoll in the shape of a hare.

That's just like the doll in the little statue's hand.

"Arok," Stefan began softly. "Where did you get that doll?"

Arok looked down at his tightly clutched prize before looking back at his companion, smiling broadly. His voice remained but the words that followed were not his own. "Oh, you mean Harriet? I've had her since I was a little girl. My mother bought her from the markets for me because I was a good girl all day!"

Stefan frowned at Arok's response and approached him tentatively. "Arok, I think it's a good idea that you put down the doll."

"No!" Arok wailed, turning away from Stefan and Lyrium, hiding the doll from view. "You can't take Harriet! She protects me from the bad men!"

"Of course she does," Stefan said, thinking quickly. *Is it a possession?*

Arok stalked across the room and hid behind the door,

clutching the ragdoll for dear life. Lyrium approached Stefan, looking confused at the proceedings, while he merely shrugged. Her brow was furrowed in thought, but her eyes held insight. The pair watched their companion as he looked down at the doll and started humming a rough imitation of the song they had heard earlier emanating from the vanity box. Lyrium approached her lover slowly as Stefan watched on uncertainly.

"May I see Harriet?" Lyrium asked softly. "I have something for her."

"No, she keeps the bad men away, she protects me!" Arok wailed again childishly. Lyrium's lips pursed in impatience for a moment before trying again.

"I understand that, but what protects her? I have something that will, but I need you to trust me," Lyrium replied, trying not to let herself be affected by Arok's immature behaviour.

"No! You'll just take her away!" Arok screamed again, stomping his foot.

"I promise I won't. I'll give her back right away. I just want you both to be safe, wouldn't you like that? I think Harriet wants you both to be safe," Lyrium responded, cooing to him as a concerned mother would.

Arok stared up at Lyrium with tears in his eyes. He seemed distressed almost to breaking point as he looked back and forth between his newfound doll and Lyrium. He seemed to struggle with himself as he stared into Lyrium's eyes. Slowly, he raised the doll from his chest towards Lyrium, who slapped it from his hand across the room.

"Hey! Why did you –" Arok shrieked before cutting off. "Wait, what . . . ?"

"I figured. The possession is limited to the person holding the object. Garnet had mentioned possession once or twice during training sessions." Lyrium stood before announcing, "Do not touch anything! Especially anything that is connected to the music box! Stefan? Do you hear me?"

Lyrium looked over to her companion to see that he was fixated on something out the window. A look of confusion was strewn across his normally calm and handsome face. Lyrium hurried over and as she joined him at the window, she said, "It's unnerving, isn't it? It's like we –"

Under the single illuminated tree sat a small girl playing with a ragdoll. A red book lay a couple of feet away from her on one of the tree's roots protruding up from the ground. Her long brown curls fell over her shoulders and bounced up and down as she threw her doll into the air and caught it while laughing with joy. Lyrium's head jerked to where she had slapped the doll from Arok's hands, only to see her lover climbing to his feet. He was confused but unharmed; the doll was nowhere in sight.

"Arok! Can you see a doll anywhere? Do not touch it! Can you see one?" she demanded.

Arok looked around in a daze. "A doll? No . . . Why are we looking for dolls?"

Lyrium quickly dismissed him with a wave of her hand, snapping her head back to the window and bringing her focus back to the girl.

How did she get her doll back? A thought that seemed unimportant as the girl outside looked up at Lyrium, smiling and waving.

"Why are you here?! You aren't supposed to be real! What

do you want?!" Lyrium yelled through the window, trying to force her way through it only to be pushed back by the window's unseen power.

The effort amused the young girl greatly as she stood up and raised her hand. She wiggled her index finger at her as if to say "no no no" before she turned away, skipping off into the darkness. The book and doll were in her hands, and a knife was protruding from her back. Lyrium cringed as she caught a glimpse of blood dripping down, coating the hilt of the blade and soaking her brown hair. There had been plenty of signs confirming her dread, but this was not so easily dismissed.

Frustrated, Lyrium turned and stormed away from the window. She punched the wardrobe hard enough to bruise her knuckles and the noise echoed throughout the room as she stormed out. Stefan and Arok hurried out into the corridor after her. They paused at the rage on Lyrium's face. It was an unexpected emotion as they were both of the assumption that everyone present was terrified rather than angry. Before either could offer soothing words to the enraged woman, she barked an order. It was the first time she had really taken charge since arriving. The men were nodding in affirmation before the message was even fully heard.

"We don't have time for the little nightmare's games! We each take a door and search the room. We know what the original looked like so search for anything different. Oh, and for the sake of all that's holy," Lyrium turned to Arok, "don't touch anything!"

The pair continued nodding, each crossing the corridor in separate directions to their own elected doors. Stefan called out, "Lyrium, you seem to have more of an idea of what is going on here than either of us. Is there something in particular you are looking for?"

The woman sighed to herself and looked down at her footwear of pelt, as if trying to recall something embedded in her mind before speaking in a barely controlled rage.

"Yes, find the accursed book! But do not touch it, and certainly don't touch any knives that you might find!"

Arok was about to question how Lyrium knew what to do when he saw Stefan shaking his head at him. His lover pushed open the door she had selected and disappeared from view.

"Remember, Arok, this is Lyrium's trial. We are merely support – we follow her lead 'til the end," Stefan reminded him and with that swung open his own door and entered, leaving Arok by himself.

He looked up and down the corridor, mentally counting the remaining doors. He realised that after exploring his room, they would still have half a dozen left unopened. With a despairing sigh, he swung the door open fiercely. It opened at the same pace as the times before, frustrating him further as he heard the door's soft, familiar *thump*.

CHAPTER 40

WHEN A NIGHTMARE BECOMES REAL

Arok rolled his eyes as he entered the room to find it exactly the same as the previous ones.

Typical! He thought angrily as he began his rounds of the room.

Dislodging his war hammer from its brace on his back, he readied it to strike anything that might decide to try to scare him again. He checked under the bed first and was relieved to find that there was no ragdoll under it this time. His next move was making his way to the wardrobe and swinging it open as he took a cautious step backwards, mimicking what Stefan had done. He wasn't used to having to be so wary; it was usually Stefan's role to watch over him. It proved unnecessary as all that greeted him was the same assortment of dresses as before.

He made his way across the room to his lover's usual position by the window, eyes instinctively darting to the vanity box on the dresser. The little box showed no interest in opening this time. He reached the window and gazed out. Nothing had changed. There was just the lonely illuminated tree surrounded by the rest of its kind clouded in shadows. He stared at the creepy image in front of him for a few moments before turning around. He stopped dead in his tracks as his eyes fell on the bed.

Cowering on the bed was the little girl, but what he saw was not the girl in her entirety. He could see through her to the sheets underneath her; she was pale, almost mist-like. The spectre of the young girl was staring wide-eyed towards the door. She was clutching her doll to her chest. The red book lay open at a bookmarked page, resting on the bed in front of her.

Arok shivered at the sight, but the girl paid him no mind. She was intensely focused on the door. Arok slowly moved towards the apparition, his weapon raised. The little girl could very well still be a threat. Cautiously shifting to the side of the bed, he noticed that her back showed no sign of a knife.

A vision? Is this from before . . . ?

His thought process was interrupted when the young girl recoiled from something in the doorway. Arok jumped back, weapon at the ready once more, eyes darting from the open door to the little girl and back again.

The transparent spectre was suddenly an image of the little girl screaming in fear, although no sound was heard. Before he could respond, something shifted in the doorway. Like a sheet of camouflage that had been hanging over it now dropped as more spectres, soldiers clad in armour, stormed into the room.

Two of the soldiers stood at the doorway blocking the exit while another moved to guard the window. The ghost of a man passed through Arok, causing him to shiver with anxiety. The sensation lingered, leaving him with a persistent tremble. One of the guards was speaking inaudibly with the little girl while she shook her head in fierce defiance. The soldier seemed perplexed at first before shrugging and stepping towards the girl.

A calm seemed to set over the young girl's face as she pointed to a line on the book's open page with her index finger. Arok watched in wonder as her ragdoll stood on its own accord with footing as sure as any human's. Harriet stood next to her owner, also pointing at the line, as the little girl mouthed a string of words unheard by Arok.

The ground below the two soldiers at the doorway shimmered. A spike formed from the stone and earth below shot up under each of the two soldiers, impaling them from the bottom of their feet through the top of their heads. The earthen glaives retreated back into the ground, leaving it as if it was never disturbed. Transparent liquid gathered around the impaled bodies in what Arok figured was a pool of the soldiers' blood and without the earth's assistance in standing, the bodies hit the ground.

Arok was mortified; but before he could even think of what he should do, the little girl snapped her book shut, grabbed her ragdoll and ran for the door. He silently cheered on the little girl, but before she reached the doorway a ghostly knife soared through his own body and lodged itself within the girl's back. Her book flew from her hands as she dropped to the cold stone floor, clutching her doll desperately.

Arok's head whirled around, so quickly his neck cracked, to see the remaining soldier, smirking as he walked through Arok again on his way to the girl, who was already bleeding wisp-like blood across the stone floor. The soldier stopped at the body, kicked it roughly and after it gave no response, continued to walk out of the doorway and from view.

Arok ran to the body, although he knew he could do nothing to help. The outline of the girl was fading and becoming harder to see by the second. Before long, there was nothing remaining of the struggle that had just taken place. The girl, the soldiers and even the blood had faded. Dismayed but hopeful, Arok realised this was the first answer the trio had received to any of the questions they had.

He raced out into the corridor and made for Lyrium. He barrelled into the room she had chosen to find his love staring at the ceiling intently.

"I know what happened to the little girl," he said, stopping short as he too looked at the ceiling.

Written across the ceiling in crimson was the message.

To gain power, two will become one, both parties combining strengths, weaknesses, hopes, dreams and above all – fears.

Arok clamped his mouth shut, confused by the cryptic message, and openly stared at Lyrium, who looked down to him and simply shook her head, muttering, "Stefan."

The two ran from the room and into the one their friend had chosen. They froze in their haste when they saw Stefan standing in the centre of the room, hunched over, with a gaping wound in his side. He was bleeding heavily and surrounded by countless hovering knives, their blades all pointed at him.

The short blades were similar to one another and more importantly, their hilts were identical to the one that protruded from the young girl.

"Don't make any sudden moves. These knives appear to have an attitude problem whenever their prey moves," Stefan spluttered with a poor attempt at a joke.

The blades started quivering at the entrance of Lyrium and Arok, as if daring them to move again. Their steel glinted in the unexplained light of the room. Only one of the knives had its shine dimmed from dripping blood. That was the one responsible for Stefan's wound.

Lyrium let the scene sink in until it was clear in her mind. Her body moved instinctively into the circle of floating daggers to stand tall with Stefan as Arok protested to his lover in vain. Lyrium looked around at the blades, which were still trained on Stefan as if ignoring her entirely. Arok reached out to grab her shoulder and the knives shuddered violently, forcing him back. When Lyrium spoke, her voice was filled with confidence and authority. She spoke with conviction.

"That's enough! This is my trial and my nightmare! Only I deserve your judgement – nobody else! You plagued my sleep all through my childhood and returned to haunt me as a woman. I understand that this is a curse I am to bear for whatever reason, but I will not stand for you hurting others!" she screamed, her voice elevating as her anger grew.

The daggers ignored her, shaking slightly whenever Stefan drew a shuddering breath. After what seemed like hours, the blades simultaneously shifted from targeting Stefan to her. She smiled to herself, indicating that Stefan was to leave with a shake of her head. Hesitantly, the wounded man stumbled to the door.

Arok caught him, sitting him leaning against the doorframe and passing him bandages from his hip bag so he could dress his wound. His hurt companion took the bandages and began to tentatively wrap them around his waist. Arok gratefully returned to watching Lyrium, who was staring down the deadly blades.

"We will get you out," Arok called.

"No, these blades want blood and I won't have anyone

suffer my curse," Lyrium replied firmly.

"But if you –" Arok began.

"No buts! This is my burden," Lyrium said before addressing the daggers once more. "Do your worst."

Arok let out a howl of anguish as he saw the blades flash forward towards his love. Arok's cry was cut short as he rushed inside and saw the daggers halt in midair. The standoff started over, with Lyrium forcing a deep breath to steady her nerves. The points of the blades pricked at her skin as the air filled her lungs. She could feel droplets of blood escaping from a couple of places on her chest, and she resorted to shallow breathing.

Each of their sharp points was now less than half an inch from her body. They held their position in the air briefly before dropping to the ground in a clatter of steel to stone. Arok embraced his surprised lover tightly, thankful for whatever mercy had been shown. Lyrium stood wordless – she was alive. Stefan shuffled out of the way, resting himself against the wall beside the door.

He was shirtless with bandages wrapped around his waist that were already stained with blood, but otherwise he seemed fine. He grimaced and announced that it was time for rest before taking out a modest amount of timber from his backpack along with a flint. Within a few moments he had created a small fire. Arok set Lyrium down across from him so the three were all facing the fire but capable of seeing a full circle around their makeshift camp.

As the fire came to life and Stefan sat back in position, Arok looked towards his companions who, like him, were letting the situation sink in. Stefan was wounded. Not fatally, but enough to slow him down. Lyrium had almost lost her life in sacrifice. She obviously knew more about what was going on in the horror show they were experiencing than either of the men.

Then there was himself, unharmed, but scared out of his wits. No conversation was had for a long while. Stefan slowly stood, asking Lyrium for the cast iron pan to cook some of the meat he had from the village. He received no more acknowledgement than her reaching behind her into her pack and tossing it towards him. Their morale was low, their fears were soaring, and they had no idea how much more was expected of them.

CHAPTER 41

A DARK WIND BLOWS

Katarina soared down towards the ground at a speed that her body would have easily given out under, if she hadn't been protected by the stone's energy. She could see the dark energy of her enemy in her mind, shining like a twisted light. As the shimmering beacon came into focus, she noticed that it didn't feel inherently evil. Violent and dangerous, yes.

But not evil.

In her rage and fury, she still managed to sense the calm of the Vassal. Surely she could feel Katarina's approach by now, yet she made no attempt to prepare, move or even flee.

This is what she wants! Fine then!

Katarina had noticed that the main gates of Neibel-Haven had been broken through; the enemy was inside. But instead of going to investigate, she continued to the main source of the chaos.

Her strategy was simple: kill the enemy before it could kill her people.

My people? Katarina let the idea entertain her rage-driven mind for a single moment. She always felt this way about those she fought alongside. If only for the current battle, they were as one. It was a sobering thought. She realised that her concentration was waning. She slowed her descent as she approached the ground and saw the woman garbed in dark clothes.

She touched down gently, taking in the enemy before her. The woman was a little shorter than Katarina, perhaps in her early twenties. She was thin but not sickly so, with curves that most women would kill for. Her face was filled with sharp features, but they were relaxed, as if Katarina's presence was inconsequential. She wore a unique violet attire of an origin that Katarina couldn't place.

While no scholar, Katarina had spent some time researching warfare and, more specifically, armies throughout history. Seeing a woman dressed like the one before her made her stomach twist. Either Katarina's research was lacking, or the woman before her hailed from a military force she knew nothing about.

The only thing that seemed animated on her face were her crimson eyes, analysing Katarina. She was taking in everything about her opposition just as Katarina was doing to her. The difference being that the leader of the invasion was giving away nothing of her feelings. With the atrocities taking place around her, Katarina couldn't hide the venom in her voice when she addressed her enemy.

"You are about to meet your end, Dark One," Katarina spat. "I hope coming here was worth it!"

"So, there was another; I thought as much," the Vassal of Darkness said, uncaring. "A shame that I missed out on seizing the other one as well. But you will make my trip well worth it."

"Who are you? What is your goal by gathering these stones?" Katarina asked bluntly.

"There is no point in hiding my name. I am Lyndell. As for why we are gathering the stones, you will know soon enough as you will be returning with me," Lyndell replied in an indifferent tone, to which Katarina smirked.

"Oh really?" she began incredulously. "If that's what you think will happen here, you are going to be disappointed."

Lyndell's eyebrows raised a fraction, the first sign of interest she had shown since the beginning of their conversation.

"Are you are electing to resist?"

"You have no idea what you are in for," Katarina replied confidently.

"I see. Answer me this, then." Lyndell started to look at Katarina in curiosity. "I've seen you fight now, and I realise that you are most likely the only Vassal, aside from myself, that has managed to control their power to this extent. Any others – even if they have found their stones – would be as feeble as babies. With such power at your command, why resist me without a clue what I hope to accomplish?"

"Because I will not stand by and let innocents be slaughtered. I may not know your goal in full, but your methods are cruel and brutal," Katarina replied without hesitation.

"Do you speak for the other Vassal as well?" Lyndell had returned to her apathetic tone.

"I don't know what she will do, and I dare not speak for her. But with my sisters by my side I will always stand for what is right," Katarina replied viciously, her vision narrowing to focus solely on her enemy.

"Sisters . . ." Lyndell repeated the word without emotion.

Lyndell stared at Katarina for a moment, letting her words sink in. If the words had any effect Lyndell still showed no reaction. Before long, she simply shrugged, raising her hands. Dark purple mist coursed down her arms while Katarina reached into her mind to ensure the connection to her stone's power was secure.

The connection sizzled in response and Katarina drew the energy to the surface. Its power sparked and blazed within, her personal tornado whipping up and lashing out at both her enemy and the side of the mountain. Within seconds, stray dirt and small rocks were lifted into the air and flung away from their home.

"You better make this more interesting than the feeble attempts from the mages," Lyndell called out, her voice louder but no more enthused by the proceedings.

"Trust me, I'll alleviate some boredom!" Katarina replied, excitement growing within her as she took her combat-ready stance, lifting and pointing her blade directly at her enemy. Her slender blade shone with thin but concentrated energy designed to cut through her enemies.

Lyndell raised her fists up, as if preparing herself for a fist fight. Katarina realised that something within her had awoken, something she never thought existed. She had the vicious desire to kill her opponent.

❖

Katarina struck first, channelling her energy to lunge directly at Lyndell, her sword's tip aimed at her enemy's chest. Lyndell disappeared in a purple flash a split second before the blade could make contact. Her energy reregistered in Katarina's mind to her left. Her head jerked towards the energy to see Lyndell with her hand encased in darkness ten yards away. Katarina barely had enough time to duck out of the way of a blast of purple light.

She launched herself towards her enemy once more, this time slashing quickly in a flurry designed to keep her opponent off-balance. Her opponent effortlessly matched Katarina's speed, weaving under and around each unpredictable slash from the enchanted blade. The pair moved off the dirt path and onto the steep mountainside, dancing over large stones and other natural obstacles as Katarina launched swing after vicious swing at the evading enemy. Their movements were a blur to the untrained eye.

The only respite from swinging her deadly blade was when Lyndell managed to put distance between them. Katarina would alter the wind around her to project herself forward and close the gap. Katarina pressed her target, forcing Lyndell back until she stood on a lip of the mountainside with a drop of sixty feet behind her. Lyndell was trapped, and Katarina took the opportunity to lunge towards her.

Her assault was bought to an abrupt halt when Lyndell raised her hand into Katarina's overhead swing, the dark energy from her hand clashing with the wind-infused blade. The mountainside reverberated with a thunderclap as the two elements collided. Lyndell drew upon the energy from the dark stone to her free hand and thrust her fist into the heart of Katarina's thinning personal vortex. Her dark energy pressed against the light – launching the swordswoman into the air away from the brawler.

Katarina latched onto the stone's energy, her tornado exploding to life around her feet. Her erratic trajectory stabilised, bringing her to a standstill in mid-air. She was unharmed physically but had felt a drain on her mind as the stone tried to give more to compensate. But even it had limitations and she had already expended a large amount of its reserves.

Lyndell sent forth another blast of dark energy towards her. Katarina dodged it easily but her opponent had used that moment to disappear again. She searched for her energy with her mind but found nothing.

Her search ended when she felt a menacing presence close to her.

Too close!

Before she could react, Lyndell descended from above her, piercing her vortex with a palm infused with dark energy. The two magical forces clashed again, the darkness ripping down the layers of magical protection that Katarina desperately tried to rally. She was forced towards the ground. She caught a glimpse of Lyndell before disappeared from existence again – a shadowy outline of her frame lingering briefly.

Katarina had no time to comprehend what she had seen as she collided with the ground, her magic only partially cushioning the blow. Her vortex vanished, along with her magic defences – she had exhausted her supply. She groaned in pain as she tried to get to her feet, only to receive a vicious kick in the side for her effort that sent her back to the ground. In the haze of red blanketing her eyes, she saw Lyndell standing over her with the same impassive expression as before.

"You are fast, and clearly well trained," Lyndell conceded. "But you are sorely lacking in other areas. I'm disappointed. But, Lucian did request that Vassals be brought before him if possible; it is not my place to question him."

"Over my dead body," Katarina spat. *Lucian . . . So, we were right . . .*

"No, he prefers the idea of you alive I'm afraid. This would be a lot simpler if not. Keep resisting and you may just get your wish," Lyndell replied dryly.

Katarina was about to snarl back but was stopped by a fierce assault on her mind. She felt an invading presence and immediately attempted to fight it off, rallying her remaining energy to combat the unknown force. It felt like a migraine instantly settling into her head. As it pressed through her defences with ease, she recognised it as the same energy Lyndell emitted every time she struck out at her during their battle.

She is consuming my mind. Impossible! she thought.

"Stand!" Lyndell commanded, and Katarina followed against her will, slowly getting to her feet, all the while attempting to force herself back to the ground. Her body refused to follow her command.

The dark energy lingering in her mind felt like searing venom, burning the very essence of her being and spreading quickly. She could feel it making its way to the back of her consciousness where the connection to the stone was resting. As the invader's influence coursed deeper, the connection's resistance flared. The union between her and the stone sparked violently once again. A brilliant flash of green emitted from behind her eyes, and it went dark. Steadily, her vision returned, revealing a room void of light.

The darkness had to be unnatural. When she looked down she could make out her body as easily as if she had been standing in the midday sun. Her location finally dawned on Katarina. The perpetual bleakness, the dissolving of her physical surrounds – the only other person there being her enemy. She was trapped inside her own mind. The Vassal of Darkness had succeeded.

"Get out of my mind!" Katarina yelled fiercely at Lyndell, who was wearing a mildly confused look.

"Hush, weakling." Lyndell dismissed the outburst with a wave as she looked around herself before spotting something behind Katarina of interest. "Ah, so you two are the reason."

Katarina spun around to see what had caught her enemy's attention. She found herself staring straight at Amelia. Beside her, a head shorter than herself, was a petite girl, about sixteen. She had golden-blonde hair curling around her face that lit up her dark blue eyes and a wide grin strewn across her lightly freckled face as she walked alongside Amelia.

"Siena?" Katarina uttered the girl's name, unable to say anything further in the stupor that had taken hold of her.

"Katty!" the young girl addressed her sister cheerfully, skipping forward to embrace the bewildered woman. "I can't believe you are actually here!"

"Well, we are within her mind, so it makes sense," Amelia said, rolling her eyes even though she was clearly pleased by the reunion. Lyndell sniffed derisively, but watched closely, arms crossed.

"How is this possible? How are you two here?" Katarina asked as Siena reluctantly let her go. "I watched you die, Amelia! I've watched you both –"

"We have been here all along, Katty! Well, I have been – Amelia only arrived a short time ago," Siena said, cutting Katarina's denial.

"It appears that when we died, our consciousness took refuge within the stone, Sis," Amelia explained. "So now we dwell within the stone, alongside the guardian."

"The guardian? You mean the one who spoke to us when we first found the stone?" Katarina asked.

"The very same. It seems we were doing the right thing all along, searching for the stones and their bearers. Now you must continue what we started."

"I'm afraid you won't be doing that at all," Lyndell finally interjected from behind Katarina. Kat had almost forgotten she was even there.

"We will help you, Katty!" Siena said cheerfully. "She won't get through all three of us."

"Siena is right," Amelia agreed. "We will help drive her from your mind. Now that we have found a way to communicate with you from the stone, we will be able to help. You must continue."

The room began to dissolve. Katarina's sight returned, showing the battle-worn landscape. She could see the smouldering mass of the deceased Talice amongst the scorched and torn mountainside. She could hear voices in the distance, indistinct though they were. Lyndell, who was once standing over her, appeared to be recoiling from her prey with a confused and pained expression. She stumbled away from Katarina, who felt control of her body returning. Lyndell cursed under her breath.

Katarina's body felt exhausted, her mind even more so. Her side ached from the sharp kick that Lyndell had delivered earlier, and her abdomen felt tight and bruised from when her enemy had sent her flying. Her head pounded fiercely, but she felt able to fight once more, however feebly. She cursed the chainmail's ineffective protection as she rubbed her side and stood shakily.

Lyndell, however, seemed to have recovered, although she didn't look uninterested as she did before; instead she looked tired. Her eyes narrowed at her enemy, searching for a weakness to exploit. Katarina could sense the malice, but she could see the hesitance in her opponent's stance.

"You still won't win this. You can't keep up with me and I'll just break your body until you succumb to your fate," she snarled.

She is right . . . Katarina thought, disheartened.

No need to be so down about it, Katty! Siena's voice rang through Katarina's mind.

Siena?

Yes, I'm here, and yes, if you keep going like this she will destroy you. You're giving her the advantage!

What are you talking about? Katarina asked, her eyes instinctively searching the landscape for the sister who wasn't there.

She moves so quickly because she is a master of the darkness . . . and strangely enough there's big old clouds covering the battlefield in shadows! It's like you want *her to win!*

Siena is right. Have the clouds disperse and she will find her disappearing act ineffective. You won't have that draining on your reserves either, Amelia's calm voice joined Siena's one of excitement.

Katarina looked up to the clouds she had forgotten about, and sensed her connection to them. The adrenaline from battle masked the exhaustion, but when she focused on them she could tell it was indeed a massive drain. As she severed the connection, she was immediately offered some relief. Her senses picked up along with the steady disappearance of the clouds.

Lyndell's scowl disappeared as she looked up curiously at the sky. Her face whitened slightly as the clouds let through the dying light of the sun.

"Hmph, you worked it out? It's irrelevant," Lyndell said, her body starting to glow in a sinister purple aura.

Katarina prepared her exhausted body and mind, drawing on her remaining energy when Lyndell stiffened, her head jerking towards the gates of the city. Katarina strained her ears to hear anything, but the effort wasn't required when she heard the booming voice of Mordrik, magically projected across the landscape.

"KATARINA! WE ARE COMING! HOLD ON!" came the succinct message.

Lyndell seemed in conflict with herself, unsure how to act. It was at that moment that Katarina realised what had happened.

"Heh, was the gamble to seize me worth losing your men?" Katarina asked triumphantly.

"Quiet, insect!" Lyndell hissed, as she produced the crystal she used for communication, muttering into it, "We have failed," before placing it back in her satchel and taking out a second stone.

This one's violet surface was alive with dark crawling tendrils racing through the confines. The stone seemed filled with shadows of countless snakes slithering through an ominous mist.

The stone may have had a foreboding aura and looked

completely different to her own, but Katarina knew exactly what she was looking at. The elemental Stone of Darkness. Lyndell channelled her energy into her hand, firing off a blast behind her, away from Katarina. The light erupted into a doorway swirling with dark shadows. The Vassal of Darkness made her way towards it wearing a smirk.

"Well done, fellow Vassal. But this is far from over. It's only a matter of time before you wind up like the Vassal of Light. Do not squander the time you have bought."

With that, Lyndell stepped through the dark doorway, which disappeared instantly. Katarina was alone and exhausted when Mordrik, along with a squad of mages, found her seconds later.

CHAPTER 42

TO FACE ONE'S FEARS

"It's from a nightmare I had almost every night through my childhood," Lyrium voiced around the party's small camp, breaking the silence that had fallen over them. They'd taken turns at sleep, broken though it was. Arok looked at her questioningly as Stefan shifted uncomfortably, his attention focused on Lyrium. "I'd walk into a long corridor full of doorways that led to identical rooms. It took me a while to place it. But when I saw the little girl playing under that tree, I knew the dream had become real."

Stefan nodded slowly, trying to understand. Arok, however, was not so calm.

"What are you talking about? We're fighting nightmares now? What kind of sick game is this?" he berated Lyrium, his voice rising in volume with each question.

Lyrium paused, waiting for Arok to calm before answering slowly.

"It makes sense, really. This is supposed to be a trial to see if I'm worthy of the stone's power, which means facing that which scares me."

"Aye, I got that. What I don't get is how we are supposed to fight a nightmare. Nightmares aren't real!" Arok insisted, thumping his fist on the stone floor.

"I have a wound that would indicate otherwise," Stefan said curtly before turning to Lyrium. "Do you remember how the nightmare ends?"

"That's the scary part. Every night that I was forced to face this, I entered the nightmare with the knowledge of what had happened in the past times. It let me change my actions each time."

"I think I understand. Did the outcome ever change?" Stefan asked, brushing his long fringe from his eyes.

"It changed slightly, but usually with my death," Lyrium answered.

"Your death? If that's the only outcome, we may as well leave now!" Arok yelled.

"I said that's how it *usually* ended. I said to look for a book earlier. The last time I ever had the nightmare, I had found the book and inside it was an incantation that banished the little girl and with her – all of this," Lyrium explained, brandishing her hand around.

"Why don't we just move on?" Arok gestured to the door at the end of the corridor. "We don't need this, we only need to find the stone. So why not just keep moving?"

"If you approach the door at the end of the corridor before laying your trial to rest, you will find only death. The death of a coward. It is inscribed on the door in my nightmare," Lyrium replied, reciting something she had read countless times as a child. "That's what is written on the door at the end. I once tried to run past and it was terrifying – never again."

The three sat tensely, allowing the gravity of the situation to sink in. Lyrium had fallen silent at the recollection of something horrible that she seemed uninterested in sharing.

The trio didn't look at each other, each lost in their own thoughts. It was Stefan who finally spoke first.

"Forgive me if I am wrong, but this isn't a problem," he said as Lyrium and Arok stared at him. He raised his hand to Arok, who looked ready to object. "Let me finish. This is no different to hunting for game. We have a target. Basically, we need to find this book that Lyrium told us about. It is most likely residing behind one of these doors."

He waved his hand in the air, gesturing at the wooden frames surrounding the party.

"The danger is great, that is true. Perhaps we shouldn't have separated but the fact is, if we don't find that book, we may as well turn back now and give up on the stone altogether. And, if we do that, what's to stop the ruins from disappearing again?"

"Stiff is right, sitting here griping solves nothin'," Arok added thoughtfully as he got to his feet and stuffed the last of his share of meat into his mouth. Lifting his mighty war hammer onto his shoulder, he asked, "How's your wound, Stiff? Are you right to keep going?"

Stefan responded by slowly rising, wincing in pain as his body stretched. He carefully stood straight, looking down at his bandaged side and nodding. Lyrium leapt to her feet. Stepping forward and stamping out the remains of the small fire under her crude boot, she turned to her companions and addressed them in a voice thick with emotion.

"You two have come here with me at your own risk. You both know that one or all of us could die. Stefan has taken a knife and Arok has been possessed."

Lyrium looked both of her companions in the eye in turn,

her own filled with gratitude. "I wouldn't have got this far without you two. I would have been killed or lost my mind in this nightmare. This trial isn't about me, it's about us and the world outside of these damned ruins. I thank you both."

"Ah, stop it, Lyrium. I'm going to get weepy," Arok laughed as the other two joined in mirth.

"So, let's try another of these doors," Stefan said after the laughter had passed and the trio started walking to the next unopened door in the corridor. Arok grasped the doorknob and turned it without hesitation.

"Too right, Stiff. We know what we came to do and we didn't come to die," Arok declared as they entered the next room.

The trio marched into the room and went about searching it as they always did – Stefan at the wardrobe, Arok under the bed and Lyrium to the window. The room was as they expected and, despite the fact that the trio had become accustomed to the similar surroundings, it made them no less uneasy. They searched the room over and over, steadily becoming more anxious and unnerved by the minute.

The difference within the room seemed to be that there was no 'difference' at all. For the first time since finding the ominous corridor filled with nightmares, they appeared to have found a normal room. A normal, ordinary bedroom that happened to be identical to the other haunted ones.

In some ways, this room being normal is worse than the others, Lyrium thought grimly. *At least the others were obvious in their differences.*

After checking their respective areas, they had swapped locations in hope of seeing anything that the others may have missed. But the music box remained silent, there were no floating knives, and the young girl seemed to have no interest in making another appearance. The trio didn't know whether to be relieved or troubled. They weren't in any immediate danger, but they weren't getting anywhere.

"Alright, what's the joke?" Arok finally asked, frustrated.

"This room appears clean," Stefan offered.

"No, there is more to this room. I know it," Lyrium said, as the two men turned to stare at her. "We are close, I just can't remember what it was about this room that was so important."

"Very well then, take your time," Stefan said, sitting on the bed so not to overexert himself or antagonise the wound too much. His eyes continued searching. "We will stay here until we decipher what this room is hiding."

Arok and Lyrium started their rounds again. Lyrium checked behind the door and Arok attempted to open the music box. They spent another half hour searching before Arok's impatience got the best of him and he spat, "This is ridiculous! Is this a test? We have to search a room for something we don't even know exists?"

"Lyrium thinks something is here, so we need to –" Stefan cut off mid-sentence, his eyes staring dead ahead at the stone wall next to the window.

"What is it, Stiff?" Arok asked impatiently.

"That wall . . . It's different," Stefan muttered, tilting his head with interest.

"What are you –?" Arok was cut off by Lyrium exclaiming excitedly.

"That's it! Well done, Stefan!" She raced across the room to the wall and traced her fingers across its surface. The smooth stone was cool to touch, slowly giving way to a grainy texture as she ran her fingertips across it. Small amounts of sand and dust fell away at her touch and she knew what was beneath.

She dug at the stone with her nails, steadily raking away with small rocks and mortar that stuck beneath her nails. Noticing thin trails of her blood on the hole, she switched to the small knife at her side. With a fierce thrust, she drove the blade into the brittle stone. With a few quick stabs at the wall she'd accomplished more than she had with her fingers. The two men walked up behind her, watching as Lyrium's efforts redoubled at the sight of something within. After a while she stopped, placing her knife away and turning to her companions with a crimson book in her hands.

"We have our weapon. Now, let's find the girl," Lyrium said, voice full of determination.

"The answer is within?" Stefan asked curiously. "Perhaps we should study the contents?"

Lyrium shook her head as she handed the book to Stefan, who immediately tried, and failed, to open it. The covers remained firmly closed despite how hard he tried to pry them apart.

"It's the bloody box all over again, eh?" Arok grunted.

"Let's find the girl," Lyrium repeated, taking back the book and heading for the door.

❖

The trio moved swiftly to the three remaining unopened rooms. Each paused with their hand on the knob of their chosen door.

"Remember, we are only trying to find her at this point in time. Do NOT confront her alone," Lyrium warned the other two. The men nodded as the three of them simultaneously turned the doorknobs and stepped inside their elected room.

Lyrium took a step into the room, stopping to stare at the sight before her. Sitting on the bed, cross-legged and smiling widely, was the small girl. She was clutching her ragdoll in one hand while the other waved in a friendly manner.

"Greetings. I trust you have made yourself at home in these halls?" the girl greeted in a sickeningly sweet tone as Lyrium's grip on the book tightened. "I wouldn't attempt that if I were you, as I only wish to speak to you right now."

Against her better judgement, Lyrium eyed the girl closely, waiting for her to continue.

"You have come a long way from the frightened child whose nightmares I once plagued. How you have grown," the girl stated.

Her tone was similar to that of a child, yet her words were those of an adult. Her demeanour was a stark contrast against the childish mannerisms and there was the ever-present aura of an older woman, perhaps older than Lyrium herself. Lyrium knew that she was not speaking to a young girl despite the facade in front of her.

"Who are you?" Lyrium asked.

"Shouldn't you of all people know the answer to that? I am dreamt up by you, after all," she replied.

"No, you are not a just a dream anymore. You are real, and very dangerous. Stefan learnt that the hard way," Lyrium pressed.

"Yes, your companion was foolish enough to think he could handle it all on his own. He got what he deserved. What you are overlooking, however, is that you could have fared a lot worse than you did when you put on that bravado. I could have ended your life. I could have ended you all," the girl grinned with a villainous smile.

"Then why didn't you? Answer my questions. Who *are* you? Why are you down here? Remember, the power to finish this is in my hands now," Lyrium replied with a wave of the book.

"Ah, yes, the book. My book, in fact. I'd like it returned," the girl said, suddenly serious as she held out her hand. A small click came from within Lyrium's hand. The book's enchantment had released at its owner's presence. Just as she'd expected.

"Forget it, kid. This book was my only way out in my dreams. Nothing you say will make me part with it!" Lyrium replied with conviction.

"Oh, but as you said – this isn't a dream anymore. You haven't grasped anything at all in your time down here, have you?" the girl replied condescendingly. "The dining room in the chamber above, and now the nightmare in this one. Have you forgotten when this was set in motion?"

"The dead would-be Chief said something about setting up this trial for me. But you won't trick me. Ever since I stepped into these twisted ruins my resolve to see this trial through to the end has grown, regardless of what that end may be." Lyrium's jaw tightened as the measured words left her lips.

"I see you are still under the assumption that this only started when these ruins appeared. Why don't you tell me what Surok and I have in common, hmm?" The girl tilted her head in curiosity.

"You are both pains in my arse that just won't quit!" Lyrium yelled, although the girl could see the uncertainty in her eyes.

"It seems you're determined to deny the facts for the sake of it," the girl snickered. "I, along with Surok, have been waiting for your arrival, longer than your life itself. Our role was to test your character before you reach the stone."

"I'm not going to trust you, so quit it," Lyrium scoffed. She was scared, but also ready to fight the girl with her bare fists out of frustration.

"Caution is all well and good, and at most times advised. However, if you never take a risk, you will get nowhere," the girl replied cryptically. "I assume you will not be returning the book then?"

"No, the book is mine now," Lyrium snarled before leaning out of the room and calling, "Arok! Stefan! I found her!"

Lyrium turned her attention back to the girl, who was climbing off the bed. She shook her head, muttering something about "hoping it wouldn't come to this". Lyrium quickly backtracked into the corridor, watching the girl closely as she advanced. Lyrium's head jerked up to see Stefan hobbling towards her. His eyes widened as he saw the girl emerge from the doorway. He halted his advance and grimaced in pain as he unclipped his bow, nocked an arrow and aimed directly at the girl.

As Lyrium was about to call out to Arok again, she spotted him running as fast as he could from his room. His face was filled with terror as he called. "Something is coming!"

From the room that he had chosen came a peculiar shadow

spilling from the doorway, clinging to the ground and spreading rapidly across the stone floor in pursuit of the man. As if called, more of the tenebrous shadows leaked from the doorframes of the other rooms, steadily gliding across the floor and clinging to the walls. Its bleakness was expanding at an alarming rate and in a few short moments all of the doorways – including the entrance and exits – were covered in the inky blackness. Arok stumbled out of the way as a stray shadow made its debut from one of the rooms. He glimpsed the room's interior, now deprived of the unnatural light it housed moments before.

Lyrium turned to the girl, who was smiling with a false innocence, only this time the expression came with a tinge of cruelty that wasn't there earlier.

"Lyrium! The book!" Arok cried.

Nodding, she opened the book to see pages lined with characters she had never seen before. It was a different language entirely, and she couldn't read a word of it. *This wasn't in the dreams!* her mind screamed as despair took hold.

"I don't know what it says!" Lyrium cried. "I can't read it!"

"Then we take her out the traditional way!" Stefan snarled, letting fly his readied arrow. The projectile sailed straight and true towards the girl.

The girl's head snapped towards the incoming threat and she smiled as a stone from the wall behind her flew from its home. The solid chunk collided with the arrow, making it ricochet to the ground as the stone remained hovering in the air.

Arok reached the girl at that moment and swung his mighty war hammer in an overhead assault. In response, he received the stone that had blocked Stefan's arrow straight into his stomach before he could bring the weapon down. The force lifted him half a foot into the air before he crashed to the floor violently. His lungs emptied of air, as if a pair of hands gripped and tightened around them.

"She knows a few tricks!" wheezed Arok painfully.

"Perhaps, but look! The shadows have retreated!" Stefan cried. His observation proved true; the shadows had retreated, but were now starting their approach once more. "If we distract her, she can't keep control of them!"

Arok pulled himself to his feet. "Easier said than done, Stiff. Lyrium! Any luck?"

"Just keep her busy!" Lyrium yelled back, frustrated as she flipped through the book, looking for anything that she remembered from her dream.

"You only delay your own demise," the girl said in a sickening tone designed to be cute. "Are you ready? *Gladirus: Stoardus Vercres!*"

More stones dislodged themselves from the wall behind her and started to circle her form mid-air. Her small frame was barely visible through the vortex of rocks. Lyrium's head jolted up at the word *"Gladirus"* and the scene in front of her.

"I know what I'm looking for! Just a little longer!"

The men nodded grimly, steeling themselves as Lyrium started flipping through the book with renewed vigour. The girl could be heard laughing as a stone the size of the head on Arok's weapon shot out at Stefan. His prior injury slowed him and a cry of excruciating pain escaped his lungs to fly freely through the hall – a perfect pitch to complement the cruel mirth coming from the little girl.

Another stone was slung from the vortex towards Arok. The

heat of the moment took hold as he swung upwards, heaving his massive weapon from the ground. Its head met the stone and shattered it into shards, which spread across the corridor. The moment of glory was dismissed by the wielder as he ran to his injured friend.

"Stiff! Get up, it's coming –" Arok's attention turned to the shadows creeping ever closer to his wounded friend, a mere yard away and steadily closing in.

"I can't!" Stefan spluttered from his kneeling position. His blonde hair was strewn everywhere as he clutched his arm. "My shoulder, it's crushed."

Blood had already soaked his companion's green tunic, staining it a dark red tinge. Stefan's arm was removed completely from its socket, branching away from the rest of his body as if it didn't belong to it at all. Arok's eyes darted over to the vortex of stones that was concealing the little girl before attempting to pick up his friend. The effort was met with heavy protest that was promptly ignored.

With Stefan under one arm and his war hammer in his spare hand, Arok carried both back towards the fray, away from the shadows. All the while, the little girl laughed maniacally and launched another volley of stones at the indisposed pair.

"Aye, I wager this'll hurt," Arok laughed morbidly.

Abandoning his weapon to gently lower his friend to the ground, he turned his back to the impending onslaught. His broad body loomed over Stefan's, a thick barrier of human flesh. The assault came in waves; the first was the lightest, barely making Arok flinch. Then the core of the barrage arrived and a dozen blunt impacts slammed into Arok's back as he struggled to stay upright. Despite the barrage that had torn his back open, not a sound of pain escaped his lips.

"Is that, is that – gah! That all ya got, little bitch?" he spat, gasping for air as his back throbbed with the sensation of being branded.

Despite his bravado, what he saw made his blood freeze. The girl had her hand raised above her head, the stones dancing above her. They were swirling faster than ever as she muttered under her breath inaudibly. After a second, she looked over at her prey and smiled cruelly. Her free hand rose and pointed towards the wounded pair as she opened her mouth once more.

"Gladirus: Virisal Grevara!"

Arok's eyes darted to Lyrium. She had shifted into in a wide stance and was shaking as if she was having difficulty just keeping herself upright. But her eyes held no fatigue as they burned into the little girl. The girl looked genuinely surprised before fear registered upon her face. The stones above her stopped, hovering in mid-air with an odd stillness. And then, they descended upon their master.

The stones were met by others ripped from the walls. They pressed into the little girl, encasing her entire body in the smooth rock, forcing a scream from her lips. The hard substance shifted in shape as it was needed to cover her features and her piercing shriek ceased as quickly as it started as the rock covered her mouth. At the end of the spell, a perfect stone statue of the girl was all that remained.

"What was that?" spluttered Arok.

"A spell. It's called the Dark Grave according to the book. It combines Dark and Earth Magic to bury the supernatural," Lyrium offered a vague description as she lowered herself into a sitting position. She noticed that all she held in her hand was loose ash; the red book had disintegrated.

Exhaustion devoured the disappointment of losing the book as the shadows disappeared and she lost consciousness. The toll of the magic was great, even with the assistance of the book. Arok raced over and, after realising she was only asleep, he laid her out, putting her pack under her head as a crude pillow and nodding.

"Rest, my love. I'll tend to Stefan," Arok said softly before returning to his friend. Concern returned as the man writhed in pain.

"Work with me, Stiff. You aren't going to die on me just yet," Arok said grimly as he reached into his friend's small satchel of medical supplies.

As the wounded man treated his injured friend as best he could, there was the soft click of a door unlocking at the corridor's end. Arok looked up at the sound and frowned, growling under his breath.

"Whatever is behind that door can wait until we are good and ready!"

CHAPTER 43

FROM PRINCESS TO MAGE

Wake up, Alicea. That is quite enough beauty sleep for one of my pupils, Garnet's voice entered the unconscious Princess' mind.

Alicea rolled over, attempting to ignore the crow at the end of her bed in the hope it would make her tutor leave her be.

You are my pupil, and a Princess no longer. Remember our agreement?

Alicea groaned, before telling Garnet to go away in her sleepy voice.

Very well, I suppose I'll allow you to sleep a little longer, Garnet replied in amusement before hopping off the bed rail.

The black bird bounced along the animal pelt mattress until she arrived at Alicea's face. Leaning her beaked face in slowly until it was an inch from the Princess' ear, she let out a loud shriek. The Princess' body jolted upright, eyes wide and etched with sleep, as Garnet flew away from her flailing arms. Alicea's blurred vision cleared to see Rufus doubled over in laughter. Her face turned to a look of angry betrayal as she noticed that even her own aqueous bird was squawking inaudibly as if amused. Getting her bearings, she snapped at Rufus.

"Mr. Thief! How dare you allow people to waltz into my room while I'm resting! What kind of guardian are you?"

"An amused one!" retorted Rufus, laughter making his body tremble more the more he tried to stifle it.

Even her pet had fluffed its water-made feathers up, hiding part of its head in fear. Alicea looked over to Garnet, who had positioned herself atop the doorway.

"Can I help you, Garnet?" Alicea asked.

Yes. Get dressed. Your training for the day is about to commence. Same place. I'll see you soon. With her message conveyed, Garnet took off, she circled the room once before flying out the window. Alicea sighed before looking at Rufus and sniping, "You are coming too, Mr. Thief. I'm going to enjoy learning new things at your expense."

Rufus' face dropped.

"I actually had planned to make a new hammock and catch up on my rest –"

"I don't remember giving you a choice, Mr. Thief! Now get out so I can get dressed!"

Rufus rolled his eyes and simply left the room, resigned to his fate for the day.

The pair breakfasted on meat and fruit that the hunters had supplied before setting out for the training field again. By the time they arrived, half an hour had passed since the Princess' abrupt wake-up call. Fortunately, she was in good spirits, smiling as she spoke to her liquid companion. It would respond by squawking silently or flapping its wings in confirmation as Rufus sighed and rolled his eyes in equal measures.

Garnet was sitting in her spot on the tree at the centre of the field. As they came closer, she underwent her transformation and although they had seen it before, it was no less of an amazing sight to them. By the time they had reached the tree, Garnet had donned the dress she left there and began speaking immediately.

"Very good, you have arrived," Garnet said as Rufus sat down with his back against the tree and closed his eyes again.

"Yesterday you demonstrated how to control your bird and while you did exceptionally well, its power is limited. You would have a hard time defeating anyone with that strategy should their focus be on you and not your bird. You'd stand next to no chance against multiple targets, or someone with the knowledge of you being a sorcerer. They would only have to attack you and break your concentration."

Garnet let her words seep into Alicea's mind before continuing.

"Today I'm hoping I can teach you how to draw from a magical object such as your stone for energy. But before that, we need to exhaust you a little. Walk with me."

Garnet led Alicea across the field to stand at the side of a deeper part of the stream, about two long strides across and deeper than the Princess was tall.

"You have great affinity with the element of water. Most people have an affinity with one or, in rare cases, multiple elements. Generally, most have very limited potential, even with their respective element, and most that find they have any real talent go north-east to Neibel-Haven for study. However, that option is not available to us right now as our first priority is gathering the bearers of the stones. It is a shame, as I feel you would flourish at the academy." Garnet's voice grew wistful for a moment before continuing. "My mentoring will have to do for now. I want you to reach out to the water you see in front of you as you did when taking control of your bird."

Alicea looked at Garnet blankly. "My bird has a consciousness, though. I'm not sure if I can command other water. The reason I can find my bird is because she calls to me as I call to her. We are in constant contact; I can feel her presence in my own mind. We are connected."

Garnet smiled understandingly. "The beauty of magic is the fact that if you know your elemental affinity, you can reach out to any source that is aligned with it. One who has an affinity with air feels a cool breeze much differently to a person aligned with, say, the Light element. But most wouldn't know they are experiencing it differently, as they grew up that way. Just like myself with Earth, and in turn, you with Water. Stretch out your mind to the water here like you would your bird, and give it a command."

Alicea looked doubtfully at the narrow stream in front of her before closing her eyes and doing as instructed – reaching into her own mind to find a now familiar energy in the back of her head, before concentrating on the water in front of her. Surprise registered as a peculiar feeling washed over her mind. It felt like an intrusion on her mind; it wasn't unpleasant, but refreshing. Once the connection was made, she opened her eyes and watched the liquid passing her closely.

She realised that the water had slowed its course – it wasn't moving through the stream as quickly. It was as if the liquid was waiting for an order from her. Alicea tried to think of a command suitable to show that she had control, but the water was already doing something.

If it's already doing something, what command can I give? . . . Stop!

The water came to a halt, the stillness spreading rapidly up the stream and branching off in all directions in its pursuit of the moving liquid. The water was steadily brought to heel until every drop visible was as still as ice.

Alicea looked at Garnet and smiled.

"I have control – oh my!" Alicea's face paled as an overwhelming drain took hold on her consciousness. Through the wave of fatigue, she heard Garnet yell, "Release it now!"

Alicea severed the connection with the water and immediately felt relief from the drain that had threatened her. She was barely standing and swaying in front of Garnet. Her eyes had erupted with the colour of sapphires at the surge of energy but were now flickering a pale grey. She looked as if she was about to pass out when some of her energy returned as suddenly as it had left. Though she felt relief from the refunded energy, she noted that not all of it came back.

She could feel that she had less reserves than she had started with, but she was able to stand and function again. It took her a second to realise that Garnet had a hand on her shoulder, steadying her student and eyeing her with concern.

"I didn't expect you to take control of the whole stream! That was unwise and I apologise. But this has shown that you have outstanding potential. For you to be able to grasp and control that much of your element, even for a second, is a feat to be proud of. It also had the desired effect. You now have a slightly better idea of your limits and what can happen if you abuse them," Garnet praised.

"What now?" Alicea asked groggily, gently pushing away her tutor's hand.

"Now you will do the exact same thing again," Garnet said curtly. "But this time you will attempt it with the stone's assistance."

"I see," Alicea nodded, unconvinced.

"It serves just as any other magical tool, the only difference being that it will only respond to you. As for how you will do it, you will simply connect with it as well," Garnet said, reassuring the confused Princess. "Perhaps I should explain further. You are able to connect your mind with multiple targets. Of course, the more connections you have, the more difficult it is to maintain each individual one. Fortunately, the connection with the stone is designed to give you strength, not to be manipulated. At least, that is my understanding. Now, try for yourself."

Under Garnet's instruction Alicea produced the stone from her pocket and stared at it cautiously before closing her eyes and reaching out to it with her mind. What she found was different to the connection with the water. It felt similar to when she connected with her bird. Then it hit her. An astounding amount of power forcefully pushed against her mind. Her thoughts clouded over, being consumed by the power. She tried to retract the connection but the stone had seized the other end and refused to let go.

Just as Alicea thought she would lose her very identity to the power of the stone, it let up, allowing her mind to think clearly once more. The two consciousnesses were beside each other in a strained harmony. Alicea uttered a gasp in alarm as the world around her began to change. Trees, streams and her tutor faded away, replace by something entirely different. The world vanished; whether it had gone elsewhere or she herself had changed location didn't matter.

She was standing in the middle of a surreal-looking body of liquid. It felt familiar, but it wasn't something to be recalled.

A pond? No, It's much too large. An ocean perhaps? Alicea pondered, unconvinced that was the correct answer either.

The liquid was unlike any known to her, with a shining silver hue that stretched for a short distance before being obscured by a light mist. What she assumed was water swirled around her hips as she slowly turned on the spot, taking in the sight before her.

Confused, the Princess began to panic before a familiar voice rang throughout the area. Though it sounded vocalised, it echoed within her mind.

Welcome, Young One. I apologise for overwhelming you in response to your attempt at connecting with me. It has been such a long time since anyone has been able to connect with me and it feels so very unfamiliar.

"You are the one I spoke to before!" the Princess exclaimed. "I recognise your voice! The one within the stone."

That's correct. You've adapted to the trials before you and you are doing well, Young One. Worry not, I will aid you in your training.

"Where am I? And who are you?" Alicea demanded.

Your inquisitive nature has made itself apparent once more, though I'm surprised that you cannot recognise this location for what it is. But it is not time for answers. You must focus on the tasks ahead, Young One. Eventually all will be clear.

"This isn't fair! You can't just simply instruct me on what to do!"

Very true. In fact, in this situation it is indeed you who is in control and I am the one who is commanded. My power is yours. As it stands, I am unable to supply you with the answers you desire. If you want them, then I suggest you follow your teacher and your heart. After all, it has lead you this far and it's what is inside you that has made you worthy of wielding my strength. Now, what will you do?"

"I will continue," Alicea replied with clenched teeth. She wanted nothing more than to ask more questions.

Yes, I assumed as much. You have a long way to go yet but you are more than entitled to my power. So, take it!

The vision around Alicea exploded with light. The water surrounding her dissipated away with the mist. Alicea found herself back at the training field and staring into the water. Her eyes were filled with determination as she turned to a concerned-looking Garnet.

"Is she alright?" Rufus called to Garnet from his place under the tree.

"Worry not!" Garnet called back, watching the focused Princess.

Alicea's consciousness lashed out at the water coursing in front of her. Her mind was ablaze with the two connections branching off in different directions, one to the stone and one to the river.

The stone connected with the stream as well, forming a powerful trinity in the Princess' mind. Electricity was coursing through her head and tying the three conduits together. The power of the stone was giving off a euphoric feeling of intense life within its master.

Her senses sharpened, ready for something more. She raised her hand, pointing at the water before calling out the command to it: "Rise and form!"

The water responded immediately, launching into the air. Liquid from along the stream systematically joined the rest of the substance, flying across the field and gathering in a massive sphere above both tutor and student. Garnet looked on in bewilderment as the Princess grinned like a maniac. The bed the water once rested in had turned bone-dry. The sphere started moving in odd angles, transforming before their very eyes as it began to take shape.

In the few seconds during the transformation, the swan upon Alicea's shoulder dove to the ground in curiosity before gazing up at a giant replica of itself.

Once its shape was complete, it fell from its elevated position, landing with a tremendous *thud* from impact. The great bird swung its head back, opening its mouth and sending a fierce jet of water into the air. It still held the youthful look of a cygnet, as it spread its wings outward in a glorious display of its expansive wingspan. It was clearly proud of its size and power. With a shake and puff of its chest, it coiled its long neck downwards to examine the Princess, who immediately burst into laughter.

It stood as tall as the trees circling the field with its neck turned down. The aura it gave off was one of strength. Alicea could feel its presence within her, much like she did with the smaller version. Grinning with pride, Alicea raised her hand and the magnificent bird allowed its master to pet its beak gently.

"ANOTHER DAMNED BIRD?!" came Rufus' distressed voice from behind the women, reigniting Alicea's laughter all over again.

Garnet turned her gaze from the phenomenon to Alicea.

"How do you feel?"

"A little fatigued, but overall I'm fine," Alicea shrugged. "I can feel a slight drain, but whenever it starts to get too much, the stone knows and lends me more strength."

"I understand." Garnet looked back at the giant bird and broke into a wide grin. "This is amazing! I've heard stories about the stone's power but this – the stories do not do justice. Release it now."

Alicea nodded, mentally severing the two connections. The bird erupted from the release, the water returning to the river and continuing its course. She felt her heightened senses return to normal, her body returning to her depleted of energy. Even with the stone's power, the drain on her body was considerable, and she hadn't even made the swan do anything. She needed more practise.

Alicea sat on the ground, her breath slightly ragged, and Garnet joined her.

"That was nothing short of incredible! It's not just the stone, either; you have a talent for this beyond any fledging mage. You have a long way to go but that was unimaginable progress. But, I do have to ask." Garnet took a breath. "Why another swan?"

"That's what I'd like to know. What gives, Princess?" Rufus said, throwing himself down beside her after approaching unnoticed. "The little bird is annoying enough. Don't think I'm going to play with a massive one as well."

"Oh, stop complaining, Mr. Thief," Alicea replied impatiently before turning to Garnet. "It's just its form. I tell it to take shape and that's what it becomes."

"Then when you gather your strength again, that will be

your next task. We have a good idea of how much power you have and it's exponential. It's just a matter of moulding it into a means of both attack and defence. Rest now. We will resume in one hour."

With that, Garnet got up and walked over to the tree. She reached behind it, producing a book from under one of its branches. Without another word, she sat and began to read. Alicea looked up at Rufus and smiled, the thief rolling his eyes in response.

"What do you want?" Rufus groaned.

"That's no way to speak to a lady, Mr. Thief. Heavens forbid I might want a civil conversation with the one I've been travelling with," came her swift response.

"I apologise, you're right. It's just been a tiring few days for everyone involved," Rufus replied in a slightly kinder tone. "What would you like to talk about, Princess?"

"That's better, Mr. Thief. I would like to discuss you going to get food from the village for me," Alicea said, laughing as Rufus got up and stalked towards the village, cursing the whole way there.

CHAPTER 44

THE FLEXIBILITY OF WATER

Alicea and Rufus were eating fruit that the thief had brought from the village when Garnet snapped her book shut and walked towards them. Rufus had grabbed a portion of dried meat for himself, but the Princess forced him to surrender it.

Garnet stood beside the pair as Rufus glared at the Princess nibbling happily on her prize.

"That's time enough for rest. Let's continue," she said briskly.

"Can we finish eating? What's the rush?" Alicea asked.

"We don't know when Lyrium and the others will emerge from the ruins and from what I can gather from the Chief and Setz, you have another task ahead of you once they do. I have to pass on as much knowledge as I can before then," Garnet stated to the disappointed Princess before sighing. "Fine, but listen while you eat.

"So far you have a decent grasp of the theory of magic. You can control it well enough, and you have a deeper energy pool than most others, even without the stone's assistance." Garnet paused a moment, as if considering her next words carefully. "And so, it is time we delve into the nature of water itself."

Garnet took a moment to gather her thoughts as Alicea reached over and swiped an apple from Rufus' pile of fruit.

"Water is the most flexible of all the elements. That means that while it is not as destructive as fire or wind, it can be moulded into many forms aside from the comfort zone of your bird. Which is exactly what we are going to experiment with." Garnet looked around before her eyes settled on a stump a dozen strides from where they were. She nodded. "That will be our target. I'll demonstrate, though my proficiency with water is rather limited."

Rufus and Alicea watched Garnet closely as she took a deep breath and muttered the words, *"Meilung: Impalu!"*

Some of the moisture on the ground from where Alicea's larger bird had erupted started to gather before levitating into the air. The liquid moulded into a small, hovering spear the same length as her arm. It shot forward, flying at the stump, impaling the tough bark and causing it to splinter around its new wound. The weapon remained firmly lodged within the wood.

Rufus nodded in appreciation of the new use for water before the magical spear reverted back to water droplets. Garnet rubbed her temples gently; it had been an effort for her to even accomplish the demonstration. Water Magic was not her forte.

"You will be required to imitate that as your next task. It will be a starting point for when you will have to show aggression. It's only basic like the rest I have shown you and any competent mage who saw it coming would be able to deflect it easily with their own energy. But it's the best starting point I can think of," Garnet said. "You will do it of your own accord; your energy alone should easily suffice. I expect someone so strongly aligned with water to be able to accomplish this task by dusk."

Alicea leapt to her feet, excited to begin. She hadn't seen water form into anything except for her birds and was eager, despite her distaste of sharp weapons. Closing her eyes, she searched for the moisture on the ground with her mind and found small glimmers of the water's essence. They were like glittering stars flecked across the otherwise dark backdrop of her consciousness as she gathered them. It proved successful: the water lifted from the ground into a small sphere. Alicea ordered the water to change form as she held the image of a spear in her head.

The sphere seemed to struggle with the idea, agitated as it started to ripple violently, before the demand on energy hit Alicea's mind and the sphere exploded in a shower. The sudden force left Alicea gasping for air as her head whirled painfully.

"What happened?" Alicea asked between gulps of air.

"A lack of practice happened. Again!" Garnet ordered harshly.

"But it doesn't want to change!" Alicea protested.

"It doesn't *want* anything! It will bend to your will. Picture the weapon you want to create in your mind as you feed it energy. Now, again!" Garnet ordered once more.

Alicea tried to form the spear again. She arrived at the same point in the spell when the sphere revolted and erupted again. Garnet pushed her to repeat it again and again until the sun started to set, bathing the sky in its crimson beauty. Its appeal was lost on the exhausted Princess as she forced herself to project her mind outwards, grab hold of the water and try to force it to change shape before failing each time.

The closest thing to success she achieved was forming the water into a wobbly and unstable stick before she, and the water, collapsed from the effort. When it failed for the eighty-ninth time, she threw herself on the ground in anger and exhaustion.

From his place sprawled out on the green grass enjoying the last rays of the warm sun, Rufus suggested, "Why don't you just tell the bloody bird to do it? Be nice if it did something useful for once."

Alicea glanced over at her relaxed companion sceptically before looking directly at her bird. The cygnet was sleeping on a tree trunk a few feet away. Sleeping seemed a ridiculous activity for a magical bird. The Princess stretched out her arm and beckoned towards her pet.

The bird awoke at the movement and flew over to its master, resting on the outstretched arm, its transparent eyes curiously staring at Alicea.

"Can you do that? Are you able to change form?" she asked it kindly.

"It can't talk!" Rufus snapped, sitting upright. "Can it turn into a damned spear or not?" Alicea stood, ignoring Rufus' outburst and pointed at the stump. She reached out to the bird's consciousness with her own and pointed at the stump before issuing the mental order:

"Change and strike!"

All eyes were on the tiny bird for a long moment before the Princess slumped back down in a heap, disappointed by its lack of change. The bird jumped from the Princess' arm and curled up in her lap. Alicea sighed sadly and looked up at the setting sun.

I can't even accomplish a basic task like this one. What hope do I stand of ever changing anything?

Rufus knelt down beside the Princess, his hand on her shoulder. The touch made her jump before realising who it was. The colour of her eyes had become an indication to the thief of how she was feeling at any given moment. If they were shimmering like sunlight reflecting off the surface of the ocean, she was happy. They turned the colour of sapphires in a dark room when she was manipulating magical energy – or screaming at him. It always had him on edge when they turned dark blue.

But when there was more grey than cerulean, it meant that sadness was eating at her. It had taken him a while to realise it; it was only on the last few nights of their journey to Tremel that he'd put the pieces together. The most frequent trigger of the grey hue of the Princess' eyes was when she was silent and fondling the small rose pendant around her neck – her mother's necklace.

"I'm a failure, Mr. Thief. What hope do I stand of ever helping anyone if I can't even do this one simple incantation?" Rufus' face broke into a grin as her face screwed up in even more pain. "If you are just going to laugh –"

"Oh, belt up and listen, Princess," Rufus said roughly before looking at her seriously. "You think this will stop you? Wake up. You aren't living in a fancy palace anymore. You can't just quit and expect a servant to pick up the slack. Understand? No, there is no time for you to wallow in self-pity like a spoilt brat – this is on you. More importantly, only *you* can do this. Do you think the only reason I came with you was because the twins had grown to the point they could look after themselves? No. I could have stayed. So, get off your royal backside and try again."

Alicea glared at the thief as a single tear rolled down her flawless face. For a second it clung to her slender jaw before falling directly onto the back of the bird nestled against her bosom. The salty moisture joined the cygnet's form with a small ripple before returning to normal. The Princess rose slowly, holding the bird in one hand and wiping away the tear streak with her other before turning back to Rufus.

"Mr. Thief, where did you learn to comfort a lady? You are terrible at this," Alicea scolded as Rufus rolled his eyes. "I'll do this regardless of what you –"

Alicea's rant was cut short when her bird began writhing in her arms. Concern was written across her face as she examined the bird. It was mutating violently in her hands, changing shape, its wings retracting inside its body. As its transformation continued, it steadily lost the features of a bird, stretching out in either direction. Alicea's expression changed to disbelief as it completed its transition, resulting in a slender staff.

Spears were originally designed to disable enemy horsemen's mounts and to slide through the gaps in chainmail. She had read about numerous weapons throughout her childhood, and they were a fascinating topic to her despite her loathing of those designed for killing.

Is that why the water refused to transform into a spear at my command? Because I don't want to wield a weapon that can kill?

Alicea knew that a staff could kill as effectively as other weapons. The blunt nature of the weapon simply helped reassure her that it was less likely to accidentally harm someone.

The biggest difference was that hers was still water. As the

Princess grasped it, it became obvious that its appearance did nothing to diminish the weapon's durability and strength. Alicea grasped the weapon like she had seen the knights do in their training. With the stance imitated flawlessly, she knew that the reason it took this form was simply because she desired it.

"My theory has been confirmed. It can sense what you feel. Now you have a weapon," Garnet said before adding with a smile, "Not to mention an exceptionally versatile friend."

"Thank you!" Alicea beamed.

Garnet turned to Rufus. "You will be playing a much bigger role in tomorrow's training, Thief. So, I trust you will prepare accordingly."

Rufus's eyebrow raised curiously but he responded with a simple nod.

"Well then, I would say that is enough for today. You have been pushed to your limit. Now go. Eat and rest. I expect you here same time tomorrow morning. Don't make me have to wake you this time," Garnet instructed the Princess briskly. Her dress hit the ground as she shifted into her crow form and took off towards the village.

Rufus turned to the Princess and smirked.

"So, are you able to walk this time? Or should I carry you again?" he asked with mock concern.

"These legs work just fine, thank you, Mr. Thief!" the Princess snapped before storming back to the village, her staff still in hand.

"Oh, you are such high maintenance," Rufus muttered as he followed.

CHAPTER 45

OF DRAGONS AND GODS

Before the exiled man and woman were the dilapidated remains of the once great city of Scourge. Chase gawked at the site in wonder. He'd heard the tales of the residents of a once powerful civilisation being eradicated in a single night after toying with an artefact far beyond their own comprehension. The similarities to his own situation weren't lost on the young man. The same artefact that obliterated an entire city was the one he forced upon the woman standing next to him. The knife in his stomach made itself known again with a quick twist of guilt.

Accompanying the guilt was a realisation.

It was the simple comprehension that the woman beside him now housed the power to annihilate an entire city. In some form or another, Temperance and the incredible power were one. It was hard to accept, and equally hard to ignore, the fact that she had been so close to bringing the same fate to Neibel-Haven that had claimed Scourge. She controlled it in the end. Sure, he had helped her reach out for her own humanity, but compared to the immense restraint and tight grip on her own will that she had displayed, his role in her accomplishment was meagre at best.

Chase glanced at the woman. His concerns vanished for a

second as he took her attire in for the umpteenth time that day. For most of the night in the inn, she had refused to wear anything besides the rags she was dressed in upon exile. Keeper had encouraged her to change into any of the dozens of clothes he showed her, but Temperance had politely refused each time. It was only when Keeper had looked at Chase, whispering something to Temperance out of his earshot, that she nodded hesitantly and picked an outfit. Chase still had no idea what had been said, but his eyes had risen at the dark skirt and light blouse she'd chosen. He didn't know much about clothes, but there was what he assumed to be a small cape draped across her shoulders, and the entire outfit was tied together by strategically placed bows. She had also selected practical boots with a platform sole and completed the outfit with a large, wide-brimmed sun hat. With a quick rummage through the remaining clothes, she had found a long piece of stray fabric that matched the other bows and tied it around her hat into a larger replica.

Chase appreciated her style, though he'd never seen anything like it. Once she'd finally taken back her half-rimmed glasses from him, he saw Temperance for who she really was. Chase appreciated her flair, though where it was born from was anyone's guess.

Temperance navigated the debris littering the road to the city with ease. The houses that were built outside the gate were burnt-out shells. It was as if something had exploded inside each one. Chase wouldn't have been surprised to hear that someone had gone into each one and personally detonated a generous amount of explosive powder.

Scorched black marks were all that remained where merchant

tents had once stood, an ashy outline and strategically placed pegs in the ground the only evidence that they'd ever been there. Unnervingly enough, their owners' remains were nowhere to be seen. The blazes had done immense damage and would have burnt away much of what made up a human's body, but to see no sign at all . . .

Were the people burnt to dust? Is the stone's power so mighty?

There were stables just outside the destroyed city where Chase assumed that horses once existed. Their masters, who had once attempted to make a living out of breeding the best of the best, were long gone, leaving the stables in shambles. As soon as any large threat was detected, a good breeder would free his stock to run for their lives. As Chase stared at it, he found himself hoping that the horses had made it to safety. An odd thought for beasts that had long since perished either way.

The pair walked cautiously through the destroyed gates and into the city. It looked as if the gate itself, along with large chunks of the stone wall, had been levelled by extreme impact. The stone crumbled away under Chase's hand as he brushed across it. Putting his palm flat against the stone, he could feel the heat prickling at his skin. Temperance glanced at him with concern before turning her head back towards the inside of the city.

Chase's awe only grew as he made his way into the ruined city. The houses on the inside of the broken walls were made from stone rather than their wooden counterparts outside. It had made little difference as most of them had been reduced to rubble. The stone from the houses still let off thin wisps of smoke; some of the debris even had a white-hot tinge lingering within them.

Chase knew better than to touch them. He already had one burnt hand from grasping Temperance – he certainly didn't need another. He glanced down at his right hand: the flesh had not started the reparation process that skin usually underwent. The burnt tissue and peeled skin had cauterised immediately at an unnatural rate after coming in contact with Temperance's skin.

The moment itself had felt conflicted, as if the flames themselves hadn't wanted to harm him but were forced to. It was a morbid reminder that reality could be exceptionally cruel.

The pair strolled through the burnt-out streets lined with scorched flowerbeds that still had the crispy remains of plants dwelling within. What was strange was that the damage looked so fresh, as if the destruction was recent. No matter where he looked, Chase noticed images of dragons of different colours, shapes and sizes in the form of etchings into stone or small statues of the legendary entities. There was a mural upon a large wall with chunks missing from its foundation. Even missing large pieces of its image, the piece of art did not fail to depict a large crimson dragon in its fierce and absolute splendour.

Of course, he'd only seen pictures of dragons in books or the occasional scroll that Lazear had left lying around. But while there were countless different styles and interpretations of a dragon's appearance wherever he looked, one in particular stood out. The large crimson one upon the mural. It was the one that made Chase uneasy; not only for its intimidating and ferocious demeanour shown in every rendition, but also because he'd seen it before.

Lazear had carried one scroll with him every time they'd

found a promising new subject. Sometimes he left it out in the open, though Chase had felt that it was unintentional. It had almost seemed careless. He'd had taken a look a few times, though once had been enough to take in the simple image of a dangerous-looking dragon sitting atop a large crystal. The only colour in the picture was blazing red within the crystal and the same in the beast's eyes.

The crystal, Chase pondered thoughtfully. *Is the crystal supposed to be a connection to the stone now dwelling within Temperance? What of the dragon I keep seeing here? Professor, how much did you know?*

Even Temperance seemed to be far better informed on the situation than Chase was. She hadn't said a single word since arriving; instead she'd hum in thought and occasionally nod at different buildings or city fixtures, as if she was confirming something for her own benefit. They eventually came to what Chase assumed was the main square, although it seemed to be more of a shrine without a ceiling. His attention was undivided as soon as he saw the main attraction.

A massive dragon statue stood in front of them, taking up the centre of the square. Its body was sprawled out in an attack-ready stance with its tail curled upwards, stretching into the sky. Its huge head was turned towards them as if greeting them and anyone else who might enter. The monster's head was large enough to devour them both in one bite.

Though the sun shone off the crimson armour formed from scales that was coating the beast, the light reflecting off the dragon's body seemed unnatural. The sun was overhead and while it may have been the unnerved man's imagination, it looked as though the rays of light reflected from the west rather than from a sun approaching noon. Chase thanked his lucky stars that it was just a statue as he took in its long fangs. Each was almost the length of the blade strapped to his back. Its open mouth looked ready to launch an assault.

Or eat, he thought grimly, as if it made a difference.

"This is Scourge, or rather a statue in his likeness," Temperance announced as she adjusted her glasses, interrupting Chase's examination.

"Scourge is a dragon? It's named after a city?" Chase asked.

"The city was named after the dragon. Scourge started out as just a small cult that grew over many decades, eventually forming this city," Temperance explained, sniffing slightly before continuing. "The tale says that more than a millennium ago, the dragon, Scourge, was summoned to this world by a group of fanatics. Nobody knows how they did it but the dragon came and torched the land with a fury that doesn't belong in this world."

"They summoned a dragon? That's impossible!" Chase scoffed.

"How much do you know about dragons?" Temperance asked.

"That they don't exist on this plane of existence and that they aren't to be trifled with," Chase shrugged.

"Dragons do indeed exist on a different plane of existence, one that even the most accomplished of mages can rarely reach. Even if they do succeed, they are generally not alive long enough to grant insight on the mystery surrounding the dragons. The fanatics who successfully summoned Scourge were sacrificed for their efforts. It is said that the combined strength of Neibel-Haven's mages was able to banish the dragon back to its own plane. That is all that is known in that regard," Temperance explained before adding in a bitter tone, "Not that their destruction was enough to deter more fanatics from taking their place. They didn't try to summon Scourge again but instead they built a city in reverence, treating the dragon as a god."

"In my opinion, the accursed thing can stay on its own plane of existence," Chase replied.

"I agree, although I cannot shake the feeling that Scourge has some form of connection here. The voice I heard . . ." Temperance trailed off.

After waiting a moment for her to continue, Chase tried to comfort her by saying, "Come, there is something you came here for. You may not know what it is yet but I'm sure it wasn't to give me a history lesson."

"Yes, you're right. We have spoken enough about that particular disaster. We must now focus on finding out how the city fell a second time. I need to get to the cathedral." Temperance shook her head as if trying to shake off something uncomfortable.

The pair navigated themselves around the large imposing statue, following the road branching out from the square in the opposite direction from where they had entered. The signs of destruction did not let up; if anything, they intensified. They saw a blacksmith's forge completely destroyed, the smithy's tools strewn everywhere across the street they walked on. The charred remains of the smithy were where his front door was, burnt beyond recognition. It was a morbid feeling, but Chase was relieved at the sight of the remains. Though, even if there had been remains after the catastrophe, they should have eroded over time . . . Maybe seeing them wasn't a good sign.

There were similar corpses littered in the shells of the houses and on the street. The smell of burnt flesh was becoming steadily more potent the deeper they went into the city. The scent didn't turn Chase's stomach like he'd assumed it would have. He remembered feeling slightly nauseous from the odour he'd taken in when Lazear and the others burned, but now he didn't feel ill at all. It was then that Chase realised he hadn't asked the most important and apparent questions in need of answers.

This tragedy happened two centuries ago. Why does it look like it happened yesterday? And how does Temperance know where she needs to go? Chase thought before voicing his queries as they forged their way through the burnt cemetery that was Scourge.

"The stone's power showed me flashes of the destruction that took place here all those years ago when I was consumed. It was like I was standing amongst it but I was unable to do a thing to help. Even the flames passed straight through me," Temperance explained. "I had this overwhelming feeling that I had to get to the cathedral, that there was something there."

Chase pondered what she had said for a moment with little understanding, so he moved on.

"And my other question?"

"The destruction from the stone is not so easily dismissed. Scourge does not follow the same route along the path of time that the rest of the world does anymore. The visions . . ." Temperance screwed up her face in concentration as if trying to recall something that happened a long time ago. "They showed a woman consumed by white-hot flames as I was and when she spoke it was a loud and cruel voice. I think it was the same voice that came through me."

"Wait, you think she was possessed and bent on destruction? That sounds a little too familiar to be coincidence."

"Yes," Temperance nodded, happy that Chase was drawing the same conclusions that she was. "And now, the town will never recover. People have travelled here and tried to rebuild, myself included. But everything I did – anything that anyone did – to restore this town was redundant. It returned to this state when they awoke the next morning. As if nothing had been accomplished."

"You tried to restore this city?" Chase responded in surprise.

"Yes, I was trying to decipher this curse when I was – let's say, 'picked up'," Temperance replied, leaving Chase to give a questioning look before realising what she meant.

"You mean dragged unwillingly to Neibel-Haven," Chase said quietly, the guilt returning like a searing blade to his gut.

Temperance didn't respond, instead quickening her pace towards the now visible cathedral towering over the ruined city.

It seemed to have weathered the destruction better than the rest of the city's buildings, with its beautiful gold engravings of dragons still intact for the most part. The bodies of the magnificent beasts were coursing across its walls, missing only small parts of their glorious bodies here and there. He was beginning to think that whatever had assaulted the city actually intended to leave the images undamaged.

Two dragon statues sat on their hind legs on either side of the great entrance, their necks coiled around each other and their heads staring down at the path. The arrangement of intimidating figures before them gave Chase the uneasy feeling he was being watched.

Temperance paused for a moment, allowing Chase to take in the figures for the first time. The dragons were slender compared to the statue of Scourge. Chase let out a low whistle of admiration before addressing Temperance.

"I'm starting to think that the residents of Scourge weren't just obsessed with Scourge himself, but rather dragons in general," he admitted.

"A fair observation. However, I'm uncertain of its accuracy. All records I've read, and there have been a lot, indicate that Scourge himself was the focus of their obsession. Other dragons make small appearances in the records but nothing of substance compared to that of Scourge himself," Temperance replied as her eyes descended on the entrance to the cathedral. "That's peculiar."

"What is it?" Chase asked, looking at his companion.

"The door was sealed when I was here last. Now it's wide open for anyone to enter," Temperance replied quietly.

"Wait, you dragged me here to a place you thought you wouldn't even be able to access?" Chase asked in mild irritation.

"That's hardly what's important here, Chase. Don't you think it's odd?" Temperance asked coolly, taking a moment to straighten the front of her dress.

Chase glanced at the entrance again. It was a little unnerving. Either someone or something had gained access to the cathedral recently, or something was expecting them. Temperance was ready to turn back when he grabbed her arm.

"No, we came here to find out what is waiting for you. This

is just another sign you made the right choice," he said softly.

"What if it is a trap?" Temperance asked.

"Then it's most likely one you are meant to fall into. Either way, if we turn back now you are just going to have it in the back of your mind. If it's a trap, I'll protect you. It's most likely just looters, and I can handle a few brutes." Chase pointed at the hilt over his shoulder with a smile that was full of confidence. "Besides, the answers to so many questions may reside within those walls. We both know you are going inside there."

Temperance met his eyes. For the first time her thoughts weren't tainted by the bitter hatred and resentment of what he had done to her. Instead she saw a young man trying to do what was right – right for the world, its people and above all – for her.

He can't be any older than me but he shows the bravery of a man who has weathered trials his entire life.

Temperance looked into Chase's deep-green eyes, full of confidence and honesty. "Very well, I will trust you."

CHAPTER 46

EVERY VILLAGE HAS ONE

The Princess was already awake and dressed when Rufus entered her room with a plate of fruit. He placed the meal on the small table in the corner and turned to leave, only to be stopped by Alicea's voice.

"Mr. Thief, is that it?" she asked, running a comb through her hair and arranging half a dozen clips and ornaments.

"Is what it?" Rufus asked.

"You just waltz in without knocking, place food and leave?" the Princess pressed accusingly.

"What was I supposed to say?" Rufus asked, his confusion growing as he ran his hand through his dirty brown hair.

"How about 'good morning'? Or at least 'hello'? I may be a Princess, but you are not a silent servant," Alicea replied as she tied her hair back.

"Not a servant? I have to say that's not the way I feel at times –" Rufus started sarcastically.

"Right! That's enough out of you. Thank you for reminding me why I should be happy that you don't speak to me. We have a big day ahead of us; I suggest you improve your attitude," the Princess snapped before storming towards the bear pelt guarding the exit and using both arms to push it aside.

Rufus shook his head in disbelief, trying to work out what he had done wrong, when Alicea's head poked back into the room.

"Are you coming, or would you prefer a royal invitation?"

An exasperated Rufus and an irritated Alicea set out for the training fields for the third day in a row. The Princess was in good spirits. She smiled broadly and waved to everyone they passed on their way to the winding path connecting the village to the training field. The people of Tremel were pleased to see the Princess walk through the village, though it was still a new concept to many. Instead of the cautious whispers and blatant stares they had received upon arrival, they were now greeted with happy words and smiles. Even the children had become comfortable enough to race up to Alicea for their chance to speak with a real Princess.

The young girls wished they were princesses like her. The boys would blush and mutter compliments before running away. Alicea always responded kindly, with a level of patience that Rufus couldn't understand.

They were almost to the gate when a couple of swaying men blocked their path. The men were both at least a head and a half taller than Alicea, broader than Rufus and drunk.

The men swaggered straight up before stopping their stagger a little closer to Alicea than Rufus was comfortable with. They showed no sign of even seeing the thief; it was the Princess they were interested in.

"How fares your day, m'lady?" the first slurred, leaning on his friend for support while he chuckled in a strange fashion.

"Very well, thank you," Alicea replied quickly. "I apologise, but I have somewhere to be. Perhaps another time."

As Alicea attempted to sidestep the drunkard, she was stopped by the large man's hand moving with surprising speed. His dirty, meaty paw grasped her wrist, pulling her close. Alicea's face screwed up in disgust at the scent of mead on the brute's breath as he looked down at his prey, panting heavily. She'd never liked the scent of alcohol in the first place – to smell it blended in with the man's foul breath was even worse.

"Now, now. For a Princess you're pretty rude," snickered the brute as his other hand attempted to make its way to the Princess' chest. "I think I deserve a royal apology."

"I suggest you don't move another inch, you drunken mule. Lest you lose an extremity," the Princess stated defiantly, causing the man to hesitate, mostly from surprise.

"Um, Marn? You should let her go," came the quickly sobering voice of the drunk's companion.

The man, Marn, turned his head slightly to see his companion's wide eyes transfixed on something. He followed his friend's gaze down to see Rufus squatting between the two men, twin daggers drawn. The first was preventing his friend from approaching. The second was an inch away from being buried in Marn's ribcage.

"H-how?" Marn growled accusingly at his friend.

"Now, Marn, let me go," the Princess said. She forced herself to smile sweetly, despite the stale smell of mead and sweat. "Mr. Thief tends to get a little carried away if someone threatens me. Best not to test him."

Marn hesitated before relinquishing the Princess, who danced backwards gracefully. The drunk then turned slowly and faced Rufus' fierce green eyes. He looked down at the squatting thief for a moment, weighing up his chances to get past the blade and place his hands on the man threatening him.

Common sense trumped intoxication and Marn addressed Rufus roughly.

"You think this is over? We have a way of making things difficult," he spat, barely coherently. "You just made enemies."

"If I had a piece of gold for every enemy I had, I wouldn't have to protect this brat for money," Rufus retorted. "You have your ways, I have my own. Now, back away slowly before I'm forced to do something that'll have the Princess whining about me being too violent."

Marn stepped backwards slowly. The threat felt too genuine. Marn scowled at the thief before turning to walk away. Rufus turned his attention to the other man, who was white with fear. The man hadn't moved an inch and was clearly not the alpha of the pair. Or of anyone.

"Name?" Rufus demanded.

"Rhept," the man squeaked without hesitation.

"I suggest you run, Rhept," Rufus snarled, and the man immediately sprinted after his friend.

Rufus sheathed his blades, looking around at the small group that had gathered.

Alicea beamed a reassuring smile at the people as she grabbed Rufus's hand and pulled him towards the rear exit of the village. She released his hand when they were clear of the gate and were walking along the familiar trail to whatever training Garnet had in store.

"Well, that was certainly unexpected, wouldn't you say, Mr. Thief? I would even go so far as to say you left quite an impression," Alicea said.

Rufus replied with a grunt, his eyes fixed straight ahead as she continued.

"You have done well in your role of my guardian."

"That's my job, of course I did it," Rufus responded shortly.

Alicea slapped his arm to stop him and he looked down to see her looking up at him seriously with eyes of shimmering cerulean. It was a foreign sight – the Princess gazing at him without rolling her eyes or glaring. The whole situation was making him uncomfortable.

"You protected me. I'm grateful," Alicea said before standing on her tiptoes and quickly kissing him on the cheek.

The Princess immediately continued walking, leaving Rufus standing in the middle of the path and unable to respond.

What was that all about?

He returned to reality at the sound of the Princess' voice and saw her a ways ahead, waving her hand impatiently.

"Mr. Thief! I am sincerely grateful that you move quicker during a confrontation than you do when simply walking! Are you coming or not?"

Rufus started at a jogging pace to catch up, unsure of what was happening anymore. He was anxious for her to get on with her training so he could sleep away the rest of the morning.

CHAPTER 47

WITH COMBAT COMES BRUISES

"Welcome once more, Princess," Garnet said as the pair approached. "You are a little late."

"Yes, I apologise. There was a little trouble back in town but nothing to worry about," Alicea replied.

"Very good. Now, your thief friend will be playing a large role today," Garnet said as Rufus sighed, halting the journey to his spot under the tree. "But first, summon your bird."

Alicea closed her eyes, reaching out with her mind to find her bird's consciousness within the distant foliage. Its essence glowed like a beacon in the distance on a pitch-black night. She could sense exactly where it was and what it was doing. The Princess allowed a moment of surprise to blossom within her as she felt the bird bouncing along some sort of tether. It took her a moment to realise that the bird was traversing the vines that hung from the trees of the dense forest. It would occasionally spot something of interest before extending its neck and snapping it up in its beak.

Is she foraging?

As soon as the bird felt its conjurer's call, Alicea felt it take off, making its way towards the training field. Less than a minute later, the bird was perched on its master's shoulder, looking around curiously.

"Very good," Garnet repeated. "Now transform it."

"I could only do that when I was upset. I don't even know when it transformed back into a bird," Alicea started to explain but was cut short when the bird jumped from Alicea's shoulder and into her hands.

It proceeded to mutate and within seconds, the form of a long staff was resting in her hands. The transformation came easier than the time before; it was smoother, as if the bird had been practising.

"How?" she asked incredulously.

"Yesterday I explained that my theory was correct. It knows what you want and feel. Thief, draw one of your blades," Garnet ordered quickly.

Rufus slowly drew a single dagger. Garnet took the long knife, placing her hand over the blade and muttered, *"Gladirus: Bentun."*

Rufus watched as Garnet's hand started to glow and the shining silver blade darkened steadily until it was the colour of rich soil.

"What did you do?" Rufus asked as he took back his weapon and turned it over in his hands to examine it himself.

"Your blade is now coated in Earth Magic and the enchantment is under my control. I have made your weapon blunt so that even when you strike the Princess, it will only bruise. It will not hurt or kill her," Garnet explained.

"Why would I attack her?" Rufus asked.

"To help her learn how to spar, of course," Garnet replied impatiently, taking a few steps back away from the pair. "How is that difficult for you to follow?"

"I don't think I could attack her. Besides, she has me to

protect her and – aah!" Rufus' sentence cut off with a cry of pain as Alicea lashed out with her staff and struck Rufus with its blunt tip. Her swing was wide and clumsy, but to the unsuspecting thief it might as well have been the precise strike of a master.

"What the hell is wrong with you?" he yelled at the Princess, who had jumped backwards, smiling widely as she bounced from foot to foot.

"Garnet is right, Mr. Thief. I need to be able to defend myself physically, not just magically. As one would expect of a ruffian, physical combat is where your expertise lies. It makes sense that you should instruct me," she said with excitement in her voice.

Rufus looked the Princess up and down doubtfully. Her petite frame was still dancing on the spot with her strange weapon held in hand across her chest.

Despite not trying to, Rufus noticed weakness after weakness in the Princess' form. She was elegant and sure-footed, but that was it. It was painfully obvious that anyone with any combat experience – and even a fair share of those without it – could murder her before she knew she was under attack.

"I don't know –" Rufus started, getting cut off again by another swing from the Princess. Expecting it this time, he parried the staff easily with his dull blade.

"Would you stop it!?" he yelled.

"No. You will fight me or end up as one big bruise, Mr. Thief!"

"Could you at least throw on some armour?"

"Armour is for those who intend on getting hit!" she laughed, jumping forward and swinging her weapon erratically.

Rufus met her weapon with his own, blocking it effortlessly before reaching out and slapping her out of rash irritation. Princess, shaman and thief alike froze in response to his choice as Alicea processed what had happened.

"You slapped me!" exclaimed the shocked Princess.

"I'm sorry, I just –" Rufus felt the wind leave his lungs and his vision blurred slightly as Alicea drove the end of her weapon into his chest.

Alicea retracted the staff and spun on the spot, bringing her weapon downwards and smashing it over his head. Pain shot through his body and Rufus backed away, just out of reach of Alicea's weapon as she swung at him again with little thought. The Princess continued, stepping toward him as he struggled to breathe and stay out of the reach of what had become a staff-wielding madwoman.

Let's give her a weapon, what a grand idea! he thought bitterly.

Rufus felt his breath slowly returning as he stumbled further backwards. When his vision had returned fully, the Princess was still pressing forward with her erratic assault. He stepped forward into a particularly wild swing of the Princess' and grabbed the weapon in mid-air with his spare hand. His leg twisted around hers, sweeping them out from underneath her body. Falling on the soft grass didn't deter her for long as she leapt to her feet again. She picked up her weapon and sprinted towards Rufus, thrusting the end of her staff directly at his face. Smoothly ducking his head just enough to avoid the assault, Rufus lashed out at the Princess' side with his blunt weapon. The dull blade found her frame. The blunt impact made her falter as the waves of pain spread outward from where the weapon had found her flesh. A small whimper left her lips as she lowered her weapon and grasped her side.

"Stop just running at me like a maniac and *think*!" Rufus ordered.

"But you move so quickly!" the Princess gasped, sweat already falling down her pretty face. "I thought that if I was fast as well, I could beat you."

"That won't work if the opponent is faster than you and has more experience, along with countless other things. Agility is only one factor in a fight – would you stop?!" Rufus yelled again, dodging another attack designed to surprise him before roughly grabbing the collar of her shirt with his free hand and pulling her close.

"Now, listen to me!" he growled as Alicea squirmed defiantly.

Rufus released her, taking a breath while watching her cautiously to make sure she wasn't going to rush him again. The Princess sighed dramatically and started tapping her foot, so he started explaining the fundamentals of his style of fighting.

"I'm quick because I've trained myself to be. I have light weapons designed for close-quarter fighting, which enables me to move unhindered. I'm also physically stronger than you. Overall, I'm stronger, faster and far more skilled than you in combat. I am also aware of your presence, making it nearly impossible for me to be surprised. Now, tell me about your weapon and abilities?"

Alicea stopped tapping her foot and thought about the question before answering.

"I have no experience except from what I've read in books. I'm not very strong and trying to attack quickly doesn't work for me as you are faster," she said thoughtfully as Rufus nodded. "But my weapon is much longer, therefore I have more reach than you do."

"Right, that's a benefit of your weapon of choice. Tell me a positive aspect about you that can be applied here."

"I just explained that I'm not skilled or strong!" Alicea snapped.

"We will not be moving on until you think of something," Rufus shrugged.

It took her a moment to sift through her talents before realising that some of her skills that she had never thought to apply to combat might be beneficial after all. Thinking back to what she'd spent her time doing in the castle as she grew up yielded little in the martial arts, yet she did have some physical capabilities that she thought could be transferred to the art of fighting.

"I am smaller than most people," Alicea acknowledged hesitantly. "Which might tempt an opponent to try to overpower me."

"I asked for positive aspects."

"I haven't finished!" Alicea yelled before returning to her thoughtful tone. "I also spent quite a lot of my life dancing. That involved a lot of skill, stamina and finesse. So, I'm agile?"

Rufus nodded slowly, a little surprised by the Princess' answer but unable to fault it.

"Anything else?"

"Yes. My memory is quite a valuable tool. I can recall anything I read, hear or witness in perfect detail. Providing I was there, of course."

Garnet shifted in the corner of Alicea's vision, but said

nothing. "Why is this a positive point for this exercise?" Rufus asked.

"Because I can recall where every inch of your body was at any given time during our spar. It stands to reason that the longer the fight, the more of an advantage I would gain by learning the style of my opponent."

"That's a valuable tool. But there is more to combat than simply remembering an opponent's motions. If you can't stop what they're throwing at you then there is no point in knowing what is coming. If you are forced to fight a more experienced opponent, you will need to at least somewhat rely on your instincts. You're very clever and your mind is what is going to allow you to adapt and learn. Your mouth is not. Now, try again," Rufus said, flicking his blade into a backwards position with the blade running up his wrist. He lowered his frame into a combat-ready stance, watching Alicea.

Alicea examined his stance and applied it against what she'd read in the past.

Low stance for a quick retreat and to minimise his chances of being hit. Reverse grip on his blade designed to exploit weaknesses but overall . . . defensive.

Alicea extended her hands along her staff so that a foot and a half of it protruded from each end before approaching slowly. She started by cautiously circling around him in an attempt to expose a weak point.

Rufus lunged forward, lashing out with his blade in a wide arc. She was barely able to parry it with the middle of her staff before flicking it downwards at his shoulder. The staff clipped the thief with enough force to make him grunt, but not enough to halt his momentum. Again, he brought his dagger under the Princess' guard to strike her side in the exact spot he had hit before, making her cringe and shudder in pain.

"Not a bad effort, but blocking one strike isn't enough to end a fight. Your counter was weak but at least you thought quickly enough to do it," Rufus commended the Princess while she squatted on the ground in agony.

Rufus waited the few minutes that were required for Alicea to stand back up. Her bruise felt like it was sprouting its very own bruise on top of it. She extended her hands into the position she found comfortable and with a nod, the pair sparred again. They trained for the entire day, barely even breaking for the food that some of the villagers brought.

Alicea felt as though her body was one giant throbbing blister as each round ended in Rufus punishing her attempts to fight back with a vicious blow from his blunt weapon. Methodically, he struck her arms, legs and stomach, but never her delicate face. When she'd realised this, Alicea became furious. She didn't want him to hold back, but no matter what she said to goad him, Rufus refused to strike any place higher than her collarbone.

By the time the sun was setting in its usual blaze of gorgeous crimson, Alicea was physically drained while Rufus had barely broken a sweat. She had improved a lot in a short time. Her strikes had become more deliberate and less of the wild swings were utilised. When she became flustered, the erratic attacks became more frequent, but she had quickly learnt that it was the lack of discipline that was punished most severely.

Overall, it was her blocking that had improved the most. She managed to parry up to eight of Rufus' attacks before he connected in some of their spars. The Princess collected a lot of information on Rufus' form in an effort to predict his next move, but it was a slow process. Every time she'd start to grasp his style, Rufus would suddenly alter it and Alicea would have a new bruise. Despite this, she quickly learnt to adapt.

"That's about enough," Rufus said, glancing towards Garnet, who nodded slightly.

"No, one more!" Alicea demanded.

Rufus sighed but fell into a ready stance. "Last one, Princess."

The two squared off, taking each other's stance once more. Alicea had developed her own form, holding her staff close to her body with one end pointing towards Rufus while the rest of its length stretched out behind her. It was a stance that Rufus was unfamiliar with. However, he did not criticise it – a different style may just be what the Princess needed to obtain an edge.

She never does things the conventional way. Why should this be any different? he thought.

It was Alicea who moved first, feigning a swing at Rufus' right side. He raised his short blade to block in response, only to realise the ploy a split second too late. Alicea thrust the end of her staff directly at him, glancing it off his shoulder again before retracting it quickly, dancing on the tip of her toes in retreat. Rufus retaliated by leaping forward, slashing at her chest but meeting only air as Alicea ducked to the ground. She swung out, her staff flying through the taller blades of grass before smashing Rufus' knee, forcing him to hobble back in an attempt to avoid further blows.

Alicea found her momentum, running at her opponent and thrusting her weapon directly at him. Rufus grabbed the staff in mid-air, barely an inch away from his face. Roughly thrusting her weapon away from his face, he stabbed at her with his armed hand, only to miss again.

Alicea had followed the trajectory of her weapon. She sunk with the swing into a squatting position and swung at Rufus' knees again. To her surprise, he lifted his leg into the air and stomped on the approaching weapon, the force ripping it from Alicea's hand. Her face turned to a look of disappointment when Rufus kicked the weapon away and she realised she had lost again.

"You win again, Mr. Thief," Alicea said bitterly, slightly short of breath.

Rufus dropped to the ground, finding himself likewise slightly panting.

"You have improved. Best one yet. I'm pretty sure I even have my very own bruise now."

"You don't need to say that to make me feel better," Alicea said quietly.

"I mean it. In one day you have grown more competent than most. Who would have guessed that a Princess could fight?" Rufus laughed.

"What exactly is that supposed to mean, Mr. Thief?" Alicea demanded.

Rufus saw a playful look on her face and they both laughed as Garnet approached.

"The thief is right, Alicea. You did well," she said. "The next few days will be focused around this kind of combat training until you are competent enough to fight Rufus with no restrictions. I want you to be able to hold your own against him even when he has both weapons drawn and doesn't hold back."

"You were holding back?" the Princess asked despairingly.

"Yeah, I'm much more comfortable with two blades," Rufus said offhandedly and Alicea bowed her head.

"I have a long way to go," she said quietly.

"But you have come so far already. Despair not about what you haven't accomplished, but appreciate how far you have progressed," Garnet said kindly before turning to Rufus. "Tell me, Rufus, are you only skilled with twin daggers and short swords?"

Rufus raised his eyebrows slightly before answering.

"I can use any blade well, especially if I have one in each hand. Within reason, of course. I couldn't wield two broadswords – very few could."

"So, longswords are fine?" Garnet asked.

"I could wield them. Daggers are more suited to my usual work. But yes, longswords are no more difficult."

"Interesting," Garnet said, lost in thought before realising that she was being watched by Rufus curiously. "That is enough for today. Everyone involved did well. I must report back."

Garnet transformed into the crow and took off, leaving Rufus and Alicea alone on the field.

"Right. Cryptic questions from crow ladies aside, I think you especially need rest. Shall we head back?" Rufus asked.

"Yes, I think so," the Princess replied as she slowly got to her feet, wincing in pain as Rufus started walking off. "Um, Mr. Thief?"

"Hmm?" Rufus said, looking back at the bruised Princess curiously as she shifted slightly in discomfort.

"Well, now that the adrenaline has worn off, I appear be

unable to move without my whole body protesting, so . . ." she stuttered, not meeting his eyes.

"Yes, that happens in a spar and bruises are a part of that," Rufus replied.

"I know that!" the Princess snapped before adopting her uncomfortable look again. "It's just a long walk."

Rufus stared at the Princess, wondering what she was getting at before it dawned on him. Rolling his eyes, he walked over to the Princess and gently picked her up before setting out for the village with her in his arms.

"You are such high maintenance, you know that?" Rufus grumbled.

"And you speak when it is not required, Mr. Thief," Alicea retorted softly, already feeling sleep closing in. "Perhaps I should invest in a *silent* servant, after all."

CHAPTER 48

GRAVE TIDINGS

Garnet was in the Chief's hut that morning, having put Alicea's training on hold after being called to Kurok's presence. The Chief spoke to his subordinate gravely, adopting a resigned posture in his chair as Garnet's face creased with worry.

"I see," Garnet said with a troubled look.

"Setz contacted me last night," Kurok sighed. "It appears that since the Princess' kidnapping, Aquiocia's damned Council has taken control of the kingdom. Word has reached them that the Princess is here. He believes they'll march soon."

"You must have known it would only be a matter of time, Chief," Garnet stated.

"Aye, it was always going to happen. But I never expected it so quickly. It must mean there is someone here disloyal to the village," Kurok sighed.

"And what of Setz? What will he do?" Garnet asked.

"I have not sent a response to him as yet. According to his message, we have a few days left at least before soldiers embark. I will ask him for assistance to be sure, but I need you to deliver the message personally."

"For what reason, Chief? I feel I would be invaluable here should things turn sour," Garnet protested.

"You would be, and you will be as I know well that the

warriors of the village respond well to your command. So, you will be quick. Inform Setz of the situation and return immediately," Kurok ordered, waving his hand dismissively. "Finish any business you have here today."

"At least allow me to see that my responsibilities here are handled before I leave," Garnet said, a mild look of reproach flickering across her face.

It wasn't lost on the Chief and he nodded slightly.

"Do as you must, but have it done by tonight. You leave at dusk, no later."

"Chief, as your advisor I simply must offer all options. We could flee. Being small in number I'd say we could outrun them and the forestland would aid us more so than the knights," Garnet suggested, hating her own words as she spoke them.

"I will not leave Arok, Lyrium and Stefan to come back to this mess. I have not given up hope."

"Chief, it has been a week," Garnet said bluntly.

"It is not just the Princess' stone they will be after should they find out about the one Lyrium is hunting," Kurok countered before adding bitterly, "Providing she returns."

"Then you have drawn the same conclusion as I. They care not for the Princess but the stone in her possession. Regardless, we will give them a fight they will surely remember. We have not one but two of the bearers to protect."

Garnet exited the hut, leaving her Chief to lean back in his chair and close his eyes.

Lyrium, Stefan and my son. Come back soon. Strife is coming, and it will be a grand fight.

CHAPTER 49

A PRIZE OF THE ANCESTORS

The trio had almost reached their limit as they trudged down more stairs. Lyrium was at the head of the group, leading Arok, who was supporting a badly wounded Stefan. Arok's wounds were bound beneath thick bandages wrapped around his middle, as seen to by Lyrium. Though the pain must have been considerable, he didn't let on to his companions.

They pressed on, down the winding corridor lined with lit torches that they no longer questioned. Being alone had become ideal to the party and, while they didn't voice it, they knew that another confrontation would likely bring their journey into the ruins to an end. There wasn't much more the group could take.

Stefan could no longer use his bow and Arok was too busy supporting him to fight, let alone taking into account his injuries. Stefan had suggested on many occasions that they leave him behind. The idea had fallen on deaf ears every time as Arok and Lyrium refused to hear of it. Lyrium was armed with nothing but a hunting knife and a limited grasp of magic, which it exhausted her to use.

They were about to take a break when Lyrium saw an unfamiliar light at the bottom of the stairs – faint but there nonetheless. The three forced themselves towards the light, weary and cautious. The light grew brighter with every step they took downwards. The closer they got the clearer it was that the light was a peculiar sepia colour.

The party stopped a few steps from where the light was resting on the stairs. Lyrium took a deep breath before walking down the remaining stairs with a false bravado, through the doorway and into the odd light.

Lyrium tentatively stepped into the new area, her companions lumbering awkwardly in behind her with puzzled expressions.

No sign of this new chamber indicated that they were within the ruins of a fortress. The room was lined with perfect walls of smooth flat stone. Simple, yet sturdy pillars were mirrored on each side of a narrow path, reaching up to the high ceiling above her. At the chamber's end stood a statue of a woman holding something precious that shone with a sepia radiance that filled the room.

The stone!

Lyrium crossed the room slowly, cautious of traps and yet finding nothing, when a voice boomed within the trio's heads.

Do not hesitate, Hunter. You have passed the trials. One more stands before you, but my power will be accompanying you for that!

"There is another trial?" Lyrium asked. She hesitated to grab the stone, looking back to her handicapped companions. "We are not ready."

Oh, but you are. Your concern for your friends will not stop you from taking the stone as the final trial is how you use this power. You will be training to use it effectively before making a difference in the coming struggles. What kind of difference is solely up to you! The voice seemed slightly humoured by an inside joke.

Lyrium resigned herself to the fact that she had no real choice. The stone was what she had come for and the sooner they could focus on looking for a way out of the ruins, the better.

The essence grew stronger the closer she got to the statue and Lyrium realised who the woman must be. Garnet's lectures came to mind, along with her conversation with the Chief beside the bonfire. The simple woman was garbed in pelts with short, spiky hair, her face perfectly intact from the past centuries, looking no older than Lyrium herself.

This is a statue of the woman who gave her life to protect Tremel around two hundred years ago, Lyrium thought before correcting herself. *No, this isn't just a statue. This is the actual woman who protected the people within the Fortress of the Forest. The woman who gave her life and turned to stone for Tremel is right in front of me.*

A sudden desire to explore the ruins made its way into Lyrium's heart. She wanted nothing more than to turn around and walk back up the seemingly endless stairs to the maze above them. She wanted to see the fortress that was once considered impenetrable and to know more of those who lived within its walls.

"I want to understand our people. I want to understand what they went through. Their strength, the terror of the battle, everything. I want to know *you!* Why were you chosen before me, and why have I been chosen now?" Lyrium asked the statue. Arok was beside her, having propped his wounded friend against a pillar. He didn't say a word, just smiled towards his lover.

Lyrium had never questioned why she had been chosen. She'd questioned the history and even questioned what she had to do, but never why. Looking into the lifeless stone eyes of the Vassal before her, Lyrium took her prize and smiled.

"Your sacrifice . . . You never asked why, did you?" she asked as she finally grasped the stone. "Then neither will I. I will give it my all and should it take my life, I will make sure that whatever kills me doesn't walk away."

Lyrium was saved the effort of finding an exit the second she had the priceless item in her possession. The stone responded to her touch, the image of restless soil shifting just beneath its surface. The movement entranced Lyrium briefly before a loud and familiar grinding sound interrupted her concentration. Looking up in relief, she saw part of the wall crumbling to rubble. From behind it sunlight leaked into the room.

The sunlight seemed to be combating the sepia haze as it forced its way into the room. Lyrium's first assumption was that the light disliked the exposure to the sun, but no complaint was heard as the peculiar light steadily faded from existence. Her mouth opened slightly as if to say something, but no words made their way out. It was the path they had taken into the ruins. She could see the pillars guarding the entrance and in the distance, she recognised the rough trail leading back towards the village.

"Impossible," Stefan muttered painfully as he tried to make sense of the sight.

The trials are complete, came the voice within the stone. *Return to your village, Hunter. Things are about to become complicated and will require your assistance.*

Lyrium nodded, placing the stone into her pack. She helped the others over the rubble and the sunlight washed over them.

The natural light was a cruel reminder that they'd been

denied it for so long, burning their eyes mercilessly. When they'd adjusted, the three slowly set out for their home.

On the rough path towards Tremel, Lyrium could not help but look back towards the ruins sadly. She was only half surprised to find that they no longer stood where they had been just seconds before. The forest was back to how she had known it her whole life.

She looked to her companions who both exhaustedly smiled back. Stefan was particularly weak and only managed a frail grimace. It was only the pride of finding the stone that quashed her disappointment from being unable to explore the ruins more.

CHAPTER 50

THE THEORY OF COOPERATION

Rufus knocked quickly on the side of the doorway leading to Alicea's room before pushing the massive bear pelt serving as a curtain aside. The Princess had moved the table across to the window. Her long dark hair shone with scarlet flecks from the early morning sun as she pored over the small mountain of books in front of her.

"Ready for today's training?" Rufus asked.

"There is no training today. Garnet came earlier and informed me that she had things to attend to that couldn't wait. She offered me these books about magic from her library for the meantime," Alicea replied absentmindedly, her eyes not leaving the pages before her.

Rufus' face flashed with irritation before he shrugged as he realised that he finally got his day to relax. They had been through a lot in a short time, after all. He made his way over to the table and sat on the chair across from the reading Princess. Stretching his legs up onto the table, he reached for an apple off the plate of fruit that had been concealed by the books.

Alicea looked up from her reading, eyes narrowing at the overly relaxed man who had taken it upon himself to come in and make himself at home in her room. Rufus greeted the look with a wide smile, oblivious to the judgemental stare he was receiving. Finally, Alicea sighed and rolled her eyes before speaking in a far more direct tone.

"Mr. Thief, do you honestly have no tact at all? This room is that of a lady. Most ladies do not like having ruffians just walk in and make themselves at home," she scolded.

"Most ladies don't try to beat me within an inch of my life with a bird that can turn into a staff," Rufus replied, mouth full of apple.

"What are you trying to say?" Alicea asked, her eyes narrowing further and adopting a darker shade of blue.

"You aren't really a lady," Rufus shrugged, crushing the core of his apple and tossing it into his mouth.

"That's it!" Alicea slammed her book down and stood. "You are so rude, Mr. Thief! I'm going to take you outside and hit you with my staff again until you learn some manners!"

"Oh, well, now I'm convinced you are a lady!" Rufus retorted.

Alicea glared at Rufus before her shoulders slumped. She threw herself back into her chair in frustration, ignoring the book that she had just been transfixed on. Instead, she stared out the window at the townspeople going about their business. Rufus reached across, grabbed another apple and bit into it before addressing her again.

"What's on your mind? Normally by now you would have tried and failed to hit me with your staff a few times."

She could barely make out what he was saying with his mouth full of fruit. As the Princess turned her pale eyes on him again, Rufus could tell that she was surprised he had even noticed.

"I've been thinking about what I've learnt under Garnet. Despite the fact that she says I've made remarkable progress,

I wonder if it's enough. I assume I'm always going to worry about that . . . I'm just not particularly confident that I was the right choice to take on this responsibility," Alicea replied.

"Well, for what it's worth, I think you were the right choice."

Alicea scoffed, looking out the window again.

"I mean it. The stone couldn't have picked a better person," Rufus offered, to which Alicea allowed a small smile. "What are you reading that's making you think like this?"

"It's called *The Magical Affinities and Their Properties*. It's a basic outline of each element. I figured it would be wise to learn about what I need to look out for when confronted by a magical opponent. While it was helpful, it got me thinking about something else entirely," Alicea answered.

"And what's that?" Rufus pressed, leaning further back in his chair.

"That almost everyone has an affinity with an element. So, what is yours, Mr. Thief?" Alicea asked.

"No idea," Rufus replied shortly.

"How enlightening." Alicea's foot started tapping under the table; she was excited. "Garnet said that Neibel-Haven has the facilities required to find out a person's affinity. We could –"

"No," Rufus replied flatly.

"Why not?" Alicea snapped impatiently, her foot becoming still.

"Because I'm no mage. I don't even like magic. All it does is hurt people. This struggle is all over power. Power that comes from the stones and magic is not to be trusted," the thief explained with a shrug.

"So, you don't trust me?" Alicea asked, catching Rufus off-guard.

"I trust you well enough given the circumstances. I just don't trust your magic," Rufus said, shooting a look at the little water-bird watching him from the bed. "So, I will not take part in magic just to sate your curiosity."

"It's not just curiosity, Mr. Thief!" began an exasperated Alicea. "Through these books I've learnt about combining two people's magic, which yields powerful results. If we had the combination of two elements on hand, we would be even more resilient when faced with a powerful foe."

"Combining magic? Why do I feel as though that would be dangerous? Besides, you will always be the superior mage with that stone of yours. I don't think I'd be much help," Rufus said, rummaging through the bowl, searching for more apples.

"It does have inherent risks," Alicea conceded. "In order to make it work you have to both be skilled and – even more importantly – in sync with one another. I think in time we could make it work."

"Us? In sync? I don't think you have had enough sleep, Princess. Where does it say this?"

"Chapter four, page thirty-seven, lines six through to twelve," Alicea replied, tossing the thief a closed book without breaking eye contact.

Rufus' brow creased at her instant response.

"That is a very annoying talent, you realise?"

"I can live with the fact that I annoy you," Alicea replied, without a hint of humour.

Rufus sighed, rising to his feet and making his way towards the doorway. Alicea leapt from her seat and raced to catch up, stopping him at the exit by slapping his arm.

"Can you at least think about it? No commitment, just think about it?" Alicea asked as Rufus rolled his eyes and stared down at the Princess waiting for his answer.

"No promises, but I will think about it," Rufus conceded. Alicea broke into a wide smile before walking back to the table.

"Thank you, Mr. Thief. Now get out. You are disrupting my reading," Alicea ordered.

"I was already leav—"

"Mr. Thief! When a lady asks you to leave her room, you do so!"

Rufus took a moment to stare blankly at the Princess, then turned and left in a confused silence. It was just easier.

CHAPTER 51

A HERETIC'S WALK

The sun was steadily rising as Rufus left the Princess' small domain and followed the dirt road leading to the site of the bonfire. As he approached the villagers' favourite place to end their day, he wished that it was night. A chill found its way under his clothes and his desire for a fire was strong. There was no fire; cold ash was all that remained of what was a splendid blaze the night before.

How did it get so cold, so quickly? Rufus thought in irritation. *It's only just coming up to autumn and this kingdom never gets colder than a small fire can handle.*

Deciding that his hammock would be an unpleasant experience during the persistent cool, the thief moved on. Taking the road opposite to the one he came from, Rufus noticed that there weren't many people on the streets. Around this time any other day, he and Alicea would be training, so he couldn't be sure of what was considered normal within the village during the day.

Through the small groups of women and children waddled an older man. Rufus recognised him, though he hadn't seen him since arriving at the village gates with Alicea. After waving to the other villagers in passing, the man named Gramere stopped at the sight of Rufus.

"Why, hello, my good man!" the older man greeted in a friendly tone that forced the thief to smile.

"Gramere, wasn't it? This village is so small that I can't help but think you've been hiding!" Rufus joked.

"Aye, care for a walk? I can't promise that I won't talk your ear off, but it's a good day for it."

Rufus shrugged and joined the older man as he strolled towards the main gate of the village.

Gramere was right, it is a great day for a walk. Rufus found himself smiling.

Despite the chill, the sun was glowing and the breeze was peaceful, gently rustling through the forest on the far side of the village. Laughter of children carried on the wind, along with the gossip of the women doing chores. The sound of conversations was enough to make him think back to his home and the twins. They were older now – soon they too would be wasting time on gossip. It was a harrowing thought.

I had better not catch them wasting time like that!

"Is something on your mind?" Gramere asked kindly, breaking Rufus' reverie.

"No, nothing. Just thinking about home a little, I suppose."

"Home is the greatest longing for a man away from it. Have you been on the road long?"

"No, not really. The brat – er, Princess and I have only been travelling a short time."

"I was referring to you alone. What did you do before accompanying Her Highness?"

"I took odd jobs. Ones that nobody wanted." Rufus found that they'd reached the front gate and were now looking at a large hole that he swore wasn't there when he'd arrived.

"I assume that way of life suited you?" Gramere asked.

"Perhaps. But there was plenty I didn't like about the jobs." Rufus shrugged as he investigated the hole dug around the front of the village. It was deep enough for even the tallest of men to take cover within.

There were hunters still digging further down the outside of the wall. Men were also patching up the palisade wall that served as the primary defence of the village. Between the wall and the trench was a natural platform of solid ground littered with countless quivers overflowing with arrows.

"Are you happy now?" Gramere asked with a smile, catching Rufus unaware.

"Happy?" the thief repeated in surprise. "What does happiness have to do with it?"

"Surely, on some level, you must be enjoying what you are doing? You do not strike me as a man who does things he doesn't like very often."

"I do things I dislike every day, but I get your point. This job is better than others I've done in a lot of ways. The client is a pain in the ass, but at least she's honest. Almost to a fault, I'd wager," Rufus replied before pointing at the trench and turning to the older man. "That is either a trench or a small moat – and the quivers littered everywhere? What's coming here, Gramere?"

"You have a way of answering questions without actually giving an answer," Gramere stated before turning his attention to the trench as well. "I'm not sure I should be telling you, but they know that Her Highness is here."

"Who?"

"The Council of Aquiocia."

"So?"

"The kingdom would very much like their Princess back," Gramere said quietly.

Rufus glanced at Gramere and noticed his serious expression. Their carefree conversation was clearly dead and buried.

"The kingdom itself might, but I was under the assumption that the Council didn't care a great deal about Alicea? They've been running things for a while now."

"That's an assumption well worth clinging to. Nothing about this sits right with the Chief, Garnet or myself. As you know, the Council took hold of the kingdom's operations when the late King and Queen passed," Gramere explained before raising his hand and pointing towards the kingdom in the distance. "Her Highness could walk into that city and scream out in the middle of the street that she would like to be crowned Queen. The people would carry her through any resistance the Council might put up and place her on the throne. It would be that simple. Aquiocians are extremely traditional in some ways and they all adore the royal family. Especially what little remains of it. They would die a thousand times each for Princess Alicea, there is no question."

"So, what's the problem?" Rufus asked, still examining the trenches. "Why not just escort her there, get her to take the throne and then she can do as she pleases?"

"It's never that simple in politics, Rufus. Especially when it involves the last of a royal lineage," Gramere said kindly. "You seem to think that seizing the throne could solve the issues buried within Aquiocia."

"I still don't see how it wouldn't help," Rufus said stubbornly. He knew he was missing something, but he couldn't tell what it was. "Alicea becomes Queen, she wields the kingdom's power."

"Ah, very true," Gramere acknowledged with a slight dip of his head in Rufus' direction. The older man allowed his company a moment to enjoy the concession before asking, "Do you think you're the only one who has thought of that course of action?"

Rufus paused.

"You see the issue then," Gramere smiled. It wasn't smug or condescending; he wanted the younger man to reach his own understanding.

"I heard a Council only acts as the head of a kingdom when the royalty is unable?"

"That's true. An example of that might be when the direct heir is unable to tend to her duties. For as long as that heir is incapacitated, the Council remains in control," Gramere nodded again, now catching and holding Rufus' gaze.

"Then that brings us back to Alicea going back and . . ." Rufus trailed off and Gramere averted his gaze. "Gramere, what happens if there is no heir within the kingdom?"

"The Council, should they come to a majority vote for a candidate, may elect one of their own to ascend the throne for as long as it takes to confirm the fate of the heir."

"And what if that heir turns up dead?"

Gramere didn't answer verbally, yet Rufus got what he needed.

"Of course. That makes sense. When she was immobilised by grief, she was easy to contain within the castle where they could keep an eye on her," Rufus conceded.

"That is our belief. The Chief will speak to her about it soon enough. Until then . . ." Gramere trailed off.

"She's not stupid –"

"We know that. Did you think that you were the only one looking out for her? Garnet has been reporting back to the Chief, the Chief has been advising Setz and myself. We know exactly how intelligent she is. But we also know how compassionate she is. She has no place on the field of battle."

"What do you suggest I do?"

"I would suggest picking her up in the middle of the night and running." Gramere shrugged and waved his hand to the east.

"That would never work. She is determined to meet with the other stone-bearer if she returns."

"Again, we know. I believe Garnet has some ideas but she is about to leave the village to meet with Setz. Ah! Here she comes!" Gramere gestured to the path they'd just walked. Garnet made her way towards the pair swiftly, a loose dress draped across her body and a small leather bag in her hand.

"I suppose I should speak to her," Rufus sighed.

"You should. Thank you for your time. I enjoyed our talk, Heretic." Gramere smiled.

Rufus' neck cracked from his head turning so fast.

"What did you call me?" Rufus asked in surprise.

"Rufus?" Gramere answered, concerned. "Am I pronouncing it wrong?"

"That's not what you said!"

"I can assure you that's what I said," Gramere squeaked, genuinely concerned that he'd angered the Princess' guardian.

"Thief!" Garnet's sharp voice came from right behind him. "If you're quite finished intimidating the people who are trying to help you, come with me. You're about to make yourself useful!"

Rufus glared at the older man for a moment before muttering an apology, to which Gramere smiled uncertainly before dismissing the event. Garnet led the thief away from the man and his battlement project, heading back the way they had come.

CHAPTER 52

A BURDEN SHARED

Alicea placed her book down when a commotion outside her hut disturbed her. Her eyes lit up with curiosity. She was about to order Rufus to investigate but she had banished him earlier. Instead the Princess got to her feet, making her way out of her personal dwelling, past her assigned guards and towards the source of the disruption.

People were running past her, cheering. There were wide smiles on their faces, but no sign of what caused their joy.

Alicea quickened her pace, only slowing to avoid being trampled by a group of large men lumbering towards the scene with the rest of the people.

Alicea ducked amongst the crowd, her small stature easily able to slip through as she weaved between the excited people.

Following the crowd, she was led to the centre of the village, where three people were walking through the gates.

One was a pretty woman with long, wavy chocolate-brown hair. She was dressed as the rest of the village and had far more muscle definition than most women Alicea had seen, yet there was an undeniable feminine air about her.

Her companions were a short, stocky man who seemed to move with pain as he supported an injured taller man on his shoulder. Oddly, the taller man's blond hair seemed to remain perfectly positioned despite the rest of his damaged appearance. The blond was the only one there aside from the Princess who was not garbed in the pelts of animals.

The crowd let out cheer after cheer as they approached.

When Alicea asked the woman beside her who the newcomers were, she replied with an apologetic explanation.

"Oh, Your Highness! I'm sorry, I didn't see you there! That is Lyrium! The shorter man is her lover, Arok. The man with the long hair is not of this village but is the couple's close friend, Stefan!"

The woman quickly left Alicea to absorb the information and followed the other villagers running up to the trio. Some villagers carried Stefan off for medical attention while the others stood and continued cheering. The man named Arok seemed to brush off the offer of assistance and limped after the ones carrying Stefan.

This left Lyrium smiling at the crowd before reaching into her pack. The crowd fell silent at the action before she thrust her fist into the air in a victorious pose.

What appeared to be a fist-sized garnet caught the midday sun, spraying a surreal, sepia haze across the village. With a mighty roar, Lyrium let all the pent-up pride and triumph fly freely from her lungs. The crowd instantly lost control and swarmed her, some offering congratulations while others joined her primal cry.

The sound startled Alicea; she didn't know the purpose of the barbaric yelling.

Lyrium laughed with her people for a long while as Alicea waited patiently. The Princess was watching the proceedings with an uncertain smile on her face when a man caught sight of her. He excitedly turned to Lyrium, saying something that made her look over curiously before telling the overexcited crowd to make room as she made her way through towards the Princess.

"Is it true?" she began excitedly. "You are the Princess of Aquiocia?"

"I am." Alicea's smile widened. "I am also a bearer of a stone like yours."

Alicea produced her beautiful sapphire-coloured stone so that the two incredible jewels could be held next to each other. Alicea's smile softened, feeling the burden of being alone lifting already. She had another ally.

"I don't believe it – you must have arrived just after I left for the ruins," Lyrium said.

"Yes, only a week ago," Alicea replied.

"What? A week?"

"Well, that's how long I have been here. Kurok said you had left the day before I arrived. So, it has been a week," Alicea explained.

"I – I see." Lyrium looked down thoughtfully. "I must see my father-in-law immediately then. Please excuse me, Your Highness. I will find you afterwards."

"Please, call me Alicea. We will speak at length when you are free." Alicea smiled understandingly.

Lyrium took one last look at the Princess, taking her in before nodding, smiling and finally darting off towards Kurok's hut. A weight fell away from the Princess' heart, one borne from the prospect of facing a great ordeal alone. She hadn't doubted Setz's advice, but she had doubted her nomination as a Vassal. She had doubted herself and her ability to do it alone. Meeting another in a similar position changed things. *I'm not the only one after all.*

❖

Alicea was back in her designated visitor's hut as the last hours of morning were passing. She was still reading the books that Garnet had left when she was interrupted by a sharp rap of knuckles on wood. Alicea looked up from her reading, calling out that the visitor may enter. Lyrium walked through the doorway. Her long, wavy brown hair had been washed and was bouncing with life. Her clothes had been changed to a cleaner variant, this time with a wolf pelt tied around her neck.

"Ah, I see you have had a chance to wash," Alicea greeted Lyrium in a friendly tone.

"Yes, it is something you never expect to miss until you find out the day you were gone lasted a week," Lyrium joked. Both the ladies smiled uncertainly, unsure of how to further address each other.

The pair sat in silence for a long while, just looking at each other, before Alicea asked, "Would you like to tell me how you came in contact with your stone?"

The ice broke with that one question.

Lyrium told Alicea everything, from why they had been looking for the ruins, to the history of Tremel. For the most part, Alicea already knew Tremel's history from books. Nonetheless, she learnt a great deal about how Tremel was divided after the great battle against a powerful force they believed to be Lucian.

"I mean no offence," Alicea started carefully as her guest

cocked her head. "Do you truly believe that Lucian, the man practically written off as a myth, returned to level Tremel?"

Lyrium shrugged. "It's what I've been taught, so I will believe it until proven otherwise." She didn't look offended by the question, breaking into the story behind the separation of Tremel's people after the devastation.

Alicea had known that shortly after the battle, the residents of Tremel scattered to other settlements. What she hadn't known was that the Tremel she had become acquainted with was the smallest of all. She listened quietly until Lyrium mentioned the statue at the centre of the ruins.

"Tell me about her!" Alicea ordered enthusiastically before adding. "Please."

"She sacrificed herself," Lyrium said shortly, taking a moment to pick her words. "She was . . . a person. A person who knew what was expected of her."

Alicea smiled faintly, allowing her guest a moment to collect her thoughts. Lyrium's expression grew thoughtful as she recited what the Chief had told her around the bonfire. While Alicea was captivated by the story of sacrifice and the woman who had wielded one of the stones before her, she could see the apprehension on Lyrium's face. Alicea had seen the look before – the look of someone working through something.

Try as she might, Alicea couldn't refrain from asking every question that came to her. The story stretched across hours as the morning became noon.

This story would be told a lot quicker if the Princess didn't interrupt so often, thought Lyrium.

Lyrium never protested, though. After being accompanied by men for what turned out to be a week, she was happy to have a woman to talk about it all with. Lyrium shifted the conversation to her trials within the ruins, giving Alicea every detail she could recall. The Princess' face shifted from wonder to horror and back countless times throughout the hunter's recount.

She asked very few questions about the trials during the time it took Lyrium to give her recount. She instead focused on absorbing it all; it was an indication of just what the stones were capable of. It wasn't until Lyrium reached the part of her tale where she found the stone that Alicea blurted out her restrained string of questions.

"It spoke to you? What did it say? Was it female? Did it give any insight as to why we were chosen?" Alicea fired off the built-up questions she had been struggling with.

"It gave little information on *why* we were chosen but I think these events have been in the works a fair while," Lyrium said and proceeded to recite some of the things the voice had said, before adding, "I've never heard a voice like it before, but I believe it is male."

"The voice that spoke to me was female," Alicea offered. "Though it gave no further information than what the voice that spoke to you supplied."

The Princess sighed, a little disappointed that even with their collaboration they were unable to further discern the motives of the stones. Lyrium, however, was quickly distracted from the conversation when her eyes fell on Alicea's tiny bird. It had been lying behind the pillow on her bed the whole conversation, its graceful neck turned to watch Lyrium.

"It *is* a bird!" Lyrium exclaimed, approaching slowly as the swan retreated behind the pillow.

"Hmm?" Alicea looked over her shoulder. "Oh yes, she's my little friend!"

"Your . . . little friend . . ." Lyrium let the words roll of her tongue as she slowly approached the bed, hands in front of her, ready to grab the bird.

"Would you like to hold her?"

"What?"

Alicea didn't repeat herself. Instead she looked over at the pillow.

Come out and say hello.

The swan's head reappeared from its shelter again, shooting a look at its owner. With a puff of its feathers, it hopped from behind the pillow and across the bed to Lyrium's waiting hands. Rather than grabbing at the bird, Lyrium took an involuntary step backwards, uncertain now that the strange bird was interested in her. The hunter raised a wary hand up and gently poked the swan's head. Soft ripples branched out from the contact, but the form held. The swan looked from the hunter's face to the pocket of her pants.

"Does it eat?"

"She does," Alicea smiled, amused by the entire scene before her.

Lyrium didn't reply immediately, reaching into the pocket that had the swan's attention and producing a few wild berries on a thin vine. The swan's head twitched from the berries to Lyrium's face and back again. After a moment, Lyrium handed the fruit over. The swan snatched the vine from her hand and immediately retreated back to its hiding place with its prize.

"Alright, I'll bite. Why does it look like water?" the confused hunter asked, returning to her seat.

Alicea broke into a laugh. "Probably because she *is* water! I will gladly tell you, but in order to do that I'll need to tell you how I came about *my* stone and my journey to Tremel, which may take a while," Alicea answered.

Lyrium leant back in her chair to get comfortable.

"I'm sure I can make time," she encouraged with a grin.

Having all the encouragement she needed, Alicea dove into her own tale. She briefly explained what had become of her parents, a story that most already knew. Alicea didn't allow herself to dwell, moving quickly onto the kidnapping and her meeting with Rufus.

"Mr. Thief?" Lyrium asked before laughing. "You mean Rufus?"

"How do you know about him?"

"I saw his hammock at the bonfire and asked about it!" Lyrium said, still chuckling and shaking her head slightly.

"Yes, well, Mr. Thief likes to think that he may do whatever he pleases," Alicea sniffed before continuing.

Alicea told Lyrium everything, from the conversation with the stone at the spring, to her training under Garnet. She gave Lyrium every detail that seemed relevant before finally shrugging and saying, "And here I am."

Lyrium sighed, taking in everything and laughing again. Alicea stared questioningly, and the hunter explained what she found humorous.

"The whole kidnapping part sounds almost romantic, don't you think? Handsome man taking you away from a castle – it's the type of story bards sing," Lyrium said through laughter.

"Mr. Thief is not a man, he is a scoundrel!" Alicea retorted, annoyed at Lyrium's perception of the situation.

"Getting angry just proves that your words are lies!" Lyrium exclaimed playfully.

"I . . . That is, Mr. Thief is . . ." Alicea spluttered before throwing her hands up, exasperated, and shaking her head. "He is not what is important in this story!"

"You're right, of course." Lyrium broke off from her laughter and looked seriously at the Princess. "I have to tell you something. The Chief, he . . ."

Alicea's eyebrows rose at her guest's sudden hesitation.

"He believes there are knights getting ready to come and get you."

"Knights from my kingdom? So, they must have caught wind that I'm here," Alicea said quietly.

"So, you expected this? What will you do?" Lyrium asked.

"I can't go back, not yet. Not until I can decipher what it is I am meant to do with this power," Alicea replied, pausing slightly before adding, "There's something you're not telling me."

"Aye," Lyrium nodded, still hesitant about sharing all she knew. "The Chief is suspicious of Aquiocia's movements."

"I'm not surprised," Alicea said cryptically. Lyrium looked puzzled, but didn't ask for clarification.

"I want you to know that Tremel has your back, Princess."

Alicea's eyebrows rose in surprise. "You don't even know what you're volunteering for."

"True!" Lyrium grinned. "I don't know what you or the Chief are thinking, but whatever you choose to do, we support you. It's our duty."

"I thank you for your support." Alicea smiled warmly, though her pale eyes reflected concern.

"Well, it was good to swap stories and compare where we each are in this whole mess," Lyrium said as she stood and made for the door. "A pleasure to meet you, Princess. I'll see you tomorrow with any further information."

"I told you before, call me Alicea. Thank you for everything."

After Lyrium had left, Alicea reflected on their encounter. There was something liberating about the way Lyrium spoke to her as an equal. Lyrium wasn't someone serving or tending to her; she seemed the sort that one could speak to about anything.

Have I made a friend?

Her thoughts were interrupted when Lyrium's head popped through the pelt hanging over her doorway. With a massive grin, she stated, "By the way, I noticed that you didn't argue when I said that Rufus was handsome."

She was gone before Alicea could react. A blush spread across the young Princess' face as she stood alone in her room.

Yes, I have made quite the friend.

CHAPTER 53

THE ELEMENTAL CHRONICLES

Rufus had barely pushed his way through the doorway of bear pelt before Alicea was berating him. She held a collection of various plants from the forest, gathered by a villager upon her request. She had taken a break from studying and was twisting the flowers around small pieces of ornate metal. With one final twist, she pulled back her hair into a ponytail and placed the ornament at the base of it. The earthy colours collected with shades of orange lit up her dark hair nicely as her eyes narrowed at Rufus.

"Odd, I'm quite certain that I told you to stay out of my room, Mr. Thief!"

"Odd, I'm quite certain that I've told you to shut your royal mouth on many occasions, and yet here we are!" Rufus snarled in response.

"What isn't odd is the sight of you two failing to grow up!" Garnet quipped as she bustled into the room.

"Garnet!" Alicea exclaimed. "I apologise –"

"Save it, I have precious little time."

Garnet placed a perfect, wooden cube on the table. Each side of the timber was marked with a different illustration in glowing – almost lustrous – ink of different colours.

It took the Princess a moment to realise that the markings

represented each of the six elements, one upon each of the surfaces of the cube. As she stared at the item, she was met with a strong sense of déjà vu and she knew what it was even before Rufus spoke.

"The Elemental Chronicles."

"Indeed." Garnet's eyebrow rose in surprise.

"My father played this game with the soldiers! He and Maxim would lock themselves in a chamber for hours. They said it was too dangerous for me to play!" Alicea exclaimed.

"Well, it's finally your turn. The thief here will be your opponent," Garnet smiled.

"Not interested," Rufus said simply.

"I don't recall asking if you were," Garnet replied.

"I researched this item in the royal Aquiocian library and came up with very few details," Alicea said with a frown. "All I managed to find out was that it is a dangerous and exceptionally rare item."

"Both statements are absolutely correct," Garnet declared. "It's addictive and I am going to allow your friend here to explain why to the best of his ability."

Rufus rolled his eyes and sighed before revealing what he knew.

"The game looks inside your mind and crafts an environment for you to compete against your opponent within."

"What?" Alicea asked in confusion. "It is a cube, Mr. Thief."

"Really? I hadn't caught that detail, thank you! Now, may I finish?"

Alicea turned to Garnet, who glared at the pair with impatience. Thankfully, Rufus broke the silence, continuing his explanation.

"You need a playing piece that resembles a small block of

wood. The more you play, the more the block takes shape. One game isn't enough and most players either don't survive or stop playing long before their block of wood changes. Of course, not just any wood will do – the player pieces are as rare as the game itself." Rufus shrugged. "The piece bonds to its owner upon starting their first game and will not respond to anyone else after that."

"And have you played enough that your piece has changed?" Garnet asked knowingly. The thief offered a glare in response.

"So, how do I acquire my own piece?" Alicea asked. "Also, how does this make the game dangerous?"

"It's difficult to explain. The quickest way would be to play a round or two," Rufus conceded, warming to the idea of playing. "But I will be playing on your side."

"You will be playing against her. It will be the best way for her to learn quickly and hone her skills," Garnet ordered with forced patience. She glanced towards the doorway, clearly wanting to be off.

"It's not safe, you know that!" Rufus insisted.

"I do know that. Now may I see your piece?"

Rufus could tell he was losing the debate so he reached into his coat and, after a few moments of rooting around, produced a small wooden statuette of himself.

It was crafted well enough. Anyone could tell that the shape of a man leaning against a wall was Rufus, but it was as if the craftsman had stopped work suddenly. From the waist down was a long rectangular base, waiting to be carved into legs.

Alicea grabbed the figurine and brought it up to her face, turning it in her fingers. Other features of the miniature Rufus were roughly carved. His hair was chunky, not pushed up on his head like the real article. His blades looked like small toy swords, blunt, with none of the dangerous gleam of the ones hanging from the original's hips.

The element that really caught the ladies' attention was a strange light within the statuette's chest that glowed black and white in equal measures. It was faint, but definitely there.

While the display coming from the figurine was of great interest to Garnet, the Princess was following a completely different train of thought.

"Where do I get one?" she exclaimed.

"You aren't getting one unless I'm on your side, damn it!" Rufus snapped.

"But I –"

"I said no!" Rufus yelled before continuing. "I will not have the blood of a royal brat who was tempted by a damn crow on my hands!"

"Rufus!" Garnet's voice rose but it wasn't the volume that stopped his outburst. It was the fact that she actually used his name.

"What?"

"This exercise will be good to sharpen her mind. The game is useless to the average mage without tutelage. But Alicea *is* rather clever despite *your* reluctance to acknowledge it!"

"I'm the first to acknowledge that she is clever – when she actually takes the time to think things through – but I –"

"Do you see how this could be beneficial to her?"

"I do," Rufus sighed. "But –"

"So, would you say that she would be better off with you teaching her? Or should I summon a trainee within the village?" she taunted.

"Are you going to actually let me finish a damned thought?"

"Just as soon as it's one that isn't borne from poorly concealed concern for her life. If you're worried about her, stop acting like a selfish child who has been forced to share his toys for the first time and actually look after her!"

Rufus' expression turned foul and for just a moment, he looked as though he might attack the older woman.

"Is that it, Mr. Thief? Is it actual concern for me? Or is it just about your reward once this is over?" Alicea asked with genuine curiosity.

Rufus looked down at the shining emblems on the wooden cube, searching for a response that would placate the pair of women staring at him expectantly. In the end, he ran his fingers through his hair and said with a resigned sigh, "Get her a damn piece."

"Here." Garnet produced a piece of timber the length of an outstretched hand with a small smile that suggested the argument from fifteen seconds ago had never transpired.

"It's not very exciting," Alicea noted as she took the block from the older woman and examined it.

"It won't be until we start playing," Rufus muttered.

"I must go now," Garnet announced. "I did not account for having to argue with Rufus, but fortunately he knows how to play so when you two are ready, you may step outside and begin. Play safe."

Garnet was out of the door almost before she finished speaking. Any other time Alicea would have been curious as to what was keeping her instructor so busy, but today her excitement to play was too much. The game her father once took great interest in.

"Can we play now?"

"Yes, on one condition," Rufus sighed.

"What is it?"

"You need to listen to me. This can be very dangerous." Rufus waved his hand at a loss for words. "Just . . . listen to me, alright?"

"I will, Mr. Thief. Now, let's begin!"

As the excited Princess and reluctant thief stepped out from the shack, they were not greeted by the midday sun as expected. Erected above them was a wide tarp made of feathers gently blowing in the breeze. Below the cover were four chairs and a medium-sized tree stump with a small cube-sized hole in the centre. Alicea stared at the orifice curiously. It was clear that it was there by design and she knew what was supposed to be within it.

"Sit down, I'll set it up," was Rufus' response when she spun around looking for the cube in his hands.

The thief took in the passing people going about their daily duties. There were few, as the Chief had organised one of the more secluded dwellings for his royal visitor. Despite the mundane nature of the chores the villagers were undergoing, Rufus did not overlook the group of three burly men staring at them across the way. Quickly weighing up the crowded table that the brutish-looking men occupied, he noticed two younger women dressed in owl feathers.

His first instinct was to analyse the group further, but he recognised one of the bigger men. The one who had spotted Rufus looking their way and was waving at him.

That's . . . Breant? The hunter from the front gate.

They were making sure there was someone overlooking

the game from a distance in case anything went wrong. The mountains of meat were to subdue either player physically, whereas he was willing to bet the women in the feathered cloaks were shamans from the village. Garnet had thought of everything. What's more, Alicea was so excited that she hadn't noticed their audience in the distance. It was a pleasant surprise. Normally she didn't miss anything.

Rufus turned his attention back to the sitting Princess, who was investigating the new arrangement. He joined her at the table, glancing at the spare chairs.

"Apparently, we were not originally meant to play alone," Rufus observed.

"Can you play with more than two people?" Alicea looked on curiously.

"Of course, but we're going to keep it simple," Rufus explained as he lowered the cube into the centre of the stump.

Alicea's eyes grew as the cube settled into the hole. The moment it was secured, brilliant rays of light shredded through the shade offered by the feathered cloth above them. Before long an aurora of light burst forth, bright enough to force Alicea to look away.

Then it was gone.

The Princess slowly turned to Rufus, following his gaze back to the table. Covering the surface of the stump was a transparent map of a dense forestland. It was taken from a bird's point of view. Alicea quickly noted a few landmarks on the map: a large coursing river, a mountain range in the east and a few villages littered here and there.

The entire map had thin white lines criss-crossing through the land in random and erratic directions. The amount of lines was denser over the rougher terrain, such as the water and the mountain range.

The more the young Princess stared at the landscape, the more her interest and intrigue grew. It seemed that more detail was being added to the map by the second and while she had no idea how it was going to work, she couldn't keep her enthusiasm in check.

"Alright! Is it my turn?" Alicea squealed, her foot tapping in anticipation.

"You're joking, right?" Rufus questioned in disbelief. "I have to give you fair warning of the risk of playing."

"Well, go on then!" Alicea snapped impatiently.

"The biggest risk is addiction," Rufus explained. "It seems ridiculous, but it is a very real possibility."

"Addiction?"

"Some people become consumed by the game. They start to lose sight of reality."

"It is a game, Mr. Thief." Alicea rolled her eyes. "I'm sure I will be able to handle it."

"Sure," Rufus shrugged. "But the second I think you are in any danger, the game is finished."

"Yes, yes, you're in charge. I'm sure that's a wonderful concept for you. Now, let's get the game going before you get too full of yourself!"

"Fine," Rufus conceded, allowing a small smile.

I am going to humble this brat!

"Alright, what do we do?"

"Simple. Throw your playing piece onto the board."

Alicea looked down at her hand and realised she was still clutching the block of wood. Her knuckles had even turned white. *Am I really that tense?*

It was a strange notion that she should feel this excited about anything after spending twelve months feeling so numb. She'd forced herself to dismiss any strong emotions; having something to look forward to now felt completely ridiculous. She brushed the thought aside, deciding it would be better addressed later when she could think in peace. She let the block of wood roll from her hand onto the strange surface covering the stump.

The landscape ruptured countless times before returning to its original state. As it settled another force collided with the transparent land. If Alicea's had made ripples, Rufus' playing piece made a tidal wave. The Princess swore that she felt the atmosphere around her adjust slightly. As if the game was drawing upon the real world.

Ridiculous, it's just nerves.

"Right," Rufus stated as the map settled. "Time to begin. You may go first."

Her opponent waved over the board with his hand and Alicea gasped as the overhead map magnified. As she stared at the image before her, she felt as though she was falling. The stream that split the forest was getting larger, but that wasn't her destination. No, the game's target was found shortly after the fall through the floral canopy of the forest's trees. The Princess' view was displayed from above the forest floor, overlooking a figure.

"My piece . . ." the Princess swallowed loudly.

"What about it?" She could hear the smirk in Rufus' voice as it came from around her.

With her arms crossed and her right foot tapping the ground

impatiently, there stood a young woman. She couldn't make out much as the woman had her back turned. Her long, dark hair was tinged with strands of red by the beams of sunlight through the trees; it covered her back and fell just below her buttocks. She knew who she was looking at, but it did nothing to prepare her for what faced her when the woman turned.

Alicea's playing piece spun, looking up at her. At first she was too alarmed at the sight of her own face staring at her to realise the piece was saying something to her and stomping her foot in irritation. Try as she might, she couldn't hear the words of her counterpart. Tearing her eyes away from her doppelganger, Alicea looked up at Rufus.

"It's me!" Alicea squealed. "I thought you said it took a few games for my piece to take shape?"

"It does. From what I've heard, it taking shape is the piece bonding with you and it grows as you do. But, it can replicate you in-game from the start."

Despite having more questions, Alicea put them aside as she noticed that her replica was becoming more irritated. "I'm – ahem, *she's* – angry and trying to tell me something?"

"Without telling me anything about your location, is she stamping her foot and pointing into the distance?"

"Yes," Alicea said as she stared down at the game.

"As the piece is a manifestation of you, I'd say she's having a tantrum and telling you to hurry up."

"I think she's angry that she doesn't have a brush – her hair is all over the place!" Alicea replied, ignoring Rufus and absentmindedly stroking her own hair.

"Are you planning on using this game as a damn mirror or do you think Princess Vanity could tear her gaze away from herself for the minute it takes to play her turn?"

"Oh, fine!" Alicea snapped, releasing her hair from her hand's gentle grasp. "How do I take my turn?"

"Firstly, you know it's your turn when the board focuses on your piece. I can't see your piece right now, and you never give away your location. Your opponent may try mind games on you to give up your surroundings but they will never be able to cheat. The game's enchantments make sure of that."

Rufus shifted in his wooden chair until he was in the comfortable pose of leaning forward with his legs apart, arms resting limply with elbow to knee.

"All you have to do is make a decision in your mind," Rufus finished cryptically.

"Make a decision?"

"Decide what you will do and touch your piece," Rufus encouraged. "The goal is to disable your opponent."

"I'm not sure I understand, but I will try." Alicea nodded, leaning forward slowly.

Uncertain, yet calm, Alicea tentatively extended her finger towards her tiny doppelganger. *Perhaps I should explore the surroundings . . .*

Her counterpart's expression changed instantly, giving her a massive smile and spinning on her heel to face the forest before her. The Princess didn't feel like she had a plan; she wasn't even sure she grasped the rules properly. But when her finger made contact with her piece, the main attraction of the game became abundantly clear.

❖

"Turn begins!" a booming voice resonated within Alicea's skull the moment her finger tapped her piece.

Her mind felt like it was dragged away as her vision blurred. The Princess' consciousness was moving fast when suddenly it came to a dead stop. The halt wasn't painful, but her mind whirled from the mental whiplash.

The next thing she saw gave the Princess the peculiar sensation of waking up all over again, like opening her eyes for the first time to a fresh, new morning. The sight before her wasn't a bedroom; it was the forestland behind Tremel.

As far as she could see in any direction was the lush, green flora akin to the circle of nature surrounding the training grounds. The difference was that she was within the brush and there was very little in the way of open plains to see, much less run across.

Because that's what she was doing – running. Her legs were moving quickly through the brush with an essence of sure footing that surprised even her. When did she become so nimble?

This *wasn't* her. It wasn't actually her, Alicea, running through the forestland.

But why could she feel the twigs snapping under the thin yet strong leather of her boots? Why could she feel the air brushing across her face while her lungs steadily tightened and relaxed? Why did she feel the anxiety of knowing that she had been pitted against an enemy in a game that had become so much more real than she could have imagined?

Because this *was* her. She was perceptive enough to realise that while she was obviously under the influence of the game, what was before her was an absolute reality in its own right. It was real, and she had to be careful.

Her legs stopped running and it took her a moment to realise the piece expected another decision. There was a massive, rocky ridge before her, and it was clear that the landmark was why she stopped running. But, she hadn't told herself to stop. She hadn't slowed her speed. She wasn't in full control unless she knew what she wanted.

"Make a decision!" The same booming voice from before bellowed across the land.

Is that the game's voice?

Alicea's eyes darted up the side of the ridge and she knew that she could climb it if she chose to. It would take time and she didn't know what she'd find at its peak. She didn't like the idea of attempting to navigate the forest. She wasn't trained in survival, and forests were known to house all sorts of beasts. Besides, she could hear something of much more interest from further up the ridge. She could hear running water.

Her decision was made and her legs were in motion, this time along the length of the ridge's base. She could guess roughly where she was on the overhead map, recalling the landscape with ease. She placed it as one of the mountainside's edges as she looked up at the growing altitude of its sheer cliff face. But that wasn't of any interest as she rounded a corner made from solid, grey stone and found the running water she'd heard.

Before her was a cascade of water falling down the mountainside. As it followed its vertical descent, the Princess realised that she wasn't on the bottom floor as the liquid fell into a chasm before colliding with the bottom in a spray of white mist. Carefully examining the stone opening, she noticed that the way the water flowed suggested there was a stream below her. The climb was steep and the idea of climbing down had inherent danger. But she knew being near water was her best chance at standing against her opponent.

Alternatively, I could go higher or return to the forest. No, I will find a safe point to work out my next move.

Alicea spun around, gently lowering herself over the side of the cliff face. Much to her alarm her body scampered down the side of the ridge with ease. She tried to tell herself to slow down out of fear of falling, but she knew her decision had been made. She could feel the game pulling at her body, forcing it to stand by her decision. Its hold wasn't as strong as it was back in the forest, but Alicea submitted to the sensation of being moved by an unseen force as it seemed reliable for getting her to the bottom safely.

She had no idea how deep the water was and whether it'd save her should she fall. She couldn't shake the assumption that it was shallow and a sudden descent would break her neck. She was a quarter of the way down when the booming voice from before reverberated around the land.

"Turn complete!"

"What do you mean?" Alicea screamed as her surroundings turned dark.

It was as if the entire process of day turning to night happened in the space of a second. Except there was no twinkling stars in the sky and there was no light from a glowing moon. All that remained was a terrified woman clinging to the wall of stone. Then the Princess was face to face with her opponent. Rufus sat before her, smirking in the same fashion that irritated her beyond measure. It was the smirk he wore when he knew something she didn't. She hated how often he found an opportunity to wear it.

"What is it, Mr. Thief?" Alicea demanded. "Have you won?"

"Won?" Rufus laughed. "I haven't even had a turn yet! Look around you."

She had been too focused on Rufus. Her face grew warm when she realised she was sitting at the game table in Tremel. A few villagers had slowed to check on the commotion, while others who knew what had happened were stifling laughter.

"Well, this is embarrassing," Alicea admitted.

"Forget it. Everyone is thrown off in the beginning. I once witnessed a man get trapped within the game during his very first turn. His sanity didn't return and they eventually found him face-down in an inch-deep puddle of water. The idiot drowned," Rufus shrugged.

"That is incredibly insensitive, Mr. Thief! That man needed help – how could you just laugh at him?"

"The risks were well known to him and he was told time after time to not play. The fool didn't listen and threw a big old bag of coin down as a wager. Nobody in the Underbelly would pass up that kind of bet," Rufus replied with a little too much indignation.

"It was you," Alicea whispered, as her expression turned to disgust. "You were his opponent!"

"I didn't say that I –"

"Admit it!"

"Alicea, I –"

"ADMIT IT BEFORE I ORDER MY GUARDS –"

"WHAT GUARDS, BRAT?" It was Rufus' turn to yell.

The pair looked ready to rip each other's heads off and Breant's group was watching closely from across the way. Sensing that they might intervene, Rufus buckled.

"Aye, I was his opponent," the thief muttered, his fingers already running through his hair.

"That man's blood is on your hands," Alicea sniffed.

"Aye, and it's blended in nicely with all the rest," Rufus snarled before adding in a softer tone, "They said they'd look after him. You'll have to forgive me if I choose to laugh it off rather than be consumed by remorse."

"Don't speak as though you know anything about remorse!"

"If you're so well-versed in the sensation, why don't you tell me the good it has done for you?"

The pair fell silent. Rufus sighed and looked away from the Princess' eyes. He knew that he'd gone too far before the words had even fallen from his mouth. Sure enough, when he glanced back, Alicea's expression was one of absolute fury. But it wasn't the rage that made a knife turn in the thief's stomach; it was the tears running down her face.

"Alicea, I am sorry. I wasn't referring to your parents."

"Then what were you referring to?" Alicea wiped her face.

"I – I don't know. I'm sorry," Rufus admitted.

"Apologising does nothing for the one who was hurt. Remember that next time you want to throw hurtful remarks around," Alicea lectured, wiping her face again and beaming.

"You little brat!" Rufus exclaimed as he realised he'd been played.

"Mr. Thief, unless your turn requires you to speak, I'd greatly appreciate it if you closed your mouth before you offend anyone else."

Rufus snickered, deciding that the fact the Princess before him wasn't really crying was the best outcome he could have hoped for. Rather than replying, he reached around to the back of his neck and yanked at the dark cloak he always wore. The fabric fell easily and the top half of his gear fell from his body to reveal a roughly spun and very basic shirt. Rufus wrapped the cloak in a rough ball and placed it on the seat beside him.

The sleeves of his shirt were cut short, ideally mutilated so the wearer could remain cool in the hot weather. While the cover above them offered great shade, the day had warmed and it was the first time the Princess had seen the thief even slightly relaxed. Sure, she'd seen him constantly sleeping, but even in those times his body seemed tense, anxious even.

This game seems to soothe Mr. Thief.

Alicea noticed that his arms were not the size of the burly men of Tremel – they were leaner. Strangely enough, it didn't make the thief seem scrawny, nor weak. The faint tan on his arms suggested that he had spent enough time uncloaked, but he didn't live in the sun like the hunters of the small village with their bronzing skin.

The Princess only realised she was staring when the surface of Rufus' skin flashed with luminous lines of black and white. They were only there for a fraction of a second and Alicea had no time to comprehend the pattern before they were gone again.

What was that? They were like tattoos, but they kept moving. They glowed more brightly than any black or white I've seen. They were not normal ink.

"Right then!" Rufus announced, stretching his limbs as if he were about to undertake a lengthy run. Instead, the thief reached out with a single finger towards the board before him. Alicea looked for any sign of the tattoos but they were not interested in showing themselves again.

Did they even exist? The Princess tried grasping at the image within her mind but it was as if the memory was being deliberately washed away as she reached out for it. *I never fail to recall – what is happening here?*

Rufus had obviously noticed nothing as his finger connected with the board and a serene look took its place upon his face. The Princess' attention returned to the game, the phenomenon completely forgotten.

Nothing about her opponent's turn was revealed to her and yet she couldn't tear her eyes away. The board reflected the map with its bird's-eye view and Rufus' hand hadn't moved. His piece, however, must have moved, as it had disappeared from her view. Nothing about the scene before her gave any information she could use, least of all Rufus' blank expression.

Was this the expression I had when it was my turn? she wondered. *Probably, up until I decided to lose my composure anyway.*

His turn was done in what felt like seconds and the thief leant back in his chair and put his hands behind his head. She had never seen the man so at ease. It was as if the game completely relaxed him.

"That's it?"

"Mm, and a fast game is a good game," Rufus prodded.

"Alright," Alicea grumbled as she reached out.

"One last tip: anything can happen from here in," Rufus revealed. "The first turn generally gives you a chance to get your bearings. Not always, but usually."

"What is your point, Mr. Thief?"

"The point is that the game touches your mind, searches through it. It searches through *you*. All players are on equal footing. The game is fair. You go in as yourself. With your capabilities, strengths and weaknesses. That's as clear as I can make it."

CHAPTER 54

EIDETIC RECOLLECTION

Alicea's feet hit solid ground. She was covered in a thin sheet of moisture, standing at the shallow end of the gathering liquid. She had finally scaled the stone wall. Now, she stood opposite the cascade filling the grand pool in front of her. Before she had a chance to take in the beauty of it all, she pivoted slowly in a full circle, searching for threats and the like.

I've been around Mr. Thief too long. I've never been this paranoid.

Relatively satisfied that she wasn't about to be ambushed, she gazed up at the natural formation that she had just scaled down. Even the path she had taken was slick with moisture from the spray of falling water. She stood opposite the constant collision, yet her clothes were steadily collecting moisture. It was time to move.

Set into the side of the wall was an arch of smooth stone leading into a cave. Along the floor of the natural opening escaped a steady trickle of water from the main body. Short of climbing back up to the top, the cave was her best bet. Glancing back at the much deeper pool of collected liquid and sighing, she took her first steps towards the only option she had.

Her footsteps were masked by the running water. There were cavities everywhere in the cave's form. While they were nothing that would bring the ceiling down upon her, there were small beams of light that slipped through that cracks.

Another light caught her eye, flickering ahead of her from around a bend. As she slowed her approach, she identified the light as the same emitted from a small campfire. *The only other person playing is Mr. Thief. Why would he set up a camp?* Her mind whirled with possibilities. *Is it a trap? Or maybe he's sleeping. Knowing him, it could be both.*

Part of her mind was already reaching out to the trickling water, grasping at small amounts of the liquid and bringing them together until the Princess knelt and picked up what had become her weapon of choice – the staff.

If he is asleep, I could secure an advantage.

Then she heard voices – men's voices.

Creeping closer to the bend, pressed up against the firm wall of earth and stone, Alicea closed her eyes to focus on the sound of the voices around the corner. They spoke like brutes, grunting in place of certain words through their sentences, but they were largely coherent.

They're drunk, Alicea figured, but it wasn't what caught her attention. They sounded familiar.

The anxiety within her told her she knew each of the five men the voices belonged to. She knew she would have to confirm her recollection. It was time to take a gamble. Inching her head around the corner, Alicea's eyes widened with dread before she hastily concealed herself again. She'd seen the small fire and large kegs of whatever nauseating substance they were drinking. She'd also seen the side of two of the men's faces.

Marn and Rhept, the drunkards Mr. Thief got rid of. She pursed her lips.

The Princess had briefly caught sight of the other faces as well, but they had been pushed further back within her memory.

Who are they?

"Who are you?" The question remained unacknowledged for a moment as Alicea pulled herself from her investigation to notice the swaying man behind her.

How?

The man stumbled toward her – whether with intention or as a result of the booze was anyone's guess as her body instinctively stepped around him and her staff found his face. She almost couldn't believe what she'd done. She had only ever sparred against Rufus and yet she attacked a man without hesitation. Was this the game controlling her? She could feel its hold weakening as her body stepped around behind the now howling man and with a fierce jab to the spine, her enemy lurched backwards into the open campsite.

That . . . That wasn't the game . . .

Shadows within the flame's light raced towards the wounded man as the Princess struck again. Her staff found another man's middle; it was the man called Rhept. He was now doubled over, winded and shocked at the sight of Alicea.

It didn't force me to do that . . .

She saw Marn's loathsome face next. His expression at the sight of the Princess was one of a starving animal when it saw a deserted carcass.

"Well, the Princess has come around –" His words were cut short as her weapon's blunt tip found the bridge of his nose. His face crumpled around the indent made by her staff. Guilt assaulted the Princess, but vanished as soon as she saw the now horizontal man writhing and screaming curses at her. She hadn't killed. Not yet.

And I won't! she screamed internally, accepting that what was happening around her was her own doing. Her epiphany was emphasised by the air softly shuddering around her. It was subtle and easily dismissed by the distracted Princess.

"My, my, my. Hasn't the Princess grown?" A familiar, smug voice caught Alicea's attention as she stepped over the incapacitated men to confront the rest.

The fire's light hit the sitting man's face for the first time and recognition found the young woman.

Memories of a market festival from almost sixteen years ago consumed her mind. At four years of age, the streamers and laughter had been too much for her to resist. She had fled the castle to partake in the festivities, eluding the knights and their regulated patrols with ease. But what she found was the torment of men who knew her worth as a ransom.

"You!" Alicea spluttered, rage and fear fighting within her. Her spare hand rose to her temple, rubbing the tender spot on her head to soothe the pain running through it. The recollection made her head throb.

"Aye, me. But that's all you know me as, isn't it? One of the men who tried to kidnap you. Do you know what happened to us?"

"Do I look like I care?" Alicea snapped.

"Bit hypocritical, don't you think? You show us nothing but hate for doing what we had to do to survive, but to the man who actually stole you from your castle, you show respect," the man shrugged.

His demeanour was aloof and even as he rose to his feet,

he kept a safe distance. It didn't seem to be out of fear, but in an attempt to keep the conversation flowing. His dark, oily hair was slicked back into a messy bun, allowing his dirty, unshaven face to be seen by the shaking Princess. Alicea looked back at the men she had put on the ground moments before. They weren't in any condition to fight, save for Rhept.

Rhept does nothing without Marn's lead, but just in case, Alicea thought as she shuffled to the side of the fire so that she could see everyone. She was surrounded, but not incapacitated.

"Mr. Thief is not treated with respect. He is yet to prove himself of being anything but a scoundrel . . ." she replied weakly after ensuring her relative safety.

"Odd that he received the chance to do so," was the man's reply.

He is attempting to warp my perception of the events, she thought. *Did he honestly think I'd buy this side of the story?*

Even with her resolve in check, the memories of the great festival leaked into her mind. She saw it slightly differently, though. Originally all she saw was happiness and joy from everyone gathered. The crowds of people at the festival had spread mirth with every dance and song. She remembered being caught up in the sheer merriment and wonder before being surrounded by the men who wished to abduct her.

At four years old, the concept that people would mean their Princess harm had not occurred to her. It was only a teenage boy with shoulder-length blond hair who managed to steal her away from the crowd. She had screamed the whole way; now that she thought about it, the tantrum probably did nothing for the boy's attempt at getting her back to the guards safely. But he had. The man had been commended, given a title within the castle. That was when Alicea had met her attendant, Locke, for the first time.

Back in the cave, guilt gnawed at her. She had run away from Locke with a complete stranger. He had always been a bother and the fourteen years between their ages made sure that, even though she was exceptionally clever, he always had the air of being a babysitter.

Now isn't the time to be thinking about Locke. Alicea snapped out of her recount of how she left the castle.

At the forefront of her mind was the memory of the festival itself. Now, the recollection seemed darker, a little forced. Thinking back, the people did seem ecstatic to be there. But there were those near the young girl who had been strangely stiff in their joy.

"There were three men there, including yourself, who wished to kidnap me, and now you are before me, you request forgiveness? A pardon for your behaviour? What?" Alicea threw questions at the man while she sifted through the memory in full. Something hadn't been right.

Her mind started by taking in her surroundings before looking at each face from the memory closely. Like anything she laid eyes on, her mind had absorbed the image perfectly. Everything from that day came back to her, even the book she had read that morning.

"It is too late for forgiveness. Even should I get yours, you will never get mine," the man shrugged.

"You are aware that *I* was the victim?" Alicea's eyebrows rose in surprise at his response. The man was smiling faintly as he shifted slightly. It was subtle, but she caught him glance at one of the other men.

A signal to his companion? No ... He was looking for affirmation!

"Who was in charge at the festival?" she demanded suddenly.

"What are you talking about?" the man smirked, answering carefully.

"Answer the questions or you will be in the same state as your friends," Alicea threatened. "Someone orchestrated that kidnapping and I want to know who!"

"You choose now to bring up wild accusations?"

"The people at that event were filled with merriment. But where I was, there were holes in the atmosphere. People were forcing their happiness, I remember now," Alicea explained her suspicion as she continued to investigate the details on the faces within her memory.

"Do not say anything further!" one of the men still sitting ordered.

Alicea's head snapped to a man in a blue tunic. She recognised his gleaming, green eyes, scruffy face and lack of teeth. His large, rotund build found its place in her memory as the wall of fat that had barred her access to an alley behind her sixteen years ago. He was the one giving orders, even at the festival. She suddenly picked up on every order he had given through nods, clicking of fingers and even tapping on wood. He didn't give verbal orders because it gave away the chain of command.

His cover was almost perfect as the bumbling idiot who had tried to lean down and grab the agile four-year-old while the other man spoke. He had lunged at her, but she had easily outmanoeuvred him before seeing the poorly hidden figure in the alley behind him. Her mind grabbed onto the brief moment in which she seen the man in the shadows. He had turned away, but she had seen his face. She knew who it was. Her memory was infallible. Although she'd never chosen to look back on the traumatic event, whatever was going on within the game's realm was forcing her to. It was forcing her to answer to herself.

"How?" Alicea directed the question at no-one. "How could he do that?"

"Who?" the man in the blue tunic questioned as the original speaker remained silent.

"My own uncle –" Alicea had no time to finish the thought as the shadows on the wall shifted.

Had she let her guard down? She could see the two men but there had been a third. She had barely acknowledged him but she remembered his brown clothing, coloured not by design, but from a lack of cleanliness. She ducked just as two arms found open air and the Princess' staff found two ribs. The man dropped with a crack that most combatants would find satisfying coming from their enemy.

The original speaker rushed her with the leader slowly following. The Princess had been patient enough. She feinted to the right and as the man hesitated to avoid stepping into the fire, her staff slammed into his middle before swiftly flicking up to meet his forehead as he doubled over.

"I'm rapidly becoming more than a helpless Princess!" she declared as she jumped over the flame to get the last man still standing. "I suggest you learn to keep up!"

The obese man's flabby face screwed up in confusion as the young woman charged him. He wasn't accustomed to his prey running towards him. His weight shifted and pain shot through both of his knees – he was already falling. It was unnecessary and she knew that Garnet would have scolded her for wasting energy on an already downed opponent, but that did nothing to calm Alicea as her staff became a blur, scoring multiple blows that marked before the man even hit the ground.

He landed with a crash that echoed through the cave. It was a satisfying sound, enjoyed as she looked around at the humbled men with a grim smile. She had been betrayed all that time ago, which suggested that the unrest in Aquiocia ran much deeper than what had come about in the past year, but she had stood up for herself, even if it was just within a board game. She didn't fully understand the game yet, nor why it had chosen for her to confront the men before her.

Yet it was becoming clear how useful the game could be. She may never have made the connection if the memory hadn't been forced. Alicea took a moment to look at the writhing mess before her that was the leader of the kidnappers. The man's fat had done little to shield him from the flurry of blows. The Princess grimaced at the trickles of blood soaking parts of the man's tunic as he whimpered.

"We will keep at it until you either understand what I am teaching you, or you collapse from exhaustion. I'm not fussy about which comes first," Alicea recited before adding, "The words of my mentor. I am thankful I got to pass them onto the likes of you."

She had barely uttered the words before rough hands grabbed her from behind. Trying to use her weapon was pointless as she was lifted from the ground and the weapon was knocked from her hand.

"It is just lovely that Her Highness can remember her amazing mentor's words. But you're training with me right now," a soft voice met her ears as she was flung to the ground. Alicea's vision blurred slightly but she recognised the diluted green eyes within the assailant's hood, glinting in the firelight just like the knives in his hands.

"Mr. Thief!"

"Rule one: *never* lose sight of your target."

Alicea had no time to think of a retort before she felt the bitter bite of twin blades buried in her stomach.

"It is finished!" boomed the voice within the game as her vision swirled with colour before fading. The pain relented steadily as the game grasped her being and pulled.

❖

Alicea burst into reality from the illusion in a sweating fit. She spent the first full minute free of the game's influence coughing and trying to regain composure.

"Breathe, woman!" It was the same soft voice she had heard before being eviscerated within the game.

"Get away from me!" Alicea screamed. She wasn't thinking clearly.

"It's me, damn it!" Rufus yelled back. The thief was behind her; he grabbed her arms, folding them inwards until he was holding the wiggling Princess in a bear hug. "It's safe, I promise."

Breant and his group had sprinted over to the pair, watching the Princess slowly give up the struggle.

"Bad disengagement from the game, all is well," Rufus

explained and the group nodded, returning to their post, leaving thief and Princess in the awkward proceedings of a tight, one-sided hug.

"You may release me now, Mr. Thief. I have finished acting like a fool," Alicea said quietly after a long, silent moment.

"You did nothing of the sort. You handled your first game pretty well," Rufus commended as he released her.

Alicea was calmer now. She produced a comb from one of her pockets and proceeded to realign each strand of her dark hair with swift swipes.

"I didn't expect you."

"The objective was to kill you – your piece!" Rufus corrected hurriedly.

"No, I understand that. I didn't expect you to just appear like that. I also never expected to be able to feel the pain of a blade within the game," Alicea added as her spare hand moved to check her middle. Relieved to find herself unharmed, she looked at Rufus directly for the first time since the game was over.

"You didn't feel the shift," Rufus stated with a nod.

"The shift?"

"The first game is always the roughest. At first we take turns to make our pieces move. Then, as the game takes a firmer grip on your mind, the turns become more and more blurred until all players are acting in real-time," Rufus explained. "Once you play more games, not only will you be able to feel the shifts, you'll be able to anticipate and embrace them."

"It felt like it was over in two turns," Alicea admitted.

"Most claim it feels like ten turns." Rufus shrugged as he took his seat again, reassured that the Princess had recovered.

"It prompted me to join during your second turn. I was surprised, but the game knows best."

"Does it matter how many turns it felt like?"

"No. At least, I don't think so. The turn count is generally a guide on how long it took the game to derive the information it required from the players. It could have been sped up by a variety of factors." Rufus shrugged, his vocabulary seeming to expand as he spoke about the game.

The pair were interrupted by the reappearance of Garnet. The older woman took the seat next to Alicea, examining the Princess' face.

"My, you look pale, Alicea," Garnet stated.

"I'm alright, just an exhausting game."

"I should think so – you've been playing all afternoon, after all." The older woman's mouth flickered with a smile.

Rufus openly laughed as the Princess looked out at the village in alarm. The sun was setting in the distance; the villagers were cleaning their hunting gear and going home, or making their way to the middle of the settlement to the bonfire they always made at dusk. Alicea could smell the start of the flames' work on the firewood, a scent she found oddly soothing. It was a foreign feeling of serenity as the aroma and sight of fire had often brought her an unexplained sensation of dread.

"I have a theory on why there were so few perceived turns in your game, if you'd like to hear it?"

Alicea nodded as Rufus made a hand gesture that seemed to say, "If you must".

"I'd say it is because of the bond between you two," Garnet revealed.

"I don't think –"

"Oh, that is horsesh— " The players' protests overlapped.

"Was I finished?" Garnet interjected coolly, silencing the pair and their disputes. "The game is known to play on the participants' bonds. In fact, I would almost say that it is one of the biggest contributing factors to why it works. Thief, surely you've had different experiences depending on who you have played?"

"Sure, although I mostly play strangers for money. Playing against her was the first time the game shifted into real-time so quickly," Rufus nodded thoughtfully.

"Precisely. There is a radical difference between playing a stranger and playing someone you share experiences with. I had a similar experience whenever I played against –" Garnet seemed to stop herself with a glance towards Alicea. "When I played against an old friend."

"I will have to play against you sometime!" Alicea exclaimed. "Oh, and against your friend!"

The older woman smiled kindly and as she rose, she grabbed the game that had folded back into its original cube and said, "Oh, Princess Alicea, I would be honoured. Perhaps after I return to the village. I must leave for now. Enjoy your night, both of you."

It was a strange response, but the Princess hadn't noticed the peculiarity. Instead she turned to Rufus as Garnet left as suddenly as she had arrived.

"There is a bonfire that we could be warm beside instead of sitting here in the approaching night." Alicea tilted her head towards the gathering crowd.

"You wish to join us all tonight then?" Rufus asked in

surprise. The Princess had been too exhausted every other night; she had simply retired to her bed to read and sleep.

The pair rose and stepped out from the table, joining a small party of villagers who were making their way towards the fire. As they walked, the villagers nodded in their direction; some even waved in a friendly manner. They had become accustomed to the pair wandering the village and, furthermore, had accepted them both.

They are loyal to both myself and Aquiocia despite the village's fall from being the size of a kingdom itself. These people do not falter.

The thought filled the Princess with pride, happiness and even courage as she playfully nudged Rufus in the ribs.

"You know what, Mr. Thief?"

"What?" the thief grumbled.

"I think I would have had you in the game if I knew you were coming."

"Oh really?" Rufus snickered. "Let's ignore the fact that no one *ever* sees me coming and skip to the part where you tell me how you would have *had* me?"

"I made a simple mistake: I found myself caught up in my own mind. I should have had a sentry to watch my back."

"I am glad that you are learning from your mistakes, but you do realise I am the one who watches your back, right?"

"You aren't the only one who watches over me," Alicea grinned as she looked ahead and beyond the bonfire to the branch that Garnet sat upon. The older woman had adopted her form of a crow and was perched next to the bird made solely from water.

"Ah, the bird. You have no idea how much it had me watching *my* back while looking for you," Rufus laughed. "It had me paranoid yet you weren't even using it."

"She slipped my mind. I was too pre-occupied, I don't even know where she was," Alicea admitted, her thoughts drifting momentarily to what she had found within the game – within herself. "So much was happening at once that I lost sight of the task at hand."

"And that is absolutely fine," Rufus said as he led the Princess around the circle of hunters who greeted them warmly.

The thief led the way to a small log that was vacant but still a part of the circle around the fire. It sat directly in front of Garnet's tree and though it looked slightly out of place to Alicea, she took her seat happily. The Princess glanced up at her bird with a fond smile as her tutor examined it closely.

Stretching out behind Garnet's favourite perch was another thick branch that had strong ropes lassoed around its girth. Hanging from the support of the restraints and branches was a hammock made from the pelt of a bear. Rufus had thrown his gear over the tree's limb and flung himself onto his bed of choice.

"Your motives are so transparent, Mr. Thief!" she declared with an irritated flick of her hair.

The thief dragged over the log you're sitting on the first night you arrived in case you needed a seat, Garnet's voice entered the minds of the pair. *The hammock was a gift from the village and he hung it afterwards.*

"I'm sure I told you not to tell her that," Rufus groaned.

"Looks like you might be a gentleman after all!" Alicea taunted the thief, but was betrayed by her eyes deepening in colour.

"Oh, belt up, brat!" the thief snapped and everyone gathered burst into laughter. Rufus' irritation was dampened when he caught the colour change in her eyes.

Amidst the mirth, Alicea smiled widely as Lyrium dropped another large wooden block, taking a seat beside the Princess. The pair immediately broke into a conversation about Alicea's first experience with the Elemental Chronicles. Alicea could feel an almost foreign feeling as she looked from Lyrium to the other villagers and, finally, to the dozing thief in the hammock behind her. She knew that soon she would have to contemplate the revelation thrust upon her by the game, but for now she focused on the warmth she felt within. Her joy almost caused her to not notice Garnet taking flight and becoming one with the night as she soared towards Aquiocia.

Almost.

CHAPTER 55

WINDRIDER

Katarina stood in the Council chambers in front of Mordrik. While a day had passed since the hostilities between Neibel-Haven and the enemy force had ceased, Katarina's body remained on edge. Part of her was still in the throes of conflict as she stood before the Council. She held that part of her close, forcing herself to stagnate within the anger a little longer. She couldn't buckle. Not yet. Not until she left the city behind.

The damage done was primarily confined to the walls and main gate, and the number of casualties could have been a lot worse than it was.

But that didn't alleviate Mordrik's grief and concern for his people.

His men and women had succumbed to exhaustion and even death from overuse of their magical abilities. The healers of the great city could only do so much but the people who had come into physical contact with the enemy soldiers were dying a slow and painful death despite the city healers' best efforts. In light of this new epidemic, the death toll of the struggle was on a slow but steady rise.

"What's the count?" Katarina asked.

"Around two hundred at this point, but it is still rising. That's not to mention the people we cannot find within the rubble," Mordrik replied stiffly, his wrinkled face wearing a stoic frown.

"I see. Then it could have been far worse," Katarina offered weakly. "You have done well."

"Do not patronise me. I wish to speak about what it is that you plan to do. An explanation for the abilities you demonstrated during the battle would also be greatly appreciated," Mordrik snapped, the venom in his voice barely dampened by fatigue.

Katarina drew in a deep breath and exhaled slowly. Normally she would offer no explanation for her abilities; there was too much risk of the knowledge falling into the wrong hands. Even those of her home only knew that she was a Vassal, and not the extent of her talents. To them along with everyone else she met, she was simply a talented swordswoman with an average grasp of the wind element.

This case was different. She knew that her display during the battle had given a lot away about her abilities. Coupled with the fact that she felt Mordrik deserved to know why his city was attacked, Katarina had decided to explain as much as the devastated man desired. His right to answers actually made it even more difficult for her to find the words. He didn't deserve a half-hearted explanation, but a conversation was the last thing Katarina wanted. In a way, the idea of talking was more daunting than going another round with the Vassal of Darkness.

"The woman who commanded those bound souls is a Vassal in control of the Stone of Darkness. As for why she came, I would assume it was the same thing that drew me. A week or so ago there was a massive spike in magical energy, the nature of which felt like someone in possession of a stone.

There are rumours going around the land that Lucian is on the move again and that the Vassal of Darkness, or 'Lyndell' as she called herself, is in his service. After all, she openly offered this information."

"Wait – Lucian? The dark knight who was defeated over two hundred years ago? What kind of fool do you take me for?" Mordrik spat at the woman trying to explain.

"One who should close his mouth and listen!" Katarina snapped back before her face set in an expression that dared Mordrik to contest her. The urge to lash out was strong; she didn't need provocation.

As Mordrik glared at her, he could see dark rings under the eyes of the woman who had saved his city. Resigned, he sighed and waved towards her as a sign to continue.

"There have been strange occurrences throughout the land. Amongst them is the rumour of a knight seen in various graveyards. It's all inconclusive but it's the best lead we have. The strange thing is that there is no pattern in where he appears, and while the knight is rarely violent, he *always* disappears shortly afterwards. Whether he destroys the dwellings or not seems irrelevant; we have confirmed that he *never* stays in one place."

"Who is *we*, exactly?" Mordrik asked impatiently.

"Myself, my sisters and the scholars of Nimbus," Katarina answered.

"Ah, so you're from Nimbus!"

"Am I?" Katarina's eyebrow rose at the Archmage's assumption.

"Nimbus knows of all this?" Mordrik asked, more to himself than anyone else. He was too tired for head games.

"Continue."

"We believe that Lucian is active, although we have no idea what he plans to do. We do know he is attempting to collect the stones again; that much is confirmed in my mind, especially after confronting Lyndell. This is only the beginning," Katarina finished cryptically, allowing the Archmage to imagine what might come next.

The swordswoman shrugged slightly with Mordrik's analytical gaze lingering on her, unsure of what else to say.

"This . . . Lyndell, was it? She had unnaturally strong dark energy. She's strong enough to control those undead warriors and wage destruction upon the city walls at the same time. Lyndell alone is all Lucian needs to make him a potent adversary. Does he have any other forces that you know of?" Mordrik asked, slowly coming around to the idea that Lucian's existence may be plausible.

"No, although the dark beasts from the sky are an indication that he does have other resources. Not to mention great strength himself," Katarina offered before adding thoughtfully, "But, I don't know. His power seems incomplete, like he can't control it properly or he is distracted. If he entered this world right now I would be powerless to even struggle against him. So, what is stopping him?"

"But the reason you came to this city has come to naught," Mordrik stated before finally remembering his manners and muttering, "Not that we are ungrateful for your assistance."

"I came as I too am interested in the other stone-bearer. I met her and her companion on the road here. My goal is to gather as many of the Vassal fledglings as I can and ready them to defend against the coming threat. I knew I wouldn't be the only one who felt the spike in magical energy, nor the only one interested in it. But we continued here expecting the possibility of a confrontation with Lucian," Katarina explained, trying to mask the pain of her sister's sacrifice.

"And what about you yourself? Your remarkable capabilities and the fact you are undergoing this task is rather suspicious," Mordrik accused and Katarina sighed, producing the beautiful emerald from her pocket. Her hand had been resting on it in anticipation for exactly this.

The Archmage stared at the relic curiously as a cyclone whirled out of control with small veins of blue lightning streaking through its confines. Katarina could see the researcher side of Mordrik was tempted to grab it out of her hand. In truth, she wouldn't have minded, if she wasn't planning to leave the city. She was ready for a break, though she knew that respite was nowhere to be found in the near future.

"You see, I too am one of the chosen. I am the Vassal of Wind," Katarina said shortly.

Mordrik, along with the other councillors, stared at the stone in awe. Katarina had forgotten that the others were even there, but moment after silent moment passed as they struggled to absorb the information before them. It was no surprise that the leaders of Neibel-Haven were captivated. They each had dedicated themselves to magic in one form or another. To see one of the stones in person was a momentous occasion for them. Serell of the Wind Tower had even risen from her chair in hopes of getting a better look at the precious stone.

"I see. Just so that you are aware, I must inform you that if these stones are indeed the source of supernatural power they are said to be, I did not catch sight of a stone similar to this when we apprehended the cause of the spike a week or so ago," Mordrik said, turning to the other members, who in turn shook their respective heads.

Katarina gave a quick look of scepticism before shrugging.

"I must still investigate. A spike of that magnitude couldn't be ignored even if it wasn't produced from the power from one of the stones," she replied finally.

"Do you even know where to start looking?" Mordrik asked.

"I've already begun. I will be going to Hearthgrim as soon as we finish this meeting," Katarina replied, hinting at the desire to leave, which was not lost on Mordrik as he clasped his hands together.

"Very well, then my final question is this. Do you require anything from us here at Neibel-Haven? Whether it be food, a caravan to travel in, clothing or knowledge. We have the resources, and I offer them to you in thanks for your help."

"I can get around more swiftly than ever now that I'm alone, thank you. However, the offer of knowledge is enticing. I would like very much if you researched these stones for any information regarding their origin. Also, if you could make a greater effort in locating them, it would be greatly appreciated," Katarina listed without emotion. She didn't expect anything from the people before her.

"This is all research that has been studied to death! There is just so little lore to work with, but we will try. Do you have anything else to go on?" Mordrik asked hopefully.

"Well, there is one thing that might help. Although, it is unlikely you would find anything," Katarina began hesitantly while Mordrik looked at her apprehensively. "In Nimbus, the scholars managed to find hints that indicate that Raymore truly did exist. I want it found."

"Raymore? The legendary city that was levelled by an unknown force over a millennium ago? That is a myth, a bedtime story for children, and you want us to locate it?" Mordrik asked with a look of disbelief to his peers, all of whom returned the look and frowned at Katarina.

"It is a request I do not expect you to fulfil if you do not wish to. After all, even with Nimbus' headway, it still stands as a legend. However, if it did indeed exist, it would be quite the boon to our campaign. In the stories it was known for its great military prowess and extensive library, which was known to house more lore than that of any other city in the land. It may have documents on the stones I'm searching for." Katarina smirked at the bewildered looks she was receiving.

"You say Nimbus has leads?" Mordrik asked thoughtfully, to which Katarina nodded. "Then if they will have us, I will have a small team from each of the towers of study join their efforts in finding this lost city. Even if the leads only find dead ends, nothing will be missed."

"Are you sure? Can you spare the mages for this study despite its incredibility?" Katarina asked, genuinely surprised by the cooperation.

"Once you leave the city, I daresay we will be left alone, if the enemy is indeed as bent on the stones as they seem to be. Truth is, if you weren't here, I wouldn't have the city we are standing in anymore. If you want us to repay our debt by chasing myths, then we will do it happily," Mordrik said with the first sign of humour she'd seen.

Katarina looked around at each of the Council members,

who were nodding and smiling, before finally grinning herself.

"Then in that case I leave my thanks and gratitude with you all now. I must get to Hearthgrim," Katarina said, turning to leave.

"And ours goes with you. When this is all over, I do hope that you will return so that we may honour you properly, Katarina 'Windrider'," Mordrik said.

Katarina smiled again at the name they had chosen for her as the great chamber doors opened behind her. With a quick bow, she made her exit. She was weary and devastated by the loss of her sister, but it didn't stop her from smiling at the civilians who waved happily at their saviour. Heading for the destroyed main gate and on to Hearthgrim, Katarina's fingers gently stroked the stone and whispered, "You always said you wanted your death to mean something. Well, it couldn't have meant more if you tried. Rest well, Sister."

CHAPTER 56

THE FIRES OF FOREVER

Temperance fidgeted as she followed Chase into the now open cathedral. Her gaze jumped around the great hall, taking in the demolished sight.

It was once a place of prayer. Some of the pews were still in place, facing towards the altar at the far end of the building. The rest of the seats had been thrown across the enclosure, leaving the visitors to navigate around their splintered and broken remains. As they stepped over the scattered stone, they noted that parts of the wall had been blasted away, leaving piles of singed rubble and smouldering debris. The only thing left untouched was the shrine behind the dais.

The shrine was flanked by two medium dragon statues while a third, far more imposing, draconic figure sat upright, staring towards the doorway they had just come through. It had the same vicious expression as the one in the city centre. It was even adorned with the same searing red scales. Another tribute to the monster that was Scourge.

The pair cautiously stalked the length of the cathedral, examining every inch for any indication of a trap. When they finally reached the altar, Chase read the plaque below the dragons: "To the mighty Scourge, both kin and man shall bow before you." Chase rolled his eyes at this sight and muttered a curse.

"While you are visitors, please show some respect to our heritage. It is all we have left, after all," a voice came from behind them. They both spun, Chase instinctively drawing his sword.

Before them stood the burnt carcass of a man. He wore little clothing over his red, raw flesh and flaking skin, with tattered rags barely keeping his modesty. He was sickly gaunt, and his eyes blazed crimson with life. Chase felt guilt's knife bury itself into his stomach, complementing the anxious grip he had on his weapon.

One of the experiments . . . No, they were all female . . . he reasoned with himself.

"Who are you?" Temperance was the first to speak, quivering though her voice was.

"I am one of the remaining residents of Scourge. I am one of 'The Nameless'," the charred man rasped, his throat damaged. "An ironic name, perhaps. But I am here to welcome you to our ruined city."

"You have been touched by the stone's power," Chase observed more than asked.

"I only appear before you now because we can sense you have the stone in your possession," the nameless man explained, barely acknowledging the question.

"To what end?" Temperance asked in a shaky whisper. Her trembling hand found its way to her chest as she watched the man. This was almost her fate.

"To assist you, of course. You have taken in the power of the stone and survived. It is our duty to help you," the man answered cryptically, starting to walk towards them unhindered despite the sound of tearing flesh. The burns had cauterised, but moving opened the wounds again.

"Keep your distance!" Chase raised his voice, stepping between the man and Temperance.

His sword was raised in front of him, ready for a confrontation, but the man stopped his advance. His face struggled into a smile, the burnt skin stretching laboriously to perform the feat. His voice slurred slightly as he spoke with the tormented smile defiantly clinging to his face.

"We mean you no harm. If we did, you would already be dead." The man somehow managed to be curt.

"We? I've seen no sign of any others. Your bluff will not work," Chase replied.

"Chase, look," Temperance said quietly, walking up behind him and pointing past the man. At the entrance to the cathedral, there were two more charred silhouettes, cautiously poking their heads through the doorway. Chase stole a quick sweep of the cathedral with his eyes. "The Nameless" populace was appearing everywhere.

Some were peering over the ruined wooden seats while others looked through the windows and holes in the walls. Chase's skin crawled at the sight; they moved with none of the handicap that the ones in the underground tower had. The charred man was right. If they attacked he would be overwhelmed.

"We only wish to be of assistance to the one with the stone. It is our obligation. But if you refuse to heed our words, we will go back into hiding and give you no grief. Just know this – we will not stand for threats." The man explained himself so calmly that it didn't even feel like a threat. His effort at smiling had been abandoned; his wounds had returned to the same state they had been in at the time of his appearance.

Chase turned to Temperance for her opinion on the situation. After looking around once more at the curious remains of the charred men she announced that she would hear any wisdom they were willing to pass on to her. Chase's sword was half away when he brought it back to the ready as "The Nameless" moved rapidly towards them.

He was ready to fight when Temperance ordered him to stop. "The Nameless" took their seats around the chamber, all with their eyes on them. They looked as if they were gathering for a day of worship and Temperance was the one they were paying tribute to.

Chase had no qualms with religion – he even partook in quiet worship of the entity of flame. But being the sole focus inside a cathedral really unnerved him. Despite this, Temperance's scolding resulted in him slowly sheathing his weapon and flashing his open palms.

"What is it that you wish to know? What has brought you here, my Flame?" the man who had introduced himself asked Temperance.

Despite there now being several hundred similarly scorched men, women and children present, it seemed that only the original man was going to be speaking.

"I'm aware of the history of Scourge, everything from its origin to its demise. But I did not know there were people still living amongst these ruins. Please tell me who you all are," she requested timidly.

The man began slowly, considering his response. "You say you know of the demise of Scourge? If that is true then you know that Scourge the Dragon was once summoned to this world and razed everything in an inferno of incandescent splendour. Our people were small in number then, and managed to escape the town before being cleansed by the power of our deity." The man's face didn't change, but his tone was one of reverence before turning wistful. "Neibel-Haven came; they had been watching us. They banished our god and turned their backs on us. We rebuilt, of course. We had laid eyes on a god, after all, and this is still our belief. By the second instance of the city's destruction, it had grown to the size of a small kingdom. However, the ruins you see here are the work of the stone you now possess. We tried to bestow the power upon one of our own, to create a weapon for battle and for our city's defence."

It was strange listening to the man's lament and see little to no physical sign that the recollection was causing him grief through his burnt features. Chase struggled to dismiss the uneasy feeling that came from the stillness displayed by the people in front of him as their "leader" continued.

"We were often attacked or shunned by outsiders. The only exception was those of Neibel-Haven to the north-west, who originally saw our dedication to magic as admirable, despite the fact we only dedicated ourselves to the path of Fire Magic. We believe this is why they were watching so closely when Scourge was unleashed. Our mages were second to none in the destructive force that is our element of choice. That includes those studying within the city's Fire Tower."

"The Nameless" took a deep breath, and Chase felt some small relief at the sign of humanity. The man's red eyes turned to Temperance to ensure she was listening before he continued with his rasping lecture.

"After Scourge first came and destroyed our small town, which at that time is all it was, we found the very stone we now sense is with you. We do not know where it came from, but we suspect that Scourge's summoning and the appearance of the stone was not mere coincidence. Even then, we knew that it was a gift from our god. After that our people tried to find a Vassal for the stone for centuries, before we finally had some success. The stone finally took to an older female mage in our midst. The power, however, consumed her almost instantly. Her actions and even her voice, from the moment the stone took her, were not her own. She destroyed the city with magic so devastating that I doubt the combined efforts of every mage in our city could have surpassed it. The sky was choked with ashes and the ground set ablaze like a sea of fire." "The Nameless" finally seemed pained as he recalled the memory.

Temperance nodded. The pieces of her studies were finally coming together.

"But what of you? Who are you, exactly?" she asked once more.

"We are 'The Nameless'," the man repeated, his stillness resurfacing. "We are the ones who saw the devastation the stone brought to our city and lived, if what you see before you could be called living."

"Houses remain smouldering . . . Why does it look like they were just burnt? I have my own theories, but nothing conclusive. If you are who you say you are, I could finally put this mystery to rest," Temperance probed, trying to appear at ease as she tried and failed to casually clean her glasses. Instead the woman quickly rearranged them on the bridge of her nose after knocking them askew.

"The woman who was consumed by the stone burnt up and collapsed and this is how the city remained. The flames slowly faded, but the damage remains. It cannot be rebuilt, for we are bound by time, forever the same as we were the day of the disaster. We have no other explanation other than it's a curse placed on us," the man said solemnly.

"You have waited here all this time? Why not seek help? Someone from Neibel-Haven may have been able to break the curse," Chase contributed, never breaking his glare at the masses.

"We made a plea to Neibel-Haven. They turned their backs on us because of what we did. The Council has never been fond of the type of experimentation we were involved in, regardless of what people sat in the seats of power at the time. Now that I look back on it, I can no longer blame them," the man explained.

"The Nameless" sitting in their seats nodded in empathy as he continued. An action that made Chase's fists clench in anxiety.

"So, we made the decision to stay here in hopes that if anyone took on the power of the stone, they might come here to learn what they could. Scavengers came and went and from them we hid the stone. Eventually scholars of Neibel-Haven arrived. I assume they thought us dead, but we allowed them to find the stone. Being a timeless city, we have seen and heard a lot of what goes on in the land. The land may have forgotten about us, but we have not forgotten it."

Chase had never asked Lazear how he had found the stone. To find out that it was simply because these people allowed it was a surprise. For as long as he'd known the Professor, he had never seen him care if he was "allowed something".

Did Lazear even know of these people?

"I see. Then perhaps you know something of the danger the world faces over these stones?" Temperance enquired.

Chase glanced at his companion. *How much does* she *know?*

"We do. We know that individuals and even kingdoms are looking for the stones – or, perhaps more accurately in some cases, the Vassals themselves," the man answered. "As far as we are aware, most, if not all the stones have been claimed by bearers."

"What? How is that possible? The likelihood of that happening is tiny!" Chase blurted out. "Finding the stones alone is a feat in itself – even Temperance only found hers by misfortune and coincidence. That's ignoring the fact they respond to very few people."

"Allow me to attempt to alter your outlook, young man, with a simple sentence," the man said before stepping closer to him. "The Nameless" man's crimson eyes bore through Chase as he stated, "There is absolutely no such thing as coincidence when it comes to these stones."

"This is still hard to believe. Chase is right in some capacity; it does seem unlikely. What else do you know?" Temperance asked before Chase could reply. She was a little off-guard from the flood of information, but her companion wasn't helping.

"We know that every Vassal is female, something that most history buffs could deduct. We can also pick up whenever powerful magic is being used. The power of the stones rings across the land as clear as day to those who are listening," he replied.

"What about the threat, though? Rumour has it that there

have been some strange goings-on. Villages have been destroyed, seemingly at random," Temperance asked.

"Ah yes, it's true that a great deal of strange incidents are transpiring. We believe it is the work of Lucian," the man replied.

"Lucian. Why do I know that name?" Chase muttered before realisation dawned on him. "You can't mean *the* Lucian who searched for the stones two hundred years ago!"

"The very same. Reports say that he has been seen in the graveyards of various villages and cities, but Temperance here already knows that. The reason seems unknown, but there is something even more disturbing than that. There is a theory we have come up with recently that we didn't want to voice out of fear. But you coming here may have sealed its credibility," the man said, hesitating briefly.

"What is it? It's best we hear all theories," Temperance pressed.

"We felt the biggest spike in magical energy we have felt in centuries come from the direction of Neibel-Haven about a week ago now. It seemed to disappear and then a few short days later we felt two different spikes. They seemed to clash before one disappeared. Our theory is that Lucian has at least one of the Vassals working under him," the man explained grimly.

"Two others there after me ..." Temperance trailed off with an uncomfortable look.

"I've got good coin that says the two women we met on the way to Hearthgrim were one side of the clash," Chase said quietly, reminding Temperance of the odd encounter and even odder way they had stared at her.

Temperance turned to Chase anxiously.

"You think they were after me?" she asked worriedly.

"I don't think so. If one of them was a bearer of one of the stones and hunting you, they would have overpowered us in a heartbeat. Besides, by the way they were speaking I think they knew you were what they were looking for. Add that to the confrontation and I would wager they were there to protect you," Chase reasoned, reassuring Temperance slightly.

"So," Temperance began slowly, trying to make sense of the information in front of her. "The logical explanation is that there were two Vassals fighting over me. Do you know which Vassals they were?"

"Which Vassals? Meaning their elemental alignment? I'm afraid we don't. Over that distance we cannot discern the alignment. Even when we felt the spike emanating from you, we couldn't tell if we were feeling the Vassal of Fire or just hoping that it was the case. But if we were to make an educated guess, the one fighting for Lucian is the Vassal of Darkness. She was at the Battle of a Thousand Blades and fought against the Vassal of Light. We also have reason to believe that the Vassal of Light has been forced out of the battle against Lucian since then," he replied, hesitating slightly on the word "forced".

Temperance turned to Chase. "We need to go to Neibel-Haven and find Katarina and Amelia. They may know what to do and know how we could help."

"No, I don't think that is a wise idea," Chase said shortly.

"And why not?" Temperance asked.

"We have been banished by the Council and if the battle there is over like this man has said, then we would only be walking into a dangerous situation. Katarina said they will catch up with us in Hearthgrim and we left a message with her friend that we were coming here. They will catch up, if they are still alive," Chase reasoned.

Temperance stopped to think about it for a long moment before nodding reluctantly.

"Then you are staying here a little longer?" The man seemed hopeful in his question and smiled when Chase nodded slowly without looking directly at him. "Well, we don't have much to offer but I think there is something within our ability to help you if you are interested."

Temperance looked up curiously. "We have the answers we came for already. What more do you have to offer?"

"I mentioned before that we were unrivalled in the art of Fire Magic. We could bestow our knowledge and techniques upon you. Chase, if you're interested, we weren't incapable of wielding weapons. Maybe you would like to brush up on your own skills by learning our style?" the man graciously offered.

"The people of Scourge had their own style of swordplay?" Chase asked curiously.

"Of course. Although we weren't equal to the commandants of Aquiocia in the art of warfare, we developed a style of fighting that incorporated fighting with man-made weapons that helped channel our magical energy," the man replied proudly.

"You mean like this?" Chase asked, drawing his sword, ignoring the twitch from his audience at the threat. He ran his hand across the blade, drawing out an eruption of flames. His sword donned its own personal inferno and Chase felt the familiar and ever-so-slight drain on his energy stores.

"You not only know our basic technique, you can enchant your blade without the incantation. Most bizarre, but impressive nonetheless," the man said incredulously. "Is it possible that you already know our fighting style?"

"I'm afraid not. My father crafted this blade when I expressed interest in swordplay so that if I chose to master both I would have an appropriate weapon. He taught me the basics of the sword but circumstances caused the training to cease early on and I taught myself from there," Chase replied.

"Interesting. I look forward to seeing what you have taught yourself. Very few can even imbue their weapon outside our city, let alone maintain it and engage in combat without exhausting themselves," he commended Chase as he released the enchantment and sheathed his blade. "So, Lady of the Flame, are you interested in learning more of the art of Fire Magic?"

"It is rumoured that I descend from the Scourge of old. Training under the ones who could be my ancestors would be a far greater honour than I could have ever hoped to have," Temperance admitted with a nervous smile.

"The Nameless" sitting around in the cathedral all rose simultaneously and started to walk towards the exit as the man said, "We shall organise food for you along with appropriate shelter. Then we will get your respective training underway."

As the legion of charred men and women filed out of the cathedral, Chase rested his hand on Temperance's shoulder. She started at the touch.

"Are you alright?" he asked.

"Yes, I'm fine considering . . ." Temperance responded stiffly as she lifted her dress slightly to step over larger pieces of debris. "I feel all we can do is wait . . ."

"Hmm . . ." Chase removed his hand and nodded slowly. "Then that settles it. We wait."

CHAPTER 57

A CORRUPTED COUNCIL

The Council of Aquiocia was in an uproar since its Princess had disappeared – or rather, had been "kidnapped", as it were. Every day since the discovery of the missing Princess the Council had come together. Every day they had ended up in a furious back-and-forth between the members. Each member of the Council had a different idea on how they should proceed; the information on her being in South Tremel had only ignited their fury.

"I say we stomp the village into the ground! How dare they!" one fiery member yelled. The outburst was met with a chorus of agreement and an equal amount of hissing. It was a suggestion that had been thrown around all too frequently in the past couple of weeks.

"If we destroy a village within the kingdom, how will the others respond? As it is now, losing our Princess has already crippled their favour of us," another chimed in against the suggestion.

The argument continued while Arissam sat at the head of the long table, watching the other eleven members squabble. Arissam was the elected leader of the Council after the death of the late King and Queen. As Alicea's one remaining uncle, what he said held more weight than all the others combined. The power was great, providing no one claimed the throne itself.

He sat in a comfortable posture, his chin resting on his closed, right fist on the arm of his chair as a content leader. His cold, blue eyes were glazed over from boredom as they slowly moved from one person to another, listening to the same short-sighted suggestions over and over again. He was one of only a handful of the royal family left and had a firm standing in the line to the throne. Given his position on the Council, even before promotion, he was well and truly within his rights to grasp full leadership of the kingdom.

If a certain Princess wasn't running free, that is, he thought bitterly. His attention fell on Locke, who was standing awkwardly in the corner. The interest in the former attendant fled a moment later; he was irrelevant.

He had done his research. A lot of the royal family had been at the Battle of a Thousand Blades and had been eliminated. Setz, a close advisor of the late King, had disappeared; with him had vanished the hope that the late King might have passed on the kingdom to him. Arissam wasn't stupid. He knew Setz was a loose end that could present an issue should he reappear.

He also knew that he had only been elected as the leader because he was thirty-four and thus the youngest – and most easily manipulated – member of the Council. It was a theory he was about to prove wrong. He ran his hands through his thinning brown hair and got to his feet.

"Ladies and gentlemen of the Aquiocian Council!" he declared loudly and with force. Everyone in the room immediately turned towards the head of the table, surprised by the sudden interest of their leader.

"Before I begin, I simply must bring the involved people in to join us. Locke, if you would, get the door?" Arissam asked with forced politeness and Locke obliged, opening the door to the chambers. Two men marched in confidently. Even without the introduction, the newcomers commanded the room's attention as they strode forth. They were opposites in many ways, yet both of their presences called for acknowledgement.

The first was a man with long, red hair. It hung down to his lower back, tied back off his face. He had honest, green eyes and a bright smile. He greeted everyone in the room with the utmost respect, ensuring that everyone present received the pleasure of locking eyes with the charismatic man holding their attention. He even bowed his head low, though the practice had never been made mandatory for Council members, even back when the King and Queen were alive. The man wore startling gold and silver, full plate armour; a gentle clink could be heard with each step of his approach to the Council's table.

Maxim, Warmaster to the knights of Aquiocia. He was a teacher of the blade to many, Locke included. He was a decorated hero of the battlefield, feared by many enemies of Aquiocia for his battle prowess and knack for command and strategy.

The second man showed no such respect as he wandered into the chambers, looking as if it was a chore just being there. His dead-straight black hair fell over his pale face, partially hiding his wicked amber eyes on its way to his shoulders.

He was dressed in black, donning long, black pants accompanied by a full-length coat trimmed with crimson, with one of the sleeves cut short. The coat was left open, revealing his torso and the countless scars across it. The man had obviously been wounded many times, yet he sauntered into the chambers without hindrance.

Slung over the man's back was a sheath holding a contraption of some sort. A thin band ran over his shoulder down to his lower back, where an odd folded object hung loosely.

Locke tried looking at it from different angles but it would not give up its secrets. The only thing he could deduct was that the item was dangerous. Locke quickly changed focus to the man's left sleeveless arm, which was completely wrapped in bloodstained bandages. The bindings were tight, with repulsive patches of blackened stains seeping blood. The dark blood looked as if it had been left to age despite it only just escaping its bounds.

The man smirked. His sinister eyes suddenly snapped to Locke, forcing the unnerved attendant to look away. The unknown man and Maxim stood at the end of the table, on display for everyone as Arissam spoke once more.

"Ah, excellent, everyone involved is now present," he said with out-of-place enthusiasm considering the day's discussion. He turned back, smiling, to the members of the Council, who were now eyeing their leader warily.

"Over the past couple of weeks since the Princess' disappearance, you have all presented your personal opinions time and time again. To be honest, I think I could recite them back to each of you word for word," Arissam said without a hint of humour across his ageing face. "But now it is time we took action instead of quarrelling amongst ourselves."

Arissam began to walk around the table as he spoke. He would occasionally pause, locking eyes with one person or another as if awaiting a response before moving on. His strides were slow, measured. Even the sound of his expensive boots touching down on the stone felt rehearsed. After completing his circuit of the chamber, he stopped to take in the massive flag which hung on the wall bearing the iconic Aquiocian Rose. He took in its blue and silver splendour upon the back wall, marvelling as if for the first time.

"With this in mind, it is apparent that the time for me to put my foot down as your Chairman is now," Arissam announced, returning to the table and leaning down on it before addressing the other members in a more forceful tone, taking the time to stare at each member in turn. The fierceness in his gaze dared them to interrupt.

"You may not have noticed, but Aquiocia is in peril. We not only lost our King and Queen, but have now also lost the one direct heir to the throne. This has left the body of Aquiocia's kingdom without a head, so to speak."

Arissam let his words sink in for a moment before continuing. It was a truth that everyone present knew but despised talking about as it was a declaration of weakness.

"The citizens are scared; some have lost faith in us. Some are even leaving the city in search for a better life and others have disappeared altogether. Nobody knows where they go but they cease to exist within our kingdom. It started out as a very small number, barely noticeable. But because this meagre trickle of people leaving has been in effect so long, it has begun to affect the kingdom. This kingdom needs guidance. It needs direction and a firm hand to lead it. It needs someone at the top. It needs a King!"

Every Council member was silent, letting the words wash

over them, still unsure of the meaning behind them, despite the obvious point the Chairman was trying to make.

"It has been over a year since the King and Queen died. Without the heir I hold the highest title in the kingdom. With these things all in mind, I have decided to ascend to the throne," Arissam finished quietly and almost instantly the room exploded with raised voices.

Eight of the Council members were on their feet in an instant and yelling their disapproval at him, but it wasn't them he was interested in. He was watching the three who remained seated, quietly reflecting. Within the chaos, Maxim met the unknown man's wicked smirk with a polite smile as the Chairman waited patiently for the aggressive members to tire of their verbal ordeal. After a while of explosive one-sided arguments, they were left red-faced and waiting for an explanation from Arissam. They were surprised when Maxim spoke first.

"My, this is quite the surprise indeed. If I may ask a question of you, Sir?" Maxim asked as the ever-polite gentleman.

"What is it, Warmaster?" Arissam asked curiously.

"I hear that the Princess has been located. What will you do with this information?" Maxim asked with a smile.

"The Princess has indeed been located. Though, for all we know, it might never have been a kidnapping at all." Arissam raised a hand to silence Locke, who was ready to protest in anger. "Almost at the exact time, the stone of power was stolen from our hidden vault. How the thief knew about its location is unknown, but the coincidence cannot be ignored," Arissam said cryptically.

Maxim refused to let it go. It wasn't a good enough explanation for the man who had watched the Princess grow up.

"Sir, you have not answered my question," Maxim pressed gently with the same polite and unreadable smile.

"She will be apprehended in South Tremel. If she resists, she will be removed," Arissam added simply. "This kingdom has been without direction for far too long. We cannot have this kind of behaviour from anyone with such a title, least of all a Princess who shirks her duties so blatantly."

Maxim lowered his head in a slight bow. His eyes were closed as if he was thinking intently before acting. His movement was a simple one; the Warmaster rubbed his temple on the left side with his fingers. To most it would look like any old habit, but those whom Maxim truly trusted knew the Warmaster rubbing his left temple was an order to remain calm and quiet. A rubbing of his right temple was to notify those present to prepare for a confrontation.

It was such a simple tactic, but efficient. It was only known to the late King and a handful of soldiers he trusted. Maxim had only told Locke of the sign about a year ago. Until now, the Princess' attendant thought of it simply as a knight's paranoia. He had been wrong. Locke's eyes darted around the room and confirmed that he was the only one there who would have understood such a sign.

He wants me to remain calm, but why? Locke's mind whirled. *If this goes poorly I could support him, I don't know anything about the man in black but the rest aren't a threat unless –*

Maxim looked up, his green eyes ablaze with rage, but his smile never wavered when he said, "Then, you will find yourself a King with no army."

To this Arissam chuckled, "I'm afraid you are mistaken there, *former* Warmaster."

With that the man in black struck, moving with blinding speed to get behind Maxim and drive a dagger downwards into his neck as the entire chamber echoed with gasps. Locke was about to advance on the man in black but stopped as Maxim spluttered the words, "An order is an order!"

He didn't look at Locke but the attendant knew who the words were for. As Maxim drew his last, shuddering breath, he gazed through rapidly blurring vision at the monster that was set to take the throne. He fell to one knee with the dignity of a true knight declaring fealty to the crown and Arissam's cruel smirk quickly changed to a scowl of fury when he realised that the dying man's smile hadn't faded.

The standard had been set for the knights of Aquiocia in countless ways by Maxim throughout his career. He had ascended through the titles of the military quicker than anyone before him until there were simply no more ranks to climb. From there he had been named "Warmaster" and was declared part of the royal family by the late King. Despite all of this, the humble man had always maintained that the most important title he could possess from the King was as his "friend". Just before his legs finally gave way, the war hero of Aquiocia showed his true colours once more through his final words.

"Long live the Rose of Aquiocia."

The entire Council was in a state of shock, unable to fully grasp what had just become of the prestigious man who had led the Aquiocian knights. His blood spread from the wound in his neck, bathing the pale blue floor with a crimson hue that rivalled his hair.

Locke wanted nothing more than to strike out at the man who had so unfairly taken his mentor's life. But he knew that Maxim had given him a silent, yet direct order – his final order – and he would see that his dying wish be done.

The man who had taken Maxim's life stood over the Warmaster's corpse and kicked it roughly between the gaps of plate armour. Finally, looking up at the Chairman, he confirmed that the Warmaster had indeed departed this world. Arissam acknowledged it with a small nod before addressing the Council once more.

"With this undesirable business aside, I now call a vote. Those in favour of my ascension to the throne will get their say, as will those opposing it. Know that I only wish to bring Aquiocia back its former strength and glory. The changes I make will shield Aquiocia from the coming threat across the land and save it from the horrid fate that so many others have faced.

"And the destruction won't stop there," Arissam continued with little pause. "It might be localised right now, but word of the stones will spread to the smaller neighbouring isles. They will see a use for the stones and mark my words, they will – and possibly already are – making preparations to come and seize them for themselves. The best thing we can do is to strike down the threats we know, start a new search to destroy those who wield the stones, and lock the stones away forever before it gets out of hand. Now, it is your turn to raise your voice – who is with me?"

Locke was ashamed to admit to himself, but he was almost

moved by the Chairman's words. He knew that he had a point, to an extent, but to threaten their own Princess? Did he really mean to turn a blade on the only pure royal blood left in the kingdom?

Say what you like, this is nothing short of madness, he thought.

Locke's heart fell when a chorus of *"Aye!"* rang out and eight of the eleven voting members' hands shot up. Clearly the death of Maxim had enticed them to join Arissam in the unsightly display of betrayal. Fear was always such a strong motivator, but not one that Aquiocia traditionally succumbed to. The other three silent Council members sat with looks of utter defiance, uninterested in betraying the crown, even in its absence.

Ah, so there is still some loyalty left within these walls, Locke thought.

"I thank you all for your support. To the remaining three who will not join, please know that I do understand your position. That's why it saddens me to ask Locke to open the doors once more. Locke, if you would?" Arissam asked.

"Yes, Sir," Locke replied, just barely concealing the loathing in his voice as he strode over to the doors and opened it to find eight armoured knights. The soldiers filed into the room with their swords drawn.

Arissam pointed at the three resisting Council members, whose faces had turned pale as the knights sworn to protect them apprehended them. They didn't scream or fight the arrest; their pride forbade it as they were roughly thrown out of the chamber and led away.

"That will be all. Thank you, Locke," Arissam said, gesturing towards the door. "You do not need to hear what I have to say to the rest here. Go about your duties."

"Yes, Sir," Locke responded, thankful to finally be dismissed.

As he exited the chamber, he heard one last declaration by Arissam. His blood ran cold as he realised just what was coming towards next for the kingdom of Aquiocia.

"Now, to the first point of business. To replace Maxim I offer you all Jex, former Lieutenant of the Sixth Division. I implore you all to support his promotion to General of the Aquiocian army, effective immediately, of course."

Impossible! Now I know who he is! I thought the man dead! The Princess has mentioned him frequently, but I had never laid eyes on him! How is he even alive? What is the Council thinking bringing a man with his history into power? How could they replace Maxim with "Jex the Reaper"?

CHAPTER 58

SWAPPING SIDES

Locke marched across the audience chamber of the castle with little purpose. The fervent pace was to make others think he was busy so they left him be. The only interaction he partook in was a slight nod towards any guard or noble who took the time to greet him. The almost foreign sight of people within the castle should have been a sign that he had a lot of work to do.

In a perfect world, the Princess would be there to greet the visitors. As her attendant, he would have seen to the preparations so the time people spent with their Princess went smoothly. Yet, with the Princess absent, both Locke and the visitors had little reason to be there.

As it was, the man had spent entire days patrolling the castle while the Princess' location was unknown. The goal had been to not draw attention to the fact that he had been present and listening in on a lot of the Council's talks. He had decided that the best way to gather information was to stand in plain sight while acting like nothing was amiss. It had worked, mostly. But if he had little reason to be there the day before, he had none to continue the facade now. He'd hoped to turn to the Warmaster for guidance . . .

Maxim . . . Damn it . . . Locke tried to push the sudden

murder of the hero from his mind, focusing on his next move.

He had no idea what to do. He knew that if he repeated anything of what he had seen to the public he would meet the same fate as Maxim. Not that death scared him greatly. He certainly didn't like the idea, but the bigger fear was that the public wouldn't believe him.

He had been in the markets regularly and each visit he had noticed that people seemed more distant, as if they were undergoing their daily routine with little thought at all. Their wide-eyed stares suggested that they were conscious, but lacked any real awareness.

He turned into a corridor with no idea where he was going. His feet moved with no instruction, yet his body held purpose as he reached the end of a portrait-lined corridor. His hand mimicked his feet in taking the initiative his mind couldn't muster, pushing open a door that led to the main courtyard.

He didn't slow his trance-like pace as he crossed the long courtyard, barely noticing a group of guards. They had gathered in a huddle; they spoke barely above a whisper and disbanded with a flurry of apologies when they saw Locke. He didn't care, not anymore. The guards could sense something was amiss in the kingdom. The difference was that the guards still had a reason to be there. They still had a purpose.

Since the day before, he had noticed there were a lot more soldiers stationed around the palace. It was only natural that the tightening of security would set off suspicion within the guards.

Locke approached the great gate to leave the castle, heading into the city. The guards raised the portcullis, giving him generic greetings in stiff tones as he set out down the streets. He barely took any notice of the citizens who had taken to whispering in their little groups between their shopping endeavours. The markets bustled with life as always, but there was a deadly quiet over the centre of trade that Locke had never encountered before.

His reverie was temporarily broken when a woman collided with him, stumbling. Locke's hand caught the woman's wrist, his other hand on her back to help her back up. She met his eyes with a vacant stare before bustling away without a word. The strange interaction was enough for Locke to take in his surroundings, noticing that there were a lot more soldiers present. They weren't just patrolling as normal; there were groups of three stationed at each small stall or vendor. What was even more distressing was that they all seemed to be watching him.

He resumed his swift pace through the crowd – it would be suspicious to turn back. Something was obviously wrong with the protectors of the city. They stood stiff and even their slight movements were rigid. It was an observation he dismissed as he reached his destination. He sighed at the sight of what his mind had subconsciously led him to.

Before him stood that tall statue of the missing Princess, smiling in one of the royal garbs. The massive figure was made from the same pale blue stone the castle had been crafted from, with beautiful sapphires twinkling as the Princess' eyes. As he looked into the priceless jewels, he felt the last of his strength leave his body. Realisation that he had failed in his duty to protect her plagued him like never before. He had always known that it was his carelessness that had led to her disappearance, but he'd never let it consume him.

Until now.

If he had kept her safe, this whole mess within the kingdom wouldn't be happening. Arissam wouldn't be succeeding the throne. Jex would not have been made General of the Aquiocian army. Whatever was threatening to follow next wouldn't occur.

"Blaming yourself will solve nothing," came a soft voice from behind him, breaking his dive into self-pity.

Locke spun around to see two young girls who couldn't be far from adulthood, and yet both stood with the confidence of burly mercenaries.

Well, two slender, rather feminine mercenaries.

Their appearance was delicate and yet an underlying fierceness was burning in their deep green eyes. They were obviously twins. At first glance they were identical in every way, with the exception that one had her long, blonde hair in a ponytail and the other let hers fall upon her face. It was the only physical difference he could pick, but the girl with the ponytail had a short bow strung over her shoulder, whereas the other had a pair of long knives sheathed at her sides.

The pair were dressed as rogues, garbed in leather dyed pitch-black.

"Can I help you girls?" Locke asked politely, despite the threat of being robbed.

"No, but we can help you. You're Locke, right?" asked the one with hair strewn across her face. Her tone was hard, barely glancing at Locke as she spoke except for a glare to prompt an answer.

"That's right," Locke replied uncertainly.

"I'm sorry about my sister's rudeness. My name is Lorinaea. This here is Torinaea," the girl with the ponytail explained with a slight frown at her sister. "Lori and Tori is fine."

"We've come to get you," Tori declared vaguely, her fingers dancing along the hilt of her daggers. "So, come along before I draw my blades!"

"This is precisely why the boss told *me* to do the talking!" Lori hissed under her breath. "So stop threatening our target!"

"Lori, was it?" Locke asked, interrupting the twins with a slight nod towards the milder-mannered twin. "Why were you looking for me?"

"Our leader has requested you. He understands that you might be reluctant to follow two strangers, but he wants us to assure you that it is for the best. That is, if you wish to see the Princess again."

"You were involved in the kidnapping of the Princess?" Locke asked, his hand shifting to the hilt of his blade.

"Yes," Lori replied calmly. "The Princess was kidnapped by Ruffie, under our leader's orders."

"Who is this leader of yours?" Locke snapped coldly.

"His name is Setz, he used to –"

"From the Council? The one who disappeared over a year ago?" Locke asked. *The King's advisor is alive? As much as I'd like to believe that . . .*

"Yes, that's correct. Although he has been our leader for a lot longer than just the past year," Lori replied shortly.

"I don't believe you, nor do I have any reason to leave my post."

"That's rich," Tori sneered, breaking her silence. "You don't even have a post now that the Princess is gone. Shouldn't you be looking for something constructive to do?"

"Enough, Tori," Lori cut across quietly. "Show him."

Tori rolled her eyes and pushed a small object into Locke's hand. He looked down at the blue and silver trinket. It was a badge with the Aquiocian emblem, the same one that had been bestowed upon Setz by the late King as a token of gratitude for his work on the Council. Everyone knew that Setz had been the King's advisor. If he was alive, chances were that the Princess was as well. The emblem was proof enough that Setz might still be alive.

"This is –"

"Yes, it proves we aren't lying." Tori rolled her eyes. "So, are you coming or not?"

Locke looked back at the statue of the Princess, uncertain of his next move.

This could be a trap, his brain cautioned. *And what if it is? What will I accomplish remaining here?*

He was an attendant to a Princess who had left her kingdom weeks ago. Every day without rank or position felt like an eternity. Perhaps it was time to take a risk. He turned back towards the twins and examined them intently. They seemed honest enough, if a little shady.

"Very well. Take me to Setz," Locke said after a long moment.

"Setz requested that I warn you that, by coming with us, you may be joining the side of the Princess. Returning to your life as you know it will prove more than difficult," Lori recited as Tori let out an exaggerated sigh.

"She means that just because you're coming with us doesn't mean you won't end up dead. You have to listen to Setz, and do as he says if you want to see the Princess again."

Locke looked back towards the castle and he saw its beauty in a different light. He was now aware of the corruption within its walls; it wasn't the same castle as when the Princess inhabited it. Its light and lustre had been fading steadily for a long time, but now it was completely gone.

"Take me to Setz," Locke repeated, this time with conviction.

❖

Locke was in a state of shock, his mind racing to comprehend the sight before him. His eyes jumped from one astonishing sight to the next as the twins led him through the Underbelly. His constant barrage of questions had ceased upon seeing the civilisation that dwelled below the city of Aquiocia. He was desperate to see everything around him, his body twisting, performing full pivots that a dancer would be proud of to take it in.

"This is . . . incredible!" Locke exclaimed as they reached the central pillar and the home of the Guilty Blade. *Is this where I would have ended up had I not become the Princess' attendant?*

His mirth was met with a small smile from Lori and yet another eye-roll from Tori.

"Yes, a truly wonderful discovery for you, I'm sure," Tori replied sarcastically as they walked through the entrance.

Locke's wonder was reborn – this time, however, with a hint of unease at the cloaked men sitting at the tables and bar. Fortunately, the men made way for the twins as they headed for the grand staircase at the far end of the room. Locke kept close to his escorts, avoiding direct eye contact with the patrons. For whatever reason, he knew he was safer near the twins.

As they ascended the seemingly impossible number of

stairs, the Princess' attendant could tell he was at the centre of everyone's attention. He heard mutters in regards to his noble attire and, for the first time in his life, his pride in wearing the clothes of the palace was replaced with concern for his own wellbeing. They eventually stopped in front of a wooden door. Locke reached out to it but Tori slapped his hand away.

"Enchanted," she muttered as the door clicked open on its own. "Don't ever touch this door unless you wanna be launched back down the stairs. I'm not worried if you do, I'm just letting you know."

Locke ignored the end remark and entered the room with the twins after Lori had pushed to the front of the trio. His eyes fell on the man sitting behind the table, who was in deep conversation with an older-looking lady dressed in a tattered shawl. Recognition leapt onto Locke's face when he saw the man sitting at the table.

"Setz, it's actually you!"

The Guildmaster's eyes darted to Locke and back to the woman, and he said, "That will do, Garnet. You have my report and my assistance. A team will be sent immediately. This was a pleasure."

"Excellent," the woman called Garnet replied, barely above a whisper. "Might I offer some insight before I leave, Setz?"

"Certainly, please do," he said, inclining his head with mild interest.

"I know that what we discussed will not be relevant for a long time, and I understand that it's for her own good. But you may not fool her so easily. She is clever, Setz. She passively remembers anything she reads, word for word. She can recall the eye colour of every person who attended an event that took place years ago, strangers and all. She has made more progress mastering the magical arts in one week than some magicians accomplish in decades. She has both her mother's aptitude and her father's ambitious ideals. She has also known great pain. Do you know what they call a woman with those qualities?"

"Some would say she is gifted."

"No, Setz. They call them dangerous. So watch your step in attempting to deceive her."

Garnet swiftly crossed the room and with barely a glance at Locke, she disappeared out the door and down the stairs. Setz seemed to be momentarily lost in thought as his new visitor approached his table.

"Setz! It really is you!" Locke repeated, unable to think of anything more tactful to say.

"Of course it is I, Locke. Did you come here expecting someone else?" Setz asked in mild amusement.

"No, I –" The bewildered man struggled to find any words worth saying when Tori chimed in.

"We told him it was you who called for him, but he didn't believe us. He's just another noble idiot," she said, blowing the hair out of her face in irritation.

"Now, now, Tori," Setz said, patiently. "Clearly he had some degree of belief to have come here."

Tori rolled her eyes and looked at her sister, who nodded back before speaking.

"The target has been brought before you with no witnesses of consequence. We avoided creating a scene as instructed and the target was warned as requested. Therefore, the mission has been a success," Lori said with confidence as

Locke's expression of disbelief intensified.

These two know what they are doing. Despite their age, they have some unreal skills.

"A mission well done," Setz commended as the twins nodded and took their leave.

The Guildmaster then turned his gaze back to the slack-jawed previous attendant of the Princess.

"Please sit down, Locke. I owe you an explanation."

CHAPTER 59

TO BE SELFLESS, YOU MUST FIRST BE SELFISH

Alicea left Chief Kurok's hut with a heavy heart, the tiny aqueous bird sitting on her shoulder as Rufus and Lyrium followed behind. Lyrium got distracted by something and called out that she'd catch up.

"Why not just send someone to talk to me . . .?" Alicea muttered, barely even acknowledging her friend's departure. The news that soldiers were marching to retrieve her had come from Kurok himself, and it didn't sit well with her.

She wasn't ready to return to the castle – she hadn't mastered the stone's power and was only just becoming aware of the deep-seated issues throughout the land.

"Even if they think I have been abducted, why wouldn't they send a messenger first . . .?"

"Why would they?" Rufus asked quietly from behind her. The sound of his voice made the Princess turn slowly; she'd almost forgotten he was even there.

"Aquiocia always tries diplomacy –"

"Even if their Princess was abducted?" Rufus cut across smoothly. "I don't know royalty, but if there was ever a reason to send an army . . ."

Rufus let the thought trail off. He'd said enough.

Alicea slowed her pace and glared at her companion. "As it turns out, Mr. Thief – I happen to know Aquiocian royalty. One might say that I would know more than you on the topic."

Rufus didn't reply.

"They, always, send, a messenger," Alicea finished with clenched teeth.

"Who are you trying to convince here?" Rufus asked quietly. It was a difficult position to be in. He wanted the Princess to be at ease about the situation, but deluding herself wasn't the way to do it.

The Princess didn't reply. She had already retreated back within her mind to ponder the situation. It didn't make any sense. Kurok had explained that it seemed suspicious that the Council knew where she was, and that they had felt the need to seize the throne in order to issue a command to bring her back.

It didn't add up.

If they knew where she was, Maxim would have marched straight to her, alone if that was what it took to bring her back. She knew the Warmaster; he'd have no issue in doing just that. In fact, if Maxim himself had come for her, she would have had a difficult time saying no to him. He was the example of the loyalty that many soldiers aspired to. He had been there throughout her entire life, one of the closest things to family she had left.

The Princess shoved the bear pelt leading to her hut violently aside as she charged inside. She threw herself in the seat she had put near the window with force; the startled little bird took flight from her shoulder. In its panic, it flew to the bedhead, where it watched her in concern as Rufus entered the room.

"Look, Alicea. I –" Rufus began only to be cut off. Alicea's mood had changed, and he was having difficulty keeping up.

"What am I going to do, Mr. Thief?" Alicea asked. Rufus opened his mouth again only to be spoken over. "No, I don't need you to answer. I need you to listen! There is something wrong in my kingdom and it runs deeper than the lack of royal blood," Alicea snapped. She turned to look out the window, her mind a blur of possibilities as it sifted through every memory relating to the situation. "Setz says that something is wrong within the castle. They have taken the throne, which is unnecessary to declare a search for me."

Alicea took a shuddering breath in an attempt to control the upset consuming her before continuing. Rufus' mouth opened uselessly as words failed him.

"No, something is definitely wrong here," Alicea said, her tone bitter as if she had just resigned herself to something unpleasant.

The one-sided conversation fell to silence, filled by the bustle of people outside. The people of Tremel were preparing for the legion marching their way and although Alicea turned away from the window, she didn't stop listening. Finally, she rose, walking over to her uncertain companion standing at the door. Rufus faltered at her expression. He'd seen it before, but not on her face. No, it was one worn by newcomers in the Underbelly, the ones who were new to the scene.

Guilt.

Looking up at his understanding face, she whispered softly, "I don't want them to take me back like this, Mr. Thief."

Rufus looked down at the distraught Princess and smirked before saying, "Who said anything about them taking you back?"

"They are coming for me now!" Alicea cried with growing hysteria.

"So say no!" Rufus said, grabbing the Princess' shoulders. "You don't want to go back? Say no. Look them in the eye and say no. Then tell them to turn around and go home!"

"It's not that simple –"

"Yes it is!" Rufus exclaimed. "You're their Princess! Their rightful Queen! Tell, them, no!"

Both stood still, eyes set in a fierce battle of wills. On one side there was a man who needed to be believed. On the other end was a woman who wanted to believe him, to just deny the sense of dread nestled within her and believe him.

Eventually, after an agonising amount of time, she smiled.

"You are an idiot."

"So I'm told." Rufus grinned and released her.

Alicea's smile faded, and the guilt returned.

"Mr. Thief, I know it is too soon to be thinking of this, but after this is over we will need to think about what I'll do about my kingdom. I am the only remaining royalty for Aquiocia. It is my responsibility, after all," she said finally, wiping away the tears that had cascaded down her face.

"That is fine. I will be there, whatever path you choose," Rufus replied reassuringly.

"Well then, I'm glad that was sorted and that you seem to feel better," Alicea concluded as a chuckle came from the door.

Lyrium had caught up with them and was pushing past the pelt.

"If all is well, Alicea. Garnet pulled me aside at the end of our meeting. She would like us to meet with her at the training grounds once you have calmed down."

"She wants us both there?" Alicea asked, intrigued. "Then let us waste no more time. I've spent enough of it feeling sorry for myself."

CHAPTER 60

THE ORIGINAL STUDENT

By the time the group approached the end of the winding forest road, Rufus was ready to drive his head into one of the sturdier tree stumps to escape the incessant chatter emanating from the two women in front of him. They spoke about everything, from the stones to themselves and their lives. They both often looked back at Rufus and giggled before turning back to their conversation. Every time they did so, it left the thief more unnerved than any enemy he had faced in the past.

The girlish conversation died off upon reaching their destination. As they walked onto the now familiar training field, their interest shifted to the crow perched in the only standing tree. Below the branches, leaning against the base of the tree, stood Arok. Lyrium walked straight up and let her lips brush his in greeting, allowing a moment with her lover. They hadn't spent any time together since returning from the ruins. She had been too busy and Arok had been tending to Stefan. They quickly swapped greetings before Lyrium turned and pointed at Alicea and Rufus.

"Arok, this is the Princess of Aquiocia, Alicea, and her guard of sorts –"

"Rufus! Good to see you again, old friend! I was starting to wonder if the guards had grabbed you. All that sneaking around isn't for me but I have to give it to you, you're good at what you do," Arok greeted cheerfully, clasping the thief's hand and shaking vigorously before glancing between Alicea and his friend. "I take it this is what you were fetching? Go in for riches and come out with the greatest jewel of all, huh?"

Rufus laughed at Arok's carefree greeting before replying, "Aye, something along those lines."

"You two know each other?" Lyrium asked with a raised eyebrow.

"And I most certainly am not some jewel for a thief to steal," Alicea added sharply, at which Rufus rolled his eyes and Arok openly guffawed. The Princess' attitude did nothing to dampen Arok's good spirits.

"If not for Arok I would still be standing outside the castle walls, scratching my head and trying to figure out how to get in," Rufus said, smiling at the burly man. "Didn't expect to see you here."

"The Chief is my father," Arok replied simply as Garnet approached in her human form, having changed during the conversation.

"Alicea and Lyrium, you are probably wondering why I called you out here now of all times." Garnet took a deep breath, adjusting her thin frock to protect her modesty. "As you both know, thanks to Setz and his men, there is an incoming threat on our town that will not stop until they seize the Princess. Setz, the Chief and I are all in agreement that since we have limited knowledge of their intentions, we should be prepared for anything."

"I am so –"

"Close your mouth. You are my student and I am speaking,"

Garnet said coolly. "In light of this, the people of Tremel will prepare for the worst. However, even the small force that I investigated rallying in Aquiocia would walk over our village with little problem. That is, unless we have something to repel them with."

"What numbers are we looking at?" Lyrium asked seriously.

I met this woman a few days ago, yet she doesn't hesitate to defend me? Alicea thought with mixed emotions.

"From what our scouts and Setz have indicated, the enemy is one thousand strong plus their new General. This is not surprising; Aquiocia regularly moves with one thousand soldiers. They are trained to move efficiently with such a number," Garnet explained. "Our village houses around six hundred, a little over a third of whom are either too elderly or have not picked up a weapon before."

Lyrium looked at the ground, her face covered in concern, when Alicea piped up.

"New General? Who is it?" Alicea asked. Rufus knew the Princess was concerned for the man named Maxim. Garnet hesitated a moment, as if weighing up which words to utilise before continuing.

"I left before we got the nobleman's report from the castle, so I have no insight as to what became of the last man who was in charge. As for the new General, his name is Jex. Though he does appear rather young to hold such a title," Garnet replied, unaware of the importance of the name.

Alicea almost physically recoiled at the name, bringing her hand to her mouth and shaking her head in an attempt to deny what was being said to her. When questioned, she just shook it more furiously, retreating quickly to a tree stump and sitting on it with a look of pure horror on her face. Garnet turned to Rufus, who looked just as confused as the rest and nodded towards the Princess.

"Go, speak to her. I'll start briefing Lyrium on what we are here for. My former student already knows the basics in magic; she was taught by myself in hopes of becoming a shaman one day."

Rufus walked uncertainly to the Princess, who had turned the colour of a white sheet. He sat down beside her on the massive stump and looked back to see Garnet lecturing Lyrium while Arok sat stiffly under the tree, watching the proceedings with crossed arms. His back wasn't pressed against the trunk, though; his injuries had been addressed but were still tender. He, like many of the residents of Tremel, wouldn't dream of complaining about wounds they considered to be minor.

"What's the problem?" Rufus asked, careful to keep his eyes forward. Somehow, he felt looking at her would worsen the situation. He was rewarded with a reply after a long silence.

"Jex is not a soldier, he is a murderer," Alicea said softly.

"Most soldiers kill, Alicea."

"No. He never rose any higher in the ranks because his methods were deemed too brutal. An incident took place where he was ordered to take a small company to a neighbouring village, investigating a trading issue. He returned alone. The reports stated that the village was left as dust and rubble," Alicea continued, her voice cracking with a fear that seemed out of place.

"It was destroyed? What about the other soldiers? Surely that's suspicious enough for him to be imprisoned," Rufus said as Alicea shook her head.

"The other soldiers were found dead." The Princess drew a shuddering breath. "He was imprisoned. It took everything I knew just to find where he was being kept."

"Did you know him?" Rufus asked.

"Since I was very young. In fact, I haven't seen him since I was around four. He was usually deployed somewhere; it was required for his training to become a knight, but he has been to the palace many times."

"Ah, so you knew him when you were children?" Rufus stated more than asked, piecing together Garnet's report of his young appearance and what Alicea was telling him.

"No, that's just it. He was a young adult then. I'd follow him everywhere because I knew something was deeply wrong with the man, something that nobody else seemed to see, or believe. Since I was very young I'd watched knights come and go from the castle. Each one I saw more than once, I'd recognise. Their face would reflect what they'd been through in the months they had spent away. Be it fresh scars, the weariness in their smiles as they bowed to me or the sorrow of loss in their eyes, I saw it. I remember it," Alicea said, a tinge of fear in her voice now as she turned to Rufus. "Mr. Thief, when I see Jex next, he will appear as he always did to me. I know this."

"How . . . How could you possibly know that?" Rufus frowned. Alicea's story had given him a chill.

"My father decreed that Jex be executed. It wasn't a public affair – Aquiocian executions rarely are. But my father wouldn't lie to me. He's supposed to be dead. Do you understand yet, Mr. Thief?"

"Are you saying the man came back from the dead?"

"No, I cannot confirm or deny that. But I know this – if there is any one person in the Aquiocian kingdom who truly loathes me, who wouldn't hesitate in killing me without a second thought, it is Jex. In some ways, he has every reason to want to. If it's him leading my people . . ." Alicea couldn't hold it together anymore, and tears began to spill from her pale grey eyes and down her delicate face. "I, and more importantly, everyone around me, is going to die."

CHAPTER 61

THE VASSAL OF EARTH

"Unacceptable! How do you expect to repel the soldiers with that effort?" Garnet yelled at Lyrium in frustration.

Her student had fallen to the ground in a series of desperate gasps for air. Her normally boisterous curls were plastered to her face, held firm by her profuse sweating. When afternoon arrived they had moved down to an open, grassy area between the stream's spider web paths. Garnet had insisted on training with her all afternoon to get Lyrium caught up with Alicea. By the time night fell, all that had been accomplished was the exhaustion of her student. It had been beautiful and untouched turf at the beginning of her training. Now there were sharp spikes of soil and stone protruding from the earth around the pair, illuminated by the moon overhead.

The ground beneath Lyrium moved, changing shape each time she attempted to control the stone's power. Each time the stone resisted violently. In a couple of instances, Lyrium was barely fortunate enough to have the small amount of control it took not to impale herself or her teacher.

Alicea watched on from her tree stump with concern. She had realised hours ago that Lyrium was indeed gifted in magic. It was why the Princess could not work out why her friend was having so much difficulty in comparison to herself.

Garnet was harder on Lyrium than she ever was with Alicea, yet Lyrium refused to complain, which impressed the Princess.

I may be more attuned to my stone, but Lyrium is a far stronger person than I, she thought with admiration.

"Take a break!" Garnet snapped angrily.

"N-No, I can –" Lyrium started to protest through wheezes.

"Do as I say. You are no use if you die from fatigue!" Garnet cut off her student impatiently.

Lyrium nodded, reluctantly letting her body relax a little. The moment Garnet had declared they would rest, Alicea was on her feet, gliding across the training field towards her exhausted friend. The Princess weaved through the glaives of earth and knelt down in front of the flushed Lyrium.

"What's holding you back? You have more experience in magic than I. Should this not be easier for you?" Alicea's hand extended towards one of the streams and the water within responded with a steady trickle coursing across the ground to her waiting hand. The liquid formed a small sphere in her palm. Upon completing its form it expelled the dirt and impurities from its confines. What remained was an orb of pristine liquid, which its conjurer passed to her friend.

Panting, Lyrium held the gift for a moment, as if pondering how to consume it. Finally, she shrugged and pushed her palm to her face where the orb exploded in a spray. After a moment of laughter from Alicea, Lyrium's breathing began to return to normal.

"It's not the casting of the magic that I'm finding difficult. I can't seem to gather the stone's power. I make the connection within my mind as I would with any magical tool, but it severs as soon as I try to put it into effect," Lyrium explained, lying down on a carefully chosen flat of the uneven ground.

"You mean to say that this are your doing alone?" Alicea looked around at the torn earth in wonder. There wasn't an inch of flat ground for yards from Lyrium gripping it with sheer will alone and calling it to pierce its earthen surface. "Well done!"

Lyrium laughed. "Thank you, Your Highness. I'm so pleased that I have met the royal expectations of the master magician – Princess Alicea!"

"Are you making fun of me when you just practically collapsed from exhaustion?" Alicea ribbed back playfully.

"What does it feel like when you connect with your stone? How did you first make the connection?" Lyrium asked and Alicea shrugged.

"I just asked for help," she replied simply and Lyrium frowned thoughtfully, staring at the stars as Alicea continued. "The stones, mine at least, do not operate as a simple tool to enhance magical capabilities. It is more like a friend that lends you power."

Lyrium sat up, staring at her friend sceptically, unsure of whether what she was hearing was a joke or if it was bizarre enough to work. Her thoughts were interrupted as Garnet stalked over.

"If you have enough energy to talk, you have enough energy to continue. Now, on your feet!"

Lyrium obliged immediately and without complaint. She nodded her thanks to Alicea, who returned to her place atop the tree stump next to Rufus. Shoving him roughly to get him to move over, she sat without a word. The Princess fingered the brown leaves of her hand-made hairclip anxiously as she watched teacher and student stand across from each other in the light of the full moon overhead.

"We are running out of time, Lyrium. Give me what I want – show me what you and your stone are capable of!" Garnet demanded.

Lyrium closed her eyes and took a deep breath.

When she reopened them again after a long moment of heavy concentration, Garnet was nodding in approval. Her student's deep-brown eyes were glazed over, her face expressionless. At first glance, the hunter appeared devoid of emotion and yet anyone who looked at her closely would be able to tell that something monumental was going on within her mind. Rufus leant forward from his spot on the stump next to Alicea and muttered curiously.

"That look . . ."

"Yes," Alicea said firmly. "I daresay she is speaking to the one within the stone."

"That's what I was thinking. You went all stiff too," Rufus replied, nodding slowly, his curiosity replaced with apprehension.

"Wait, she is talking to the one in the stone?" Arok's voice came from beside the spectating pair. He had moved closer when he realised his love was seemingly paralysed.

"It appears that way," Rufus said, before grinning to his friend. "Prepare for something big."

"We are not animals at some circus to be gawked at, Mr. Thief –" Alicea started to scold before being cut off by the spectacle in front of her.

Lyrium had fallen to all fours and was now surrounded in a peculiar sepia aura, which steadily devoured the pale moonlight that filled the training field. Moans of pain could be heard even from the tree stump that the three spectators had gathered around.

"She is in pain!" Arok cried in distress as he made to run to his lover's aid.

"No!" Alicea yelled, stepping in front of him, despite lacking any way to physically stop him. On her shoulder, the Princess' aqueous pet had its wings outstretched as a sign for him to halt. *Speaking with the being within my stone helped me . . .*

"This is part of it. She needs to do this."

Conflict was written all over Arok's face as he looked from his suffering lover to Alicea before reluctantly stepping back. Rufus pointed at the proceedings, making the pair turn towards the cause of his sudden movement. Alicea gasped as the aura surrounding Lyrium started to take shape. The Vassal let out a wail of anguish and Arok grunted, still fighting the urge to run to her. The tormented woman was struggling to get to her feet, the aura mutating. When she finally forced herself to stand, the bizarre light erupted. The burst bathed the entire field in a hue of burnt sienna, erasing the moonlight's rays from existence.

As Rufus and Arok stared at the newly coloured surroundings, Alicea muttered, "Oh my," staring at Lyrium.

Lyrium stood within the aura, holding the same confidence she exuded naturally. The aura surrounding her had taken on the form of a great beast. Its face looked like the adult offspring of a wolf and bear. While it had a canine-shaped jaw and eyes that reflected great intelligence, its body was much more muscular in appearance. The torso was viciously torn with muscle and yet, still lean enough to appear agile. With legs as thick as any female adult bear, the aura's limbs made Lyrium's own seem miniscule as she stood within the confines of the transparent, bestial body.

Even from her view Alicea could see the details of the coarse, brown hair standing on end from the beast's back. Its tail appeared to be just as long as its body and was flicking back and forth with the enthusiasm of a dog being praised. Contrary to the friendly wagging of its tail were sharp, serrated teeth lining its ferocious jaw, coupled with claws big enough to crush a child.

Garnet had taken several steps back in uncertainty at the sight of the beast and now approached Lyrium cautiously.

"Is this the stone's doing?" Garnet asked Lyrium in wonder.

"Is this not what you wanted? Have I not done well?" Lyrium's voice rang out, seemingly louder than intended. Her voice echoed hollowly around the field.

"This is more than I ever expected!" Garnet exclaimed. "The stone's power is nothing short of incredible!"

Lyrium smiled, clearly proud of her effort. While its conjurer appeared to have an almost casual conversation with her tutor, the beast was looking around curiously. The stunned audience of Alicea, Rufus and Arok watched closely as the wolf-bear twisted its staunch body to take in its surroundings. The Princess noticed that the beast never moved in a way that would separate it from Lyrium.

Can it not exist without her? Alicea wondered. *Is she the conduit it requires to take form?*

"How do you feel?" Garnet asked quietly, as if not wanting to be overheard.

"I feel different. I can feel so much," Lyrium tried to explain uncertainly. "I can hear things I couldn't before; my eyesight is so much clearer. I feel so calm, yet more energetic than I ever have in my life."

"You can feel the magic's nature as Alicea can?" Garnet asked thoughtfully, trying to comprehend the sensation of the connection.

"It's like energy is building up within me – I feel like I have to let it out or I'll explode," Lyrium said, looking down at her hands covered in the sienna aura in the form of large paws. Each of them had four thick extremities adorned with sharp blade-like nails, each easily six inches in length. Garnet nodded and looked back to the three spectators. She judged that they were indeed a safe distance away before responding.

"A fine idea. I will join your friends and you can release this energy in whatever way you deem appropriate. Just try not to lose control . . . or destroy the forest."

Lyrium nodded and Garnet could see the great excitement in her student's eyes. As her tutor set out towards the others, Lyrium tore her eyes from her hand and embraced the energy coursing through her.

I feel so strong, so fast and so energetic! This . . . Oh . . . This is going to be fun! Lyrium thought excitedly as the great beast stopped its examination of the field and joined its conjurer in concentration, a transparent tongue lashing at its own teeth.

CHAPTER 62

WITH GREAT POWER . . .

Lyrium's body felt as if it were about to explode. Energy and excitement coursed through her almost violently and her mind was ablaze as she became one with the stone's power for the very first time. She noticed that the aura around her was becoming less transparent, the deep hue growing slightly darker. Her vision was bathed in its presence, but it did nothing to obscure her new keener eyesight.

She honed in on a spider crawling up a tree at the edge of the field before adjusting her sight back to what was in front of her. How'd she do that? How did she know there was such a tiny creature in that exact spot? Furthermore, how could she *see* it from this distance?

The spears she had raised from the earth seemed a pitiful effort compared to the way she felt now. Her gaze drifted from the sharp lances of earth to where Garnet was. Her instructor had crossed the rich grass to where Arok, Alicea and Rufus were. The four were engaged in a conversation. From where Lyrium was standing, Garnet appeared to be doing the majority of the talking. After a quick exchange, Garnet turned back and signalled for her to begin with a wave.

Yes! This is it! she thought.

Concentrate on controlling my power, Lyrium, lest it consume you. The deep rolling voice from the stone directly entered her mind.

I know, I know, Lyrium responded impatiently and the voice fell silent, though a sense of disdain washed over her consciousness. It appeared that the stones had a way of expressing their feelings without speaking.

Lyrium called upon the power of the stone and was met with an almost overwhelming rush of energy. It felt as if a landslide had found her body but rather than being crushed, she was brought along for the rocky descent. It was rough, and the pangs of blunt projectiles started to make steady, dull impacts against her mind. There was no pain, though; rather, it felt magnificent. With the connection came an assault on her mind, but with the combined efforts of her and the stone, her consciousness was protected. It was as if a migraine had come to plague, but had been forbidden entry.

The aura surrounding her intensified in colour, becoming more distinguished in shape as her mental connection with the stone violently sparked within. She felt the stone's nature seep through her defences and her instincts sharpened. The sensation threatened to take control of her as her body slowly lowered into the stance of a prowling cat.

I have to release some of this right now, Lyrium realised as she shifted her focus to the spider she had spied.

It was spinning itself a web from its place on the side of the large tree, unaware of the predator watching it. Its glimmering silk web protruded from its backside as its front legs feverishly molded it into shape. It was a target as good as any other.

Lyrium released the pent-up energy and the result astounded everyone present – including herself. Her body flew across the training field at breakneck speed, closing the distance between her and the target within a second. As she violently collided with the thick tree, it splintered and snapped as her ethereal claws buried themselves into the tough bark. She realised something peculiar as she stared back the way she had come. She had felt no impact and only a deep sense of satisfaction as her body had connected with the tree, which now stood on an apparent lean.

Lyrium attempted to let out a triumphant cheer, but what was heard was a fierce, guttural growl. Before she could ponder the unexpected sound, she spotted an ants' nest in the brush. She couldn't look away from the mundane image as the resident ants crawling about their duties involuntarily became targets. Lyrium shoved herself from the collapsing tree with such momentum that it was driven into the ground almost instantly. The collision was heard from where Alicea and the others sat. The sound of a lightning bolt striking the ground ricocheted for leagues as Lyrium landed, collapsing the ants' intricate tunnels underground.

Feeling no recoil from the assault, she proceeded to lash out at the tiny fleeing prey with her great claws. Her claws were becoming darker and more solid to the eye as they raked away the earth beneath her, leaving only gouges in the forest floor. She only stopped her vicious onslaught when her ears picked up a distant sound from within the forest. She stood up straight and looked around with her superhuman eyesight. The sea of trees seemed endless as she searched for the source before, finally, spotting a great stag two hundred yards away.

The innocent beast had been grazing on the greenery before hearing the commotion. It appeared that the only reason it hadn't fled was that it had no idea where the sound came from. Before she could begin to comprehend the fact that she had heard the beast eating from such a distance, Lyrium's body was back in motion, using both arms and legs to propel herself across the floor of the forest. Fallen branches were trampled in her stead as she navigated the maze of flora at a pace that no beast could hope to match.

She wove through the trees, picking up more speed as she went, sidestepping at the last second to narrowly avoid a thicker-than-average trunk. The effort forced her into the direct path of another tree of gargantuan girth. The small rational part of her mind that still existed braced for impact, yet her body refused to slow. She smashed headlong into the solid obstacle with a resounding thunderclap, her wolf-like aura emitting a bright flash as she collided.

To Lyrium's surprise, the great tree was lifted from its deep-seated home and flung skyward. She didn't know where it landed, and it wasn't important. Her priority was the stag fleeing from the threat. She launched herself at the prey from afar, closing the gap between them in less than a second.

The stag's death was instant as Lyrium tackled the now seemingly fragile beast, sending them both sprawling across the ground. The bestial woman was on her feet instantly, unharmed and looking at the mangled corpse of the pathetic animal she'd slain. Another triumphant cry from her throat was mutated, this time in the form of her throwing back her head and howling at the moon almost like a rabid wolf.

But Lyrium knew she was something else entirely while connected to the stone. The wolves of the forest seemed like harmless puppies compared to the power surging through her. She was stronger, faster and more resilient than they were ever portrayed and – while a small part of her was terrified – the much larger part was invigorated. Her thoughtful reflection was interrupted as instinct took hold of her once more. Her aura's ears were on end as they picked up the sound of running water from the streams stretching across the training field.

Water! So thirsty! Her rabid thoughts were the cue for her body to bound towards the sound.

The break in the trees could be seen within seconds of her rushing back the way she came. With an almighty leap, she propelled herself the remainder of the distance. She broke free of the sea of flora and landed in the training field roughly, rolling along the turf before crashing into a deeper part of the stream. She thrashed at the waist-deep water, snapping at it like a wild beast under attack. The refreshing liquid was sent in all directions as Lyrium sprayed more than she actually drank. The interior of her mind was wild and uncontrolled with only the thought of quenching her thirst.

The thumping upon her consciousness had intensified, each collision more painful than the last. Before long, the pain began to numb; Lyrium was becoming accustomed to blocking it out. Her last thought as a rational human was laced with fear when she realised exactly how she was able to block out the pain.

The relief I'm feeling . . . It's coming from my mind taking a step back and allowing the stone full control! No! Release me, damn it!

Alicea and the others stared in wonder and anxiety at what their friend was becoming. They were all equally at a loss as to what they should do but it was Rufus who first spoke.

"What is wrong with her?" he muttered before all colour drained from his face as Lyrium stopped her onslaught against the water. Her neck snapped towards him, her aura's eyes ablaze with a vicious hunger.

Lyrium crouched down in the same way she had before, starting to slowly prowl towards the small group. Rufus quickly took stock of the situation as he always did before a confrontation. They had about forty yards of grassland and a few streams of water between the party and the beast. The smaller streams branched out of the biggest pool coursing through the centre of the field, an almost equal distance between himself and Lyrium.

Nothing that will stand in her way of getting at us, he thought grimly as he drew his short blades.

"Princess, run," Rufus ordered slowly as he stepped forward between beast and prey.

"I think not, Mr. Thief," Alicea replied defiantly.

"Would you listen to me for just once in your life –"

"Enough, you two! She comes!" Garnet cried.

CHAPTER 63

AWAKENING

Rufus moved quickly, swift steps taking him towards the fast-approaching threat. He stopped a couple of feet from the edge of one of the streams, in hopes of somehow getting the advantage of having more stable footing than his opponent. It was a hopeless strategy after seeing what she had done to the trees, but he knew he had to at least attempt to distract her while Alicea and the others fled.

If I survive this, she had better give me the damned bonus I deserve.

Lyrium was steadily closing the gap, the aura's hungry eyes relishing the fear of its new prey.

Rufus' stoic expression masked the fear that threatened to topple his facade and body. It was a strange sensation, watching what could very well be his death charging towards him. He'd stared death down many times with an air of complete indifference. He had always reasoned with his fear, trumping it with the logic that there was always a way out. By pushing aside fear, he was able to escape any unfavourable situation.

Apparently, my limit is a wolf-beast stalking towards me.

Lyrium's aura had never been more prominent. Its colour was so deep that her body was almost entirely consumed within the rabid aura. The growl of the deadly beast clawed at his bravado, but it held. There was too much behind him to buckle now. After covering most of the ground between them her powerful legs launched her through the air at Rufus.

Gripping his blades with white knuckles, he couldn't help closing his eyes as he waited for the impact. An ear-splitting crash was heard along with a surprised yelp of pain. It took a moment for him to realise he wasn't dead. He opened his eyes slowly, taking in the unbelievable sight in front of him.

A rippling wall of water stood in front of him. Taller than the trees surrounding the field, it stretched along the entire length of the stream. He could see through the liquid barricade to the beast that was clambering to its feet. Its wolfish face twisted with shock and anger as it started to pace in front of the barrier that had denied her.

"I'm almost certain that gawking at my magnificence is not productive use of our time right now, Mr. Thief!" came the strained voice of the Princess from behind him.

Lyrium occasionally lashed out at the wall with little effect. Anything her great claws raked off was replenished immediately as the wall corrected itself, waiting for the next attack.

"What in the world?" Rufus asked curiously.

"Stop staring at it and come up with a plan, Mr. Thief!" Alicea berated.

Rufus whirled around to see the young Princess' arms outstretched towards the wall with open palms. The tiny bird flapped its wings and danced supportively upon her shoulder as Alicea's face screwed up in concentration and something akin to pain.

"Unbelievable – a completely solid wall comprised only of

water," Garnet stated in wonder. "This is so advanced . . ."

"This is amazing!" agreed Arok, staring likewise in awe at what the Princess had achieved. He had remained silent during the proceedings. The lines of good and bad had blurred too much for a man who attempted to keep things simple.

The beast let out a desperate wail and hurled itself into the barrier again. Its powerful body bounced off the surface, falling roughly to the ground. Alicea grunted with the effort of keeping the wall intact, her face reflecting more of the pain that Rufus had noticed before.

"Talk about how amazing it is later, she can't hold the beast at bay forever!" Rufus roared.

Garnet nodded in agreement, her face turning serious as she approached the wall and looked out at the consumed woman that was Lyrium. In return, the beast snarled at Garnet viciously as its prey within struggled. Mentally focusing on Lyrium herself was not an easy task as Garnet attempted to reach out with her mind. She found barely a glimmer of her student within the haze created from the rage of the beast. The tutor knew that the only reason she felt her student's presence at all was the fact that her terror was so strong.

With a shuddering breath, Garnet turned to Alicea and spoke slowly.

"Alicea, you are the only one here gifted with enough strength to overpower her at this point. You need to sedate the beast, but not kill Lyrium. Can you do that?"

"I – h-how?" the Princess stuttered with a frown.

"Relax," Garnet said kindly, ignoring the inadequacy of the command compared to what she was requesting. "Command it as you would your swan . . ."

The Princess didn't reply; speaking was an exhausting non-necessity.

All eyes were on Alicea as she moved her right hand through the air slowly. The wall recognised the motion and immediately responded. Downstream, the party could see the barricade bending around in a large arc. It kept level with the ground as its journey continued slowly until it had bent enough to form behind Lyrium. Within a few seconds, Alicea had managed to mould the wall of liquid into the shape of a crescent moon.

The beast had begun to bash against the same spot with renewed rage, each attack causing Alicea to flinch in pain as she devoted more of her energy to repair the damage. She knew there was little point in making a wall expand if its foundation was easily crushed. Her left hand moved in the opposite direction of her right and with it, the other end of the wall began its effort to be united with the other side. Rufus realised what Alicea was doing at the same time the beast stopped its relentless assault and noticed the movement of the walls around it.

The beast finally took notice of the enclosing prison. The aura's face was twisted in rage, letting out the shriek of a conflicted animal. It was as if the human side of her knew what Alicea was attempting, but it only angered the beast further.

As the two edges of the aqueous barrier closed in on each other, Lyrium lowered her frame and kept her eyes on the closing gap to her freedom. The beast's tail flicked back and forth in the same way a snake warns off predators. Rufus knew that with the beast's speed it could run out of the prison before it closed. The small part of Lyrium that was left was holding the aura within the liquid wall. Somehow, she had complete and absolute faith in Alicea, but the beast only saw its exit.

The thief started yelling curses at the top of his lungs. He strode straight up to the wall and slapped his chest in an invitation to strike him. Alicea's lips curled slightly at Rufus' taunts. They were effective; the beast's head snapped around in confusion between the aggravating man and the closing gap. The distraction lasted seconds before it shook its massive head violently and lunged towards freedom.

Its superhuman speed swiftly carried it across the plain but it fell just short of freedom as the edges melded together. The beast couldn't stop in time, and it didn't want to, as it collided with the barricade so forcefully that the entire wall rippled, threatening to collapse. Alicea emitted a whimper, barely holding it together. She gasped for air as the beast picked itself up off the ground and ran back towards the party hiding behind the wall.

"No . . . Not another . . . I can't . . ." Alicea squeaked, sweat running down her delicate face.

As Lyrium closed the gap, Rufus took his place between the Princess and the threat. He was aware that the wall could very well fail and its rippling surface was ready to collapse.

"Gladirus: Natarus Gimrel!" Garnet's voice was heard.

He stared in surprise at the charging Lyrium as the ground started to stir a few feet from where he was standing on the other side of the great water wall.

As it closed in, the earth burst and countless vines erupted from under its surface at the beast. The restraints wrapped around its limbs and neck with blinding speed and forced it roughly to the ground, continually restricting its movement.

The beast thrashed against the surprise attack, ripping vines violently only to have them replaced by others. As more and more of the long tethers joined the effort, Rufus could see Garnet tiring at an alarming rate.

This is the difference in stamina between a stone-bearer and a normal mage. It's extraordinary, he thought.

Alicea, however, did not allow the effort to be in vain. The great wall she commanded started to ripple less, growing more stable by the second. With every ounce of energy she gave, her face grew more fraught with exhaustion and panic.

I need more strength! she called out to the stone.

Too much and you too will be consumed, Young One, was the soft but firm reply.

It's a risk that must be taken. We will die if you don't help!

I cannot allow you to be taken hostage by power like she has. Every Vassal is important, but none more so than you, the voice said, trying to calm the Princess with little success.

What kind of excuse is that, one person being more important than the others? Ridiculous! I'll never accept that as a reason to not help someone in need! Alicea replied viciously.

Whether you accept it or not is irrelevant. It is the way of this world, the voice replied calmly.

Perhaps you're right. But that is one of the things I wish to change. It's part of the reason I'm here!

I see, the voice replied softly.

How am I supposed to help the entire world by finding the stones as you say, if I can't even save the people in front of me? Alicea asked desperately.

The voice didn't reply, and Alicea felt alone once more in her ordeal. She stabilised the wall with what energy she had left, then felt as if she had hit a dead end. She was trapped between the options of holding the wall there to be broken down by the beast or releasing it and embracing death. She knew that to push it further would surely kill her. There was also the risk of the magic going haywire and hurting others. But it was her only chance to prevent the beast from destroying them.

After the beast kills us, what will it do?

It will make its way to the village. The truth ran through the Princess' mind.

Alicea took a deep, shaky breath and began to weave the energy needed for the next stage of her plan. The wall responded by closing in on the entangled Lyrium. The beast was still thrashing on the ground, growling and snarling as its captive watched on with dread. The wall of liquid began to move in tighter, the excess water being pushed to the top, the formation growing taller.

Alicea felt faint. She knew she couldn't hold onto the power much longer.

Even if I make it through this . . . what damage will I be left with?

Her vision was growing dark and her head ached unbearably as she pushed the wall inwards more and more.

What are you attempting, Young One? the voice asked, allowing its concern to spill over.

I will never abandon a friend just because I'm supposedly more important! Alicea snarled back.

I could give you the power to flee to safety, the voice offered.

You are not listening! I will not abandon her! I will not abandon Rufus! I will not abandon my friends!

Alicea could sense the presence of the being within the stone, although it had fallen silent. Its silence felt like eternity in an instant when she felt new power flood through her body.

You have grown, Young One.

Then the voice was gone.

Alicea's vision cleared, the splitting headache receding to a dull throb, and she redoubled her efforts. Through the haze of the bestial aura she saw her friend. She wasn't stupid; it was obvious that the euphoric sensation was only masking the damage being done to her body, but she had been given a chance. The wall was rapidly closing in on Lyrium, who had almost broken free of her bindings. When the last vine finally gave way, she was on her feet and looking around frantically at the prison that had become a measly ten yards wide.

Both beast and Lyrium gazed up at the top of the hollow pillar of water, their expressions reflecting irritation and hope respectively. Alicea felt her heart tear when Lyrium lowered her head and gazed at the Princess miserably. Her forlorn attempt at escaping her confines had yielded nothing. Her eyes screamed in fear. Even the beast's anger seemed to be simmering as it took in the situation.

The beast has consumed her completely, Alicea realised in despair as the beast's anger resurfaced and its whole body started to quiver with blind hatred.

Tears spilled down her face as the Princess called to out to her trapped friend.

"Please, just trust me!"

Lyrium's eyes widened before she threw her head back in a howl tinged with sadness. The sound was heard for leagues and tore at the group's heartstrings. Arok fell to the ground, cursing Alicea out of distress. Rufus stepped between them, growling at the distraught man to keep it together. Alicea looked at her hands in front of her, then brought them together.

The effect was instant and the top of the wall started to collapse inwards. The water cascaded downwards onto Lyrium as it filled her prison. The beast roared, lunging at the falling water. There was no pattern to the manic thrashing; the demented creature only wanted to destroy the offending prison. It thrashed at the liquid that was flooding its compound.

The water rose over the aura's head and kept rising. All the while Alicea kept the sides of the wall solid. As the prisoner attempted to thrash above the flood, Alicea mentally sealed the top and the lid became as resistant as the walls around her. There was no escape as the bestial form writhed within.

Lyrium lashed out at the clear lid of her liquid coffin, but to little effect. She was being consumed by both the water and Alicea's magical energy. The effort of striking at the walls only expended the precious air remaining in her lungs. Arok was on his feet within a moment and ran at Alicea, only to be intercepted by Rufus, daggers drawn.

"Get out of my way or –"

"Trust her," Rufus said simply. "I swear on everything I hold dear that your love will get out of this alive."

"What makes you so sure?"

Rufus had no response, yet Arok understood why the thief trusted Alicea. It was the same reason he trusted Lyrium – he just believed in her. It was just that simple.

Alicea was unaware of the men's silent exchange as she watched the air escape from her friend's lungs. The beast's attacks became steadily less forceful; each blow to the walls of her prison became easier to repair. The aura started to fade, along with her life force, before finally disappearing entirely.

Lyrium's eyelids started to droop. Her body fell limp before Alicea released the magic, severing the connection to the water and then the stone.

The prison of water exploded, showering everyone there in a cascade of liquid. Lyrium fell to the soaked earth, coughing and choking up water as Arok and Garnet ran to her.

Lyrium looked past Garnet and Arok to the exhausted Alicea with a weak smile that could be seen through the saturated hair sprawled across her face.

"Thank you, my friend," Lyrium spluttered.

Alicea only had time to smile back before her head whirled and her body gave up, collapsing into Rufus' arms.

CHAPTER 64

A KIDNAPPER'S CONCERN

Rufus appeared to be dozing off in his seat inside Alicea's room, but his mind was still more active than ever. The Princess was lying unconscious on her bed, her face serene, which only made it harder on him as he checked on her every few minutes to make sure she was still breathing.

Just move a little, curse you! he thought vehemently as he scratched at the scar near his eye. Alicea didn't budge.

Arok entered the room quietly, along with one of the village's shaman healers. The healer looked over Alicea briefly, nodded and left swiftly as Arok placed a plate of meat and bread down next to Rufus, pulling up a seat next to him.

"You need to take a break," he said quietly.

"Not going to happen and you know it," Rufus muttered, clearing his throat roughly.

"It's been five days, Rufus. She may not wake up for some time yet, and we will need you at your full potential for the fight," Arok insisted.

Rufus didn't reply. He knew Arok was right, but that didn't change anything. Why was she still asleep? Lyrium recovered within twenty-four hours and immediately resumed her training with Garnet.

Arok stared at Rufus, noting the growth of hair spreading

across his face through neglect. His eyes were dark, almost calculating, beneath his perpetually furrowed brow. The man's body sat rigid in its vigilance of keeping watch over the Princess. Arok saw his friend for what he was – a broken and worried man.

What is between him and the Princess? Why does he care so much if it was originally just a job?

"Why do you care so much about her wellbeing? My father told me your story, and you sitting by her bedside for days on end doesn't make a lot of sense," Arok voiced.

Rufus looked at his friend darkly.

"She is my current contract. As long as she survives, I get paid," Rufus replied shortly.

"So, what you are saying is that the only reason you care whether the woman in front of you lives or dies is because of gold?" Arok pressed.

"Yes," Rufus replied.

Arok stood, pushing the chair back into place. Just before leaving, he placed a hand on his friend's shoulder.

"Just a personal opinion but, as a friend to a friend," Arok began before grinning. "You need to work on your acting, because no one is going to buy that performance. You should let yourself care about someone. It keeps you going."

Arok was gone before Rufus could even reply.

It IS why I'm here, isn't it? he thought. *No, that was the reason at first, but no longer. Somewhere along the lines I came to believe in the spoilt Princess.*

The exhausted thief leant back in his chair, staring out the window with eyes blurred from fatigue.

You could make a difference, so don't you dare go and die on me yet.

❖

The training field was a disaster zone around Garnet and Lyrium. The earth was damaged beyond measure from countless small, web-like cracks spreading outwards from the field's centre. The newest, and worst, addition was the gaping fissure that now cut through the centre of the field, wide enough to comfortably fit two caravans side by side. On opposite sides of the chasm stood mentor and student, calling out to each other.

"This is progress, Lyrium! How do you feel?" Garnet called.

"Why do you keep asking that? I feel fine!" Lyrium snapped back.

"After what happened the other day we need to take it slowly. We don't have Alicea here to stop you again," Garnet warned for what felt like the thousandth time as she looked over her student.

Lyrium looked at the chasm in front of her that she had made with the stone's assistance, thinking back to the day her mentor was referring to. She couldn't remember much – her memory skipped from her taking down a stag in one strike to a blinding rage, before finally looking up to see a smiling Alicea. There was only a blank void after that. She had awoken the next day as refreshed as if she had just enjoyed a wonderful night's sleep. With one exception. Once she'd awoken and washed her face in the clear rivers of the forest, she'd caught sight of her reflection ...

From the top of her head were two long, brown, furry ears, akin to a rabbit's, protruding from her chocolate curls. The fur of the ears matched her hair and – though they were a new addition to her body and obviously a manifestation of the magic that had been coursing through her almost a week ago – they suited her. At first they had simply flopped and drooped all over the place, but, as the days passed, she was gaining more control of them. As she became more accustomed to them they integrated into her person.

Lyrium had come to love them, claiming that she was so in touch with nature itself that she was becoming part of it. It was a joke that was well-received by the other villagers as they cheered. She'd had a small moment of doubt when she first broached the subject with Arok, but the burly man had erupted into laughter, dubbed her "tough *and* cute", and not another anxious thought had crossed her mind about them.

"It's fine, damn it! I just tried to take on more than I could handle. It was a simple matter of too much too soon!" Lyrium yelled in irritation. Normally she'd have never dared to raise her voice to her mentor, but the past week of training and guilt had taken its toll. Thankfully, the older woman understood and accepted this.

Garnet nodded thoughtfully and after a moment she declared, "If you are certain that you could reproduce today's efforts at any moment, then the only thing we can do is wait and hope that Alicea wakes up soon!"

"You still haven't told me what your plan is, or why you need us both!"

"And I'm still not ready to divulge that information. I'm not even certain it's plausible! Very soon, I promise – providing she wakes up. Patience, Lyrium!" Garnet called back, ending the conversation by abruptly transforming into a crow and taking off towards the village.

"I swear she gets more cryptic the older she gets," Lyrium sighed as she looked around herself at the damage she had done.

The training field looked like an obstacle course. It had large earthen glaives protruding from the ground and the massive drop directly through the middle. Even the water had stopped flowing through most of the streams due to the tearing of their walls.

She had found that it wasn't difficult to do such feats with the stone's aid. The difficult part was controlling it, not taking in too much of the power. Garnet was right: if she had failed in controlling the power this time around, she could have wiped out her entire village with the fissure instead of confining it to the training field. As she looked up and down the length of the earthen tear, she realised that some of the trees from the forestland had been uprooted at one end. She still didn't have full control.

What is her plan? I could just bury the soldiers with my power and the problem would be solved. Why is Alicea needed? Lyrium thought.

Your teacher wishes for a peaceful resolution to all of this, as does the other Vassal. The voice of the stone entered Lyrium's mind for the first time since she had lost control.

Back off! I don't want to speak to you after the other day! Lyrium snapped.

What happened then was your own doing. I warned you, but instead you took on too much of my power at once. Be patient and her intentions will be revealed, the voice continued, unperturbed by its Vassal's outburst.

You speak as if you know her plan! Lyrium accused.

I have a theory on what it might be, yes.

Then spit it out already!

I will not meddle in your affairs; I am only here to aid you in the part you will play.

Aid me? You have done so well at that so far! Lyrium responded sarcastically. *Can't you give me any idea of what to prepare for?*

You will need the other Vassal, the voice replied and Lyrium rolled her eyes before it continued. *You are not taking me seriously.*

Why should I? If you hadn't let me take too much energy then she wouldn't be unconscious right now! You nearly killed them all! Lyrium screamed in her head.

The voice was silent. The Vassal felt wave after wave of calm frustration and restrained impatience coming from the stone. The emotions weren't particularly strong, yet to Lyrium they were so familiar that the feelings threatened to become one with her own. She had worried that she might have inadvertently killed the voice during the rampage, despite being able to feel its presence. But she didn't want to speak with it.

Resisting the stone's influence with all of her willpower, she attempted to close the voice off from her mind. Before she could do so, it spoke again.

Take me to the other Vassal.

Why should I do that? Lyrium demanded rudely.

Because you are not going to take responsibility for your actions until she awakens and you know she is unharmed, the voice replied impatiently.

Are you saying you can wake her up? Lyrium asked, trying to keep her excitement in check.

I'm saying that I'll attempt to, the voice replied coldly, its patience for the impetuous attitude of its Vassal all but gone.

It wasn't a promise, but it was enough. Lyrium sprinted towards the village, weaving through the great spears of the training fields. She could feel an ever-so-slight sliver of hope breaking through the guilt that had been gnawing at her. She was soon on the winding path back to the village, her feet slapping against the patted-down dirt.

I'm coming, my friend.

CHAPTER 65

EYE FOR AN EYE

Rufus was standing over Alicea, watching her with concern. Every now and then she seemed to stop breathing for a couple of seconds before resuming. He kept reassuring himself that it was probably nothing, but it did little to ease the worry. He was about to fetch a shaman to have another look when Lyrium burst into the room. She was slightly short of breath, which startled Rufus more than the unexpected entrance.

"What is it? Is the enemy here?" Rufus asked quickly.

"No – no enemies," Lyrium replied distantly.

Rufus stared at the woman as she walked across the room to Alicea.

"What are you doing?" Rufus demanded, stepping between the two Vassals.

"The voice in my stone believes it may be able to help her," Lyrium said shortly as she looked over to her unconscious friend.

"The same stone that nearly killed us all? You must be joking," Rufus scoffed.

"We must have trust in it," Lyrium replied, her frowning face darting from the thief and back to the Princess.

"Forget it! It probably wants to finish the job!" Rufus snarled, moving towards Lyrium to bar her path. "This is why magic can't be trusted."

"That's not what it wants!"

"And how can you be so sure?" Rufus yelled back.

"Because it wasn't the stone's fault, it was mine!" Lyrium retorted and fell silent, turning away to hide her face. "I just kept taking its power. It told me not to, but I thought I was good enough to take it all at once."

"How am I supposed to trust what you say?" Rufus asked.

"I know I don't deserve to be trusted but at least listen to me! I couldn't bear the idea that I had threatened everyone. I needed a little time, but I want to fix it and so does the one within my stone!" she cried, her voice thick with emotion from a guilt-ridden wound.

Rufus looked Lyrium up and down before stalking over to the window and sitting on its sill. Crossing his arms and watching her closely, he pondered his options. For a multitude of reasons, the Princess needed to wake up. He could do nothing but watch her in a comatose state, and in the passing days nobody had come forth with a viable solution. Their only real option was using the same power that had put her to sleep to awaken her.

Rufus spoke in a whisper Lyrium could barely hear. It was so soft that she scarcely made out the words, yet she received the message from his menacing voice alone.

"If I get the impression that what you're doing isn't in her best interests –"

"Then I expect you to run me through with those blades hanging at your sides. I mean it – kill me. Because if I hurt her again then the guilt will destroy me in little time anyway," Lyrium revealed and Rufus nodded grimly, falling silent.

It wasn't an empty threat and he resolved to uphold it. He'd had enough experience at escaping unharmed to know he'd be able to quietly assassinate the hunter and leave the village without raising any alarm from the villagers.

Lyrium took a breath and connected with the stone, feeling its comforting presence wash over her with none of the previous rage. She attempted to banish the feelings of guilt to focus before realising it was that exact bitter sensation that was fuelling her desire to heal.

She took only a little energy, enough for the connection to remain stable, before giving the go-ahead to the stone for whatever it had planned. Lyrium felt her surroundings melt away as her consciousness was yanked from the small room. Bright lights of various colours danced in front of her eyes right up until she tried to focus on them, then they dispersed.

It felt as though she was travelling at high speed, but she knew she hadn't moved an inch. She felt two other consciousnesses coming towards her at an extreme speed. One was forceful and full of unmitigated strength while the other felt sedated, as if it was dozing peacefully.

Before Lyrium could question the stone's resident, the new beings collided with her mind. Her vision returned as she felt gravity take hold and as soon as she realised she was falling, she looked down to see a massive expanse of water coming up to greet her. She hit the water hard, but there was no pain. She clambered to her feet, looking around to see nothing but waist-deep, clear water as far as the eye could see. The air was blanketed in a thick fog that held an unnatural presence.

Confusion clouded her mind until a voice resounded around her and she realised who the new paired consciousness must belong to. It had to be Alicea and her stone's resident that she had felt. Unlike her own stone's voice, this one was more refined, smoother and definitely female.

Welcome, Vassal of Earth. Please excuse the image of mist but I cannot allow my own Vassal's innermost secrets and feelings be on display to anyone who might try to invade her mind. I hope you understand.

"So, you're the one in her stone . . ." Lyrium trailed off, lost as to how to begin.

I am, the voice replied shortly, confirming Lyrium's theories. *What business do you and your guardian have within my Vassal's mind?*

This is Alicea's mind?! The realisation finally hit Lyrium before she replied vocally.

"My own guardian – as you call him – said he may be able to help her awaken?"

The voice didn't reply at first and Lyrium started to look around for anything that wasn't water or mist. Whatever the voice was doing to obscure her surroundings was working; there was nothing. A dreaded thought occurred to her.

How do I get out?

Do not worry, Vassal of Earth. I could throw you out of here in an instant if I so desired, the voice replied, replacing Lyrium's worry with outright fear. *If your guardian was to offer his strength, it is possible I could awaken her. But we guardians rarely offer each other support in this manner. I know that I wouldn't make the same offer of assistance if the roles were reversed.*

"What is wrong with her?" Lyrium blurted out her words again, unable to control her own voice.

She expended a terrible amount of energy, to the point that the magic started to drain her life-force to pay the magic's toll. My strength is enough to keep her alive in this state but no more. Because my own consciousness and hers were linked when she underwent the ordeal, she failed to sever it completely when she collapsed.

"What does that mean?" Lyrium asked.

It means that when she attempted to do what she did on her own, she should have died. The only thing keeping her in this world is her connection to me. Our connection is currently being used to hold her life in balance. Even if we could shift the connection to take energy from myself to replenish her body, she would die immediately before the transition was completed.

"I killed her?" Lyrium spluttered. "I drained her life!"

Lyrium fell to her knees, the water now reaching her shoulders. The guilt that had been plaguing her for almost a week struck with renewed force. She had awoken the day after the incident and immediately thrown herself into more training with Garnet. Part of it had been to prepare for the coming legion of Aquiocian soldiers, but the much greater motivation had been to exhaust herself so she couldn't think of the Princess' sacrifice.

She saved me and in return, I killed her.

Get a hold of yourself, Lyrium! Her own guardian's voice boomed into existence.

"Why should I? I killed her!" Lyrium wailed uncontrollably. The guardian's feelings of distaste that met the distraught woman's mind did nothing to help the flood of tears washing over her face.

Humans are ever so dramatic when it comes to their trivial feelings, the feminine voice noted in mild amusement.

"Trivial?" Lyrium sobbed. "That's rich coming from one of the beings who expects us to fight for them! I'm human, I'm entitled to cry for my friend!"

You are entitled to nothing. You cry because it is all humans are truly capable of. They consume what isn't theirs and cry like infants when they do not get what they desire.

The guardians seemed to be waiting for a rebuttal from the broken woman but all they received was silence. After a moment, the female voice spoke again in the same condescending tone she had before.

I met you at the same time my Vassal did. It wasn't very long ago, even by the standards of a human lifespan. You would spend your time crying about someone you barely knew?

"Shut up!" Lyrium snapped between sobs. "You don't get it at all! It isn't the length of the friendship that matters, it's what is shared between the people in that time."

Lyrium – her guardian started.

"Shut up, I wasn't finished!" she snarled with a voice husky from emotion before addressing the invisible female voice again. "Alicea is one of the most pure-hearted people you could ever hope to meet. She was hard on Rufus, that's true. But she wouldn't let harm come to anyone. She didn't deserve this! You should know – YOU PICKED HER, DAMN IT!"

You weren't listening. If I offer my support it is possible to bring her back, the male voice said simply.

She couldn't see the beings, but the reminder made her look up through the mist. She spoke as if the two people were right in front of her.

"How would that work?" Lyrium demanded, her voice filled with desperation.

Her guardian will hold her life-force in check as she has been doing and I will connect with the Vassal's mind and body and rejuvenate it. If she's receptive, it shouldn't take long.

"I thought you could only connect with the one chosen by you," Lyrium protested.

And who do you think does the choosing? the voice retorted. *We can work together, we just dislike doing so.*

Why are you offering my Vassal support? the female voice asked, accusation barely concealed beneath her cool tone.

It is not given freely, I assure you. The one who has been training these two, Garnet, has a plan for the coming assault, the voice said.

Of this, I am aware.

Then surely you have drawn the same conclusion as to what it is.

I can see where this is going. Very well. If it comes to that, I shall co-operate in the plan's execution. You have my word, Alicea's guardian replied.

Then the deal is made, echoed the satisfied voice of Lyrium's own.

The voices were gone, and Lyrium's mind was abuzz with energy as new connections were made. She felt her consciousness connecting with the slumbering Alicea. It wasn't an unpleasant sensation, but she could feel that her friend's rest was not as peaceful as it appeared. Lyrium felt as though she had just been drenched with cool water as Alicea's guardian connect with her own mind. When the Vassal reached out with her mind to investigate the new connections, the energy repelled her with force.

The message was clear: it was for her Vassal alone.

She felt her own guardian gather strength before channelling it towards Alicea's consciousness. The build-up felt like it was preparing for a vicious attack, but once the stored energy was released, it was welcomed by the Princess' consciousness.

Lyrium felt her mind being ripped away from its location again. She knew what was happening, though it did nothing to prepare her for the visions that met her. As her mind was pulled away and the sight that was Alicea's mind started to fade, Lyrium's head was filled with scenes she couldn't place. She felt like her brain was on fire as she saw person after person she didn't know from location after location she didn't recognise.

There was one constant. In each of the images was Rufus, regardless if he appeared to belong to the scene or not. Whether sleeping or doing some mundane task in the background, he was there. In the brief instances that she looked directly at the thief, she could feel the warmth and comforting sensation of protection. Something about the shady man being nearby made the entire experience easier to endure, though she couldn't understand why. Rufus had barely spoken to her, much less comforted her.

Through the thousands upon thousands of incomprehensible images, she saw a man walking towards a small stall selling chilled drinks. As her focus was forcibly shifted to the man, he was replaced with a plump woman who was sitting in a chair as a child tended to her shoes. Countless scenes rested in the background, a clashing opposition between what she was being forced to look at directly and the seemingly endless flood of other images.

The larger woman shrank in stature, replaced by the petite form of a teenaged version of Alicea. She was standing in front of a mirror with a wide smile, pleased with the cerulean and silver garb that she was wearing. The smile faded as the image of the Princess steadily became more youthful. The mirror that stood before her had vanished; in its place was a slender man in dark clothes with pitch-black hair falling over his face. Though his face showed confusion, his amber eyes emitted a malice that seemed absolute.

Rufus was absent, and the sheer terror that Alicea felt hit Lyrium like a battering ram, ending the confusing series of events. Alicea's small room back in Tremel came back so suddenly that even the small beam of sunlight coming through the window was harsh to her eyes. Her legs gave away and she fell into one of the chairs, exhausted and confused. Rufus ran to her, looking her over as she attempted to make his face take shape through her blurred vision.

"What happened? Is she going to be okay? What did you do?" Rufus demanded.

"Oh, stop badgering the poor woman, Mr. Thief!" a familiar voice scolded and Rufus spun around to see Alicea sitting upright and rubbing her eyes. "Honestly, you have no idea how to talk to ladies!"

"You ... You're awake!" Rufus stammered incredulously.

"My, aren't you observant today?" Alicea replied sarcastically as she turned to Lyrium. "I know you were in here with me. I could feel you. Thank you."

"No, I put you in that state – it was only right that I get you out," Lyrium replied with a bitter resentment for herself as Alicea shook her head. She could feel tears welling in her eyes; she had heard everything.

"I was too reckless with –"

"We both were," Lyrium cut Alicea off. "But friends look out for each other."

Alicea was nodding and about to comment on Lyrium's

new ears when Garnet bustled into the room, interrupting the conversation.

"Ah, here you are, Lyrium, I've come to – oh, you're awake," Garnet said, addressing Alicea in surprise.

"Yes, thanks to Lyrium." She smiled widely.

"An explanation is in order, but now is not the time. I've come to inform Lyrium, and now you as well, Alicea, that scouts have reported that the soldiers are about two days' hard march away. The numbers that had been estimated were accurate at around one thousand. I suggest you both prepare and please keep me informed of where you are at all times. Above all, now that Alicea is awake, do not separate from each other," Garnet lectured and turned to Rufus. "I trust you will ensure that they remain together and where I can find them?"

"She never listens to me but you have my word, as much as that counts," Rufus replied as Alicea rolled her eyes and Garnet nodded before disappearing out the door.

"How long was I asleep for?" Alicea asked, just realising that a lot of time had passed.

"The better part of a week," Rufus answered and Lyrium nodded in confirmation.

"Unbelievable. So much time lost," Alicea reflected before quickly producing a brush and running it through her hair. Noticing the absence of her hair ornament, she scanned the room until she saw the wilting wildflowers on the table. She regarded them sadly before nodding towards the door. "But, enough of that. I think it would be wise to see what preparations have been made in the time I've lost," she said when her stomach growled violently. The Princess grimaced as Rufus stifled a smirk.

"Food first. Then we will look at the preparations," Lyrium declared as the three of them left the room.

Alicea seemed to have energy to burn as she skipped towards the dwelling of the village cooks. During the day, the villagers would bring their game to the cooks and they'd prepare it, store it or trade for it. Rufus figured what the Princess was after as he had heard people asking for their daily game to be cooked and dried out.

She is going to eat their entire stock of dried meat, he thought in amusement. *She has a less sophisticated palate than some mercenaries I've met.*

Rufus was smirking when Lyrium stepped in front of him. They were both exhausted and each could see it in the face of the other as they weighed each other up uncertainly. Rufus had no idea what Lyrium had just been through, but even he could appreciate how worn her nerves were.

"What happened wasn't what I wanted," Lyrium began stiffly.

"It has been made right," Rufus replied simply.

"Then why do I feel like you're still angry about it?"

"Don't push it, Lyrium," he advised quietly, attempting to sidestep the woman.

"No, answer me. You're friends with my lover and obviously care about the Princess. What is it about me that you dislike?"

"You're a mage," the thief finally snapped.

"I am a shaman," she corrected. "But that is exactly the same thing to you, isn't it? I'm not going to waste my time pointing out the flaws in your attitude, as I'm sure you're already aware of them. I will say that hating someone for such a reason is stupid."

"Stop saying that I hate you. I distrust your stone and your magical abilities. That's it. I don't hate you. There is a big difference between hating someone and being cautious of their existence."

Lyrium simply shook her head in response and sighed as she looked around at the scurrying village before responding.

"You're an idiot," she muttered before adding, "But so long as you're an idiot who looks out for the Princess, I will accept that you will be around. I want you to know something, though."

"What?"

"I personally have no idea why Alicea cares for you but, by the name of Gaia, you sure don't deserve it," Lyrium said, glaring up at the taller man.

Rufus was about to bite back at the mention of her religion's deity when Alicea was heard calling to the lagging pair. Lyrium and Rufus looked up to see the beaming smile of the Princess for the first time in a week as she waved a hand filled with dried meat. For a moment, they were forced to forget the issues between them.

"Aye, you're probably right." Rufus grimaced as he pushed past the hunter.

CHAPTER 66

PRINCESS VERSUS BARBARIAN

Despite the fact that she had been unconscious for the better part of a week, Alicea found herself exhausted and falling asleep as soon as dusk arrived. It was something a lot of people were thankful for: they could finally stop worrying about her and get some sleep themselves.

The remainder of the afternoon had been spent taking a tour of the battle preparations – an investigation that had been cut short by Garnet banishing them to the confines of the village. At first Alicea had protested, but fatigue shortly caught up, forcing her to retreat to her bed.

Now, as dawn made its debut for the new day, the Princess was walking towards the bonfire circle with her tiny bird sitting in her hands. She could hear voices laughing and she had grown bored of resting. As she got closer to the circle, she could hear Arok and Rufus bursting into roars of laughter as Lyrium told the entire gathering something funny. When her eyes fell upon the group, Alicea realised that the circle had been broken by a bunch of the hunters moving the logs so they could sit around a large stump being used as a table. Arok was the first to notice her presence, getting to his feet and waving her over.

"Ah! The Princess! What an honour!" he laughed before turning to a man beside him. "Show some respect, get her a chair!"

"No, that is fine, I can –" Alicea started and gave up as the man pushed over a large, flat chunk of wood for her to sit on. With a smile and a quiet "thank you", she took her seat next to Lyrium with swan in lap. A few of the villagers gathered were watching her intently, thrilled by the idea that the Princess might wish to partake in their humble group's activity.

After waving to everyone, she noticed what had caught their attention. On the table was a large deck of cards held together by a thin silver string, along with several steins of alcohol and a few hundred gold coins stacked in little piles. The group was gambling and obviously Arok was doing well for himself with a pile the combined size of the other players' hoards.

"A game?" Alicea piped up. "May I play?"

"Unless you got a secret pocket full of coins in those fancy clothes, I'm afraid not!" Arok grinned in his shameless smile from across the table. "Coins are shown at the beginning of the game and ya need twenty coins at least."

"Mr. Thief has coins, I shall use them," Alicea shrugged as everyone laughed.

Rufus was ready to protest when he looked at the deck of cards and realised exactly who was asking to play. With a small smirk he pushed the coins across the table to the Princess.

"Before you begin," Rufus held up a hand to the crowd. "If Alicea wants to play, then I will have to pass. I also get what I loan her back in full along with fifty percent of her winnings."

"Mr. Thief, you can have it all back along with all winnings I might accrue. I have no use for gold; I'm already a valuable enough target to those outside these walls," Alicea said dismissively.

"You got a lot of faith in the Princess," Arok noted, his grin never wavering.

"I just want to ensure I get paid," Rufus grinned back, only his eyes darting around at the group. Alicea had never seen him smiling that much, though she could tell he was still keeping watch regardless.

Mr. Thief almost appears at ease. It's nice.

Arok shrugged, satisfied by the answer, and tossed six cards to each of the five players. Alicea took note of the images on the cards; there was one for each element.

"I will scatter this deck onto the table and then count to twenty. Then I will quickly sweep them up and you all guess what element I will draw by placing one of your six cards face-down in front of you. Each draw a player guesses right gets twenty percent of their bet back – continuing on to make profit. I take any outstanding gold once everyone bows out or guesses incorrectly. If you're the last man – er, woman – standing, you can choose to guess the next card for double or nothing," Arok explained. "It is a game of memory."

It was the last line of Arok's explanation that made Alicea look up at Rufus with an accusing glare. He knew exactly what he was doing by letting her play in his stead. He had played into her love of games but she couldn't be angry at him.

"Follow the chain," Rufus advised, ignoring the look he was receiving.

"How'd you come across so much gold?" Alicea asked the host, still glaring at Rufus.

"This is nothing," Arok chuckled, taking a deep gulp from a stein that was sitting beside him. Whether it was his or not seemed irrelevant. "These are just our personal stashes. Since the old fortress was destroyed, Tremel has had an agreement with the Council of Aquiocia. We supply them regularly with game from the forest and they pay us a measly amount of gold. Saves us paying taxes."

"An agreement like that pays very little. To have an immense sum of coins like you do, it would have taken years of consistent work," Alicea noted, finally turning back to the game.

"Aye, but my pile is so large because *I* know how to gamble," Arok said, taunting the other players with his endless mirth.

"The villagers here have very little need for gold," Lyrium revealed. "So, what else can we do but stash the bulk of it and hand out a few coins here and there in case anyone decides to travel to a city where they can't hunt?"

"Enough!" Arok declared, his lips dripping slightly with stray mead. "Let's begin the game!"

Everyone fell silent when the man banged his fist onto the table and cards sprayed across its surface. To Alicea's surprise, they all landed face-up for the players to see. Arok had obviously been doing this for a long time. The Princess' eyes darted from card to card as Arok steadily counted to twenty. Each of the images matched one of the cards in her hand, and she noticed that when they were sprawled out, a shiny tether extended between each card in succession. It linked them together with a small clasp in the middle of the sequence.

Ah, undo the clasp and you can shuffle the cards, Alicea realised. *Everyone has an equal chance to guess the next card if their memory fails them. But it would be unwise to rely on odds like those alone.*

"That's time!" Arok declared, gathering the cards.

Alicea was startled by the sudden call for the cards, but shrugged it off. She had seen all that she needed.

"Gold and cards!" Arok called loudly.

In response, four piles of gold were pushed forward, along with four face-down cards. Everyone was waiting on Alicea as she picked a card and pushed her pile of coins forward to join the others, a task much more difficult compared to the bigger hunters at the table. Arok nodded approvingly and flipped the first card. Alicea smiled when she saw the image of small fireball on the card's surface. The five players flipped their cards to reveal their own copies of the card.

"Well, it wouldn't be much of a wager if everyone got the first draw wrong," Lyrium laughed as she looked at Alicea.

The players picked their next bet and card before the second card was drawn by Arok. The card showed a pleasant stream of clear water. One of the hunters groaned and stood up from the table. Alicea watched the large man walk over to the tree and throw a mighty punch into its bark, causing it to shake.

"Don't mind him. He never knows when to quit and his memory isn't his strongest resource," Lyrium whispered to the giggling Princess.

The game continued and before long, all but the Princess and one other hunter had either folded or lost their small fortunes. After the sixth draw, the last of Alicea's competition folded, claiming, "I've won my gold back and a little extra – I am satisfied."

Arok pushed a pile of gold in front of Alicea. It was somewhat larger than her original bet while most the other players' hoards had dwindled greatly in a single game. Then Alicea's eyes fixed on the small mountain that Arok had gathered for himself. It grew regardless of how the game went. Sooner or later, every player's memory faltered and he became wealthier.

"Well, there is your prize, Princess. Shall we try again?" he asked the other players.

"I would like to request the double or nothing offer!"

Arok looked as though he'd been slapped. Nobody ever pushed their luck while they played with him.

"If that's what you want. Call them!" Arok shrugged, recovering quickly.

"Light!" Alicea announced as Arok drew a card adorned with a picture of countless rays of light falling upon an open field.

"Another?" Arok asked with a smirk. He was goading her.

"Earth," Alicea winked.

Another card, this one reflecting tall spires of torn earth and stone reaching for the sky. They looked like much larger versions of the ones Lyrium had summoned on their first day of training.

"Again? Let's speed this up!"

"Water!"

"Again!"

"Fire!"

"Again!"

"Dark!"

"Damn it!" Arok suddenly threw the deck down so forcefully that the sturdy stump rattled. "How?!"

The entire group burst into laughter, but none more so than Arok's lover. "Calm down, Arok!"

"Lyrium! She took it all! How is she doing this?" Arok whined.

"It is a game of memory!" Lyrium said between waves of laughter. "Of course you were going to lose!"

Arok, unaware of the Princess' ability, stared back in confusion. He seemed ready to launch the stump that served as a table in frustration when he burst into hearty guffaws that rang throughout the village.

Pushing the massive pile of gold in front of him forward, he commended Alicea, "Now THAT was a good game! Not playing this one with you again, but there are a few private games I'd like to take you along to in Aquiocia! You could be the key to winning big!"

Alicea smiled slightly, masking the pain from her city being mentioned. In truth, it didn't hurt as much coming from Arok. He was loud, uncouth and always smelt faintly of ale, but he was blindly confident that everything would be fine. She needed that blind confidence. She needed Arok. No, she needed everyone who was sitting at that table. From the hunters spilling ale as they slapped each other on the back between bouts of mirth, to Lyrium, who had proven her loyalty to the cause and even as her friend. Even the thief, currently eyeing her mountain of gold on the table, had proven that he was in it for the long haul. The desire for riches was blazing within Rufus' eyes, but the Princess knew why he wanted the gold.

He isn't as selfish as he'd have me believe.

"Arok, please divide this gold so that everybody has what they started with and send the rest to Setz. He will see that it gets to the right hands," she announced as Rufus smiled gratefully. When he looked at her, his eyes were slightly unfocused and his face was somewhat pale.

He's still exhausted.

The moment was cut short when a loud horn was heard from the front of the village. It blasted twice. The first sound was short and sharp and the second long and drawn out, at which everyone got up and trudged to the front gates. The enemy wasn't due to arrive for another day, which meant it was time to fill in any holes they could in their defences. Arok brushed the mound of gold into a large sack and headed towards the Chief's hut. His father wanted him by his side for the coming battle and they hoped for a peaceful resolution. However, they knew that might never happen.

That aside, there was no better place for a father and son to bond than in battle.

CHAPTER 67

A CONFIDENCE BETWEEN VASSALS

The Princess was walking around the inside of the village wall. Accompanying her was Lyrium, along with the occasional sighting of Rufus. The thief was taking Garnet's request seriously, if only to the extent of trudging along behind Alicea and groaning about her inability to stay in one spot.

"Charcoal," Alicea said with her hand out to Lyrium.

"Check," Lyrium replied, handing over a dark chunk of burnt wood.

The Princess took the charcoal, turned to the wall and raked it across its surface before handing it back. She had ordered Rufus to point out any flaws in the village's walls and the Vassals marked any spot he'd feel confident in exploiting if he was to try to break through. It reminded them of why they were glad he was on their side. Alicea had begun the exercise in a frustration that was born from being forbidden to leave the walls. She knew why they restricted it, but it bothered her more than it should.

It felt like she was back within the castle walls again.

"It's ridiculous that walls are made for protection and yet they make me feel vulnerable," Alicea mused. "After everything that has happened, I'm uneasy behind walls even if they are a fraction of the size I grew up with."

"If it makes you feel any better, most of the villagers feel the same," Lyrium replied. "The only reason we have walls at all is to deter animals. The people of this village feel more at home within the forest itself."

"Right. I have to ask you something." Alicea turned to her friend, subconsciously wiping her hand on her dress, smearing it with charcoal.

"Hmm?"

"This isn't the first time you've referred to the villagers with an air of separation. Are you not originally from Tremel?" Alicea asked.

Lyrium blinked a few times in stunned silence before replying slowly.

"Did someone tell you?" she questioned, shaking her head before she got a response. "No, of course they didn't, you worked it out yourself. You're partly right. I'm not from this Tremel."

"This Tremel?" Alicea repeated, her mind a blur of passages from books she'd read on Tremel. "You're from one of the other three!"

"That's the belief, although we don't know for sure. Kurok was delivered a bundle one morning; that bundle was me. According to the Chief, the person who had brought me to him was dressed as a hunter, but not one of our own. He said they were dressed very differently but he cannot recall anything else."

"I'm not surprised. If I was just handed an infant, I wouldn't be very certain on how to act." Alicea laughed and Lyrium joined in. She was thankful to not be a source of pity to her friend. She had spent most of her childhood treated more delicately than the other kids, as if she would break if someone scolded her.

"It has been a mostly good life," Lyrium conceded, still smiling. "I would like to know about my parents, but I have family here. Between that family and the skills taught by them, I was able to claim the stone. Thanks to all they've given me I can live a life that means something."

"So that's what it is, then." Alicea nodding knowingly.

"Hmm?" Lyrium probed again.

"The way you hold yourself – your unmitigated confidence. It comes from knowing what you want, right? I remember that feeling . . ." Alicea smiled sadly.

"Ah, your parents?"

"Yes." Alicea broke away at Rufus' gesture to scrub the dark dust across the wall before continuing. "But it is not only that. People assume that I only grieve for them, but almost all of my family was in that battle. I had no one for quite some time . . ." Alicea paused before hurriedly adding, "This is not a cry for sympathy."

"I didn't think it was."

"It runs deeper than the royal family. In the same way you consider this entire village of people your family, I consider the kingdom of Aquiocia my own," Alicea explained before sullenly adding, "One thousand members of my family were obliterated that day. That is the exact number that marches now and there is a strong chance that Jex himself is leading them. I feel as though that number is not a coincidence."

"Why didn't you just jump on the throne?" Lyrium asked.

"Because it isn't what my mother would do," Alicea muttered.

"So, your mother would do what you're doing now?"

"No, but I am not my mother."

"You're confusing me," Lyrium admitted, reaching up and stroking her long ears.

"My mother would protect her people from the frontline – the same thing she attempted on the day she died, the same thing that I will do tomorrow."

"So . . . what is the difference?"

"I'm not my mother," Alicea repeated with pursed lips. "I will not kill. I just can't. Mr. Thief said that holding back might get me killed, and I accept that."

Rufus grunted but didn't comment.

"Killing isn't easy, but it is all very different when it is a case of life and death. Do you just refuse to or is it something you just can't do?"

Alicea was silent for a moment, as if weighing up whether or not to share the information. With a shaky breath, she spoke.

"I spent a year wishing I wouldn't wake up. I hoped I would die and take the small chance that what they teach in churches was true – that I would be reunited with them. I was too much of a coward to kill myself and so here I am. But on a battlefield –" Alicea trailed off as she composed herself and changed tact slightly. "Day to day, I see a desire to live in the eyes of the people around me. I'm only now beginning to care for it myself. Still, what right do I have to take away someone's chance to live just so I can continue to wallow in self-pity?"

The pair were silent as they walked for a bit before Lyrium announced, "And, that's enough time!"

Alicea looked up only to feel her friend's hand clip her over the back of her head.

"What was that?!"

"That was the end of your self-pity, and I will continue to slap you whenever I think you're preparing to throw away your life. I didn't know you before. But, the way I see it, you've got stuff worth living for. Now, do you need another?"

"No, I am fine, thank you. I get the message," the Princess replied in irritation as her smiling friend kept walking.

It was an unpleasant way of supporting her but Alicea appreciated it even as she rubbed the back of her head. Rufus was making an obvious effort to seem unconcerned and aloof as he waited for the Princess to start moving again. Smoothing out her long hair, she followed Lyrium as they continued to canvass the defences of the small village. They both knew that at any moment they would be called back to prepare for the coming soldiers. Garnet had insisted that everyone gather a full day before the expected time of arrival.

Scouts were in the forest, watching the soldiers march and reporting back to the Chief and his advisors. They had brought back consistent information that suggested the knights would arrive early afternoon on the following day. Despite the impending confrontation, neither of the Vassals spoke about it. Lyrium knew exactly what was expected of her from the village and despite the Princess' pleas, she'd never give her friend up.

Alicea had made it clear that she wouldn't have blamed Tremel for handing her over. All that had produced was bouts of laughter from her friend and the Chief of the village. To them, the suggestion of running and abandoning the Princess was their idea of a ludicrous joke.

As a result, when the horn blasted through the village for

the second time, both Alicea and Lyrium simply nodded to one another and made their way towards the centre of the village to discuss their next move. Rufus, seemingly relieved by the horn's call, followed them with more enthusiasm than he'd shown throughout the entire stroll.

"Lyrium?"

"Yes, Alicea?"

"I really like your ears."

"Thank you, my friend."

Nightfall made its mark across the sky far quicker than anyone within Tremel would have liked. Many of the residents found themselves wishing for a few more hours of daylight. Some wanted more time to prepare the fortifications; others wanted more time to prepare the warriors themselves.

If Alicea had her way, the night would not have come at all. Everyone contributed to the tension as they crowded uneasily around the bonfire. Everyone had gathered; there was hardly enough room as some of the hunters squished together on the logs while others stood nearby in a sign of solidarity. Many of the elder men and women had led the children deep into the forest. At first Alicea fretted for their safety, a concern laughed off by Lyrium. The young hunter knew that those in the forest would come to no harm.

Those patrolling the small village were the only others absent, resulting in a majority of Tremel's occupants huddling around their traditional fire, telling stories and laughing together. It was easily the biggest crowd they'd had in a long while.

It was precisely what the man skulking in the shadows had been waiting for. He'd been forcing himself to be patient for almost a week now for a chance to flee. He knew well that his best chance would be the night before the knights arrived. He'd heard plenty of rumours from outside of the hut he'd been bedridden within. The shamans loved to discuss the Princess within the village and the drama she had brought with her. On top of that, Arok had visited many times and offered information he'd never share with the other villagers.

Another reason he had waited was that his injuries were far worse than he'd first thought. His shoulder had been realigned, but his shattered arm had a long way to go. Fortunately, with tremendous effort and an equal amount of pain, he could now draw his longbow.

Things wouldn't have been so dire had I not been so careless, the man scolded himself internally as he used his unharmed arm to push his long, blond fringe from his eyes.

His plan to wait until everyone was gathered seemed to be working, having only crossed paths with one villager making their rounds. He'd managed to stash himself behind one of the huts just in time before moving on.

One thing had surprised him, and it was something he hadn't considered. There were far fewer holes in the village's walls from the work that had been done on them in anticipation of their knightly visitors. It wasn't a big setback, but it took a little longer for him to reach a suitable exit from the village. Fortunately, he was able to remain concealed from the villagers' view as they huddled together.

When he reached the back entrance of the village, there were two hunters standing guard. They were not slacking off for once, as they gazed out to the forest with vigilance. He didn't want anyone to see him leave. While he did have a way to leave the village quickly, the chance of being seen was far too great.

With his back pressed against the wall of the dwelling, Stefan's head poked out from safety and he crafted a small plan. He didn't like it, but it was the best idea that he could think of to lure the guards away from the entrance.

Grimacing, the man grabbed his longbow from its place over his shoulder and pulled an arrow from the quiver on his back. Holding them both in one hand, he reached into his pocket and found a small bottle of pitch along with a tiny flint. With a flick of his thumb, off came the cork on the bottle. He gently placed the bottle on the ground and dipped the arrow tip in the black liquid. With a bracing breath and one fluid movement, the archer clipped the arrowhead with his flint, pulling back the arrow as the head burst into flame and releasing it from his hiding place. The flaming projectile soared past the opposite side of the gate and buried itself in the timber of another hut.

Then he waited.

"Can you smell – get water!" one of the guards spat as he turned to see a small fire steadily eating at the side of the hut.

The guards leapt into action, oblivious to the arrow within the flame. The guards' response was enough for the man to disappear, running through the gate after they left their posts. By the time they realised it was a distraction, it was already too late. Discreetly, the other guards were told and a search was conducted, but they knew there was little chance of finding anything more than the strange, scorched arrow without a bow.

It was as if the culprit had fired the arrow and flown away.

CHAPTER 68

FRIENDS IN WAR

The village was in a state of strained calm as Alicea led the party consisting of Rufus, Lyrium and Arok out the main gates and onto the fields separating the village from the forest a mile or two away. The turf near the gate and along the timber walls had been ripped into trenches designed to trip any invaders. Within the trenches, pointing in all directions, were large, sharpened stumps of wood to impale any careless charging soldiers.

The sight concerned the Princess. It was the kind of fortification that was designed to protect them by killing. She couldn't help but wonder just how much of the reason she was hidden away within the village's confines was borne from Garnet not wanting her to see what they were preparing outside the walls. It was hard to imagine that Garnet and Kurok would want to keep her in the dark about anything to do with her people, but it was harder still to imagine that the thick glaives of wood within the pitfalls were for anything but bloodshed.

There were several gaps in the defence, Alicea noticed, attempting to divert her attention from the possible betrayal of her trust. Some of the places she had marked had clearly been reinforced properly, whereas others had scraps of timber crammed into the holes.

With a grimace, she looked out to the prairie and saw large patches of upturned soil. At first glance it seemed like nothing was amiss, but her keen gaze missed nothing, and that included the small piles of dirt that were out of place on the otherwise flat ground. There were traps dug in everywhere, but there were still clear paths that would offer safe passage to the village.

They were obviously short on time; it is sloppy work from hunters who have been trained in the art of trapping, Alicea thought critically before realising what they had planned. *Ah, no, it is in case they charge the village. The hunters will be able to fire upon them while the soldiers navigate between the traps even after some have fallen in. They will attempt to avoid the traps, which will leave them limited ground to stand on.*

It was a vicious tactic and it surprised Alicea that she saw it for what it was so quickly. She obviously had a knack for combat strategy and wasn't entirely sure she was happy with the gift.

Well, I inherited a lot from my mother. It is only fitting that I received something from my father's side as well. He always encouraged me to read books on warfare . . .

Flicking her hair in irritation, she fixed her gaze to the ends of the village's walls. Branching out from the walls were tall barricades of wood that had been stacked high in front of the thin waterways. She remembered when she'd first arrived at Tremel and there had been a small stream making its way past the entrance and around the village. Now it was completely blocked off and the ground in front of the village left dry. The hunters assembling nearby gave it a wide berth, as if wary of it exploding and sweeping them out onto the plains.

Water was leaking steadily from the gaps in the makeshift timber walls – it too had been done hastily.

Did they reroute the water . . .? For what purpose? Alicea frowned.

Why the villagers had blocked off their water supply that came from within the forest completely eluded Alicea. The only thing she could be certain of was that there had to be a reason.

The plains in front of them seemed all too peaceful for what was about to happen. The gathering warriors had donned animal pelts that were completely intact, serving more as a statement than a need of clothing. Even those with talents outside of hunting specifically had small animals attached to their clothing. Alicea caught sight of the man who saw to the dry stores with the pelt of a rabbit clasped to his belt next to a long skinning knife.

"Why does everyone wear animal pelts? Would they not get in the way?" Alicea asked. The question was answered by Garnet, who came up behind the group with a cape of owl feathers that shifted slightly in the wind. She was being followed by two large men both donning bear pelts and carrying two additional ones.

"To be recognised in this village you must first prove that you can hunt. In any battle, a warrior is to wear their first kill," Garnet explained as Lyrium and Arok took the pelts from the men.

Alicea was a little surprised that she hadn't read that about the Tremel people. If it was such a traditional practice, then it stood to reason that it'd have been mentioned. Alicea's mind spun as she recalled everything she'd read about the people of Tremel. One particular passage stuck out in her mind more than anything else.

Fighting against the people of Tremel is similar to trying to quell a stampede of ferocious woodland beasts. A stampede of ferocious woodland beasts who also happen to be adept in stringing a bow and wielding the formidable magic of their deity, Gaia herself.

Lyrium had thrown on the pelt of a red deer as Arok wrapped the long arms of a black bear around his shoulders. The choice of attire bewildered Rufus as he stared at his friend.

"You killed a bear?" he asked in surprise.

"With only my hands, if ya'd believe it!" He grinned as he lifted his massive war hammer into his hands proudly.

"First you hurl me over a castle wall and now you tell me you killed a bear without a weapon? There must be something in your diet that I'm lacking," Rufus replied despairingly.

"Wait, *that's* how you got into my castle?" Alicea asked suddenly, to which the two men laughed in spite of the impending events.

"Lyrium, Alicea – your attention, if you will," Garnet started and the two Vassals turned to listen, their focus undivided.

"Lyrium, the plains themselves will be your part. You must control every part of earth that the soldier's feet are on when they come. Do not attempt more than you can handle. If you lose control again, it will mean the end of us. You will have assistance from the shamans of the village as well, though I fear their support in this instance may be meagre at best."

Lyrium nodded, trying to understand her teacher's cryptic instructions without asking more questions she knew would go unanswered as Garnet turned to Alicea.

"You will have the water we have hoarded at your disposal.

You will have a large amount to use at first and a constant smaller influx thereafter. We have made the dam for the sole purpose of you having a large volume of water to begin with, as you have demonstrated that you can command a lot of your element at once in an effective manner. That said, you also have your limits. Consider this a head start, nothing more. Look to the pits on the field of battle for more."

"You expect me to use my power against my own people?" Alicea asked in despair.

"Yes, but not in a violent manner. I understand your wishes, as painfully idealistic that they might be. I want both of your powers to come together at the very feet of the soldiers."

"I don't understand," Lyrium admitted as Alicea eyed the older woman closely.

"I've been studying magic a long time and you should trust me. What I have planned should work, if both casters are in harmony. You have become close friends rather quickly; we have a chance."

Alicea knew exactly what Garnet was thinking.

"Unison Magic!" she blurted out.

"You did read the books I gave you, then."

"Yes, how could I not? I've wanted to attempt this since I read about it! I only wish it wasn't under these circumstances . . ." Alicea finished sadly, her enthusiasm dying as quickly as it was born.

"You will both grasp your elements and bring them together as one when I give the order." Garnet pointed towards the open expanse as she spoke. "You will combine your powers out there and we will rout the enemy. Since neither of you wish to harm the enemy, the result *should* reflect that. If it goes well, then very few will be hurt. We all want this resolved peacefully, I assure you. This course of action was devised because of this."

The Vassals looked at each other and nodded. They both knew that the trust between them was mutual.

"I'll be back shortly. I wish to make sure that everyone is where they should be. Please prepare yourself accordingly," Garnet said, attempting to leave.

"Wait, what's my position?" Rufus piped up.

"And mine?" Arok asked as Garnet turned back and looked at the pair as if she was confused by the question.

"Where are your positions?" Garnet repeated back to them. "Your positions are next to the ones you will fight to the death to protect. I'd thank you to save any more stupid questions you have for me until after this is over."

Garnet had left and was calling out to a group of warriors before they could think of a response. Arok turned to Rufus with a grin.

"We will crush anyone who gets near the ladies, right, Mr. Thief?" Arok said, laughing as Rufus scowled at the nickname.

Instead of responding further, the thief watched on as Alicea stalked up to Arok and slapped him across the face before storming off.

"What was that for?" Arok demanded as Lyrium and Rufus doubled over in laughter. The mirth was welcome, yet short-lived as Garnet called everyone to order at the top of her lungs. It was time to assemble and wait. So began the longest few hours any of them had ever experienced.

CHAPTER 69

UNISON MAGIC

The plains were deadly quiet and the sun was high in the sky as the warriors crouched down in position with the archers standing restlessly behind them. Not a sound was heard as they waited for the expected cohort to emerge from the forest to greet them.

Alicea's small party sat in the middle of the gate, staring out over the plains. Garnet's original plan was that the Princess wait within the walls, but she had refused, claiming that she'd look her kingdom's men in the eye. Garnet had compromised by letting her sit directly in the gateway, able to retreat inside at moment's notice if they could make her.

I can't do this ... But I must! I could run – no! I will see this through!

Alicea's feelings were wreaking havoc from the possibility of having to fight the ones who originally protected her. She didn't like the idea of anyone fighting anyone, but the idea of confronting her own soldiers made her glad for the opportunity to rest her shaky legs by sitting on the dusty path with her swan nestled in her lap. As she gently petted the sleeping bird, she reached out with her mind to the great volume of water hoarded for her. Her eyes darted towards Lyrium and saw her serene and glazed-over expression, the same expression Alicea assumed she held.

Alicea knew she was doing the same thing with the earth that made up the expanse in front of them. Her friend was reaching out and feeling the calm essence of the soil beneath, to get an idea of what she had to work with. Their eyes met briefly and they shared a small smile before returning to their own thoughts.

The Princess' reverie was interrupted when Rufus reached into his pocket and produced some dried meat wrapped in leaves. The relaxed thief unwrapped the leaves and tore off a shred of the spiced meat before throwing it into his mouth casually. As he chewed loudly, he looked up, realising that Alicea was staring at him with a frown on her face.

"Can I help you, Princess?" he said quietly, unsure why he was whispering.

"How can you remain so calm, knowing what is about to happen?" she asked as the man shrugged.

"Nothing to get worked up about. No one wants this to happen but there is very little anyone can do about it," he replied.

"I wish I was as brave as you. You are never scared. Even back in the castle when you could have died, you just shrugged and did what needed to be done. I'm always so afraid," Alicea confided softly and Rufus smiled.

"Never scared? That's a nice sentiment, but I'm always scared. Especially when those soldiers were chasing me," Rufus admitted casually, surprising the Princess.

"But you always seem so brave ..."

"You can be scared and brave. To not be scared of anything is not bravery – that's idiocy. Bravery is measured by your ability to stand up for what matters to you, even when you are terrified," Rufus replied, throwing another shred of meat into his mouth.

"That was surprisingly profound, Mr. Thief. Coming from you, anyway," Alicea replied curtly.

"It's the truth," Rufus insisted. "And by that logic, I'd say you're the bravest person I know."

Alicea smiled at the compliment and leant over to kiss Rufus on the cheek.

"Thank you, Mr. Thief. That was very sweet. Now, share your food like a gentleman."

Rufus rolled his eyes, tore off a big piece for the Princess and handed it to her. They both ate quietly until the food was gone and Lyrium's head snapped up from her solemn reflection.

"Can you feel that?" she asked and Alicea nodded with an unsteady gulp.

There was a tremendous amount of magical energy coming from the forest in the distance. It was a new feeling to Alicea; it felt malicious, chaotic.

"They have mages?" Lyrium asked to which Alicea shook her head.

"No, Aquiocia has very few gifted mages. I would guess that the energy is coming from Jex himself," Alicea replied. They could both feel a cold malice filling the air around them as they sensed their adversary getting closer. He was doing nothing to mask his energy or presence.

The Vassals' conversation was cut short when a cruel voice broke the silence, booming from the forest across the plains to the gathered warriors. Alicea had never heard someone project their voice magically, yet she could still tell that Jex had to be enhancing his somehow.

"Mongrels of Tremel! Throw down your weapons and surrender the Princess along with her stone! Do so quickly and I'll consider sparing your lives." Alicea shuddered at the voice she recognised as Jex's. Despite knowing he would be there, she had hoped that Maxim was still in charge.

His absence only reinforced her fears regarding the Warmaster's fate.

Garnet was on her feet before the warriors could even move. She spoke back to the threatening man, using the same technique to project her voice across the plains, though her voice was far more calm and diplomatic.

"We shall not. Any attempt to take her from us will be met with resistance," Garnet said with strength. When she had finished, the villagers cheered before quickly becoming silent again. Alicea could only smile sadly at the situation.

Kurok and Garnet whispered with grave expressions, the Chief nodding first at Garnet and then a small number of warriors. With a massive grin towards Alicea that she couldn't return, he set off at a jog into the village towards the rear gate with half a dozen warriors in tow.

He must be checking on something . . .

The field was silent once more. Five minutes passed and the warriors began to grow restless. Alicea and her party were on their feet. Both Lyrium and herself were connected mentally to their respective stones – Lyrium's focus on the earth in front of them as Alicea's grip tightened around the water in the dam. She had no idea if there was any point; she didn't know if she'd be able to convince herself to use it against her people.

I have to believe in Garnet's plan . . .

The Vassals were struggling to grab hold of their targets.

The sheer size of both resources was more than they had ever tried to work with before. Only with the stones' aid did they have full hold.

The silence was finally broken by Garnet yelling.

"It begins! Stay true!"

Soldiers emerged from the forest, running towards the village. The vast numbers made her nervous as the steady trickle of men turned into a flood of silver and blue as more soldiers exited out of the forestry and onto the open plains. The people of Tremel held their ground, anxiously waiting for their leader's order. The first soldiers had reached about halfway across the plains when Garnet yelled, "Alicea and Lyrium, now!"

Alicea's tiny swan took to the sky as her hand flung out towards the dam, taking control of the water while the stone offered energy. The connections secured themselves to Alicea's mind and she ordered the water to go forth. The magical backing was all the water needed to break through the weak barricades. Garnet issued an order to the hunters to remain calm, but they hadn't even flinched. With Alicea's aid, the water was directed through the gap in the warriors' ranks in a great wave. Despite her discomfort, every time the liquid swell seemed to lose force, it was driven forward towards the oncoming soldiers by Alicea's command.

She was becoming fatigued as rapidly as the water flowed outwards, forcing her to apply more effort to the task. She shuddered with each mental push, her face flushed from the effort. She shook, but didn't fall. Each time she felt panic rise within her chest, the stone offered her its own energy and kept her at a comfortable level.

Meanwhile, Lyrium reached out to the earth under the hundreds of soldiers' feet. It shifted slightly as she grabbed hold and the soldiers stumbled uncertainly before continuing their charge relentlessly.

As the great swell of water closed in on the legion of soldiers, Alicea found the reserves of water littered over the battlefield. She had been so fixated on the main body of liquid that her mind tripped over the other hoards, much like misjudging a step. The hidden pools burst upwards and the identical forces became one as Alicea pushed it further towards the coming threat. Right before the water reached the soldiers, she halted its advance, instructing it to form a great wall like she had done a week earlier. This time, Alicea wielded the full co-operation of the stone. It was a fortunate development; she could now craft a clear wall of the transparent substance from afar. Despite being much further away from structure, it was easier to replicate her efforts from the last time.

The wall grew in both height and girth as wave after wave joined the effort. Before long she successfully erected a wall of water, standing a hundred yards long and still growing. Alicea felt the ordeal starting to take a toll on her as the being within the stone hesitantly fed her extra energy. Garnet realised the familiar look of exhaustion and yelled to her student.

"Now, Lyrium! Connect with Alicea!"

Alicea felt another consciousness push against hers, asking for permission to come in. She recognised it as Lyrium's and welcomed it, Lyrium's feelings colliding with her own. She could feel her stone's resonance emitting strength within her as Lyrium's took the stone's place next to her. She briefly felt the disdain between the two supernatural beings within, yet they did not refuse access to each other's power.

The earth beneath the soldiers' feet started to shift again as they reached the great wall. In panic they started to stab at the water with their spears and swords. Some realised that assaulting it with weapons was ineffective and attempted to push through it with force.

I can't hold a wall this large for long with them attacking it! Alicea called within her mind.

Just a little longer, Alicea! Lyrium cried back, her voice surprising the Princess.

Alicea felt the two stones' consciousnesses disappear and they were replaced with another. This one was different, yet the same as the two previous ones. The biggest difference was the power emanating from within it. It wasn't just a simple case of two forces combining and becoming a new one that was twice as powerful as either separately. The new being was far superior to either alone.

Alicea and Lyrium felt that this new consciousness possessed a power far greater than either could imagine – a power that threatened to crush the two Vassals' minds. They knew, without any explanation, that should the being decide to hurl them into a state of oblivion and insanity, it could do so with minimal effort.

We are one at this moment, an unknown and sonorous voice reverberated within their heads. *You have fulfilled the appropriate prerequisites; it's now in our hands.*

Rufus and Arok were staring at the two Vassals. Their eyes were glazed over like painted glass. Rufus looked back at the fields where the great wall was erected and, in sheer amazement, he watched what happened next.

The earth shook with the ferocity of an earthquake as the water that made the wall collapsed as heavy rain.

As the water fell, bright lights were emitted in the colours of lightest blue and contrasting sepia. The flashes became more frequent during the water's downpour until finally, as water and earth became one in entirety, the full force gathered at the front of the village was compelled to look away from the blaze of ethereal light that devoured everything.

The light retracted after a few seconds and Rufus' eyes adjusted slowly as he looked back at the two Vassals who were doubled over, already exhausted. Alicea fell into Rufus' arms as Lyrium did Arok's. It had been too much for them.

Garnet raced over. "Rest, you have both done marvellously. Now gather your strength."

Rufus looked up at what had the Tremel force in a stunned silence. The entire plain had transformed from stable, if uneven, turf and dirt roads to a thick swamp. The firm ground had turned to viscous sludge and the soldiers were waist-deep in mud and trying desperately to push forward. Their efforts were awarded with minimal progress and sore muscles weighed down from both their armour and the muck's stubborn resistance.

Garnet projected her voice once more towards what was now swampland. The soldiers seemed almost relieved to stop a moment and listen to the message. It was an undesirable situation to be in and any reason to take a break from the struggle was a welcome one.

"Surrender now, lest I give the order to open fire, and I assure you – Tremel's hunters rarely miss."

The response from Jex was almost immediate, and came

in the form of a sadistic laugh, as if the helplessness of his knights was genuine entertainment.

"Unison Magic, is it? And of that magnitude. There must be more than one Vassal here. It seems that our sources were right. I'm sure my superiors will be delighted when I haul both back to Aquiocia." Jex's laughter resounded throughout the ranks of the two forces as the knights' heads twisted between the origins of the two voices.

"Your men will die here if they insist on continuing this foolish attack!" Garnet insisted.

"And who cares? They live to serve! Weak and useless unless they gather in a large number and even then, they are only to be used. So, stop gaping at the enemy's magic trick and CHARGE!"

The soldiers seemed to hesitate before resuming their struggle towards the small village. They advanced slowly, even with the unfavourable terrain taken into account. They were cautious of any traps hidden within the bog. Alicea looked at the men attempting to charge through the marsh. It was a painful image for the Princess, watching her people trudge through filth.

What are they thinking? Alicea thought sadly. *Why do they persist? Are they so scared of what has become of the kingdom that they blindly march when ordered?* The Princess stepped out of Rufus' arms, walking to Garnet.

"Please, project my voice like you did to yours."

Garnet nodded and waved in the direction of the soldiers, gesturing for the Princess to continue.

Alicea cleared her voice and it could be heard through the entire swamp by every soldier.

"Please stop!" Alicea said, voice ringing with desperation. "The man commanding you is a servant of a corrupt kingdom. You may not think of me as your Princess any longer, but my only desire is to help. I was kidnapped. I won't deny that, nor will my kidnapper, who is here by my side. He is also trying to make a difference."

Garnet's lips pursed as Rufus moved to stand beside Alicea. It was his uncertain way of showing solidarity, an act that encouraged the pleading Princess.

"I have no right to ask for my throne back, nor do I want it if it means that my people are troubled. I wasn't ready to be the Queen of Aquiocia and I'm a far cry still from being prepared for the responsibility. But I can't allow harm to come to these people who took me in. The people who protected me and are now aiding me in a task I must see through!"

Save for Alicea's plea, the plains housed a silence that was absolute. Some of the warriors peered from their places within the ranks to catch a glimpse of their Princess. They saw her shaking legs, they heard her wavering voice and they experienced a moment of the sadness she had endured throughout the past year. As guilt pulled their heads down into bows, their Princess held hers high.

Alicea's voice cracked and the warriors stiffened. They didn't dare look again at the Princess' tear-stricken face; their shame wouldn't allow it.

"Many of you have served or trained under Maxim, and I don't know what has become of him. But can you look me in the eye and say he would have led you against the people protecting me? Maxim is an example of what made Aquiocia magnificent! I ask you to look to it now!"

Every soldier had stopped their march. There was a faint murmuring amongst them. As they turned to one another, each was as unsure as the next. The Princess' words had brought the entire legion to a standstill.

Jex's voice broke through the confusion, stopping the commotion.

"What are you maggots doing? Bring me the Princess' head!" he ordered viciously.

The murmuring amongst the soldiers escalated into an outright ruckus in response to Jex's latest order. The soldiers were no longer conflicted; one by one they threw down their swords. Garnet spoke once more.

"Our village is small but we welcome all who would show their loyalty to the Princess. Make your way towards the village unarmed and you will be treated with compassion. Those approaching with a weapon will be fired upon," Garnet declared before turning to the Princess and releasing the magic. "Minimal casualties. I trust you are pleased, Princess?"

"These men did not deserve to die, and thanks to your plan they didn't. You have my eternal gratitude," Alicea replied happily, to which Garnet shook her head.

"Even with your title, stone and power, I'd have never placed the fate of this village in the hands of one so young if I didn't have faith in you," Garnet said kindly and added before turning away, "When you are finally ready, you will make a truly wonderful Queen. As was your mother before you."

Garnet's words touched the Princess. She turned slightly away out of embarrassment. Rufus was about to remark on her performance when Jex's voice rang over the battlefield, his cruel tone tinged with dark amusement.

"Look at that, Princess! You still have control over your army of insects!" his voice boomed across the marsh. "But things have changed in Aquiocia, and furthermore, the world. The more visible changes started with the precious Aquiocian army. Allow me to demonstrate!"

The approaching unarmed soldiers froze in place, a short sprint from the gates of Tremel. Some had even made it out of the swampland's shallows when the force came to a standstill.

Alicea looked out at the frozen army. She grabbed a telescope from a scout and brought it up to her eye, directing it at the now stationary force. She chose one soldier in particular, focusing in on only him. As she examined the armour-clad man's helm, she could see his brown eyes. She imagined they were once warm and kind; now they were motionless and devoid of life.

Alicea was about to choose another soldier to investigate when the man's eyes flashed a bright and sinister orange. The soldier's head snapped up; there was a dark mist leaking from every break in his armour. Alicea removed the telescope from her eye slowly and looked at the army as a whole. Her despair was driven further as she noticed that almost all of the other soldiers were going through a similar transformation.

"What . . . What is this?" Alicea spluttered.

"It appears to be a curse," Garnet answered shortly, her voice bitter at the cowardly tactic.

"A curse? How can – why is –?" Alicea struggled for words as she tried to understand.

But she knew exactly what was happening. The Princess couldn't help but comprehend the situation entirely. Her eyes saw everything; her mind involuntarily combined the pieces before her.

They had come to rescue their Princess only to find her safe. Now, their Commander had done something, forcing them to march against their will. It was a march that would force the hunters to shoot them down – a suicide march.

She knew their Commander understood the implications. He was sending them to die. It only took a moment for her to realise exactly what Jex was trying to ensure.

"We could help –"

"The curse has devoured their humanity," Garnet said coldly, misty eyes analytical as she concentrated on the afflicted knights. "They cannot be saved."

The soldiers were never going to leave here alive, Alicea thought, hopelessness roiling within her. *They never do when Jex is involved. This was going to a bloodbath and now that his plan has been foiled, he is going to make sure there is as much death as possible. Whether they are his men who die or his enemy's is irrelevant.*

"You want to know what this really is, Alicea?" Rufus asked abruptly, grabbing her shoulders and turning her to face him with a stone-cold expression. "This is the time where we must face what no one wanted to happen. You need to remain focused. Don't lose your head here, understand?"

Alicea looked up at Rufus with a confused look, her pale blue eyes looking into his as if searching for an answer that she had no hope of ever obtaining. To the thief's surprise, her expression turned to one of fierce determination.

"You're right, Mr. Thief. I can grieve for the losses after this is over. These men are not the ones who once guarded my life – now they only seek to take it. This is something that I simply cannot allow."

CHAPTER 70

A CURSE UNDESERVING

No one had any idea what the soldiers were, or how they had come about the curse that had now taken hold of them. What the warriors of Tremel did know was that an enemy was charging directly at their village and it was "kill or be killed".

Garnet ordered the attack and the hunters obeyed without hesitation. The air was filled with a storm of arrows as archers let fly deadly projectiles from their longbows. The fierce war cry that accompanied the volley drowned out the Princess' barely restrained sobs. She attempted to remain stoic, achieving mixed results as her people were shot down.

The arrows punctured holes in the enemy force and Alicea could tell that the oncoming army had thinned in places. The tears on her face fell freely as she picked out some soldiers who remained unafflicted by the curse. They had removed their helms to show they were unaffected and were moving away from the fighting, struggling to get out of the massacre. Thankfully, the accuracy and perception of the archers allowed these people safe passage from the onslaught.

These men and women are unbelievably skilled, Alicea thought, unsure whether she was proud, happy, miserable, or just devastated.

The enemy was a mere twenty yards away when Garnet

turned and nodded towards Rufus and Arok. The two men immediately grabbed Alicea's and Lyrium's hands, pulling them back within the main wall of the village.

Garnet's voice was heard booming across the battlefield again. "Show him why the warriors of Tremel are unmatched! Crush them!"

Alicea resisted Rufus' grasp as he dragged her to safety.

"Let me go! I want to help –"

"Belt up, woman! You aren't going back!" Rufus growled. Alicea was about to scream at him when she saw Kurok running towards them from the centre of the village with a score of warriors behind him.

"Got caught up. Few of the bastards tried to flank us and – Arok! What in blazes are you doing? The battle is that way!" Kurok greeted his son roughly.

"Garnet ordered us back!" Arok said, looking down at his feet. Outside he could hear sound of steel meeting steel. The clashes of weapons and armour could be heard within the cries of battle. The two forces had met. That was where he belonged.

"Leave Lyrium here. No son of mine is missing out on a grand brawl such as this!" Kurok exclaimed.

"If Arok goes, I go!" Lyrium replied with determination.

"So be it! Arok, you're responsible for her safety, now let's move!" Kurok conceded quickly before his son and daughter-in-law joined the Chief's entourage and charged back towards the gates.

Rufus watched in awe as Arok reached the entrance and, with an overhead swing, crushed a soldier who had come too close to the village's interior. The thief entertained a fleeting sensation of relief when he saw dark smoke expel from the mangled suit of armour. He was still dragging the protesting Princess deeper within the village when he noticed that the back entrance to the village was wide open with a few armoured bodies on the ground, smouldering with black smoke.

I thought Garnet had made sure the rear exit was closed off. Is this what the Chief was doing ...? he thought before spotting a shining silhouette walking through the gate, followed by two more.

The men entering were oozing a dark mist from the joints in their armour. The figures ran towards the pair as soon as they laid eyes on them. Rufus stepped between them and the Princess, drawing his twin daggers as he braced himself for combat. He wasn't sure what the cursed men were capable of, but he had seen them die.

The man who entered the village first was also the first to reach the thief, swinging a fist as his weapon had been abandoned earlier. Rufus sidestepped almost casually around the wide attack of his enemy and buried his blades in the side of the soldier's neck.

Seems my luck is looking up.

The second man had barely reached Rufus when he was hit from above by an unknown projectile. The distraction allowed Rufus to move in and thrust one of his slender blades through the soldier's eye. The first two were dead before they even hit the ground, but Rufus' attention was caught by an odd puddle that seemed to be moving from its place next to the latest corpse. He then realised what the unknown assistance had been. Sure enough, within a second a small bird made of water was taking off into the air again.

"I . . . I struck my own . . ."

"Keep it together, Alicea. These are not your people," Rufus grunted.

Rufus smiled grimly at the final soldier, who was now watching him warily. To him, it was obvious that whatever was controlling the knight was breaking his will. The knight's movements were hesitant, nervous. With the same shakes Rufus had seen in opponents before, the all-over trembling that told you to run. Run away and don't look back. But the soldier didn't have that choice. Before either could move the man's body stiffened, crumpling into a heap on the ground, revealing another soldier behind him with a single, bloodstained dagger drawn.

Rufus looked over the knight – this one was a head and a half shorter than the ones who had just met their ends. More importantly, there was no darkness extruding from the soldier's armour. It was only when Rufus' eyes fell on the dagger and he noticed the design on its hilt guard that he smiled and spoke to the newcomer.

"Quite the entrance there. Where's your sister?"

The soldier pulled off the helmet to show the mischievous grin of Tori beneath it.

"Over there, at the rear gate. Now admit it, Ruffie, I'm good. Like, REALLY good." Tori laughed and Rufus grimaced. The urge to chastise Tori for being there was almost irresistible.

Tori followed the thief, happily explaining to Alicea how thrilled she was to see her again. The twin took the Princess' state of shock as awe towards her sudden appearance and relished her own perception of the event. When the three reached the gate, Rufus spotted a knight the same height as

Tori wielding a short bow, fending off a small band of enemy soldiers who had attempted to encircle the village. Rufus ran up behind the bow-wielding soldier. She spun around in alarm before exclaiming, "Ruffie!"

It was all the confirmation that he needed. For a moment he lost himself in the realisation that the twins were both there with him. He was mad, no, *furious* that they'd voluntarily stepped onto a battlefield. But that could wait. Everyone he cared about was now caught up in this fight and Rufus was ready to tear the entire enemy force apart to protect them. As he sidestepped Lori and marched towards the handful of cursed knights, he felt more invigorated than he ever had before.

This is what it's like fighting for something you care about? The thought crossed his mind as he smirked to himself. *Not bad. Not bad at all.*

Amongst the cursed soldiers was a single knight slashing out at the others with an ornate longsword. Rufus had no idea who it was, but the man had no dark aura coming from under his armour. The thief drove his daggers up under the chest plate of one of the knights seething with black mist. The man fell to the ground as arrows and the small, aqueous bird swooped at the others in an attempt to distract them. Rufus used the element of surprise to debilitate another one of the enemies. Tori mimicked his efforts as she dove into the fray a moment later, leaping up to drive her dagger into another soldier's neck. Manic laughter was all that could be heard from the nimble, now dual-wielding twin. Striking back at the knights she loathed alongside the ones she loved was the greatest thrill she could imagine.

The struggle was ended by the mysterious uncursed soldier bringing his sword through and crushing the armour of the last enemy. The winded man fell and was quickly dispatched by the knight with the glorious longsword.

"I don't know who you are, but you have my thanks," the soldier addressed Rufus. The grateful knight kicked at the lifeless bodies while glancing around for more. Completely engrossed in ensuring his enemies were dead, he wasn't prepared for introductions.

"This is Ruffie," Tori said to the soldier before turning to the approaching Alicea. "And I'm sure you know this particular Princess. Our guild has kept its word."

"Your Highness!" the soldier exclaimed, quickly taking off his helmet and kneeling.

"Locke!" Alicea exclaimed, staring at the man whose shoulder-length blond hair fell messily across his scarred face.

"There will be time to get reacquainted after this battle ends. We need to get back inside," Rufus said quickly, eyes darting back into the village.

The group ran back inside the walls. As they reached the centre, they saw a large group of warriors returning. Garnet's voice echoed over the din of the warriors with a report for the Princess.

"It's over! Setz's men were within the ranks! Jex seems to have fled, it is finally –" Garnet's cheer ceased abruptly as she spotted something behind the group, her face turning white at the sight.

Rufus spun around to see Alicea frozen to the spot, staring across the dirt road. Terror was etched across her face at the sight of the man walking towards her from between the dwellings.

Where did he come from? Rufus thought in confusion.

The man moved quickly, far swifter than any normal human, and only stopped when he was within lunging distance of the Princess. His movements were unnaturally fast, as if time moved slightly quicker for him than it did for the world around him. His long, tattered coat and hair were the only things shifting with the wind and that sight held an unnatural air about it. Even those completely unattuned to magical wavelengths could sense something horribly wrong with the man before them.

"Rufus, don't!" Garnet cried as Rufus lunged forward. He halted, uncertainly watching on as the man turned towards him, smiling cruelly.

"Yes, Rufus. Stay there like a good dog," the man said mockingly, his sinister, amber eyes alive with excitement. "I'm afraid your Princess is in quite enough danger as it is. Best not to invite more."

CHAPTER 71

THE REAPER

Everyone was frozen in place, not confident enough to attempt moving to the Princess' aid with Jex so close to her. He was too fast for even Rufus to have any hope of getting to him before he harmed the Princess. The wind had picked up ever so slightly; it was the only sound that remained bold enough to be heard as the warriors returning from the battlefield froze at the sight of Garnet's raised hand.

There was a peculiar item strapped to the enemy's back that looked like a folded battle staff, and the left sleeve of his cloak had been deliberately torn away to accommodate the blood-soaked bandages wrapped tightly around the entire length of his arm – a grotesque tourniquet. The enemy's choice of dark attire did nothing to alleviate their concern for the Princess' wellbeing, but it was the foreboding air about the man that had everyone unwilling to move against him. Rufus quickly assessed that should he be forced to attack the man before them, he'd most certainly lose.

Jex seemed content just staring at Alicea, with a cruel smirk across his lips before the young Princess swallowed painfully and spoke. Her voice quivered almost as if it danced on the breaking point from fear. Every other time she'd spoken to Jex, she had held the upper hand. Now that the roles were reversed, she was out of her depth.

"Jex –"

"The Reaper, yes. What an inventive name the people have thought up for me." He laughed, a raucous sound that was full of malice.

Alicea remained silent and waited for him to continue. It was partly an attempt to avoid provoking him and partly because her sharp tongue had nothing witty to hurl at the man. Between the soldier's curse and his appearance before her, he had effectively shut down the Princess' mental process. The shock of the day's proceedings had left her a hollow husk of her usual self.

She could barely think, let alone speak.

"You really made this difficult, Princess. I was to come here, crush the town and take you back to Aquiocia. It seems the Council and I didn't give you enough credit. That was our own failure. But the fact that there was another Vassal here, well, that was unforeseeable. The rumours were insubstantial as no one knew whether or not the other Vassal would emerge from some trial she was undertaking. Tell me where the other is!" Jex yelled the last line loud enough for anyone who wanted to respond.

"Do not give her up!" Alicea yelled back, her confidence somewhat rallying at the idea of putting Lyrium in danger.

"You realise that you are not in a position to bargain, Princess?" Jex chuckled, his gaze returning to her. "I could end your life right now."

"And yours will be ended with it. You will die at the hands of these people and you will have secured neither of the Vassals, nor their stones," Alicea replied defiantly. She didn't know where her nerve was coming from but at this point she didn't care.

"Do you not value your life, Princess?" Jex asked with curiosity. Alicea noticed his genuine interest and realised something. As a child, she had been morbidly fascinated by the man before her. It wasn't a typical attraction, and it certainly wasn't romantic. But there was something about Jex that she felt compelled to figure out. She hadn't realised at that young age that he might feel something similar, but she could see it now.

"I do, but no more than I value another's. If I'm to die here, I will do so happily and in the process, it will ensure that your mission will be a complete failure," Alicea answered coldly.

"My mission is not to return with the Vassals, just the stones. They said to try to bring the Princess if I could, but it is the stones they ultimately desire," Jex replied dismissively as he reached behind and fondled the strange contraption strapped to his back. "The Vassals could end up as collateral damage."

"Like most of the soldiers you have commanded? It seems collateral damage is a given with the likes of you," Alicea accused, to which the cruel man shrugged.

"Hand over both stones and I'll leave without any further trouble," Jex replied with an air of indifference, but Alicea could tell that he was hesitating. She had found some leverage, as small an amount as it might be.

"I think not, Jex. You may have struck the initial blow to this village, but even you must realise that you don't hold the upper hand," Alicea said, standing up straight to try to seem more confident, though the effort barely brought the top of her head to his chin.

Jex glared at Alicea for a long moment in silence, his ominous gaze running over her entire body as if he could see through her facade to the fear threatening her. Suddenly, he moved towards her with such speed that he could barely be followed by the onlookers' eyes. Alicea flinched, her eyes closing as she waited to meet her end. It was an end that didn't come; instead he grabbed her arm, pulling her towards him. He lowered his head so that when she opened her ashen eyes, they were met with the amber blaze within his own.

"How peculiar," Jex said in barely above a whisper. He didn't want anyone else to hear. "One of the reasons I am called 'The Reaper' is that I can see a person's life end before I take it. Needless to say that I had a glorious vision running through my head when I saw the troops I was to bring here to this hovel."

"So?" Alicea squeaked in return. It was a superhuman effort for her to say anything at that point.

Jex didn't answer; instead he thrust her away from him with so much force that the Princess fell straight to the ground. From her new place in the dirt, Alicea looked up at the tall man and was confused to see him walking away towards the rear exit of the village. Jex's unnatural pace allowed him to reach the exit and disappear from view in seconds. Rufus was beside her instantly and helped her up from the ground, before looking over her in concern.

"I'm sorry, I let my guard –" Rufus' apology was cut short with a wave of Alicea's hand.

The Princess wrapped her arms around Rufus and he could feel her entire body shuddering in horror. Rufus returned the embrace, holding her tightly as she shook erratically. Rufus was about to offer words to console her when Jex's voice resounded around the village, causing the cowering woman to stiffen within his arms.

"Well done, Princess!" came his mocking tone. "You have delayed the inevitable. Know this – Aquiocia will only worsen. As the dark hold around it tightens, where will you be? Were your selfish actions worth the fate you left behind for your people?"

With that, Jex's presence dispersed as he left in defeat. Tremel's warriors, along with those under Setz's employ, cheered in triumph. They had won. It only took moments for them to throw down their weapons and begin their search for the nearest ale available.

The celebration wasn't heard by Rufus. All he could think about was how badly he had failed to protect the vulnerable woman who was crying in his arms. In that moment, Alicea wasn't a Princess, nor a Vassal. She was a tormented and guilt-ridden mess who had hit her breaking point. All Rufus could do was hold her a little closer as she broke into violent sobs within his embrace. It didn't matter to the thief how long she needed it; he would hold her until she stopped blaming herself for every horrible thing that had happened that day – and many of those before it.

I'm here, he thought miserably. *I may not understand, but I'm here.*

CHAPTER 72

A QUEEN'S RESOLVE

Alicea awoke the next day feeling as though she hadn't slept at all. The night before had been a blur as her eyes filled with tears time and time again while the villagers celebrated and worried for her in equal measure. It had been well over an hour before she had even removed her buried face from Rufus' chest.

All but Arok and Lyrium had dispersed at the Chief's order. After a while, they too reluctantly plodded off towards the rest of the gathering. Each time they offered words of reassurance, the Princess' sobs intensified. Finally, Rufus shot them a look that told them to back off as he made to move. Rufus' body had become rigid from the awkward position he had been kneeling in. But that did nothing to stop him from lifting the devastated woman's limp body into his arms and carrying her to her room so that she might grieve in privacy. He had placed the Princess upon the bed gently and taken a seat across from her. It tore at him to watch her gaze past him to the wall.

He said nothing. There were no words he could possibly offer the woman with her pale, grey eyes now swollen red. He only left the room when his eyes met hers.

Without a hint of emotion, she said, "Please leave."

There had been no spite, edge or wit within the words. Just

an immense amount of sorrow and regret that made the thief simply rise to his feet, nod and leave. Alicea didn't know when she had decided to lie down. Her memory offered nothing, which meant that her mind had temporarily shut down – she had buckled. It would have been quite the fascinating sensation could she feel anything but the dull emptiness that came with being emotionally paralytic.

Back in her room, she dressed herself in a trance.

Thinking of nothing, her mind a blank slate, she pushed away the giant bear pelt that had served as a door to her room for the past few weeks. Her personal guards offered friendly greetings, all of which fell upon deaf ears as she walked slowly towards the Chief's hut. Gramere was at the door; he nodded towards the Princess. His wide smile vanished as he saw the look on her face and quickly stepped aside to let her enter.

Alicea barely registered the group of people already gathered within Kurok's hut. Lyrium, Arok, Garnet, Kurok and Rufus all turned and smiled at the Princess as she entered and took a seat. Garnet was in the middle of the battle's overview and, after seeing that Alicea didn't plan on speaking, she continued the report.

"We had minimal casualties due to Setz's forces within the enemy's ranks. Very few soldiers made it within the walls. Almost a third of the enemy force was in fact Setz's men in disguise and unaffected by the curse. They were briefed about the traps and were able to avoid them, unlike those cursed. That, coupled with the fact that the enemy dropped their weapons in the marsh, brought our death toll to less than a dozen," Garnet reported.

"Very good. Those who died will be given an honourable

burial, regardless if they were friend or foe. We will return them to Gaia's embrace," Kurok said grimly. "What of the enemy Commander?"

"He is long gone, Chief. He has fled. Our scouts have been sent out to see what they can find, but they have seen nothing out of the ordinary. I have also asked the shamans but they cannot sense his presence any longer," Garnet offered briskly.

"What of Setz's men?" Lyrium asked.

"Most of them have returned to Aquiocia," Garnet answered, turning to Lyrium. "Some have chosen to remain in the village a little longer, but the core of the Guilty Blade's units have returned to their base."

"All in all, I'd say this was a sound victory," Kurok announced. "Now, to the next point of interest. I will be issuing the order for the villagers to gather their belongings so that we may move to a new location. We need to avoid further attacks so that Alicea and Lyrium may continue their training."

Garnet's eyebrows rose slightly with curiosity before nodding in agreement. The people of Tremel had been settled in their current camp for almost two hundred years. Some had gone their own way, whether in search of the other villages or to make their own path in the world. When the fortress of old had fallen, many of their ancestors had moved on and left an almost negligible amount behind. The populace had grown and, while the numbers were by no means that of a town let alone a city, they had rebuilt a home.

"No," Alicea said quietly, drawing the attention of the room onto herself with a single word.

"What?" Kurok asked with all composure lost from surprise.

"There is no need for you all to leave this place," Alicea muttered, her eyes flickering as if her mind was beginning to gather its bearings.

"Why is that, Your Highness?" Kurok asked curiously. "We will move so that you will be safe. It is in your best interests while you train."

"No," she replied again softly before rising from her seat and walking over to Rufus. Standing in front of the surprised thief as she looked him dead in the eye, Alicea spoke. "You have stood by me through all of this. Everyone has, yet none more so than you. Will you continue to do so?"

"Of course, you don't even have to ask," Rufus replied without hesitation. *Almost feels good to admit it isn't just for the gold . . .*

Alicea nodded gratefully, turned back to the group gathered within the Chief's hut and looked at each in turn with a measured gaze.

"I have lost so much – my family, my kingdom, my . . ." Alicea looked away for a moment as the emotion caught her voice. Taking a deep breath, her hand found her mother's jewel around her neck and she continued.

"I have also gained so much as well: power, comrades and most importantly of all, I have found some friends. Each of you here and everyone just outside of this room has put everything on the line for me. Even when they had little to give, they gave it willingly."

"What are you trying to say, Alicea?" Rufus asked.

"I'm saying that I have found something to live for – something to fight for," Alicea replied firmly before slamming her fist down on Kurok's makeshift table of animal bone, looking at her friends with newfound determination. Rufus noticed that her eyes were the deep blue hue he had seen on the first night he had met the Princess. Through the dark bags of fatigue and sadness, they twinkled with the same shine that had put the stars that night to shame.

"It feels as though I have been trapped in a long slumber. Now I have awoken, I will take back my kingdom," she said fiercely and Rufus was forced to grin as he finally realised just what it was that she was saying.

"I'm in," Rufus declared before she could continue.

"As are we," Lyrium chimed in as Arok nodded, directing his wide grin from Rufus to Alicea.

"Myself, Garnet and the rest of Tremel are at your disposal, Your Highness," Kurok added, surprising Alicea. Even then, she hadn't expected the immediate support from the entire village.

"I would be honoured to assist the rightful Queen," Garnet confirmed with a small smile that suggested she had more to say, but now wasn't the time.

Alicea took one last proud look around the room at her friends. She had known that Setz and his guild would be on her side, but she hadn't expected anyone else to risk their lives to confront her own kingdom. She had a village of hunters, an underground city of rogues and a handful of new and mismatched friends at her side.

This, she thought, her mind fully operational once more. *This is what my mother would do!*

She could barely contain the tears of gratitude that threatened to spring forth. The only thing that held them at bay was how much she'd cried the night before.

Instead, she issued an order with all the authority of a Queen-to-be.

"What they have done to both myself and countless innocent lives is unforgivable. I will topple this corrupt hierarchy from its ill-gained place of power. Inform Setz and begin the preparations. This is war."

ACKNOWLEDGEMENTS

The path to getting *Awakening* here has been a long one. Along that path has been countless people showing their unwavering support and as we look upon the final product; I wish to thank you all.

Thank you to my family and friends for listening to my ideas. In particular, thank you to my mother who has been on the other end of the happiest moments and those most trying. To all of those close to me; your support means the world.

Thank you to my editors. Kaitlyn Smith and Claire Bradshaw both brought their A-games to *Awakening* and refined it into something we can truly be proud to present to its readers. Without these two, *Awakening* would likely still be a mess.

Thank you to every single artist that leant their expertise to *The Elemental Chronicles*. It has been a delight working with you all. I look forward to further works alongside you all.

Next is the pledgers from *Awakening's* Kickstarter campaign. I've been trying to find the words for months. I knew from the moment *Awakening* was funded that I'd struggle to find the appropriate words to thank you all and yet they still fail me. Thank you, truly. Because of you, *Awakening* is ready. I hope you enjoy it and although we are at the tail end of the campaign, know that my gratitude will never fade.

In order of their pledges; the names of those who helped bring Awakening to life.

Allan & Ann Kearney, E. Hoeft, Sarah Imhoff, Cheryl Mcmonagle, Rebecca Johnson, Scott Cunningham, Monica B, Boot Frogro Guevara, Sandy, Gail, Sam, Mark Walker, Con 'Bacon Pope' Orfanos and Emma Andrews, Design in 365 days, Sarah Kingdred, Christine Halter, Kaitlyn Smith, Adrian Said, Michael, Jodie Grayson, Beth, Scott, Adam Menary, Aidan Dunn, Nick Kington, Amy, Matthew Lewis, Michelle Butters, Isaac Rayward, Benji, Kait Halter, Paula and Rob Kearney, Blairy, the Ogle Family, Jacka, Jake Timm, Regina, Shadow, Matt Chalk, Danial, Kircard Productions Australia, Elise McDonald, Jason F. Broadley, Natalie Manahan, and SwordFire.

There were others who also helped but have asked to remain anonymous.

Thank you all once more! I look forward to working on the second book and hopefully bringing it to you all next year. Here's to *Awakening* and those who helped make it happen.

Ross Kingston.

Milton Keynes UK
Ingram Content Group UK Ltd.
UKHW011841050324
438776UK00001BC/10